A SETH & RAIDER NOVEL

SILK

& SAND

KATHERINE DIANE

SILK & SAND. Copyright © 2024 by Katherine Diane. All rights reserved.

Cover Illustration and Design Copyright © 2024 by Katherine Diane. All rights reserved.

No part of this book was created with generative AI.

No part of this publication may be reproduced in any form or by any electronic or mechanical means, including information storage and retrieval systems and AI, without the prior written permission from the author, except in the case of brief quotations for review purposes.

This is a work of fiction. All of the characters, organizations, and events are either products of the author's imagination or are used fictitiously.

ISBN-13: 979-8882718984

BOOKS BY KATHERINE DIANE

The Vampire Defense Agency series
Blood Lust
Dark Hunger
Night Shade
Day Break
Last Breath

Seth & Raider series
Silk & Sand
Silver & Gold (forthcoming)

Standalone novels
Beautiful Beast
Her Lord of Death

Author's Note

If you've read my work before, you know that my romances tend to be dark, raw, intensely emotional, and erotic. They contain what may be triggering content for some readers. Please know how very important your emotional experiences are, both in real life and in your reading. Take care of yourself and make no apologies for your own boundaries. Don't worry about some book that isn't right or good for you and toss it away, even if it's one of mine.

If, like me, you crave that sort of emotional and erotic intensity, you're in the right place. Maybe, like me, you can't really *feel* a story without all that darkness and depth and the kind of vulnerability that can only emerge in a complicated and intensely sexual relationship.

That's what you're in for with *Silk & Sand*. That, and some good laughs—because what is life without humor?—and plenty of action. This book gets a bit dark, but I promise you it's fun too.

I won't go into detail here because I don't want to spoil anything, but if you're concerned about the type of content you're about to experience, do know that this book contains elements of BDSM. While everything here is consensual, Seth and Raider have a lot of internal issues to work through, and their intensely sexual relationship is one of their avenues for that.

I hope you love their story. I hope you love them.

Enjoy the journey. I'll see you on the other side.

CHAPTER 1

THREE HUNDRED MILES of roads and rutted tracks. Weeks of hunting markets and inns. Seth was used to all that. He didn't mind blinding sun and lumpy beds and a dozen dead ends—because they never really were dead ends. There would be a crack, a hole, a hidden door. There would be a clue, and Seth would find it. As a Curator for the Arcanum, that was his job.

But what Seth usually hunted was artifacts. Arcane ones. Objects of interest to the scholars of the Arcanum College, things of power and danger and often incredible beauty. He followed trails that whispered from the fading ink of crumbling scrolls and the lore of fireside tales, into forests and far-flung cities, down back alleys and tomb shafts.

He did not, usually, hunt people.

But here he was in the dusty, desert-edge town of Shalaa, tromping into the bazaar with questions about a man instead of questions about a mystery. Of course, *why* an arcanist wanted for murder would have come to this little spot of nowhere was a mystery all on its own.

Mudbrick buildings squatted on either side of the not quite straight alley, their faded awnings drooping in the heat and the red govaa fruit at one merchant's stall visibly shriveling. A town as remote as Shalaa couldn't hope to enjoy the arcane advancements of a city-state like Masir, where the Arcanum birthed so many wonders.

No cooling boxes preserved the fruit. No arcane fans lifted the blanket of heat. In fact, Seth was likely wearing more arcane technology than existed in the entire town.

Without the cooling properties of the arcane fabric, his rugged black pants and sleeveless shirt would have been unbearable in this heat, especially with the added burden of his forearm bracers, utility belt, and thigh sheath. And of course there was also the heavy sword strapped at his back, its pommel jutting above his right shoulder.

The vendor with the shriveled govaa fruit woke with a snort, toppling from his cushion as Seth passed his stall.

Maybe he should have thrown on his kaftan after all, but it had seemed pointless. In a town like Shalaa, it wasn't just Seth's clothes that screamed foreigner, nor his clean-shaven face. He was too tall, too muscled, and too fair with his short brown hair and green eyes.

Even in Masir, his size and coloring marked him as *other*, and Seth preferred to think that those traits were responsible for the stares he got everywhere he went.

There was, however, another possibility.

He had been told (on many irritating occasions) that he walked like he was on his way to deliver a beating.

Seth found this unfair. He walked like he had something important to do. Which he *did*. And that important thing was finding out where in this gods-forsaken land a certain fugitive arcanist had vanished after murdering a fellow scholar.

Outside the Arcanum, such an event would hardly shock Seth, but arcanists tended to fight with words, not bludgeon each other with stone busts of the Arcanum's founding father.

But Julian had done just that, and Catalus, head of the Department of Alchemy, was understandably upset. He had insisted that Julian be returned to the College for questioning and justice.

And so Seth had been yanked away from his much more interesting pursuit of a golden bird rumored to foretell the future and had been assigned to this dusty, thirsty, frustrating manhunt.

When Seth had protested the assignment, Catalus had only scowled at him from across his desk and said, "You're the only Curator sufficiently tenacious and brutal for the job."

Seth resented that. He was not *brutal*. He was skilled with his weapons, yes, and willing to use them, yes. And … yes, fine, he had a history of losing his temper. But he did not *enjoy* violence, and he had learned years ago to control himself. (Truly, he had no idea why he still ended up in so many fights.)

Feeling the startled gaze of the govaa vendor on his back, Seth moderated his pace with an effort. He even stopped to admire the finely woven baskets hanging from the awning of the next stall.

Set back from this fringe of baskets, the weaver sat in the mudbrick doorway of his house/shop. Beside him, a woman fanned herself with a palm leaf. The weaver's nimble fingers worked the brightly dyed cheffah grass through a sturdy frame, making the humble item into a work of art.

Seth chided himself for his earlier thoughts about Shalaa. Even in this remote location, people worked wonders with the materials they had, even if those materials were simple grass.

Besides, the town wasn't *that* small. He'd seen a bathhouse riding in, and though this might be the last town before the

Kesh Desert, it was also the first town outside of it. People traded here.

When Seth stepped under the awning, the woman set aside her fan and levered herself up with a walking stick. She stumped forward, bent over the stick.

"You want to buy?" she asked in the trade tongue, the default speech of trade towns like this one. "My honored husband is the finest basket weaver in Shalaa."

"His work is beautiful," Seth agreed. The woman raised a gray eyebrow at his Masiri accent. "But I'm actually looking for someone."

The woman planted the stick in front herself and craned her neck to look up at Seth's face.

"Ah. So you want to buy information."

Seth's mouth twitched. Everywhere he traveled, people were the same.

But he couldn't blame her, standing before him in her kaftan of faded purple cotton with its mended cuffs. He fished a drahm from one of his many pockets and passed it to the woman. The copper coin vanished into her wide blue sash with astonishing speed.

Seth said, "I'm looking for a trader named Jamil."

"That jumped-up young desert dog? Thinks he is suddenly too good for us folk of the bazaar. As if I didn't once swat his bottom for stealing figs from my tree."

"And what makes him think so highly of himself all of a sudden?"

"One lucky trade and he is strutting about like a sultan."

Seth breathed a sigh of relief. This didn't confirm that Julian had been in Shalaa, but it gave Seth hope that his guess was correct. The arcane scope cinched into Seth's utility belt had caught his eye in Demir's bustling market four days ago. It was a rare and valuable item, something that had likely been owned by a prince—or an arcanist.

The Demiri merchant had commanded a high price for the scope and the story of its acquisition. It was a good thing the Arcanum had given Seth a letter of credit, or this manhunt would have dead-ended in Demir. But the scope had been one of those cracks in the dead end. The merchant had bought it from a Shalaani trader name Jamil. No prince would have sold an arcane scope to a trader in Shalaa, but an arcanist on the run might have.

"So where might I find Jamil?"

"Go past Agra's flatbreads then past the striped awning of Yusef's shop. There you will find the stall of Jamil. If he is there, I cannot say. *Some* of us have work to do."

With that, the woman stumped back to her cushion. Instead of resuming her fanning, she made a point of taking up a piece of crimson braiding. Squinting ferociously, she set to work beside her husband, who had never looked up from the crisscrossed strips of his basket.

Seth found Agra's stall, where the delicious scent of warm flatbread made his stomach growl out a reminder of missed meals.

Later. He would eat later.

After he got some answers.

Next came the shop with the striped awning. Beyond it, Seth found an empty stall. The awning was up, but the door was closed. No one answered Seth's repeated knocking.

He backtracked to the previous shop with the striped awning. Under its shade, an assortment of cheap goods—flimsy brass lamps, amulets of paste and paint—cluttered a table. The open door, however, offered a glimpse of better wares inside.

Seth stepped into the cluttered shop, where a middle-aged man in dark robes belted with a white sash was seated before a low table. He was drinking what smelled like kahve from a glass cup.

"Yusef?" Seth inquired, recalling the name the basket weaver's wife had mentioned.

"I am Yusef. You have goods to sell, or you seek to buy?"

On the surrounding shelves, household goods mingled with antiques. Among them, Seth spotted a few works of artifice, including an arcane hotplate and what looked like part of a water pump.

"I'm seeking information on the whereabouts of the man named Jamil."

Yusef steepled his fingers. Sending Seth a bland look over the tops of them, he claimed, "I do not know this Jamil."

Seth had a nose for lies, but he certainly didn't need that talent to sniff out this particular one.

"And how much for you to know him?" Unlike the basket weaver's wife, this man would yield nothing for a mere drahm.

"I am but a humble and honest merchant, harib. If you seek to purchase goods, I can help you."

Harib. Stranger. Meaning: Seth would have to abide by the social rules that the basket weaver's wife had dispensed with in the interests of economy.

Here, Seth would have to pretend that he was a customer. Depending on what goods Seth was willing to buy, Jamil's location might come up in the course of their conversation.

Prevarication tried Seth's patience at the best of times. His being hungry, thirsty, and frustrated did *not* make for the best of times. But he would have to play along.

"Since I am here," Seth gritted out, "I might as well look at your offerings."

Yusef positively beamed as he rose from his cushion. Beckoning for Seth to follow, he led the way through a curtain of colorful glass beads and into a back room. Yusef gestured to the rolled carpets standing against the mudbrick wall.

"All the way from Aqarat, beyond the Kesh. Beautiful, are they not? And these." Yusef indicated a shelf of porcelain vases and bowls. "You will find nothing better in Shalaa."

"And nothing more expensive, I imagine," Seth noted dryly, but Yusef only blinked as though uncomprehending.

Seth was on the verge of telling him to take both his rugs and his information to Hasa, goddess of the Underworld, where he could feed it to her crocodiles, when a man's voice called from the front.

"Where are you, Yusef, you old son of a goat?"

A sudden, greedy light sparked in Yusef's eyes. Without sparing Seth a further glance, he practically dove through the curtain, setting the colorful glass beads tinkling.

"Raider, my honored friend!" Yusef greeted the man. "The sun rises in your footsteps. Come, drink kahve with me."

"Kahve! Raaki would go down better."

"Alas, I do not partake of spirits."

"Uh-huh," came the sardonic reply in a smooth, rolling voice. "Pour the kahve, then, and take a look at the treasures I brought back from il-Kemsa."

Seth peered through the bead curtain into the shop's front room. A man was thumping down a stack of cloth with the same telltale luster of silk as the red kaftan he wore, though his own garment was dusty and travel stained. A kaffiyeh of darker red had been thrown back from his head to rest on his broad shoulders, baring a striking bronze face with hollow cheeks, a fine, straight nose, and startling amber eyes. A scruffy dark beard marred the otherwise-handsome face. Wavy dark hair, roughly scraped back, came to the man's nape.

Picking through the stack of silks, Yusef hedged, "I do not know that I would call these *treasures*."

The man in the red kaftan—Raider?—grinned at the game, white teeth flashing and amber eyes dancing with humor.

With a fluid motion, he swept his dusty red kaftan open, making its gold trim gleam in the light. The move exposed a leanly muscled torso and loose shalvar pants of dark blue silk. A violet sash encircled his waist. From this he drew a curved dagger in a jeweled sheath.

"That is either fake or stolen," judged Yusef, an assessment with which Seth entirely agreed.

Raider's flashy looks and flamboyant manner marked him as an opportunist and rogue. Seth knew the type.

Raider gave a careless shrug. "If you're not interested, I'll talk to Jamil."

"Jamil is a cheat, sand seeker," protested Yusef, laying a possessive hand over the silks. "How else could he have so profited from one trade? Sit. The kahve cools as we speak."

Throwing his red kaftan out behind him, Raider settled on a cushion as Yusef poured steaming kahve into a glass cup.

"All right then," Raider said, "eighty denari for the silk."

"You jest, my honored friend."

As Yusef and Raider haggled with obvious enjoyment across the low table, it took Seth longer than it should have to draw himself away from the bead curtain. He didn't know what held him there, watching the desert trader smile as he flicked away Yusef's counteroffer, listening to his smooth, rolling voice recount the trouble he'd had bringing that silk from il-Kemsa.

Raider showed off a slash in his kaftan sleeve, which he claimed had been made by a bandit's scimitar. He took Yusef's skepticism in stride, the humor never leaving his eyes as he laughed, "It's true!"

"Then Roth must smile upon you that there should be no blood."

The light seemed to catch Raider's right eye, making it flash. The laugher in his face briefly took on a sharp edge. Then, his easy manner returning so quickly that Seth wondered if he'd imagined the shift in mood, Raider casually pointed to what Seth supposed must be a small bloodstain on his kaftan. Yusef rolled his eyes.

Mastering himself, Seth withdrew to look for a back door. The dusty trader, handsome or not, was of no consequence, and Seth would not pay Yusef an obscene price for information on Jamil, a man clearly notorious in the town. Someone else would tell him.

No exit presented itself, only Yusef's living quarters and workroom, where a scroll was in the process of being artificially aged and a statuette awaited its final coat of gold paint. No wonder Yusef had been so quick to suspect the dagger was fake, given that he himself was clearly a counterfeiter.

Humble and honest merchant indeed.

Seth returned to Yusef's back room of valuables. (Assuming the term "valuables" even applied after the revelations of the workroom.) He scanned the wall beside the shelf of vases and bowls. A back door was likely hidden to prevent people from slipping out.

Seth had just decided to give it up and tromp out the front when the bead curtain rattled and a smooth voice inquired, "You're considering a vase?"

The roguish man, Raider—yes, the name spoke *volumes*—slid past the bead curtain, his amber eyes running up and down Seth in undisguised appraisal. Seth was used to being sized up, but this felt like something else entirely. It felt … well, it felt *sexual*, and it had Seth bristling even before the man stepped rudely close. They were nearly the same height, which meant Seth could see the exact shape of Raider's lips as he smirked.

"Such ... receptacles don't look like your style," Raider said in that rolling voice of his.

He held out the sheathed dagger that he'd tried to sell. He held it not *quite* at his groin but pretty damned close, which meant that it *almost* brushed Seth's groin. "Don't you think this might be more to your liking?"

"No. It looks flashy and useless."

With an arrogant quirk of his lips, Raider lifted the dagger to chest height and ran his thumb along the curve of its jeweled sheath.

"Oh, not at all," Raider purred in a way that Seth, annoyingly, felt in his cock. "It's silky smooth, perfectly honed for sliding deep—"

"Step the fuck back." No one toyed with Seth, not like this. He didn't care if his dick was into the game. In fact, that only made it worse.

Raider didn't yield right away, and it pissed Seth off that the challenge in those amber eyes had his body lighting up in a way that made painfully clear why he'd hovered so long at that curtain.

It didn't matter. The man was attractive—so, what? He was also, patently, not Seth's type.

Besides, Seth had work to do.

Finally, smiling a little, Raider stepped back. He swept his kaftan aside, flashing his bronze-skinned abdomen. He made a show of sliding the dagger into his violet sash.

"You're not from here," he observed.

"Clearly," was all Seth offered. He wanted to shoulder past the man and storm out, but his work came first, so he forced himself to say, "I heard you mention Jamil. Know where I can find him?"

Raider's amber eyes danced with amusement. "Is that what you came here to ask Yusef? No wonder he put you in the back room."

"He is going to buy a rug!" Yusef shouted from the front.

Raider called over his shoulder, "I do not think so, my friend. He was looking for your back door."

"I signaled you to stop him!"

"And I did, but he doesn't want to be held"—did Raider linger on the word like Seth thought he did?—"and he's not stealing anything, so I think I have to let him go. As for Jamil"—that rakish grin flashed again—"I'd try Ahmet's tavern."

Chapter 2

Raider let the raaki burn a delightful path down his throat. It had been a long week of sun and sand guarding his haul. A lone traveler with laden packs tended to attract attention from thieves and bandits, and this trip had been no exception. Only Raider's unique abilities—and certainly not Roth's divine intervention—had saved him.

Still, the payout had been worth the trouble, even if the silks and dagger were the least of what he'd earned.

Raider had told that besotted il-Kemsan lord he could get into the palace and deliver the man's lovesick message to the lovely Sheqel without her father, Prince Faisel, being any the wiser. A good thing Raider had been right—because he'd needed the better part of the lord's payment to clear a gambling debt.

Had it been his own gambling debt, Raider might have skipped out on it. But it would have been a shame to see such a fine pair of legs as Nadju's broken. Raider had spent many pleasurable hours with those legs wrapped around him. So when Nadju had pleaded for Raider's help with trembling hands and such sweet kisses, what choice had he had?

Besides, Raider loved a challenge, and slipping into the palace had fit the bill. The gold-sheathed dagger had been an unexpected bonus. (What had Prince Faisel been thinking, leaving something like that lying around?)

Raider slid the pottery cup back across the bar, along with one of the drahms he'd gotten from Yusef. The haggling had gotten ridiculous by the end, and Raider had very much enjoyed reaching a settlement that included both denari and drahms. (Yusef had been very annoyed by then.) The merchant hadn't been willing to buy the dagger, but that was all right. Raider kind of liked it.

Even if it was flashy and useless.

"Something funny?" Ahmet asked as he refilled Raider's cup from the jug of raaki.

"Oh, just a pleasant memory."

As Raider threw back the second cup of raaki, Ahmet raised a bushy dark eyebrow and indicated the jug. "You want me to leave this?"

"You have such good ideas. That's why I come here."

Amusement played across Ahmet's broad face. "That's not the only reason you come here."

Raider grinned. He *had* been pretty obvious about scanning the tavern for potential company.

"You know me so well."

"I doubt anyone knows you well, Raider, not even the gods."

"How could they? We're not on speaking terms."

Ahmet shook his head woefully and slung a damp towel over his large shoulder. Turning toward the kitchen, he promised, "I will pray for you."

"I cannot imagine that *your* prayers would do me much good, my friend."

Ahmet huffed a laugh and vanished into the back.

As Raider poured himself another cup of raaki, he considered his afternoon. He would love to get delightfully drunk, but he had sand in places it was not at all welcome. Perhaps at the bathhouse he would find the kind of company that was absent from the tavern this afternoon.

No one, unfortunately, was likely to interest him quite like the magnificent man he'd encountered in Yusef's shop. So serious. So intense.

What a delicious challenge.

But Raider would need to look for an easier prospect if he wanted to feel hands on his body tonight—and he did want that. He hated his nights alone. He wanted to laugh. He wanted to drink raaki and fuck and listen to a voice that wasn't inside his own head. For that, he needed someone playful and flirtatious.

Yet, when he twisted on his barstool to give the tavern's prospects a second look, there, in the dusty light of the open doorway, stood the man from Yusef's shop. Raider couldn't help but grin.

"You took my advice," he said as the powerful body came striding his way, boots thumping across the mudbrick floor.

Raider never wore boots. Not only were they far too hot for the climate, his toes, like the rest of him, required more freedom. He loved the billow and glide of his silk kaftan and pants, the unrestricted movement.

Even though the man—gods, that *face*. Broad but refined, well-cut jaw, brilliant green eyes …

What was he saying? Oh, yes. Even though the (distractingly attractive) man looked perfectly capable of any movement he pleased, the structured black clothing was so unsuited to the climate that it could only be arcane. Add to that the heavy shoulder guards and forearm bracers, the utility belt strapped with oddities that included a razor-sharp, circular chakram for throwing, the hunting knife in his thigh sheath, and the sword strapped across his back?

There was no question of what he was.

"I did not take your advice," the Curator said. "I asked two other people, and this was identified as one of three probable locations for Jamil. Because it was the closest, I stopped here first."

"What an exhausting mind you have! But no matter. Here you are! Raaki?"

That perfect jaw clenched visibly, and the green eyes seemed to spark with emerald fire as the man scanned the tavern. "Where is the proprietor?"

"Turning the lamb spit, I imagine. Raaki?"

"It's too hot for alcohol."

Raider scoffed. "It is *never* too hot for alcohol. And it looks like you're having a rough day. Or are you always this uptight?"

Those green eyes locked on Raider with an intensity that meant trouble, though what sort was yet to be seen. That kind of heat generally led to fighting or fucking. Raider had his preference, but he was flexible.

The man's iron jaw unclenched enough for him to say, "I can see how someone like you might consider me uptight—"

"Someone like me?"

"—but I am simply focused on my work."

"For the Arcanum?"

The man's powerful body stilled briefly then loosened in the telltale way of an experienced fighter readying himself, his hands going loose while his gaze sharpened. Well … sharpened *more*. If it got any sharper, it might actually start slicing things, and then where would they be? That would make a terrible mess of the tavern. Not to mention Raider.

He turned in his seat and propped an elbow on the bar top. He made a show of looking the man up and down, from his close-cropped hair and clean-shaven face to the well-muscled arms shown off so nicely by the buckled black vest with its heavy shoulder guards. The formfitting top made a fine display of an obviously muscled torso, and the pants hugged his powerful thighs enviably.

It wasn't just the clothes giving him away. There was also the arcane scope strapped into the utility belt, the sword and chakram, and the thigh sheath with its not-flashy, not-useless knife.

"You didn't imagine yourself in disguise, did you, Curator? I've seen your kind before, and he looked exactly like you."

"Is that right."

It wasn't. It was a bald lie. The other had been a thin-faced weasel of a man, but the clothes and gear were distinctive.

In any case, the Curator's words hadn't been inflected as a question. Raider knew a give-me-more-information-or-else tone when he heard one. He would gladly oblige. But first:

"We've chatted quite long enough without me knowing your name."

See that? Raider could ask questions without actually asking questions, too.

The Curator seemed to consider. Then his curiosity got the better of him—or could it have been Raider's dashing looks?—because he said bluntly, "Seth."

"Seth," Raider echoed, trying it out. "*Seth.*" Mm-hm. He liked it.

His savoring repetition had the Curator's eyes narrowing.

"I'm Raider."

"I heard. Not the name your mother gave you, I assume."

"A Curator ought to know better than to make assumptions. And he ought to know that he's easily recognizable."

"I do know that. I just didn't expect—"

"That anyone from this ignorant spot of nowhere would've seen such a rarefied individual before?"

The Curator scowled attractively. "Where have you encountered a Curator?"

"Adiri."

"Ah. Makes sense."

"Yes. The tombs there are just the kind of thing to attract Curators. Plenty of arcane artifacts to steal for your university."

"We don't steal."

Before Raider could get in a proper scoff at that outrageous lie, Seth's eyes traveled down to the jewel-studded dagger peeking out from Raider's kaftan. "And who are you to judge?"

Seth had him there. Raider grinned and threw back his kaftan to show off the dagger to full effect. It looked fantastic behind his brilliant purple sash, jewels sparkling at his hip and golden pommel gleaming against the bronze expanse of his torso.

Was that a hint of red flushing along the Curator's admirable cheekbones? Raider was certain it was, so he left his kaftan swept open. The man was either prudish (and therefore deserved teasing), or he was attracted to Raider.

In Yusef's back room, Raider had flirted shamelessly, and while Seth hadn't exactly played along, he hadn't hit Raider either. Of course, that might mean nothing with a man so controlled. Glaring seemed to be the only release he allowed his temper.

Seth looked pointedly away, but the cords of his neck strung tight. Gods, the man was intense. So rigid. But powerful, too, and the brief looseness of his body when he'd readied himself for a fight—

A mental image, unbidden but not entirely unwelcome, assailed Raider: that body, stretched out, tied up, bare, arching in frustration, all but begging for relief …

Raider gave himself a shake. He hadn't been *that* long on the road. Besides, assuming Seth was even inclined toward male lovers, Raider could not imagine a man so controlled allowing himself to be made that vulnerable.

A shame. It was a pleasant little fantasy. Of course, Raider might be persuaded to explore it in reverse …

Seth's noisy exhalation dispelled the intriguing image.

"How long does it take a man to turn a spit? I've half a mind to proceed to my next point of interest."

"He'll be back any minute. And if anyone in Shalaa knows Jamil's location, it will be Ahmet. He knows everything in this town. Take a seat! Don't you know to rest when you have the chance?"

The Curator glared into the middle distance, then, to Raider's surprise and delight, he came forward and settled on the stool. In truth, he kind of perched on the edge of it, but it still counted.

Raider leaned over the bar and snagged a clean cup from the shelf below. After pouring two fingers of raaki into it, he slid the cup to Seth.

When Seth drew a breath, likely to repeat his earlier injunction against alcohol on a hot day, Raider said, "Ahmet makes the best raaki west of the Kesh."

"You clearly want to chat, but it's obvious you have nothing useful to offer."

"Must everything be useful? What about beauty, pleasure, experience? Aren't you Curators constant travelers? That ought to inspire a bit of curiosity about the places you visit. Or are you too jaded for delight?"

"Curators are not tourists. We have work to do."

"Work and pleasure are not mutually exclusive," Raider argued enjoyably. "I accomplish both seamlessly."

"I seriously doubt that what you do constitutes work. You're clearly an opportunist. Among other things."

The Curator's gaze drifted to the dagger. Or perhaps to the exposed sliver of Raider's torso?

Raider grinned. "Have you been talking to Ahmet already?"

Seth answered with that lovely scowl of his.

"I like to see places and be on the move," Raider said. "Not unlike a Curator."

This comment clearly offended Seth. "We are nothing alike. You serve no purpose but your own."

"Should I instead serve someone else's? Why should someone get to own me?" Raider bristled at the idea.

"Is that what you think I am, owned by the Arcanum?" Seth shook his head irritably. "Gods, why am I even having this conversation with you? It's over, by the way. Where the hell is the proprietor?"

Seth glared around like Ahmet might be hiding behind one of his customers.

Raider argued, "You deliver valuable, likely dangerous, arcane artifacts to the Arcanum. Either they own you, or you have a naïve faith in them."

Seth turned his glare on Raider. Unable to resist the conversational bait, he shot back, "The Arcanum is one of many colleges within Masir University. There are checks and balances—"

"Oh, I'm sure that works *so* well."

"The Arcanum might not be perfect, but it's better than most. There are good people there. And to think you were calling me jaded!"

Raider poured himself a fresh cup of raaki. The conversation was getting too serious. He was starting to actually care about the subject and, for some reason, the Curator's perspective.

This was why he should stick with easy, playful, flirtatious men. It didn't matter how well the Curator's clothes fit his powerful body or how much his deep, gruff voice turned Raider on.

The best thing in the world was a cup of raaki—he threw one back—a smile—he let his return—and the prospect of a long, luxurious bath. And a bowl of spiced lamb, which he could smell approaching.

Ahmet emerged from the kitchen bearing a laden tray on his shoulder. He snagged a steaming bowl from it as he passed Raider, raising a bushy eyebrow at the sight of Raider's company. Before Seth could stop him with questions, Ahmet swept on through the tavern with his tray.

When Seth's stomach growled audibly, Raider said, "Oh, so you are human."

Seth muttered something that Raider couldn't make out.

Spirits lifting at the sense of gaining the upper hand again, Raider offered, "I'll share."

"I'm perfectly capable of getting my own food if I want it."

"And equally capable of denying your needs as well as your wants."

Now color really did bloom across those perfect cheekbones. Interesting. So what was it the rigid Curator wanted?

Or was that flush the effect of raaki? Because at some unnoticed point, Seth had downed the drink—and had slid a coin Raider's way to pay for it.

Rude. The drink had been a gesture of hospitality. Or something like that.

Ahmet returned to the bar and set down his empty tray. He shot Raider a suspicious look.

"You're not harassing my customers, are you?"

"I must protest, Ahmet. I've worked very hard to keep him here. You were gone a long time. Smoking?"

Ahmet grinned then turned to Seth. "Lamb? Raaki? Wine?"

"Information," Seth said. "And a room."

A room? What a fabulous turn of events.

"My best room is available."

"*Ahmet*," Raider protested. "You promised *me* your best room."

Seth turned to him. "You're staying here? I thought you lived in this town."

"You are just full of assumptions, aren't you? But, yes, I live in this town. Sometimes."

Ahmet offered, "Raider, you can have my second best room. And a free breakfast!"

"Eggs and pork loin," Raider bargained. "Plus those delicious little hotcakes you made once, forty-seven years ago. The ones with the sesame seeds?"

"That was two months ago," Ahmet corrected. He turned again to Seth, promising nothing in regard to breakfast, and said, "One denar per night."

Raider kept his face still as Ahmet set about fleecing the Curator. Seth's wry expression said he knew very well that he was being fleeced.

"I'm looking for the trader Jamil," Seth said. "Know where I can find him?"

Recognizing the question as part of the haggling, Ahmet said, "He's at the bathhouse."

Oh, delight. This day just kept getting better.

"You're sure?" Seth challenged.

Ahmet looked offended. "I shared a hookah with Nemea barely a moment ago."

"She's works there," Raider supplied helpfully.

"Fine," said Seth and levered himself off the stool to dig a denar from his pocket. As he slid the silver coin across the bar, he noticed Raider's grin. "What's so funny?"

Raider considered mentioning his own plans to visit the bathhouse, but he decided the Curator would derive far greater enjoyment from discovering that fact for himself.

"Oh, nothing," he said.

Chapter 3

S HALAA'S BATHHOUSE WAS, actually, surprisingly nice. It might not match the grandeur of Masir's bathhouses, but the large domed building boasted fine mosaic tilework throughout its honeycombed space, where steam rooms opened onto the central chamber.

As Seth walked through the large space, a blue and white patterned towel knotted at his waist, the humid air was a balm to his parched skin and lungs.

He twitched at the thought of his valuable clothes and weapons under the care of the bathhouse guard, but there was no help for that. He had to trust that he'd made himself sufficiently threatening to ensure that nothing would go missing while he located Jamil.

A steam room door opened to the left, emitting a burst of steam and three nude men. None of them matched Ahmet's description of Jamil.

The men made their way to the stone benches along one of the six pools. Each lay face down to await a vigorous exfoliating scrub by one of the bathhouse attendants.

In each of the pools, other men sat soaking, some of them enjoying the (paid-for) attentions of the bathhouse prostitutes. A few male prostitutes worked the floor, but most of them were women. They were the only women present on this side of the building. Female visitors enjoyed their own pools.

Seth scanned the pools' occupants. Ahmet had described Jamil as thirtyish and slightly built. While that could describe a number of the men present, the "little triangle chin beard with a thin mustache, like this"—Ahmet had drawn his fingers slightly up his face—was more distinctive.

Raider had (helpfully?) added that Jamil had a habit of smoothing said mustache with his finger. He'd demonstrated with what Seth hoped was comedic exaggeration.

Ahmet had also said that Jamil would likely have female company.

A man meeting every element of Ahmet's description was reclining in the second pool on the right, making the overpriced room Seth had reserved worth the money.

Of course, there was the unfortunate fact that Raider would also be staying at the tavern. How a man could be so rootless was beyond Seth. Despite his own orphaned childhood, Seth had found a place that was home. It might only be a cramped apartment in the Arcanum's dormitories, but at least it wasn't a seedy tavern room.

Then again, that probably suited Raider just fine. A man like that, all smirking lips and silk? A rogue, as Seth had first judged him.

By Roth's divine scepter, that violet sash was outrageous, not to mention the absurd dagger. Any man who needed that much ornamentation was likely much plainer than he seemed without it. Even a handsome face could be an illusion with enough flash around it.

Another look would reveal the truth: Raider was simply a bronze-skinned man with unruly hair that was begging to be grabbed. (In a *fight*, Seth told himself, not for ... other reasons.)

One of Jamil's two female companions gave a little screech at Seth's approach. He moderated his pace and made an effort to soften his expression. Maybe he should have taken the time to eat first. Hunger was undoubtedly responsible for the scowl that he was undoubtedly wearing. Hunger and impatience, but at least the latter was about to be resolved. Jamil would give him answers. Seth would leave him no choice.

"Jamil?" Seth inquired.

The man was trapped in the pool, his back against the wall, but he still managed to give an impression of leaning away. Of course, that might have been thanks to the naked woman sitting on the ledge of the pool behind him. Her legs, which had formerly been draped over Jamil's shoulders, had gripped the man's neck so tightly at Seth's approach that she was all but choking him.

The other woman clung to Jamil's side, as though that slim reed of a man could protect her from Seth. Not that Seth would ever harm a woman.

Yes, he definitely should have eaten. He rolled his shoulders to loosen them and tried to look nonthreatening.

"You are Jamil?" Seth prompted. "I have a few questions. Your answers would be valuable to me."

The woman seated on the pool ledge relaxed her legs and adopted a sensual pose, propping her hands behind herself and leaning back to display her impressive breasts to full effect. Too bad it was entirely wasted on Seth.

Leaving one leg draped over Jamil, who was giving his throat a gentle massage, she extended the other and used her toes to playfully flick water in Seth's direction.

"I have all the answers you could need," she teased.

Seth, who could not be rude to a woman as he would be to a man, looked away uncomfortably.

Why the hell he had to look in *that* particular direction at *that* particular moment, he did not know. Apep, that devious little god of mischief, must be having a laugh at him. Because at that exact moment, a certain bronze-skinned man went walking—no, not walking, *sauntering*—by.

Seth caught only the briefest glimpse of Raider's face, but there was no mistaking it: the interesting angles and straight nose, the sharp cheekbones. His thick dark hair remained a mess of waves, but his beard had been trimmed close to enhance the line of his jaw and his hollow cheeks.

Part of Apep's prank, clearly, was making Seth stumble over his earlier insistence that it was the flashy clothes that made Raider striking. There was no ornamentation to catch Seth's eye this time. No gaudy dagger. No billowing kaftan or violet sash. No clothes at all, in fact, and soon that glimpse of Raider's face was gone—and Seth found himself staring at the man's broad shoulders and muscled back, his firm ass flexing as he walked.

"Maybe I *don't* have the answers you need."

Seth ripped his gaze away and returned his attention to Jamil and his companions. The woman who had spoken pouted playfully.

Seth scrubbed sweat from his eyes. Why the hell was it so hot in here?

"My beauties," murmured Jamil, "come back in five minutes. That is"—he narrowed his eyes at Seth—"assuming you understand that it's not only my answers that are valuable, but also my willingness to interrupt my bath."

"Of course."

The women withdrew from the pool and set off toward the curtains that likely shielded the women's area. They, too, were naked, like most of the pools' occupants. Somehow, though, no one seemed to be on display quite like Raider.

In the absence of ornamentation, he used his movement to draw attention. Carelessly confident, obnoxiously sensual—

"Your questions?" Jamil prompted.

"Right." Seth crossed his arms and focused on the matter at hand. "You sold an arcane scope in Demir. Where did you get it?"

Jamil stroked his thin mustache with a finger, just as Raider had described. Gods, could the man not stay out of Seth's head for two minutes?

"It is hard to remember," mused Jamil.

Seth extracted a denar from where he'd secured it in the folded edge of his towel. He flicked it Jamil's way. Like a fish jumping from a pond, Jamil lunged and snatched it from the air.

"Ah, yes," he said, admiring the silver coin. "A slim young man, almost boyish. Brown eyes. Brown hair, not much darker than yours."

Being fair was unusual anywhere in the Sands, the arid region that stretched from the western edge of Masiri authority all the way to the Golden Empire east of the Kesh Desert, then farther still into the near-mythic lands of the djinn. But it wasn't enough, not without a mention of Julian's most distinguishing feature.

"Tell me more about him," Seth pressed. "Everything you remember."

"Why? Is he your lover? Or he owes you money?"

"I just need to find him."

Jamil snorted. "That is not likely. The fool is surely dead by now."

When Jamil subsided and adopted a distant, thoughtful look, Seth dug out another denar but didn't toss it. "*Everything* you know."

Eyeing the gleam of silver in Seth's fingers, Jamil said, "He had a reddish birthmark." Jamil indicated the approximate location on his own face, at his left temple. "He tried to keep it covered, but I saw it."

Seth didn't allow the relief to show on his face. Confirmation, finally. He'd come all this way, afraid it was for nothing, afraid he'd lost the trail.

"Is he still in Shalaa?"

Jamil continued eyeing the coin. "No. He traded the spyglass for supplies. Then he headed into the Kesh. So you see: surely dead."

Maybe, maybe not. Julian had never struck Seth as particularly rugged, but he was actually quite a brilliant alchemist. In fact, he had worked with the artifice department to develop the compact alembic that Seth himself would be relying on to purify water … in the Kesh.

It was too much to have hoped, of course, that Julian would still be in Shalaa.

Seth asked, "Did he say anything about his destination or what he was after?"

"No. He was wary. Nervous even, like maybe someone was after him. It seems he was right. But he is dead anyway. Only the Sudai tribesmen cross the Kesh. And one other."

Seth yielded the coin, flicking it to Jamil. The man was telling the truth. Seth had a good instinct for such things.

Besides, this was the most information he'd gotten from anyone in weeks. It was, finally, a clear indication of direction. And it was a confirmation of what he'd suspected all along: that he was going to be slogging his way across the vast, sandy waste of the Kesh.

Seth said, "I'll need any information you have on the Kesh. Directions to oases, distances, that sort of thing."

Jamil gazed fondly at the coins in his hand and replied sadly, "I wish I could help you, O Generous One, but there is only one who can, only one crazy enough to travel the Kesh."

Seth closed his eyes as an awful premonition overtook him. "And who might that be?"

"Him."

Seth opened his eyes to follow the direction of Jamil's pointing finger. Then he closed his eyes again to compose himself.

Of course.

Of *course*.

Because who the hell else could it possibly be?

Chapter 4

RAIDER WATCHED THROUGH slitted eyes as the Curator came striding across the bathhouse. The man's bare torso was deliciously carved with muscle above the blue and white patterned towel. His powerful legs flexed below it to pleasing effect.

Raider couldn't imagine what had the man moving his way, but he wasn't about to complain. He didn't even mind that the Curator looked half inclined to violence. On the contrary, that aggressive stride and the emerald fire in his eyes had Raider's cock stirring under the water's surface.

With the pool recessed into the floor and Raider reclining to offer a full frontal view, Seth would easily be able to see Raider's reaction to him if he looked down. However, when the Curator halted on the opposite side of the pool, he also halted his eyes at Raider's face.

"You found me!" Raider exclaimed, stretching his arms out on either side along the pool's ledge.

"You're staying at the tavern?"

"Are you trying proposition me?"

The Curator's body went positively rigid, and the flush in his cheeks deepened. Raider let his gaze drop to Seth's groin, just in case, but the Curator's towel hung flat.

"Don't be absurd. I need to speak with you but would rather not do that while you're naked in a pool."

"It *is* a bit awkward when you're not naked in the pool as well."

"Absolutely not."

"Why so shy? You have a fantastic body. Unless … not all of it's fantastic?" he baited.

"So you *are* flirting with me."

Raider laughed. "Were you unsure before?"

Those green eyes narrowed. "Did you follow me here?"

"There's only one major street in Shalaa, so … technically?"

"You know that's not what I meant."

"Would you get in the pool already? It's uncomfortable talking to you up there. I'm getting a crick in my neck." Raider rolled his head to demonstrate.

"Answer my question."

"I just got in from six days of desert travel. Where else would I go?"

Seth's nostrils flared. He didn't acknowledge that salient point but didn't argue it either.

"You'll be at the tavern tonight?"

"Hard to say. I don't like to sleep alone, so it will depend on what invitations I get. You're free to make one."

Raider knew he was pushing the man, but tension like this couldn't be wasted. The two of them needed to fuck or fight. Raider would accept nothing less.

But Seth displayed the same control of himself that he'd shown earlier. "Fine," he bit out, glaring. "We'll just have to do this here."

"While I appreciate your confidence in my ability to find a welcoming bed and thus be unavailable tonight, I do have to ask: do what?"

"Have a conversation."

"Aren't we already having a conversation?"

"You keep pulling me off task. I have questions—"

"*Seth.* You stormed in here bursting at the seams with business, but look around! This is a *bathhouse.* Enjoy the steam room. Get a massage! You're as tight as a miser's purse strings. At the very least, get in the damn pool."

Seth stared at Raider. Raider stared back. Yes, he could be stubborn too.

And he had the upper hand, which he wasn't about to waste. Seth had found Jamil then had come straight to Raider. That meant he wanted something.

But Raider wanted something too. He wanted Seth to get in the pool. At this point, it was a matter of principle as much as one of attraction. Raider's arousal, which had only intensified as he continued staring at that half-naked, heavily muscled body and listening to that gruff voice, was starting to be less fun—and so was his mood.

Seth, however, showed no signs of acquiescence. He stood in rigid refusal, his severity at odds with the lush surroundings of steaming water and relaxed voices.

But.

But.

His towel no longer lay entirely flat. He wasn't fully hard, but he was clearly turned on. By Raider's defiance? The man liked a little fight with his fucking, did he?

Unfortunately, the Curator proved himself capable of ignoring his arousal in the same way he'd ignored his audibly growling stomach at Ahmet's tavern.

"Look," Seth said, "I need information on the Kesh. I hear that you're the 'only one crazy enough' to travel it. What you know, I need to know. Distances. Directions. Probable dangers. For that, I'll get in the pool, but not for anything else."

All the teasing went right out of Raider. Before he could even think to lure Seth into the water with false promises, he said, "I will not give you that information."

"I'll pay."

"I will not sell you that information either. Any advice from me would only get you killed more slowly."

"With or without your information, I will be crossing the Kesh. I would ... appreciate"—the man really could grind out a word, couldn't he?—"any details you are willing to sell."

Raider felt his lips peel back from his teeth. "*I* am made for the Kesh. You are not. Whatever it is you're after, it's not worth dying for. Go back to your college, and leave the Kesh to the likes of me."

Seth's nostrils flared with obvious frustration. "I thought you liked money."

"I like money only insofar as it brings me pleasure. I would get no pleasure from selling you your own death."

Seth appeared on the verge of walking away, but Raider wanted to do it first. His afternoon was spoiled anyway, the joy of the bathhouse gone. Besides, he had one last play to make.

Raider levered himself out of the pool. As he climbed to his feet on the ledge, he kept his eyes locked on Seth, wondering if the Curator would refuse to look.

But, oh, he looked.

Those green eyes dropped to Raider's groin. At the sight of Raider's arousal, Seth's nostrils flared.

Mollified at having caught his prey, Raider snatched up a towel from the stack on a nearby stone bench.

Seth's eyes jerked up to Raider's face as Raider wrapped the cloth around his waist. He secured his dick against his abdomen with the towel, then he walked past the silent Curator and through the steam of the bathhouse.

It was time to get delightfully, disgustingly drunk.

Chapter 5

RAIDER SLID FROM the mattress to the floor with a groan and began the process of levering himself up. Cocooned in the wool-stuffed luxury of Ahmet's (second best) bed, he'd slept like a rock.

He had, unfortunately, also slept alone.

He had only himself to blame. Sour and frustrated after his exit from the bathhouse yesterday, he'd been half drunk on raaki by the time the Curator had stalked into Ahmet's tavern. While ordering food for his room, Seth had pointedly *not* looked at Raider, which had been very annoying.

So Raider had decided that his best approach was to shamelessly stare at the man.

Ahmet, consequently, had found himself the focus of an increasingly intense green-eyed gaze. By the time the Curator had stalked off to Ahmet's (first best) room, the tavern keeper's heavy eyebrows had climbed nearly at his hairline.

Raider did not achieve his desired state of full, delightful drunkenness until much later in the night, probably around the time the raucous music in Shalaa's fountain square had driven the residents of the surrounding houses to shout for the town guard.

Of course, it might have been the increasingly raunchy jokes or the nude dancing that had been the last straw. Whatever the case, the four men who constituted the town guard had finally been persuaded to peel themselves away from their dance partners, remove the strings of colorful beads from around their necks, and disperse the crowd.

Swept along in the exodus, Raider had stumbled his way to Ahmet's back gate, where his staggering entrance had been greeted with a slurpy dog kiss and wagging tail. At least *someone* had wanted him.

In truth, several someones had greeted him with (less sloppy) kisses, but everyone had seemed so … uninspiring … after the Curator.

Usually, Raider *liked* soft, easy, and flirtatious. Seth had put him in a strange mood.

Raider's mood right now was little better. Sleeping drunk meant sleeping like the dead. The absence of dreams was marvelous. Waking as stiff as a corpse was not.

Raider rolled his left shoulder carefully and stretched his spine.

Kahve. That was what he needed.

Clothes might also be a good idea, though his were not in evidence. Ahmet, however, had left him a thigh-length skirt of green-dyed linen.

When he put it on, the skirt revealed itself to be slit to the hip on each side. Raider tried to gauge how it looked, but his neck was too stiff to allow a good view. He trusted that it was magnificent.

Jutting back from its main room and kitchen, the tavern had two wings, one for guests and one for Ahmet. These sections made a three-sided enclosure of Ahmet's courtyard, with a gated mudbrick wall dividing it from the alley. The gate, through which Raider had staggered last night, was almost always open. Ahmet did most of his cooking (and gossiping) in the courtyard.

Raider emerged from the kitchen to find Ahmet, wearing a leather apron over his striped robes, stoking the fire under the spit in the middle of the open space.

Ahmet's heavy-jowled, tawny dog, known improbably as Jasmine, didn't budge from his hopeful place by the cook, though he did give his whip of a tail a wag at Raider's arrival. Jasmine guarded the courtyard from riffraff, which, naturally, did not include Raider.

Not that there was much to steal, even with the motley goods crammed along one wall: a spare bed, a broken table (that Ahmet had been saying for years he was "about to fix"), rugs, pots, and the ifrits only knew what else.

Ahmet made a grand gesture toward the spitted meat. "Pork tonight, as requested."

"I requested it for breakfast," Raider reminded him grumpily, making his way to the social side of the courtyard. There, beside a bench, a low table held a steaming carafe and several glass cups. "And what about my sesame seed cakes?"

"There's kahve," Ahmet informed him, flapping a hand in the general direction of the carafe.

"You're horrible, Ahmet. And it wasn't a request, it was a deal. You promised me."

"I did no such thing. And there are almond biscuits in the jar, so stop being a child. You're awful in the mornings."

Grumbling, Raider bent to pour himself a cup of kahve and extracted four biscuits from the pottery jar.

"Mind the slit on that skirt please," Ahmet said.

Raider glanced down. He'd loosened up enough on the walk from his room to get a decent look. The skirt revealed a flattering section of his flank.

"You're the one who took my clothes. I'll make no apologies to you."

"They stank."

"The pants were clean!"

Ahmet shot Raider a they-most-certainly-were-not look over his heavy shoulder. Raider decided not to argue the point.

Settling on the low bench beside the table and leaning back against the wall, he extended his legs and crossed them at the ankles. He held out a biscuit.

As Jasmine trotted over, Ahmet ordered, "Don't give him that. He's getting fat."

"Too late. I already promised. Some of us keep our word."

Ahmet rolled his eyes to the heavens.

Jasmine's powerful jaws looked capable of biting Raider's hand off, but the dog's teeth closed with extreme gentleness on the offered biscuit. Then, as though Raider might change his mind and snatch the biscuit back, Jasmine spun away and trotted to the kitchen with his prize.

"Ridiculous," muttered Raider.

Ahmet was rummaging through his stack of pans, making Raider wince at the noise. Ahmet returned to the fire with what he referred to as his "magic skillet." He slid it onto the grate below the spitted meat then disappeared into the kitchen.

With the promise of food comfortably in his future, Raider sipped the kahve and munched on one of the almond biscuits.

Ahmet returned with a basket of eggs, a platter of leftover lamb, and Jasmine at his heels.

"No," Ahmet said firmly as he scraped the lamb into the skillet on one side and began cracking eggs into it on the other.

Jasmine walked over to Raider. When the hopeful wag of his tail was met with an I'm-sorry-friend shrug, Jasmine settled on the ground by Raider's feet.

Ahmet said, "He thinks you are the easier mark."

"I am. I'm very easy. Just look at this skirt."

Ahmet sent him a wicked grin. "I thought you would like it."

"Too bad it's just you and Jasmine here to admire the view. Don't you have some other overnight guests?"

"Only one, as you well know, and he left early this morning."

"Ah."

Raider swirled an almond biscuit in his kahve, busying himself to conceal his disappointment. He knew he should be pleased. After all, he *had* told Seth to go home. Even though the man looked tough as hell, even though he was built to fight and well-armed for it, it didn't matter. The Kesh was a thousand dangers, a thousand ways to die.

Besides, the sooner Raider forgot about the Curator, the better. He never got hung up on a man, and he didn't like the feeling. Sure, it had been fun at first, but fun had turned into frustrating, and that wasn't Raider's style.

"Ooh, yum," he said, setting his kahve aside to take the plate Ahmet held out to him. He scooted over on the bench to make room for Ahmet, who settled in with his own plate of food.

Jasmine propped his chin on Raider's crossed ankles and gazed up at him forlornly.

"Oh, that's not fair, Jasmine," Raider complained. "How can I resist such beautiful, pleading eyes?"

"Don't you dare," warned Ahmet.

"Just look at him!"

"Raider, no." Quickly recognizing the futility of such an injunction, Ahmet said, "Jasmine, no."

The dog let out a heartbreaking sigh and curled up in a sad ball.

Raider shook his head. "Cruel."

"He already ate."

Raider chuckled and spooned up a steaming bite of lamb.

"Gods, Ahmet," he said around a mouthful, "it's even better today."

"It is very good," Ahmet agreed, and Jasmine sighed again. "But you, invoking the gods?"

"When I'm in a good enough mood, sure. And nothing puts me in a good mood quite like good food. Or raaki. Or handsome men. Sometimes music will do the trick."

"The gods make good and bad. You do not receive one without the other."

Raider groaned. "You want to ruin this delicious lamb with your sour-sauce words? I won't forgive you."

Ahmet shook his head despairingly. After a few more bites, he said, "He paid for another night."

Raider's heart skipped, but he didn't raise his eyes from his plate. "So this means I'm still stuck with the second-best room, huh?"

"I see I anticipated your disappointment correctly," came Ahmet's sardonic reply. "Good thing I gave you food first."

"It is *always* best to give me food first."

"Yes. You and Jasmine are much alike."

Raider held out a piece of egg for the dog, which was accepted with great care and a pleasing tail thump.

"If you're trying to insult me, try again. He's glorious."

Ahmet snorted then said, "Don't give him any more."

✱   ✱   ✱

While Raider had enjoyed Ahmet's little prank with the skirt, he was glad to have his own clothes back before heading into the streets. The laundering had been worth paying for. His neatly mended kaftan was gleaming like a ruby, and his sandals felt clean and supple on his feet.

The scent of flatbread stalled him on his way to Jamil's shop.

"Agra!" he called. "What are you making, dear woman?"

She sent him a gap-toothed grin over her thin shoulder as she used a long-handled wooden peel to remove flatbread from her round-bellied oven. "Cinnamon and a secret spice."

"You wicked temptress."

Agra tipped the flatbread onto the wicker table. "It's almost midday. You need to eat, Raider. You are thin."

"Hardly, but that's of no consequence. I'll take two."

Agra practically hopped over to the oven again, expertly sliding the peel under another flatbread. "You are my best customer—when you're in town. Why must you leave all the time?"

"I'm a feather on the wind, Agra. Hopeless."

Agra wrapped the flatbreads in a palm leaf. "You are restless. Your soul is uneasy."

Raider smiled to cover his discomfort. "I'm just curious about the world. I like to see things."

She patted the back of his hand in a motherly sort of way. "Other things matter too."

"Yes, like food. Now hand them over, woman."

Agra extended both the palm leaf-wrapped bundle and an empty hand. Raider pressed a denar into the latter and was rewarded with another gap-toothed grin for his overpayment.

It wasn't far from Agra's stall to Jamil's shop, so the flatbreads were still steaming when Raider ducked inside to find Jamil haggling with a heavyset woman in dark robes.

She made him work hard for the sale, pointing out every imperfection in the lamp she sought to purchase. By the time they agreed on the price and she left with the lamp in hand, Jamil looked harried. He'd smoothed his thin mustache so many times it was a wonder the thing hadn't been worn clean off. Raider handed him one of the flatbreads.

"Ah!" Jamil brightened. "Cinnamon and … pepper?"

"Apparently it's a secret."

Jamil's thin lips split into a smile. "There is always a 'secret' in Agra's flatbread. And she always charges extra for it."

Raider shrugged. He didn't mind. He'd pay for Agra's hard work and delightful grin any day. What else was money for?

"So—" Jamil settled on a fringed cushion in the corner, where his hookah's glass belly billowed with steam. "You sold to Yusef yesterday."

Raider took a seat on a cushion beside him. "You weren't available. Besides, I sold to you last time. Remember the bracelets?"

Jamil waved this away and tore into the flatbread. Around a mouthful, he said, "I know why you're here."

"You do?"

"The man from yesterday. You want to ask me about him."

"What gave it away?"

"You have nothing to sell me—" Jamil paused as though hoping Raider would contradict him then went on, "And I sent him your way in the bathhouse. It did not look like you had a happy conversation. Though it did look … stimulating."

Usually, Raider felt no embarrassment about such things, but he found his cheeks heating. He made himself smile anyway. "He's very attractive."

"He seemed to have similar thoughts, given the way he was staring at your ass when you first walked by."

Raider sat up straighter. "Oh?"

"Of course," Jamil added, "you walk like everyone should be staring at it."

"And why shouldn't they?"

"One of these days, Raider, you will attract more attention than you know what to do with—maybe his."

Raider sighed. "Everyone is making portentous comments today. Can we not simply enjoy a bite of food and a smoke?"

"And answers to your questions?"

"Well, if you're offering ... But first—was he really staring at my ass?"

"He was staring at you. I cannot swear to the precise target of his gaze."

Raider consoled himself with a bite of Agra's delicious flatbread. "What did he want from you yesterday?"

"Why didn't you ask him that yourself? You were certainly talking long enough."

"We mostly argued. He wanted to cross the Kesh. I told him he was crazy and talked him out of it."

"No, you didn't. He was in here not long ago, ordering supplies."

"*What?* Why the hell did you sell him supplies that will only get him killed?"

Jamil shrugged. "I am a simple merchant. If he is crazy, that is his trouble, not mine."

Raider gritted his teeth. "Where is he now?"

Chapter 6

"A RE YOU *INSANE?*"
Seth released the hoof he'd been inspecting and straightened beside his horse's shoulder. Raider was standing outside the stall, his eyes blazing with fury.

So. There was a temper underneath all that rakish charm.

Not that Seth found him charming. And not that there hadn't been a few hints of the temper already. Sharp words. A moment when his eyes, at least the right one, had seemed to flash as they spoke in the bathhouse yesterday. It had happened in Yusef's shop, too, though Seth assumed it to be a trick of the light, something in the way it sometimes caught the amber, giving it a flare of gold.

Seth calmly crossed his arms, pleased to be the one in control this time. It helped that he wasn't starving. One thing he'd say for this town: the food was good.

It also helped that he'd finally dealt with his cock.

He'd done his best, his very fucking best, to resist, refusing to take his hand to himself even when he'd woken hard and aching and grinding unconsciously into the mattress. Normally, Seth didn't deny himself release because that only ever turned him into an asshole—which was exactly what he'd been this morning.

The self-denial had been a matter of principle (and maybe a bit of stubbornness) because when he'd woken up grinding like that? He'd had some very disturbing images in his mind. Images of the man standing in the stable aisle right now. In those images, though, Raider hadn't been wearing his ruby and sapphire silks. Hell no.

The images that had had Seth's cock leaking had been pretty fucking raw and pretty fucking dirty—and inspired very much by what he'd seen yesterday at the bathhouse. Mostly, Seth's sleep-addled, uncontrolled mind had imagined Raider's bare, muscled ass taking a pounding from Seth's cock. But then there had been the full frontal view that Seth had gotten when Raider had emerged from the pool, his cock jutting out stiff and thick and so fucking perfect that Seth's brain had conjured images of that cock spurting cum while Seth fucked him.

Seth hated that he'd dreamed that shit. Not that he'd never had sex dreams, but he didn't like them being about a man like Raider. A thief and a rogue, Raider was nothing that Seth should be attracted to.

So Seth had told his dick no, and he'd dealt with his swollen balls all damn morning. Until he'd walked by the bathhouse. Until those images had come back. Cock aching, pissed off, Seth had found a quiet place and had dealt with his problem.

He didn't like how he felt about it, especially with Raider standing four feet away. For fuck's sake, he didn't even *like* the man.

But at least the physical release made Seth capable of leveling a steady gaze and saying calmly, "I don't know what you mean."

"Get your ass out here."

"What makes you think you can order me around?"

Raider's right eye brightened to gold as it had done before. Another trick of the light? The sunlight cutting through the stalls' square windows was certainly lighting up those silks, especially the gold trim on that kaftan. The silks were noticeably cleaner than yesterday, and the man's skin gleamed like polished bronze.

So damn flashy.

But maybe not as fake as Seth had first thought. Raider's anger, at least, was very real. Though why the hell anything about Seth should upset him was a mystery.

Raider snapped, "I am going to speak with you regardless of where you are, but I prefer not to scare your horse."

Damn it. It torqued Seth to comply, but the bay gelding was already reacting to the tension. When the horse let out a nervous snort, Seth stepped out from the stall, hooking the rope behind him to keep the animal in.

The boys who had been tending the horses had all mysteriously vanished, and even the public square beyond the open stable doors looked empty.

Raider made a slashing gesture. "You cannot go into the Kesh."

"You cannot prevent me, nor do you have any reason to attempt doing so."

"You fool, you have no idea what's out there!"

"I made clear that I would pay for information on 'what's out there.' You are the one who has refused to tell me, so you are the one—"

Pain crashed through Seth's jaw. He staggered from the force of Raider's punch. It wasn't often that he got taken by surprise, but that had come out of nowhere.

Seth stepped back to make space for his weapons. "Listen, you fucking lunatic—"

"You think you're tough enough for the Kesh?" Raider made a come-at-me gesture. "Prove it."

"I don't have to prove anything to you."

"Then I'll make you a deal. If you can beat me, I'll tell you whatever you want to know."

Seth briefly considered. On the one hand, he could practically feel the disappointment of his mentor across all the miles between here and the Arcanum. How many times had Marcus dragged him away from some boyhood tussle to lecture him on needless violence? How many times had Marcus led him through breathing exercises or told him to unclench his fists and hold a book instead?

On the other hand, this was a path to vital information. And maybe a chance to replace those images of Raider with ones less ... stimulating.

Apparently, the acquiescence showed on Seth's face because Raider unfastened the golden cloth toggles of his kaftan. In a single, fluid motion, he shrugged out of the red silk and slung it aside. Above the loose blue pants, Raider's build was what Seth vividly recalled: one of lean power, like that of the finest athletes in Masir's annual games.

That was all well and good, but Seth was heavier, stronger, and better armed. He had his sword at his back, a knife strapped to his thigh, and his chakram at his belt, the circular weapon razor sharp and delightful to throw.

Seth also had his arcane bracers and clothes to protect him from at least light damage. Raider had nothing but silk and that absurd dagger peeking out from his violet sash.

"Just remember," said Seth, "you asked for it."

He snatched his knife from its sheath and lunged.

Raider spun aside with shocking quickness, somehow grabbing Seth's wrist with one hand and slamming his other into the crook of Seth's elbow. Only a clever twist of Seth's wrist prevented Raider from relieving him of the knife.

Sweeping the weapon safely away from those clever hands, Seth slammed his other fist into Raider's chest, sending the man staggering back.

Seth rolled his shoulders and studied Raider in a new light. The teasing, playful look was gone from his amber eyes, and in its place was a sharp intelligence that Seth had not perceived in their previous encounters.

He should have noticed. It was the very kind of thing he usually *did* notice: that someone was not what they seemed, that they were hiding something. His instincts rarely failed him, but Raider had a way of getting under his skin, of distracting him.

Not anymore.

Feinting left, Seth slammed his knee into Raider's hip. He didn't pause to glory in Raider's bark of pain, instead grabbing for the man's throat.

But Raider had already ducked to deliver a breath-stealing punch to Seth's gut, doubling him enough that Raider somehow got him levered—and flipped Seth over his shoulder.

Seth slammed onto his back on the stable's packed-earth floor, stunned—then furious. No one had put him on his back in years.

Raider was too smart to go after Seth on the ground, likely knowing it would only get him tossed over Seth's head, or maybe knifed. He only watched as Seth got up slowly. Seth used the moment to recover his self-control.

Even knowing himself in check, he was sure the anger showed in his face, probably in his body too. Most men would have backed off. Raider's eyes, however, sparked with excitement, and he drew the curved dagger from his sash, tossing the jeweled sheath aside.

Motioning an invitation to Seth, he challenged, "Show me."

Seth feinted, lunged, parried. The two knives—one straight, one curved—clanged and scraped. Raider might be quick, but so was Seth, despite his size.

They fought for dominance, hunted for each other's weaknesses, set each other up for mistakes. Briefly, Seth lost himself in the enjoyment of an excellent opponent, someone who could take everything he had to give, someone who forced him to dig deeper than he usually had to.

Despite his excellent footwork, Raider was losing ground, backing toward the stable doors. When they reached the entrance, Seth spun in close and slammed his elbow into Raider's throat. At least, that was what he tried to do. Instead, he caught the fast-moving man in the jaw.

Before Raider could recover, Seth kicked him in the chest. The blow sent Raider flying back into the empty space of the public square.

One might have thought Raider's enthusiasm would have been dimmed by that, but he rolled to his feet, grinning.

Seth sheathed his knife and reached above his shoulder to yank his sword from its scabbard. Clear of the stable, he could now wield the powerful weapon. And end this.

Seth spun, slashing right and left, sweeping the blade in deadly arcs. Raider ducked and wove around every cut. He was a flash of blue silk and bronze skin. He was mesmerizing.

Seth focused even harder, putting all he had into the fight. Anticipating Raider's sidestep, a move he'd pulled before, Seth intercepted him with the sword. Seth nearly sliced into the man's side, but Raider curved away from the blade at the last second. On his spin, Raider snuck in a slash at Seth's upper arm.

Seth barely felt the pain—but he did feel the anger of allowing an opponent to cut him.

Picking up speed, he lunged and slashed with ruthless strength, forcing Raider toward the well.

When Raider stumbled against the stone, partially losing his balance, Seth brought his sword down in a brutal, fight-ending blow. He had enough control to check the weapon, to not kill or maim, but he had every intention of giving Raider a mark to remember him by.

But even that didn't happen.

What did happen was hard to understand.

His sword rang against metal.

Where a second ago there had been only bare skin, gleaming metal appeared, ridges of it overlapping in a shoulder guard. The metal had a pearlescent sheen, and the light played over it in a way that made it seem to move, almost like liquid.

Stunned, Seth didn't even see the coming sweep of Raider's leg. It took Seth's feet out from under him and he slammed, once more, onto his back.

Raider was on him in an instant, bringing that curved dagger to Seth's throat. Raider's lips had peeled back to bare his teeth in a snarl. That right eye flared fiercely, undeniably—but the left was even stranger.

Its pupil spun and dilated with arcane precision.

What the fuck—

"There's far worse than me in the Kesh," Raider said.

Then, before Seth could even form a question, Raider shoved himself to his feet and stalked off across the square. The metallic shoulder guard had vanished from sight.

Chapter 7

Seth stepped from the tavern's kitchen into its courtyard. The evening sun cast a mellow glow through the square space, where a cooking fire smoldered under a heavy iron pot and junk was stacked along one wall.

Along another wall, a low table held a jute-wrapped pottery jug and several cups. Beside the table was a bench. On the bench was Raider, bare chested and slumping against the mudbrick wall behind him. A big tawny dog lay at his feet, canine chin resting on Raider's crossed ankles.

Raider's head, resting against the wall, rolled Seth's way. "I told Ahmet I wanted to be left alone."

"I told Ahmet I would pay for a third night."

"Bastard." It wasn't clear whether Raider meant Ahmet or Seth.

"What are you doing?" Seth asked, even though the answer was obviously that he was in the process of getting drunk. Well, drunk*er*.

"I'm cooking."

"Is that so."

"I stirred it recently. Though why I would help Ahmet turn that beautiful pork into stew, I do not know."

Seth walked to the cooking fire and used the long wooden spoon to stir the stew, inhaling the delicious scents of pork, onion, chili, and spices. His mouth watered.

"I'm the one who's cooking," Raider said.

"It was about to burn to the bottom, which Ahmet said was likely—with you cooking. He told me to stir it."

"He doesn't trust me," Raider complained.

"Probably because you're drunk. Do you ever spend a day sober?"

"Not if I can help it."

"So. A thief, a cheat, and a drunk. Fantastic."

Damn it. Seth had been determined to be civil. He'd spent a solid hour lecturing himself on the subject.

Because …

Because he needed Raider.

Seth hated that fact, viscerally. It knotted his gut, set a fire in his heart, made his jaw clench so hard his teeth ached. He wanted to get away from this man. He wanted to be done with this mission.

But he needed one to accomplish the other. More than one god, it seemed, was having a laugh at him. This kind of cruel joke went beyond the mischievousness of the squat little trickster Apep. This felt like a divine conspiracy.

On a certain level, Seth knew that his reaction was extreme, even unreasonable. But he couldn't control how he felt. Every time he interacted with Raider, it was like all the years he'd spent learning to so carefully govern himself puffed into smoke. It was like he was once again the boy with bruised knuckles, disappointing Marcus, disappointing the Arcanum, wondering if he was about to be tossed onto the streets where Marcus had found him.

But even if Seth couldn't control his feelings, he needed to control his actions—and his mouth. Because he'd come here, unfortunately, to hire Raider. Which meant he probably shouldn't sling insults at the man.

Raider's eyes had narrowed slightly, though he looked more assessing than offended. Maybe he wasn't as drunk as he looked. What the hell was Raider thinking about?

Instead of giving Seth any clue, Raider rolled his head to look at the dog and said, "Jasmine, he's not being nice. You're supposed to keep the riffraff out, you know."

The dog sighed against Raider's crossed ankles and offered a tail thump.

When Raider lifted his eyes to Seth again, he focused on the blood-red bundle in his hand. "You brought my kaftan?"

"And the dagger sheath." Seth walked over to him and held out the items.

Raider, frowning, didn't take them.

"What?" Seth asked.

"I left them. You could easily have sold them."

"That doesn't mean I would. I'm not a thief. Or a cheat."

Gods, why could he not get control of his damn mouth? The points were relevant; maybe that was why. Because working with someone so unprincipled, *relying* on him?

Frustrating at best. Downright dangerous at worst.

But the man was still Seth's best chance of completing his mission.

Raider had to peel himself off the wall to take the kaftan and sheath from Seth's hand. He did it with a grunt of effort. His abdominal muscles contracted and the drink sloshed in his cup. Setting the bundle on the ground, Raider settled against the wall again.

Apparently, it had been too much to hope that Raider would put the kaftan *on*.

Raider said, "If you think it's cheating to use one's natural advantages, even by surprise, then I was definitely right and you don't belong in the Kesh. Because she's a nasty bitch with more tricks than me. And I only survive her because of my natural advantages—which you don't have."

"So that was your point? With the fight?"

"That was my point. Doesn't mean I didn't enjoy it. So did you." When Seth didn't respond, Raider pressed, his voice sharpening, "Admit it."

Definitely not as drunk as he looked. Too much focus in those amber eyes, which narrowed at Seth's stubborn silence.

"Fine," Seth admitted. "I enjoyed it."

When Raider's usual grin returned, Seth was struck by how different Raider's face could look. It was the same almost-too-prominent cheekbones over hollow cheeks, the same fine, straight nose, all of it somehow so damn striking, so damn hard to look away from. But that face could look charming and easy—or it could look pretty fucking dangerous.

Raider seemed to prefer the former. Body loosening, clearly pleased by Seth's admission, Raider patted the bench beside himself.

"Sit. Have a cup of raaki. And if you try to fucking pay for it again, I swear on the head of my boy Jasmine—"

"Wait. Jasmine is … not a girl?"

Raider looked to the dog again, who rolled soft brown eyes at him.

"Should we even let him drink with us?"

"Who the hell named him Jasmine?"

"When he was a puppy, he slipped his collar one night and broke into Nadja's perfume shop, where he had a nice little romp. The evidence of his guilt was overpowering. He positively reeked—of jasmine."

Seth surprised himself with a laugh, which did something funny to Raider's grin, softened it somehow. That softening triggered a strange feeling in Seth's chest. One that was even less comfortable than his usual annoyance.

Needing something else to focus on, Seth crouched to meet the dog. He was really more of a cat person, but he let the dog sniff him then scratched Jasmine's chin when he lifted it from Raider's ankles.

Meanwhile, Raider leaned over to the table and poured raaki into another cup. He held it out to Seth.

It was lucky, Seth knew, that Raider kept making these openings. Seth needed them—because he needed Raider. And because he was having such a hard time accepting that fact.

It was easy enough, though, to accept the cup. Slightly harder to make himself sit on the bench beside the man, but Seth managed it.

The bench wasn't very big, so they were almost touching, especially with the extra crowding from Seth's gear and weapons. Seth felt far too aware of that fact and of the other man's body, bare from the waist up, muscles carved under smooth bronze skin. Heat crept its traitorous way down through Seth's chest and gut.

"Your advantages," Seth began before that heat could reach its destination. "They're hardly natural. They're arcane."

When Seth had recovered from his surprise, when he'd thought about that shoulder guard, the truth had been obvious. He'd never seen quicksilver used like that, but the smooth liquidity, the pearlescent gleam?

It could be nothing else.

Quicksilver was a subject of controversy. Like every college within Masir University, the Arcanum broke down into departments: artifice, alchemy, language, divination, transmogrification. Though crossover wasn't uncommon and many arcanists worked within multiple fields, quicksilver was unique in being of interest to all of them. No one fully understood it, and it couldn't legally be used in humans. That was the law in Masir and in every other civilized state.

Because of that, at first Seth had thought that the quicksilver must be housed in an external arcane device, as it was in Seth's bracers and the glove that summoned his chakram's return. But as soon as he'd stepped into the courtyard and had gotten a good look at Raider, he'd seen the wound in Raider's left shoulder, where the quicksilver had pierced through his skin from within.

Whoever had implanted that quicksilver had done it illegally—and unscrupulously.

And what did it say of Raider, that he'd participated in such a thing, had accepted it into his body?

That he was also unscrupulous perhaps. That he had a high tolerance for pain.

There was the question, too, of why he had wanted it. Who had a need for such armoring?

A thief? Maybe.

A … raider? Yes.

And *this* was the man Seth needed to complete his mission? *This* was the man he kept getting hard for?

A cruel joke indeed.

Seth almost threw back the whole cup of raaki just to fortify himself, but Raider was doing that very thing (notably *not* having replied to Seth's observation about the quicksilver). The sight of Raider draining his cup stopped Seth from doing the same.

Yet, even in the wake of his unflattering assessment of Raider, Seth couldn't stop himself from watching the way the man's throat moved as he swallowed. He couldn't stop the image that flashed through his mind. His teeth, biting that neck, holding Raider down. Raider gasping, arching up into him with the gorgeous cock that Seth had glimpsed in the bathhouse.

Raider startled him out of this unwanted fantasy by thrusting his emptied cup at him.

"Can you refill this?" When Seth didn't immediately move to take the cup, Raider added, "It's that or I crawl over your lap to do it myself."

Before *that* could become an image as well, Seth snatched the cup from Raider's hand. He refilled it, using the moment to think. He wanted, desperately, to push Raider for an explanation of the quicksilver. Why he had it. Who had done it. How the hell it worked like that. Seth had never seen such a thing. But none of that mattered right now.

All that mattered was that, between Raider's quicksilver and his knowledge of the Kesh, he was uniquely suited to traverse it. As he had told Seth from the beginning.

Thus … Seth needed him, and not simply for his information. Seth needed the man himself. He had almost worked himself up to saying so when Ahmet spoke from the kitchen doorway.

"Two of you. *Two* of you out here to mind the stew."

Seth winced inwardly as Ahmet bustled his burly way over to the pot, but the man's glare fell solely on Raider.

"If it burns, I will scrape your supper from the bottom."

Raider said, "I was just about to—"

"No, you were not."

Ahmet continued to glare and stir for a long, pointed moment before returning to the kitchen with a loud sniff.

Raider sighed dramatically and regarded the dog. "Jasmine, one of them is mad at me and the other won't give me my raaki."

Jasmine moved his chin consolingly to Raider's knee. As Raider petted the wide dome of the dog's head, Seth held out the cup. Raider smiled. It was incongruous, such a playful-seeming man and that vicious arcane technology.

"I was only trying to help you, you know," Raider said. "In the stable."

"By attacking me? You have a very unhelpful way of helping."

"But you enjoyed it, remember?"

Movement in the kitchen doorway had both Seth and Raider glancing over. At the sight of Ahmet peering out, Raider pushed himself up from the bench with a grunt, dislodging the dog, and went to stir the stew. The dog followed him.

Raider gave every appearance of being relaxed as he stirred the stew and sipped his raaki, but Seth sensed the man's alertness. He was a little drunk, yes, but he was also waiting for something. Like he knew Seth had come here for a reason other than returning his kaftan.

Seth really wished that Raider would have put that kaftan on. The sight of muscle moving under that bronze skin as Raider tended the stew was damned distracting. It also made Seth keenly aware of the fact that if Raider agreed to guide him across the Kesh, they would be spending weeks together, just the two of them: riding, cooking, sleeping. Seth would see that body all the time.

He would just have to deal with it. With any luck, eventually his annoyance with the man would overpower his illogical, unwanted attraction.

"So," Seth began. "About the Kesh—"

"*What*, on the gods-forsaken earth, is so important about getting across the Kesh? *Why* can you not stop working for one minute? It's a beautiful goddamned evening. You have a cup of the best raaki west of the Kesh in your hands and the promise of pork and chili in your future. Why can't you just *enjoy it*, you obsessive, stubborn mule?"

"Because I have a job to do, you lazy asshole!" Damn it, this was hard enough without being challenged at every turn. "That's why I'm *here*. What the hell else could *possibly* induce me to voluntarily enter a conversation with *you*?"

Seth didn't know when he'd gotten to his feet, but he was on them, and Raider was stalking his way, that right eye brightening to gold. Was it, too, arcane, maybe in a different way from the other one? It must be. It had flashed too often for Seth to continue telling himself it was a trick of the light.

Raider's grin turned feral as he crowded into Seth. Seth's temper was still riding him, tempting him to grab the man. His instinct should have been to shove Raider away, but Seth knew that if he let his hands come up, that wasn't what he'd do.

"I have a feeling, Curator, that you're more capable of blending work and pleasure than you think."

"Step *back*."

"Tell me why you're here."

"I was about to, you colossal prick. Step the fuck back."

Raider's lips quirked, though he still looked predatory. "You're not here for information on the Kesh. You're here to hire me."

"Yes, I am. But if you don't step the fuck back—"

Raider shook his head, tsking. "You're going to have to get over this sensitivity about space."

"You're going to have to learn boundaries. And you'll have to read my next words off my fist because I won't say it again."

Raider snickered then all but purred, "Don't tempt me like that."

But he did step back. He returned to the cooking pot. He stirred again and sipped his raaki, his mood as mercurial as the quicksilver in his body.

Seth's mood was less easy to shift, so he started one of his breathing exercises. He was careful about it, tried to keep it subtle, but the way Raider glanced at him said that he knew what Seth was doing. The way Raider's lips twitched said he found it amusing.

What an asshole.

Stirring with a casual air, Raider asked, "Tell me then. What artifact or dusty scroll or scrap of arcane history could possibly be worth getting yourself killed for?"

Jasmine, who had popped to all fours, tensing at their almost-fight, resumed his position of hopeful readiness. Somehow that, more than Raider's easy tone, helped Seth calm down. Animals usually did that for him, which was one of the reasons he always left his apartment shutters open for the Arcanum's resident cats.

Seth sat on the bench again. His cock, half hard, was torqued uncomfortably in his pants, but he wasn't about to draw attention to it by adjusting it. Hopefully it wasn't obvious. Hopefully it would go the hell away.

He got back to business. "I'm not after an artifact. I'm after a man."

Raider frowned. "Is the Arcanum in the habit of abducting people? Is he to be taken back for *study*?"

Seth scowled. "I'm not going to abduct him. I'm going to arrest him and take him back to the Arcanum to stand trial for murder. He's an arcanist who killed a fellow scholar."

"It seems like a lot," Raider remarked, "sending a valuable—I assume you're valuable?—Curator haring across the Kesh after a fugitive."

Seth ignored the thrown-in question about his value. "The Arcanum takes murder very seriously. Most moral people do."

Raider waved that away. "Morals always have their limits. This is a fool's errand. You don't strike me as a fool."

Refusing to be baited, Seth confined himself to a simple, "I will complete my assigned mission."

"Why the hell don't you just go back to the University and tell them the trail went cold? Your arcanist is long gone. You're risking your life for nothing."

"I won't go crawling home, lying to save myself."

Raider huffed and stirred the pot again. "I take it back: you *are* a fool."

"It's a matter of principle. I wouldn't expect *you* to understand."

"Your principles must be strong indeed if you're willing to endure weeks of my—" Raider's eyes dropped pointedly to Seth's groin, where his arousal was, apparently, obvious. "—unwelcome company."

Raider had spoken with a distinct note of sarcasm, baiting Seth again, trying to either pressure him into an admission—or a fight. Seth wasn't even sure which the man would prefer, but he wasn't going to get either of them.

"All that matters is that I get across the Kesh."

Seth heard the flatness of his own tone. It was never good when that happened. It meant that if he snapped, it was going to be bad. He needed this settled so he could get away, walk this off, be alone.

He explained, holding himself level by force of will, "I know Julian came to Shalaa, and I know he headed out into the Kesh from here."

"He likely headed to Aqarat," Raider said, proving that he was capable of focusing on business after all.

"That's my thought as well. I will pay you five hundred denari to get me to Aqarat. We leave the day after tomorrow."

"I just got home. I'm tired."

"You weren't tired this afternoon."

A smile flickered across Raider's face. Seth, like an idiot, had opened a path for Raider to take the conversation off track, but the man, for once, didn't make use of that opening. He simply countered, "Eight hundred."

"Six."

"I'll tell you what. When we get to Aqarat, I'll let you decide what my help has been worth."

"That's ridiculous."

"I often am. As you may have noticed."

Something about the man had shifted again. This was a new mood, one Seth didn't know, but he wasn't in the right headspace to analyze it at the moment.

"So you're agreeing?" Seth pressed. "To guide me across the Kesh to Aqarat?"

"If I can't talk you out of it." Raider raised an eyebrow, seeming yet to hope.

"You can't."

Raider sipped his raaki. "Then, Curator, it seems we're going to be spending a lot of time together."

Chapter 8

Sitting on a jute rug in the shade of Gangi's tiny mudbrick house, Raider blew out a stream of smoke and passed the dokka pipe back to its owner. Gangi had cut the dokka with something bitter, a common practice in poor households, but the dokka still sent a soothing current through Raider's bloodstream.

Gangi set the pipe to his lips, puffing expertly. Eyes squinting in his thin, weathered face, the old camel breeder gazed across his dusty yard, where chickens scratched for whatever the hell there was to eat there. Raider's chestnut mare, Umae, dozed under the shade of Gangi's fig tree, hip cocked, one foot resting.

"Someone's coming," Gangi said.

Raider was already aware of that, and he didn't need the telescopic function of his arcane eye to identify the figure approaching along the road from town. Not with that aggressive stride. Not with those distinctive black clothes on that powerful body.

Even so, his eye zoomed in automatically, giving Raider a close-up view of Seth's face. He blinked it away.

It certainly hadn't taken the Curator long to find him. Not that it was a surprise. Shalaa was full of loose lips, and Seth was tenacious. He was also, as Raider's telescopic view had shown him, pissed off.

For once, Raider wasn't pleased to see the Curator. He had hoped Gangi would invite him to lunch with the family so Raider could share the salted pork he'd brought. As charity, Gangi would refuse the meat, but he'd accept it as a host gift. Rather, his wife would, and Raider wouldn't mind a bowl of the woman's fantastic tabbouleh.

"My traveling partner," Raider informed Gangi, who handed him the pipe again.

"Ah. Is it true he's a barbarian?"

"Who said that?" Raider took a deep draw of the dokka. Barbarian tended to be a catchall term for 'not from here,' but the way Gangi said it attached a less flattering meaning.

"Four different people. They say he has a very big sword."

Raider choked on the smoke. As he started hacking, Gangi rescued the pipe from his jerking hand and slapped him (unhelpfully) on the back.

By the time Raider was scrubbing his streaming eyes against his kaftan sleeve, mostly recovered, Seth was striding across Gangi's yard. Squawking chickens fled in every direction.

"Well," Raider drawled, eyes flicking from the sword pommel jutting above Seth's right shoulder to the man's groin. "If four people said it, I will dare hope it's true."

Now it was Gangi's turn to choke. As the man hacked smoke from his lungs, Raider gave him the same unhelpful pat that he had received.

"So *this* is what you're doing," Seth accused as he came to a halt in Gangi's yard, planting his fists on his hips, somehow fitting them amid the clutter of gear and weapons on his utility belt. "Smoking."

Had a word ever been laced with such contempt?

Raider was so torn between amusement and annoyance that he decided to keep to himself why he'd come to see Gangi. Let the man stew. He deserved it.

Eyeing Seth warily, Gangi climbed to his feet, dispelling Raider's last, faint hope of a lunch invitation.

"First light?" Gangi asked.

Refusing to get up just yet, Raider said, "Thank you, my friend."

Gangi hustled away on bare feet, robes flapping around his skinny legs as he ducked around the side of the house and out of sight.

"Must you be such a brute?" Raider asked lightly, hoping to see those green eyes spark with that delicious temper. (He would definitely take the temper over this steely judgment.)

Instead, Seth's gaze went flat. "I don't have time for games—"

"Or manners, apparently."

"—because I am on a schedule," Seth went on relentlessly, "which means that *you* are on a schedule."

Climbing to his feet, Raider let out a dramatic sigh designed to annoy Seth. "Back to work, it seems."

As Raider headed toward Gangi's fig tree to collect Umae, Seth bit out, "I need to speak with you."

Raider could guess why, and he didn't want to get into it here. He knew Seth's flat tone for what it was: the calm before a storm. He'd heard it yesterday in Ahmet's courtyard. He'd eased up on Seth then, had let him off easy. Raider wouldn't be so nice again.

But Gangi's yard wasn't the place for them to ... well, who knew? Fighting seemed most likely, but there were other possibilities.

"I need to take Umae back to the stables," Raider said as he untied the sleek chestnut mare and led her clear of the tree. "If you're fast enough, you can catch me there. If not, I'd try the tavern."

"Raider—"

He swung onto Umae's bare back, touched his heels to her sides, and enjoyed the look of blazing frustration on Seth's face as the mare leaped into a canter. Raider sent a parting grin over his shoulder.

✧   ✧   ✧

In Ahmet's (second best) room, Raider was packing a few final items into his saddlebags when the approaching tromp of heavy boots had his grin returning. He straightened as Seth whipped the doorway curtain aside and ducked inside.

Between the mattress on the floor, the washbasin, and Raider's strewn belongings, the cubby-like room offered little space for two men, especially when one was bristling with weapons.

"Do come in," Raider said pleasantly, as though he couldn't feel the tension practically vibrating from Seth in the cramped quarters.

"Don't fuck with my gear again." Seth crossed his beautifully muscled arms over the buckled front of his vest, his bracers creaking with strain along his forearms. "I hired you to guide me, not to tear my shit apart."

"When you hired me, I felt it was implicit that I was to get you across the Kesh *alive*. You and your horse, ideally. Some of your tack and gear was getting in the way of that." Raider tacked on, smiling, "You can thank me later."

Green eyes bored into him. "Let's get something straight. *You* work for *me*. If you have a suggestion, bring it to me, and I will consider it."

The man wasn't used to working with people, was he? Then again, neither was Raider.

"First. I do not have *suggestions*. As your guide, I will make many decisions, some of which you won't like or see the point of—because you lack my knowledge. Isn't that why you hired me?"

It was a rhetorical question, but Seth's mouth opened immediately with a reply, so Raider had to speak quickly over him. "*Second.* I thought you were in a blazing hurry, so it makes no sense to waste time hashing out every single detail."

"Oh, now you want to be in a hurry. I found you hanging out with some old man, *smoking.*"

"Yes, and you wasted time tracking me there," Raider drawled then emphasized, "Gangi is a camel breeder."

It was a test. Of the Curator's travel experience. Of his intelligence.

Seth closed his eyes as realization dawned. "You were buying butter."

Oh, good, so the man *was* high functioning. Not that Raider had really had any doubts.

He grinned. "How many times do I have to tell you that work and pleasure can be accomplished seamlessly?"

"You could have said that from the start. Any of my shit you wanted to change? You could have said. When I saw you drinking kahve in the courtyard—"

"I'm like the newly raised dead in the morning."

"—or when you saw me later in the bazaar." Seth's pulse beat visibly, deliciously, in his neck. "I know why you didn't."

Raider couldn't stop his grin from turning wicked. "Oh?"

Two short steps brought Seth's crossed arms almost close enough to brush Raider's chest. The proximity had Raider's skin prickling with anticipation. His cock stirred with interest.

"You enjoy needling me," Seth accused. "Admit it."

"With pleasure."

The easy admission didn't seem to satisfy Seth. "You get some kind of twisted thrill out of seeing me angry."

"I wouldn't call it twisted. You're gorgeous when you're angry. Didn't you know?"

Those green eyes sparked with some of that gorgeous anger—but it wasn't anger staining the Curator's cheekbones red. It wasn't anger that had his lips parting slightly.

"You don't think that's twisted, liking that?"

"Not in the least," Raider answered. "But I do think all this intensity is being wasted—when it could be put to mutually pleasurable use."

Seth's voice turned gravelly. "That's what you think you want?"

Eyes still boring into Raider, Seth uncrossed his arms and reached up with one hand. He gripped Raider by the throat and pushed him back against the wall. It wasn't a grab or slam, but it was firm, dominating—and it took Raider's cock from interested to rock hard in an instant.

Eyes burning, Seth squeezed slightly, cutting off Raider's air. Raider grabbed Seth's belt, narrowly missing the chakram's sharp edge, and yanked the Curator against him. Even through the heavy arcane fabric, it was obvious: that hard cock was every bit the magnificent one he'd hoped for.

As Raider's fingers skipped along Seth's utility belt, Seth squeezed his throat and ground into him. Raider's body roared to life. Fuck, he needed this. He'd needed it for days.

Seth's grip loosened to let Raider breathe, then it tightened again. "You like this?"

Yes. Absolutely.

Concealing whatever it was he'd lifted from Seth's belt in a closed fist, Raider slid his other hand between their bodies and grabbed Seth's dick through his pants.

"I like *this*," Raider answered, words rasping through his constricted throat.

The storm Raider had been waiting for flashed through Seth's eyes. Instead of unleashing it, however, Seth yanked away.

For a moment, the Curator stood in the middle of the cramped room, chest heaving, fists clenched, cock straining against the lacing of his pants. Raider's own cock was less constricted but no more satisfied.

Raider stared at him, baffled and pretty damn annoyed. It wasn't often that Raider was at a loss for words, but this was one of those occasions. Before he could figure out what the hell to say or do, Seth turned—and stormed from the room.

CHAPTER 9

IN THE PREDAWN dimness, Raider wedged the wrapped butter into his saddlebags, bid Gangi farewell, and climbed stiffly into Umae's saddle.

The early start had meant a cold breakfast and no kahve. It also meant chilly air, and that meant Raider's body hadn't warmed up enough to get supple. He shivered miserably (and stiffly) in his kaftan as he guided Umae onto the dirt track that would take him and Seth away from Shalaa.

The path lay wide here, where Shalaa's livestock, including Gangi's camels, frequently plodded back and forth to forage the nearby scrubland. Rocky hills lumped high in the distance, standing sharper against the sky as it lightened. Even though there was enough space for Seth and Raider to ride abreast, Seth kept his horse behind.

They hadn't spoken more than a handful of necessary words since yesterday, and those without flavor. That wasn't Raider's style and it wouldn't last, but he'd been … well, he'd been a bit upset.

Seth was so damn *stubborn*. He couldn't possibly deny that he wanted Raider, and Raider had no intention of denying that he wanted Seth. So what was the problem?

This was *simple*. Nothing on earth, in fact, could be simpler.

But Seth apparently, was determined to make it complicated and agonizing—as though it wasn't obvious what was going to happen.

Raider would *make* it happen. The alternative, giving up and giving Seth his space, wasn't to be considered. (Raider wasn't that nice, and it would be pointless in any case.) At the moment, though, Raider was inclined to sulk—and damn the man for making him do it!

As they reached the craggy, scrub-covered hills, the path narrowed, cutting around humps of tawny, crumbling rock.

When a rain of sandy debris fell pattering behind Raider, making Umae dance, he heard a familiar *shiiing!* and twisted in his saddle to see that Seth had yanked his sword from the scabbard angled across his back.

Above, a bell clanged dully, and Raider glanced up to see a goat leap its nimble way up the rocky slope. Somewhere in the distance, a boy shouted.

Raider chuckled. "We're still in civilization."

"This," said Seth, "is not civilization."

Seth sheathed his sword. He did it expertly, sliding the weapon home in a single, smooth movement over his shoulder.

He'd donned a white kaftan, which hung open over his Curator's garb. The hood framed his broad, handsome face, and the whole ensemble was a delicious mix of masculine power and elegance. Once again—damn the man. How was Raider supposed to stay mad at him when he looked like that?

"Ah, yes," Raider drawled, feeling more like himself. "How could I forget that our little town must look like a cluster of hovels to a big-city man like you?"

Seth frowned. "I'm not a snob."

"Yes, you are."

"We're on a goat track," Seth said pointedly, "not in Shalaa. Besides, is it really your town if you don't really live there?"

"I live there more than anywhere else, so, yes."

Seth frowned again, like a new thought had occurred to him. "Where *are* you from?"

"Oh, here and there." Raider untwisted himself and settled back into his saddle. "I'm a feather on the wind."

It was Raider's standard answer. People usually accepted it easily, gave a laugh or shook their heads, but the Curator made a contemplative sound that said the subject would come back up.

Raider's gut knotted briefly at the thought, but he turned his attention to the crystal clear morning and the rhythm of Umae's walk. He started working through the micro movements that helped loosen the quicksilver in his joints.

Around midmorning, Raider turned Umae south along the foot of a familiar hill. "There's water up here."

"I can see the birds," Seth replied, his tone ever so slightly short.

Raider smiled, even though Seth couldn't see it. Birds usually indicated water. The point, then, was that Seth could have found the well on his own.

Raider had nicked Seth's pride yesterday with his changes to the gear and supplies, and the man was still a bit touchy, it seemed, on the subject of competence.

The watering hole was a natural well tucked behind a rocky outcropping. A scrub hawk that had been drinking spread its brown wings and flapped away at their approach.

Raider leaped down from Umae and led her to the pool. She swung her haunches into the path of Seth's horse. She snaked her head around to send the gelding an ears-back warning for good measure.

"There's enough room for both of them if you'd make her behave," Seth grumbled, throwing back his kaftan's hood.

"He can wait for one minute. You don't hassle a mare unless you have to."

Raider knelt to scoop up the clear water. It made a lovely, cool track down his throat.

Seth muttered, "Geldings are so much nicer than mares."

"Geldings argue too," Raider pointed out, sucking down another scoop of water.

"Yes, but you can tell them no and they'll listen ninety percent of the time. Mares require constant negotiation."

"And a little finesse. I can see why they'd be a poor fit for you."

Seth flushed and looked away. He didn't say anything more, and Raider had the distinct feeling that he'd shamed him. Raider frowned. That hadn't been his intention.

When Umae had drunk her fill, Raider drew her away to let Seth bring his gelding to the water. After attaching the reins to Umae's saddle so they wouldn't get stepped on, Raider let the mare set to work cropping at the tough grasses surrounding the small pool.

He went to settle in a patch of shade and watched idly as the Curator tended his own horse. Then, water skin in hand, Seth headed toward the only other patch of shade.

It was tempting, oh so tempting, to let the man sit under the yellow-flowering quiva. The shrub, in full, intoxicating bloom, was dripping its pollen all over the ground.

But …

Raider called, "Don't sit there."

Seth halted and frowned, scanning the area. "Why? The bush?"

"Quiva."

"Toxic?"

"An aphrodisiac." Raider grinned. "Potent enough to be dangerous."

There was supposedly an antidote that rich men kept on hand so they could indulge without the risk of overdose—which could overstimulate the body into delirium, or oblivion.

Seth looked skeptical. "Most supposed aphrodisiacs don't really do anything."

Raider felt his grin turn wicked. "Then by all means, test it out."

Seth still didn't look convinced, but he turned away from the quiva. With a sigh of resignation that might have wounded a more sensitive soul than Raider, Seth came to join him in the quiva-free shade.

Because fresh grass wasn't to be wasted while traveling, they would stay until Umae and the gelding had mowed the area. The two horses would clear it in a quarter hour. Plenty of time for Raider to capitalize on having Seth trapped in the shade beside him.

Yet, somehow, Raider didn't want to. The man was pensive. Raider knew how to deal with intensity, even hostility, but he had no idea what to do with this.

So he stretched himself out on the ground, folded his hands behind his head, and settled in to rest. He'd taken the liberty of unfastening his kaftan to let the air cool his skin. Hopefully Seth would enjoy the view—and maybe consider the opportunities he was wasting.

But the Curator, Raider saw through slitted eyes, was gazing into the distance and fiddling with the cork of his water skin. Raider closed his eyes, opting to ignore the brooding silence.

Raider had just started to doze when Seth startled him with, "So … about yesterday."

Raider's eyes popped open. Seth was still staring out across the scrubland but instead of pensive he looked stiff. When Seth didn't go on, Raider prompted, "What about yesterday?"

"I … apologize."

"You did leave me pretty frustrated."

"No, I mean …" Seth swallowed visibly. "I choked you."

"Which I clearly enjoyed," Raider pointed out, confused. How had that not been obvious?

"Look, we don't need to discuss it," Seth said, as though he hadn't even heard what Raider had said. "I just need you to understand that I know it was wrong, and I'm sorry, and it won't happen again."

Raider sat up. "Well, I *don't* understand that because there's nothing wrong with that kind of thing if both people—"

"You think that's *okay*?" Seth's head whipped toward Raider. "You think it's okay for me to grab you by the throat and hold you down and fuck you?"

Raider's body rocked as arousal flooded him. He closed his eyes at the image that flashed through his mind. "Fuck, Seth."

Raider opened his eyes to find that Seth was staring out across the scrubland again, his expression grim. Raider snatched the water skin from him, mostly to get his attention.

Seth's eyes came back to Raider as he lifted the water skin to his lips and tilted his head back to drink. And, yes, the man watched him, watched his throat.

And, yes, his eyes drifted down to where Raider's cock was tenting his loose pants. A flush hit Seth's cheeks.

Raider lowered the water skin and corked it aggressively. "It's absurd, making us both miserable. What's the *point*?"

"The *point* is that, with you, I don't trust myself. I don't know why the hell I respond to you like I do."

He was responding now. Raider could see it, the ridge of his erection inside his pants.

"And, what?" Raider challenged. "You think you're going to hurt me? I hate to break it you, but you don't have a *prayer* of hurting me. I assume you've been fucking fragile little flowers, but I promise you, that's not what I am. Anything you can give, I can take—and I want to. And you want it too, so stop being such a damn coward."

Raider was sorely tempted to grab at Seth, to press his point, but that would give Seth something to fight, to push away, and the man had already proven himself fully capable of self-denial.

Besides, the horses had eaten the available grass, and it was time to go. As they finished up at the well, refilling the water skins and checking tack, they didn't speak again because, surprise, the overthinker was thinking. It was in his brooding scowl, his tension. He was still visibly aroused, but he refused to meet Raider's eyes.

Fine. Let him agonize. Surely his overly complicated brain would eventually circle around to the simple truth and he'd realize that Raider was right.

They headed out across the scrubland again as the sun climbed. Distracted by his frustration and the ache in his groin, it took Raider longer than it should have to notice the prickle of warning along the back of his neck.

Startled, he scanned the rocky hills mounding around them, using the telescopic range of his arcane eye to hunt for threats.

"What is it?" Seth asked.

"I'm not sure. Something."

Raider caught a flash of a movement. Even with his enhanced vision, the animal's tawny coat was almost impossible to distinguish from the craggy slopes, but Raider would know one of those anywhere. And where there was one, there was a pack.

"Shit."

"Bandits?" Seth guessed.

"Jackals."

"Oh."

Raider raised an eyebrow at Seth's dismissive tone. "You've clearly never met a black-jawed jackal. Hopefully they'll decide we're not worth their trouble."

It was too much to hope, of course, and it wasn't long before the horses started to prance and snort.

Raider unwound his kaffiyeh and shrugged out of his kaftan, letting the silks drape Umae's back. He drew his scimitar from its saddle scabbard. The curved dagger he'd lifted in il-Kemsa was good fun, but he preferred the scimitar's range for black jaws.

When they neared a rocky outcropping, Raider leaped down from Umae and held the reins out to Seth. Instead of taking them, Seth demanded, "What are you doing?"

"I want to look around that outcropping. She's not quiet enough, and neither are you."

"Bullshit. Tell me—"

"Did you hire me simply for the perverse joy of ignoring everything I say? Take the goddamn reins and let me do my job."

Seth snatched the reins from Raider's hand.

Without a backward glance, Raider crept toward the outcropping. He peered around it, his arcane eye picking up movement along the rocky, quiva-studded slope overlooking the path on one side. Hills mounded high on the other side, funneling travelers and passing prey into this channel.

If Seth and Raider proceeded, the jackals would stalk along until chance opened the perfect angle for them to spring.

Even alert and ready to defend themselves, there would be injuries, either to them or the horses. Better to control the situation. Better to be the hunter than the hunted.

Raider slashed the scimitar's curved blade across the inside of his left forearm, cutting deep enough to get the blood flowing. Then he headed up the craggy slope, scrambling from rock to rock, picking his way around the yellow-flowering quiva. He squeezed his arm to drip a trail of blood and ensure the jackals would choose him over Seth and the horses.

Raider worked his way toward a ledge of stone that would narrow the jackals' path of attack. When he reached his destination, Raider lay down on his back, bloody arm extended and scimitar angled across his bare torso.

Black jaws were keen opportunists and highly aggressive, so it didn't take long for them to move his way. Seth had no doubt been imagining jackals like the golden ones common in the west, but black jaws were twice the size of their more timid western cousins.

Two tawny-coated, black-faced jackals picked their way down the slope, sprinkling Raider with sand and pebbles. Several others followed in their wake.

The first two paused, sniffing. One snarled and snapped its jaws. When Raider didn't react, the jackal leaped down—and met his scimitar.

The jackal yelped and thrashed, but Raider was already rolling, slinging the attacker off his blade and down the slope. He was on his feet to meet the second jackal as it lunged. An upward slash slit its throat.

Two more jackals leaped for Raider. His scimitar caught one across the shoulder. The other snapped at Raider's bloody arm—and locked its jaws on quicksilver.

When the quicksilver responded like that, without his conscious thought, Raider was never sure if it was his own instincts triggering the armor's emergence—or if the quicksilver had a mind of its own.

Whatever the case, the arcane metal had burst from Raider's shoulder joint, slicing through his skin to form the ridged shoulder guard before cascading down his arm in an intricate pattern of shimmering ridges and gleaming studs.

It was beautiful. As much as Raider hated the quicksilver, he couldn't deny that. His body was a work of art.

The jackal's teeth screeched on the quicksilver as it slid off, but the brief grip on Raider's arm had yanked him off balance. Before he could recover his footing, the remaining jackals leaped down on him.

As the pack slammed into him, they all went flying off the ledge. Raider tumbled with painful thumps down the rocky slope, crashing through the quiva and sending up clouds of yellow pollen.

Raider thudded to a stop. Coughing on pollen and dust, dizzy and lit up with pain, he made himself get up. He tried to anyway. He was only halfway there when a tawny shape leaped for him.

Unable to bring his scimitar around in time, he braced for slashing claws and snapping jaws. But the jackal crashed into him limply—with a distinctive circular weapon lodged in its skull.

Raider shoved the body off him and staggered to his feet, but the pack had had enough. The survivors took off, leaping from rock to rock, vanishing up the slope.

Ten feet away, Seth slammed his sword into its scabbard and shouted, "What the hell is wrong with you?"

Chapter 10

Seth had followed Raider's order at first, staying back with the horses while Raider scouted ahead. At least, that was what Raider had claimed he'd be doing. Where Seth had seen him fall from?

That wasn't scouting. That was lying in wait. Which meant—

"You lied to me," Seth snarled, stalking toward Raider, whose bare torso was a mess of yellow-brown dirt, nasty scrapes, and fast-blooming bruises.

Raider's quicksilver shoulder guard was out, this time extending down his left arm in complex ridges and brutal studs. Seth only got a quick look at the intricate, pearlescent armor before it retracted with a slithering sort of movement and a hissing *shhhhkt*. It left a bleeding puncture wound in his shoulder—and its absence revealed a clean slash inside his forearm.

Seth pointed at the cut. "Unless one of those gigantic fucking jackals had a knife, you did that to yourself to lure the pack. What the hell were you doing?"

Raider squinted at him. "My job."

"The hell that's your job! Your job is whatever I say it is!"

Without the least reaction to Seth's words, Raider went to put one of the jackals out of its misery.

With a growl, Seth stalked over to the dead jackal whose skull was housing his chakram. He yanked the weapon free and wiped it clean on the jackal's coat. After hooking the weapon onto his belt, he triggered his bracer to retract its glove. Without the glove, the chakram's razor edge would cut his hand when thrown—or when the glove summoned it back. Lodged in bone, however, the weapon hadn't been able to answer the glove's call.

The mechanism unfurled from his hand and slid into its housing, not unlike Raider's armor. At least the glove didn't cut him every time he used it. What on earth could induce a man to accept such a thing into his body? How the hell had it even been implanted?

Finished dispatching the jackal, Raider straightened, swaying. Seth wasn't surprised he was hurt. He was lucky he hadn't been killed in a fall like that—a fall that had been completely unnecessary. If they had worked together, made a plan, divided the pack, it wouldn't have happened.

"Sit the fuck down," Seth ordered. "I'll get the horses and my medical kit."

He didn't wait to see if Raider complied. If the idiot fell on his ass, that was his own fault.

Relief flooded Seth when he found the horses where he'd left them, hastily tied to a scrubby tree. They sidled and whinnied at his approach, clearly unnerved, but at least they were there. He'd been afraid they might break their reins and bolt—and what a goddamn mess that would have been.

They had enough of a mess as it was.

Seth needed to get his temper under control and deal with whatever injuries Raider had sustained. He had to be coolheaded, objective, goal-oriented. Raider's lying and endangerment of himself (and by extension, Seth's mission) could be dealt with later.

When Seth returned with the horses, he found Raider leaning against a boulder. The man squinted at him.

Seth handed him the reins and went to dig through his saddlebags for his medical kit. He barely had the flap open before his horse started wandering off.

Raider had dropped the reins and was crawling his way onto his own mount.

"What the hell do you think you're doing?" Seth called, lunging for his horse's reins. "Get your ass down here and let me look at you."

"Every scavenger within a mile will be here soon," Raider said as he flopped into the saddle, his words slow but coherent. "Worse than jackals. We need to go."

"Is anything broken? Because if it is, we need to go back to Shalaa, not onward." Seth gritted his teeth at the idea.

"I'm not hurt."

"You're clearly hurt."

"It would take more than that to hurt me."

"Don't be absurd. That was a serious fall."

Raider set his mare into a walk. "We have to go."

Unbelievable.

Grumbling, Seth mounted his horse and followed Raider through the channel between hills until they emerged into open scrubland. Seth pulled on his white kaftan and told Raider to do the same. Raider fumbled his way into the red silk.

Seth was tempted to see how far Raider would make it before he fell, but after a mile of Raider swaying in the saddle, Seth grabbed Umae's reins, stopped both horses, and dismounted.

"Get down."

Raider gazed down at him. His face was flushed, his eyes partially closed. His lips were parted slightly.

When Seth tugged his arm, Raider slid from the saddle, falling heavily into Seth. Seth lowered him to the ground and pressed two fingers to Raider's jugular. His pulse was elevated and his breathing shallow.

Seth peeled open Raider's partially closed right eyelid. His pupil was completely blown and had all but swallowed the amber iris. Seth checked the other eye, but it looked normal. Then he realized he was looking at the arcane one.

It was a good piece of artifice. He could hardly tell except for the barely visible lines within the mechanical pupil and the fact that it wasn't reacting like the other eye.

Of course, the right eye was clearly also arcane, given the way it sometimes flashed, but it seemed to function more like a natural eye. In any case, it was reacting as the left was not.

But reacting to what?

A head injury most likely. But when Seth lifted Raider's head to feel around his skull for blood or swelling, he found none. Then Raider reached up and grabbed Seth's neck. When Raider pulled him down, Seth was so surprised that he didn't resist. Not until Raider's lips met his own.

Then Seth froze.

He stayed frozen as Raider's mouth began to explore his, as Raider's tongue sought entrance. Then, with a mind of their own, Seth's lips parted.

Raider's tongue swept hotly into his mouth.

Arousal, always barely repressed around Raider, surged into Seth's groin, thickening his cock for the second time in less than an hour.

Seth gripped Raider's hair at the scalp, as he had so often fantasized about doing. He tugged Raider away, half thinking to end this, half thinking to expose the man's throat and claim it with his teeth.

It took Seth a long, long moment to decide.

Raider's lips were parted, his eyes still partially closed, his striking face flushed along those gorgeous cheekbones. Surely

Atri, goddess of the erotic arts, had made this man. He was the most tempting, sensual feast Seth had ever seen.

Whenever Raider was needling him, arguing with him, it was easier to keep that at the edge of his thoughts, to mask it with irritation. But now, with Raider vulnerable before him, with Seth hard and aching, it was undeniable.

Raider was breathing shallowly, his stomach contracting, his hips lifting. At the sight of Raider's cock tenting the loose blue silk, the flared crest outlined so erotically, Seth let out a sound of raw desire.

It was hearing himself that snapped him out of it. Seth closed his eyes and took a few practiced breaths.

Something wasn't right here. He needed to be objective and in control—because Raider clearly wasn't.

Seth gently lowered Raider's head to the ground and released his hair. Sniffing away a sudden tickle in his nose, Seth flicked open Raider's kaftan to hunt for clues as to what ailed him.

With no external evidence of a head wound, Raider's confusion made little sense—and his arousal made none.

Though Raider's right side was scraped and bruised, neither that nor the cut to his left arm explained his strange state. His torso and face were speckled with dirt and grit, but that also failed to explain—

Seth sneezed violently. Eyes watering, he scrubbed his kaftan sleeve across his face—and left a yellow streak on the white fabric.

What the …?

Seth swiped his hand across Raider's face and studied the powdery yellow dust that came away on his fingers. The dust was mixed with sandy grit, but there was definitely a yellow powder there. It was all over Raider's torso as well. His pants too.

Not powder.

Pollen.

Quiva pollen, like Raider had warned him about at the well. Seth thought back to the scene of the jackal fight, picturing the craggy slope. It had been studded with yellow-flowering scrub—with quiva—and Raider had fallen straight through it.

Shit.

Raider didn't have a head injury. He was high. On what he'd described as a potent aphrodisiac.

Seth had dismissed the idea because bazaars were always full of powders and elixirs reputed to induce lust. They were always fake.

But maybe quiva wasn't.

When Raider grabbed at Seth's belt, the arousal that Seth had managed to ignore for the past minute surged hotly. He closed his eyes, trying to suppress it.

As Raider hauled himself up on Seth's belt, Seth made a half-hearted attempt to fend him off, but he was pretty damn preoccupied fighting his own internal battle. So he didn't notice when Raider's knee wedged into his hip.

The joint gave at the pressure, and Seth found himself, once again, with his back hitting the ground because of this man. But this time …

"Fuck," Seth gasped as Raider rolled his hips, grinding his hard cock against Seth's through the layers of fabric.

Raider's teeth found Seth's throat, biting possessively, as Seth had imagined doing to him. Seth rolled them over, grabbing Raider's wrists and pinning them to the ground above his head.

"Stop it," he gritted out but had to close his eyes as Raider arched up into him, pressing his erection against Seth's.

"Fuck me," Raider rasped. "Make it hard, make it hurt, make me come."

"Stop!" Seth shouted.

But *he* was the one who needed stop. He was the one who needed to be in control, to get himself and Raider and the horses someplace safe while this shit worked its way out of Raider's system.

Raider arched into him. "Choke me, bite me, hurt me—"

"Goddamn it!"

Seth wrenched himself away, shoving to his feet. Leaving Raider lying in the dirt, he walked off. He needed a second to calm down, to think with his head instead of his dick.

He worked through his breathing exercises. He tried to separate his thoughts from his feelings. He did not allow himself to touch his throbbing cock.

When Seth could think, he looked around. The horses had wandered off to forage among the scrub.

He went to collect them. He drank some water. He looked back to where he'd left Raider.

Raider hadn't moved. He was lying in the hot sun, skin exposed, out of his head. Seth needed to take care of this—to take care of Raider.

Seth's cock was still hard as hell. He couldn't help that, but he could take care of his responsibilities in spite of it.

He led the horses back to where Raider lay in the sun. Raider's arousal had eased, though his cock still lay partially swollen under the dark blue silk. Seth made himself look away from it.

Grabbing a water skin and linen towel, he knelt beside Raider, using his body to block the sun. He poured water onto the cloth and scrubbed the pollen from Raider's face and neck.

After a brief hesitation, he dampened the cloth again and cleaned the pollen off Raider's chest and belly. Raider sucked in a breath as Seth worked toward his navel. His back arched slightly, though his eyes remained closed.

Seth closed his own eyes as fresh arousal spilled through him. Somehow, this was almost worse, touching Raider like this, gently caring for him. Seth knew himself to be rough and aggressive, but he also loved to be tender.

That tenderness scared him almost as much as his aggression. Aggression was dangerous to others. Tenderness was dangerous to Seth. It was the part of him that got attached, the part of him that could get hurt.

Seth forced his mind into cool objectivity. He had to care for Raider because he needed Raider. That was all.

When Seth had cleaned away all he could of the pollen, he assessed Raider's cuts and scrapes. They needed tending, but they could wait.

According to what Raider had said this morning—when Seth had forced him to lay out the day's plan—there should be a meadow within another five miles or so. Raider had intended it as a place for an afternoon rest, but it looked like that would be their overnight stop, assuming Seth could find it.

But first, he had to get Raider on his horse.

The process would likely have been easier with Raider entirely unconscious rather than partially so. As it was, there was a lot of leaning and heavy breathing and wandering hands.

Despite all that, Seth managed to get Raider's foot in the stirrup. He did, however, have to put a hand on Raider's ass to boost him up. Did Seth grip that ass a little harder than was necessary? Probably so. Did he have bad thoughts while he did it? Most definitely.

Regardless, he got the job done, got Raider in the saddle, even got the man's kaftan straightened and his kaffiyeh up to shade his head. After that, it was two hours of leading that nasty mare, keeping his elbow and foot ready to block her attempts to bite his horse.

Seth spent those two hours trying, unsuccessfully, not to think about Raider's arguments this morning at their water stop, his acceptance of how Seth was. (Or rather how Seth, deep down, wanted to let himself be.)

Not just acceptance. Enjoyment.

Preference.

I assume you've been fucking fragile little flowers, but I promise you, that's not what I am. Anything you can give, I can take—and I want to. And you want it too, so stop being such a damn coward.

Then there had been his erotic demands:

Make it hard, make it hurt, make me come.

Gods, Seth was hard as shit thinking about that. But all of it went directly against what he'd spent a lifetime telling himself. He'd worked so hard to get where he was, to achieve the control he had.

Besides, he had to consider the source. An unprincipled man. A thief. A liar. A rogue and reprobate. A man with (illegal) quicksilver in his body.

Seth's attraction to Raider didn't change those facts.

And it didn't change the fact that Raider was a necessary but unreliable part of his mission. (The man's actions today certainly proved *that*.) Seth needed to stay focused so he could manage that mission and all its elements—including Raider.

As the afternoon heat intensified, Seth found the meadow situated between two rocky hills. The presence of grass suggested water, but Seth saw none above ground. That was all right. If they ran out, the compact alembic could filter urine or extract moisture from plants. It could even, with a bit of humidity, draw it from the air.

After pulling Raider down from his horse, Seth unsaddled and hobbled both mounts. Next, he set up the tent, wanting to get Raider out of the afternoon sun and beneath the silvery arcane fabric.

As Seth dragged Raider into the tent, the movement roused him into a bout of distressed mumbling. He'd mumbled like that off and on for the last hour of the ride.

Seth had tugged him upright once when he'd slumped over his horse's neck, making a bad sound, but Raider had flinched away so hard that he'd almost toppled from the saddle. Seth had left him alone after that.

Seth got the tent rolled up on one side to let in some air, but he needed Raider out of that kaftan so he could cool down. Holding Raider in a sitting position, Seth undid the cloth toggles.

As he slid the garment off Raider's shoulders and pulled his arms free, Raider's mumbling clarified into a distinct, "*No*."

Frowning, Seth laid Raider down on his bedroll—and stared. The cut to Raider's left forearm was gone and the wound in his shoulder was much improved. What in the name of Kasha, goddess of mysteries, was going on with this man?

Seth thought back. Raider had had this same shoulder wound two days ago, after he'd used his quicksilver in their fight. But it had been gone yesterday. Seth should have noticed. Raider always distracted him, but he should have noticed that.

Was there some kind of healing property in the quicksilver? Surely that would be known by the Arcanum, subject to study. Maybe it was known, just not to Seth?

The scrape was also gone from Raider's side, and the bruising had yellowed. If Seth had sustained those injuries, he'd be nursing them for a week or more.

Though half healed, the shoulder wound was speckled with grit, so Seth dug into his medical kit for disinfectant. As he set to work scrubbing, Raider tried to pull away.

When Seth automatically pinned him down, Raider gasped, "*Please. Don't.*"

Seth took his hand away. Was this nightmarish delirium an effect of the quiva? Or was it driven by something deeper, something ... darker?

Seth shouldn't care. Shit with Raider was supposed to remain strictly business. Besides, a man with quicksilver in his body likely had some disturbing reasons for it—and maybe deserved his nightmares.

But none of that reasoning stopped Seth from reaching out to smooth away the worry line that had formed between Raider's eyebrows.

None of that reasoning stopped him from murmuring softly, "It's okay. Hush now. Everything's okay."

And only when Raider had eased into peaceful sleep did Seth leave the tent. Only then did he start putting his logic back in place—and reminding himself of all the facts that Raider kept tempting him to forget.

Chapter 11

Raider opened his eyes to the cool dimness of a desert evening. Dusky light spilled over him from the left, but above the sky was dark. Not dark, exactly. Obscured by cloth.

He was in a tent. Seth's tent.

He knew this for two reasons. One, Raider didn't own a tent. And two, Seth's rich, earthy scent was very much in his awareness, despite the fact that Raider was quite sure he was alone.

These facts he could sort through. The rest, however, was a blur.

Raider stretched to wake himself up and test out his body. The minimal stiffness said he'd been asleep only a few hours. The ache in his balls said … what, exactly? Obviously that he'd been hard, but what had happened?

He tried thinking back, but his brain was a foggy landscape. Images popped up through the fog, vague and disconnected.

Jackals leaping at him.

Tumbling down a rocky slope.

A jackal with Seth's chakram in its skull.

Seth's lips parting against his …

Raider closed his eyes as arousal spilled through him. He breathed steadily until it faded, not wanting to get hard again. His balls already felt bruised.

Sitting up with a supreme effort, Raider scrubbed at his face, trying to dispel the haziness. He needed to move and get out in the fresh air and figure out what the hell was going on.

The dusky landscape visible beyond the raised tent flap was familiar. He knew that rocky peak and the slope down to the scrubby meadow. He could see both horses grazing.

Raider shivered in the cool of approaching night. In the desert, days were hot and nights were cold. He found his silk kaftan nearby and pulled it on, but his saddlebags, which held his cloak, were nowhere to be seen.

Firelight, however, bled the promise of warmth through one of the tent's closed sides, and he could smell roasting meat. His stomach growled.

Raider crawled out of the tent with general success, but as he tried to get to his feet he swayed dizzily. It took a minute for the world to stop sloshing around. When it did, he found Seth's eyes on him from where the Curator was sitting on the far side of a campfire.

Seth didn't say anything. In fact, his expression was positively stony as he reached up to turn the spit where three rabbits were roasting above the flames.

The Curator was wearing no kaftan or cloak, only his black arcane clothing. Below the heavy shoulder guards, the firelight did an admirable job of highlighting every contour of his bare arms.

Despite the fact that Seth looked perfectly unalarmed, habit made Raider scope out his surroundings. His horse looked fine, and Seth's gelding was grazing at a wise distance from her. There was no sight or sound of danger. The stars were just pricking their way into the deepening blue of the sky.

Spotting his saddlebags in the tidy campsite, Raider walked over to them, feeling steadier with every step. Crouching, he dug for his wool cloak, marveling at the fact that Seth had not been through his things. Of that Raider was certain because Seth's multi tool lay undisturbed at the bottom.

(It went without saying perhaps, but had his and Seth's positions been reversed, Raider would absolutely have gone through Seth's bags.)

"It's still in your system," Seth observed as Raider slung on the blue cloak and plopped down by the fire.

For some reason, the sound of that voice, deep and not entirely happy, made Raider's heart skip.

"What happened?" Raider asked.

"You don't remember? Any of it?"

"I remember the jackals. And falling."

Seth focused on the spitted meat. Raider had been out for a while if Seth had had time to hunt and dress three rabbits.

"You fell through quiva. You were out of your head."

Raider closed his eyes, remembering. Ah, yes. He could see it now, the quiva-studded slope and its clouds of pollen. More details started coming back: riding away, then lying on the ground. Had he fallen off his horse?

Other things too, though they had a feverish quality that made him unsure if they'd been real: his tongue stroking into Seth's mouth. Seth's body, hard and hot against his own.

Then later, darker things. Less welcome images. The ones that always intruded when his mind was vulnerable.

"It's coming back to you," Seth said. "The bad parts."

Raider's stomach twisted briefly, half tempting him to ask what he'd said or done, but he didn't really want to know. Instead he studied the handsome Curator in the firelight and said, "Not all of it was bad."

Seth scowled and rotated the spit. The man's face gave little away.

"Did we fuck?"

Seth's head whipped Raider's way so fast it must have cricked his neck. His eyes blazed with ... something. Raider couldn't tell if it was anger or desire. Maybe both?

Seth's nostrils flared. "What you did today was reckless—no, it was *stupid*, and it was completely unnecessary. You *know* I'm an experienced combatant. Why the hell did you go off on your own like that, baiting the jackals on purpose, instead of working together? We could have made a plan, one that could have been executed without injury. Instead, you endangered yourself—and that endangered my mission."

"But did we fuck?"

Seth's eyes glittered in the firelight. His expression was so intense, so burning that Raider felt his body heat, felt his breathing shallow, felt his blood move down to swell his cock. All that even before Seth spoke.

"If we had fucked, you wouldn't be asking. You'd feel where my cock had been inside you. You'd feel where my hands had gripped your legs, your ass, your wrists. You'd feel where my teeth had been at your throat."

Raider's body rocked at the onslaught of arousal, the fierce stiffening of his cock. He grabbed himself through his pants and squeezed. "Fuck, Seth."

"No," Seth said severely, "there will be no fucking. We're out here together *only* because I hired you to help me complete my mission. We're not here to fuck. And we're not here for me to waste an entire afternoon taking care of you in the wake of your stupidity."

Raider took his hand away from his cock with a sigh. "You can be quite cutting, you know. And you might consider thanking me instead of being an asshole."

"*Thanking* you?"

"Yes, thanking me. You lost half a day to the *revolting* task of taking care of me, but if you had gotten bitten or clawed by a black jaw? It could have ended your hunt on day one. I can take a lot more damage than you."

"You lied to me. You said you were scouting."

"Because I know how fucking proud you are! You would never have agreed to my plan."

"Which was *my* decision to make. You work for me, Raider, and you will do things my way!"

"I certainly will not. And if you believed that when you hired me, then you're a terrible judge of character."

"No, I judged your character rightly," Seth snarled. "A liar and a rogue. I won't trust you again."

"You stubborn asshole, why can you not appreciate that we're on track, a mere half a day behind, and you weren't hurt?"

"Because you *were!*"

"So *what?* It did not endanger your precious fucking mission, no matter what you think. I *told* you: I can take the damage. You can't. I told you that *from the beginning.*"

Seth fell silent. His eyes remained locked on Raider, but something shifted in them. The anger left, but what replaced it was worse: a calm, thinking, questioning look.

"You did tell me that," Seth acknowledged, "and I saw how your body healed. But I don't understand it."

Why the hell had Raider taken the conversation in this direction? If his brain hadn't still been half fried from the quiva, he would have better heard the words coming out of his own mouth, would have realized how much he was admitting to Seth.

Fuck. He'd backed himself into a goddamn corner. He would have to say something. So he said, "Neither do I, so don't expect an explanation."

"What do you mean, you don't understand it? Is it the quicksilver?"

Raider felt himself lock up inside, the resistance familiar and automatic. "I have no idea."

"Bullshit. You weren't born with quicksilver in your body. An arcanist implanted that for you. I find it impossible to believe that you don't know anything about it."

"Well, I don't. You can believe me or not."

Frustration flashed through Seth's eyes. "Why can't you just be clear—"

"Because it's not clear to *me*. Because *I don't know*, I *don't remember*."

Raider looked away, breath suddenly raking through his lungs, heart suddenly hammering. Fuck, fuck, fuck.

Seth was silent for a long time, still for a long time. Then he started working on the food. He slid a steaming rabbit from the spit onto the unused cooking pan, turning it into a plate.

Raider was aware of that peripherally, but he didn't look at Seth. He didn't want Seth to see the fear that might show in his eyes.

Maybe Seth saw it anyway. He certainly saw something, judging by the shift in his manner and tone. Almost caringly, he held out the food in Raider's direction. Almost gently, he said, "Here, eat."

When Raider took the laden pan, Seth next held out a water skin. Raider took that too.

Usually, Raider very much enjoyed his food, and there was a lot to enjoy about the rabbit. Seth certainly knew how to cook, including how to make sparing but excellent use of spices. But fear had a bad flavor, and it took a while for Raider to swallow enough of it down that he could really taste the meal.

Seth expressed little enjoyment himself, eating in a businesslike manner. Then again, he probably always ate like that.

Still thirsty from the quiva, Raider lifted the water skin to his lips then stopped himself. "You found the well? It's not dry?" In the desert, you never knew.

"I found the well," Seth confirmed, and Raider drained the water skin.

The silence having been broken, Seth circled back to their original argument.

"Raider, I need you to discuss plans with me. Coordinate. I need to be able to trust you."

"You can trust me to get you to Aqarat. How else would I get paid?" he added glibly, hoping to redirect the conversation.

Seth, however, was not to be sidetracked. "Get this straight: I am not going to wait behind like a goddamn princess in pearls while you take on dangers alone."

A laugh burst from Raider. Now *that* was an image.

Even Seth couldn't suppress a huff of amusement at the picture he'd inadvertently drawn. Then he pressed, tone softening, "Don't do that again."

Somehow, that soft tone got to Raider in a way that the harshness had not. It prodded at a tender place inside him, one he hadn't known was there. The sensation brought with it a sense of foreboding.

That was a tone he might listen to.

He said in surprise, "This is going to be a difficult trip."

Seth snorted. "Are you just now realizing that? We're a terrible match."

"Maybe so," Raider said, even though that wasn't what he'd meant. "But we're both here. We're both fine."

"Are you, though? Fine? You were really out of it." Seth added, as though he couldn't help himself, "Out of it in a dangerous place. If you'd been alone—"

"Good thing I had you, then. Even if we are a terrible match."

Chapter 12

R*AIDER, SETH HAD BEGUN* to realize, had a lot of different moods. He'd been in a strange one for several days now, ever since the incident with the jackals (and the quiva). He'd been ... withdrawn. Actually, he'd been entirely normal, but compared to Raider's usual flamboyant manner, normal *was* withdrawn.

The days had been uneventful, quiet—and painfully dull.

Seth should have been pleased. With Raider riding silently ahead of him, Seth should have settled into the rhythm of travel, the particular emptiness that came with traversing endless miles without stimulation.

The trouble, Seth thought, was that, even silent, Raider was stimulation enough to keep Seth's mind from settling. Being Seth's guide, Raider usually rode in front, and that meant he was almost always in Seth's direct line of sight. Which meant Seth spent a lot of time observing him.

Raider was an excellent rider, a fact that had been proven many times when his reactive mare had shied at a darting lizard or a rustle in the scrub. Raider sat her beautifully, his body lithe and supple. He was kind, too, with his hands and voice.

And the longer Seth watched Raider in his brilliant silks, the more right they looked. The red kaftan gleamed like a ruby. Flashy, yes. But beautiful.

When Raider's darker red kaffiyeh was thrown back, his wavy dark hair, curling against his nape, made a striking contrast to the colors. And when his head turned as he tracked a sight or sound, his unsmiling profile was a sudden shock of beauty.

Even when they camped, Raider didn't speak much. He answered questions, but mostly he just did his work—and he worked hard.

It surprised Seth, shamed him a little after his harsh assessments. But Raider hunted and gathered fuel for a fire anywhere that deadfall existed. He looked after the horses. He was knowledgeable about flora and fauna and shared information freely.

And, gods, he was attractive.

Not just his striking face, not just his gorgeous body. His gestures. His voice. His laugh, when he'd let Seth hear it these last few days.

Seth wished Raider would resume his teasing so Seth could resume fighting him. He wished Raider would make himself aggressively irresistible again—so Seth could resist him.

Seth had a harder time resisting the impulse to watch Raider. He had a harder time fighting himself.

It was that damn quiva incident. The kiss. The hot press of Raider's sensual body. The erotic words and the images they had conjured.

But similar things had happened in Shalaa without Seth reacting this way.

No, it was something else.

It was that moment in the tent when Raider had been out of his head, when he'd said, *Please*. When he'd said, *Don't*.

It was Raider's voice when he'd said he didn't remember how he'd ended up with quicksilver in his body, the way he'd looked after.

Vulnerable.

Even, Seth had thought, afraid.

Seth didn't know what to make of that. He tried to tell himself that Raider was a liar, but … was he?

And was he really a rogue, as Seth had argued?

A little, maybe. Something of that was in him. He was reckless, certainly, but he might not be quite the rake that he pretended. Not when there were so many other facets to him.

Like the way Raider had risked himself with the jackals. Seth still didn't like what Raider had done and didn't want him to do anything like that again. But the fact was inescapable: Raider had put himself at risk to protect Seth.

It pissed Seth off because …

Because that was *his* role. To take risks. To protect others. It felt wrong to have someone do that for him.

Yet, there was truth in what Raider had said about being able to absorb more damage. His body healed amazingly. Seth envied him. Seth didn't mind pain, but he hated the tedium of recovery, the weeks or months of limitation.

But why didn't Raider know more about his healing ability? Why did he not remember anything about his quicksilver implantation?

Seth needed to ask him. He hadn't yet because … he was afraid. To open that door. To talk to Raider that earnestly.

Seth knew, deep down, instinctively, that once that door was open, once he walked through it, he wouldn't be able to walk back out. He didn't know why that was the case, but he was damned sure of it.

Seth had said they were a terrible match. On a certain level, it was true. They clashed. And yet—

"Watch out."

Seth jerked to attention, startling his placid gelding into darting up beside Raider's chestnut mare. In response, the mare sidled, dancing her haunches into Seth's horse. Seth's knee banged into Raider's.

"Wool gathering?" Raider inquired.

Seth scanned the flat, barren landscape. The rocky hills they had traversed the first few days had crumbled into nothing. Now, it was just dull, hard-packed earth here in the last stretch of the borderlands. Seth was almost looking forward to the rolling sand dunes of the Kesh.

"What am I watching out for?"

Raider pointed a little ahead to a large, slightly sunken, nominally darker patch of the same hard-packed earth that they had been traveling over since dawn.

"Whatever that is, it's twenty feet ahead. You made me jump on purpose."

Raider's white teeth flashed in a grin. "Maybe. But you were so deep in thought I wasn't sure how long it might take to reach you."

"Don't pretend there's an emergency when there isn't one."

"Well, it *would* be an emergency if you set foot on that little patch of hell. But that's why I'm here: to look out for you."

Seth closed his eyes briefly, internally berating himself for his thoughts on the dullness of Raider's silence. A few seconds of conversation, and Seth could already feel the familiar pressure in his chest that made him want to throttle the man.

Raider asked, "Do you get this wound up with everyone, or is it just me?"

"It's just you."

"Because you dislike me so very much?" Raider asked lightly.

"Just tell me what that 'little patch of hell' is."

"Quicksand."

"Really? It looks dry."

"The top is. That's why I walked across a patch like that once, trying to get to the govaa tree growing in the middle of it. It's a soupy, nasty mess under that crust. Dislocated my knee getting out."

"You could have died." Seth's hands tightened on the reins. The risks this man took were outrageous.

Raider shrugged. "I got out."

"Reckless," Seth muttered, shaking his head.

"I was *starving*."

"Reckless to have been out there alone."

"Have you already forgotten that you were planning to cross both this and the Kesh alone?"

Seth swung down from his horse. "If that's quicksand, I can draw water from it with the alembic."

"Did you just ignore my question?"

"Hold these reins please." Seth thrust them in Raider's direction.

Taking them, Raider grinned. "A *please*? You must be warming up to me."

Seth dug into his saddlebag for the compact alembic. It was a sophisticated and valuable arcane device that looked a bit like a small hookah, though the canister was copper instead of glass, and it had two hoses.

Such a brilliant piece of artifice. Julian's inventions had done so much for the College, so much for *people*. It was hard to imagine such a man murdering a colleague.

But then, Seth didn't really know Julian. Seth had caught the young arcanist watching him from a distance a few times, but Julian had never engaged Seth in conversation. In fact, Seth had always felt like Julian avoided him. Once, passing the young arcanist in a hallway at the College, Seth had said, "Good morning," and Julian had frozen like a hunted rabbit, clutching a stack of books to his chest.

Seth had always assumed that Julian was afraid of him, but what if Julian had actually been afraid of Seth discovering his activities? What had Julian secretly been involved in?

After all, he had apparently fled the murder scene with a book. When Catalus, head of the Department of Alchemy, had assigned Seth to this manhunt, Catalus had ordered him to bring Julian and that book back to the Arcanum for thorough examination.

For Seth to do that, however, he had to get across the Kesh, and that meant weeks of smaller concerns: sun, sand, food, and, above all, water.

While Raider kept the horses back, Seth made his way to the quicksand with the alembic and a leather bucket. When Seth was still two feet from the edge, Raider called, "That's close enough."

"I can't reach it."

Seth tested the solidity with his toe then took another step.

"Stop! Lay on your belly if you want to get any closer. You're too heavy to be on your feet anywhere near that."

Seth halted, both at the words, which were probably true, and at the panicked tone. He did as Raider said, lying flat and edging forward until he could dig through the crust with his knife.

When he hit the slop of quicksand, he plunged the alembic's extractor hose into it and flicked the switch for the pump. Creeping back, he guided the dispensing hose into the leather bucket.

When the bucket was full, Seth carried it back to where Raider waited with the horses. As Seth's gelding plunged his nose into the water, Seth eyed Raider. His dark eyebrows, instead of having their usual, teasing arch, were down over his amber eyes.

After the gelding had drained the bucket, Seth turned to make another foray with the alembic.

Raider stopped him with an intent, "Be careful. It's dangerous."

Seth might have said something about Raider being one to talk after the jackal incident. He could have kept it comfortably argumentative. But Raider was genuinely worried. Raider was looking out for him—and it wasn't the first time.

So Seth promised, "I'll be careful."

And Raider, damn the man, said earnestly, "Thank you."

✵   ✵   ✵

"Last chance to turn back," Raider said as the hard-packed earth softened to sand a few hours later. Dunes rose in the distance, cutting an undulating line against the blue sky.

Seth urged his gelding onward. "You say these things to irritate me. Can you possibly imagine me responding with, 'Oh, Raider, you're right, let's turn back'?"

Raider grinned, undaunted. "If you're going to develop an immunity to my teasing, I'll have to try harder. All I really meant was: there's nothing but trouble ahead."

"There's plenty of trouble behind—and more than enough right beside me."

Raider's grin deepened. "You know, I wasn't sure at first, but you do actually have a sense of humor, even if it is a bit dry. Is that a Curator thing? Do you all sit around at the tavern, zinging each other with your wit, totally stone faced?"

Seth raised an eyebrow. "Is that how you imagine my free time?"

"How *do* you spend your free time? Please tell me you don't just train with your weapons all day."

Rather than admit that, yes, he did often do that, Seth said, "I like to read."

"*Read?*"

"It's a simple process. You open a book—"

"Don't be an ass. It surprised me, that's all. So why aren't you a scholar if you like to read? You could have studied something instead of running errands for the Arcanum."

"First of all, being a scholar isn't about enjoying reading. It's about focused study of a single subject for *years*. That would bore me. I like to learn new things, and I don't care about being an expert in any of them.

"Secondly, I do not *run errands* for the Arcanum. I research and track down arcane objects. This mission," Seth raised his voice when Raider tried to interrupt, "may be slightly different in focus, but it's still important."

"Is it though?" Raider asked skeptically as he led the way to a ridge that proved to be a stony shelf, the footing easier for the horses than deep sand.

The ridge forced them into single file, so Seth had to speak to Raider's back. "I realize that you don't think bringing a fugitive to justice is important, but—"

"Important enough to send you on a deadly trek across the Kesh?" Raider twisted in his saddle to look at Seth. "Hell no."

"A man was *murdered*."

"And this is unusual? It happens every fucking day."

"Not at the Arcanum. The rest of the world is a goddamn mess, but the University is a place of sense and reason. I won't see that tarnished."

"Oh, for fuck's sake." Raider untwisted himself in his saddle, putting his back to Seth. "How can you be so naïve?"

"Why are you so cynical?"

"So you *want* to be on this mission?" Raider challenged.

"Answer my goddamn question."

"Answer *mine*."

Seth glared at Raider's back. Seth had asked his question first, but pointing that out would sound childish—and *Raider* was the childish one, not Seth.

So Seth took a (somewhat) calming breath and said, "No, I don't want to be on this mission. I wish someone else had been assigned to it. But *I* was assigned to it, and I will complete it. Now answer my question: why are you so cynical?"

"We're not done talking about your mission"—infuriating man!—"and how ridiculous it is. *Too* ridiculous, Seth. Something else is going on. I refuse to believe that the Arcanum would send you haring across the Kesh just because one weaselly scholar killed another."

"And why do you think one scholar would murder another, Raider?"

"Rivalry? Lovers' spat? How the hell should I know?" Raider stopped his mare and turned her to face Seth. "Why? What haven't you told me?"

"Nothing that affects you. But since you won't let this go, the Arcanum is full of dangerous objects and dangerous information. Julian may have a book in his possession that belongs in the care of the College."

"So this isn't about a murder, not really. It's about something the Arcanum wants—big surprise. Why the hell do you trust them so much?"

"I'm done answering your questions until you answer mine: why are you so cynical?"

From within the shadowy hood of his dark red kaffiyeh, Raider's right eye flashed. "Because good people rarely hold power. It gets taken from them by others who are greedier and crueler. Good people get killed."

"That doesn't answer my question."

"Why should I need to answer your question? You're hunting a scholar who murdered another over a book that may have dangerous information. Isn't that what I *just* described?"

"Don't twist this around. We're talking about you, not about my quarry. Is this why you refuse to attach yourself to anything? Because you don't trust anyone for more than a meal or a fuck? Is that why you're a—what did you call it?—a feather on the wind?"

Rather than answer, Raider made a sound of disgust and wheeled his mare around, leaving Seth to watch that red silk and wonder: what the hell was Raider, a man who healed so fast, a man with quicksilver in his body, so damn afraid of?

When they stopped during the heat of the day and put up the tent, Seth could no longer hold back his question. It was a compulsion of his, to dig at mysteries. It was what he did as a Curator. He opened doors and boxes and tombs. He looked inside at the secrets. So even though this was the very door he'd been afraid to open with Raider, Seth couldn't stop himself.

His question was a thousand pieces and parts but only a few simple words. He asked, "What happened?"

The silvery tent was propped up as an awning, unsided but high and wide enough to shade both men and horses. Its arcane material not only dispersed the sun's heat but also drew heat upward from within, keeping the interior cool.

The horses were dozing in their loosened tack. Seth was using the alembic to purify urine that he'd managed to collect from the animals. With the oasis nearly a week away, nothing could be wasted.

The alembic hummed softly and pure water splashed from its dispensing hose into the clean leather bucket.

Raider, who had been lying back on his sheepskin, bare from the waist up, hands clasped behind his head, jolted at Seth's question.

"I told you," Raider said quietly, his gaze locked on the awning above. "I don't know."

"You said you don't remember. You don't remember the reason for the quicksilver? Or who implanted it for you?"

Raider shuddered but didn't shift his gaze from the awning above him. He didn't answer.

"What about your life before it?" Seth asked. "There must be some clues."

"I don't remember anything. From before."

Seth frowned. "What do you mean?"

Raider sat up abruptly, muscle tensing all through his body. "When I said I was a *feather on the wind*"—this time, he sneered the words—"I meant it. Because I *don't remember anything*. There is *nothing* before this *shit*." Raider gestured in a way that seemed to mean his whole body.

Seth gaped at him. "You can't mean … your *whole life*? Nothing?"

"That's what I said!"

"Okay. Okay." Seth lifted a hand in a placating gesture then had to turn his attention to the alembic, which was gurgling out the last of the purified water. He withdrew the hoses from the two buckets and took the alembic to the edge of the tent to run it through its purging cycle.

Seth knew that memory loss happened. He had some holes himself. But to not remember anything? He couldn't wrap his head around that.

Raider said to his back, "I don't like talking about it. Please don't bring it up again."

Seth frowned, focusing on the alembic so Raider wouldn't see his expression. He didn't want to make that promise. It wasn't in his nature to let things go. And this … it felt important.

But then Raider said, "Please, Seth. Don't." Like he'd begged when he'd been out his head from the quiva, delirious and afraid.

Please. Don't.

Seth turned to look at him and found a hint of that same fear in Raider's amber eyes. So Seth had no choice but to say, "All right."

And when Raider lay back down, clearly relieved but clearly still upset, Seth added, "I'm sorry."

But Raider didn't reply and didn't look at him. And even though Seth knew that he'd made a promise, he also knew that he'd been right. He'd opened that door—and he wasn't going to be able to close it.

* * *

After six days of shifting sand dunes, Seth also knew that he couldn't have done this without Raider.

Seth had no idea how the man was tracking their direction in this disorienting landscape, didn't know how he navigated from sand ridge to sand ridge. Seth would have been lost.

Seth was also forced to acknowledge that Raider had known better what supplies to bring. Seth was used to rough traveling. He was even used to desert environments. None of it could have prepared him for the dizzying landscape, the crushing heat, and the absence of water.

Raider had admitted that Seth's alembic was pretty handy, but the butter and dates that Raider had packed were about all they could eat. Seth knew the value of butter when traveling, but his life had never depended on it before.

Their dried meat would have to wait until they reached the oasis—this evening, Raider had promised—because it required too much moisture to digest. Most of the water that Seth's alembic could filter from urine went to the horses.

Dehydrated, overheated, and nearly starving, Seth was starting to get a loose, floaty feeling, like he was drifting in his body.

When Raider had slapped him this morning, it had taken him a good, long minute to understand why, to realize that he'd been wandering off in the wrong direction. He'd been drawn to a mirage of water.

Now, resting in the tent's shade during the worst of the day's heat, Seth felt a little guilty. Raider had expended a lot of precious energy chasing him down, and Raider was the one forced to focus for hours every day. All Seth had to do was follow—and even that he'd messed up.

The horses were dozing under the awning and Raider was dead asleep. They hadn't talked much for the last several days. It took too much energy. Even when Raider had caught up with him this morning, he'd only pointed in the correct direction and rasped, "Follow."

Lately, Raider had vocalized more in his sleep than when he was awake. Usually, Seth fell asleep before Raider but often woke to hear him mumbling, to feel him twitching.

Today, Seth was still awake. He didn't know why, but he just kept sitting on his bedroll, awake but not really alert, staring out at the golden dunes. But when Raider started mumbling in his sleep, Seth's mind sharpened a little.

He looked down at Raider stretched out beside him.

As usual in sleep, Raider was stripped down to just his loose dark blue shalvar pants. He'd lost weight. Every muscle was highly defined, and his belly had a sunken look. His cheeks had hollowed more deeply above the dark beard, lending his face an even more exotic look than usual.

Raider's lips, dry and cracked like Seth's, were moving and Raider was making sounds too slurred to be intelligible, but the expression on his sleeping face was easy enough to interpret. He was having a nightmare. He had them a lot.

Seth did what he usually did when he was awake during one of these. He laid his hand on Raider's chest, feeling the thud of his heart, trying to still him without waking him. That was usually enough to make the dream fade, but today Raider's chest rose sharply under Seth's hand.

Seth rubbed Raider's chest in a soothing circle, as Marcus had sometimes done for him when nightmares of his mother's death had haunted him.

When Raider let out a shuddering breath and settled into peaceful sleep, Seth lay down on his own bedroll. His hand was still on Raider's chest. He left it there.

Chapter 13

Raider's arcane eye had locked on the oasis fifteen minutes ago, but he hadn't said anything. He wanted to see Seth's face when it came into sudden view. As Umae crested the last dune, Raider pulled her to a stop and waited.

"Oh gods," Seth murmured in exhausted relief as his gelding drew alongside Umae.

Seth's beard had grown in since they'd left Shalaa. Raider kind of missed seeing the delicious line of Seth's jaw, but the beard gave him a rugged look that suited him just as well.

Raider, did not, however, like the over-brightness of his green eyes or the dark circles under them. Seth had scared him this morning when Raider had looked around to find him gone.

If not for his arcane eye, Raider might not have found him so quickly. He might not have found him at all.

That eye had paid for its pain today. Raider was forced to be grateful for it.

"Come on," Raider rasped and urged Umae down the slope, sand spilling in their wake.

The oasis sparkled in the golden light of early evening, a paradise of green and blue, a promise of rest and renewal. It stretched through the valley like an island in the sea of sand.

A deep spring fed the main pool that was the heart of the place, but precious underground water supported the grass and scrub that would feed the horses. That underground water also fed the trees that would provide shade and fruit. There would be small game as well.

Raider led the way into the trees along the smoothest path to the water. He slid down from the saddle, gripping it for support, and watched Seth do the same.

The horses plunged their noses into the pool. Because the horses had gotten most of the water the alembic could produce, they were not as dehydrated as the Seth and Raider, so they got to drink their fill. The men would have to be more careful.

Seth dropped to his knees and scooped water into his mouth. Raider watched closely then kicked his boot.

"Enough," he rasped. "You'll be sick."

Seth drew back reluctantly. "Damn it."

"You need to eat. You need salt. Then you can have more water."

Seth got to his feet with a grunt. "I know. I know that. You drink."

After Raider had drunk a little and they'd filled their water skins, they led the horses to where they would make camp, unsaddled them, and turned them loose to graze.

While Raider dug up the dried meat from their provisions, he kept an eye on Seth. Seth was exhaustedly laying out the bedrolls, not even bothering with the tent. Finished, he sat with a thump beside Raider.

Raider handed him a piece of salty camel jerky and a water skin. Seth began to chew with the slow deliberation that said he didn't feel hungry but knew he needed the food.

Raider did the same with his own portion, and they ate the last of their dates. They still had farro but were both too tired to cook the grain. When Seth stopped eating, Raider pushed one more piece of jerky at him and made him finish the water skin.

When they lay down on their bedrolls, Seth was out in seconds. Raider took a little longer.

The nightmares had been creeping in the last few days, taking advantage of his exhausted mind. Raider didn't want to dream. He wanted peace. He wanted ease. He wanted to feel good.

He lay down beside Seth. It was hard to be that close and not reach out. Raider liked to touch and be touched. He laid his hand on his own chest, letting the weight of it soothe him, his body remembering something that his mind did not.

✯   ✯   ✯

Raider reclined against the pool's rocky ledge, sitting on a shelf of stone and letting the cool water dissolve the memory of several days of weariness and deprivation.

After a long night of rest, after food and plenty of water, he was feeling much more like himself.

He and Seth had both woken late. After eating, Seth had wandered off to check on the horses and to take a look at the oasis. There were no signs of other visitors, so Raider had let him go alone, opting to come here. He'd been here for quite some time now and had no interest in leaving.

This was the kind of bliss he lived for.

Raider sighed and closed his eyes. He kept them closed even as the rustling of undergrowth announced Seth's approach. The light scuff of boots on stone said he'd reached the edge of the pool.

Then silence.

Raider opened his eyes to the sight of Seth, soap and scrubbing cloth in hand, standing on the rocky ledge. The man was staring at him, looking stalled. He had expected, perhaps, to find the pool empty, to bathe alone.

Raider met his gaze with mild challenge. It reminded him of that day in the bathhouse, when Seth had stood at the edge of another pool, demanding answers, refusing to bare himself, refusing to enter the water with Raider.

Would he still refuse?

Raider waited for Seth to drop his eyes, to turn away. The clear water obscured Raider's nude form a little with its wavy distortion, but the fact of his nudity was plain enough. Seth's eyes remained on Raider, not dropping to the bareness of his body but not dropping to the ground either.

Seth was going to turn away, leave, seek another, more private cove. Raider was sure of it, so sure that he smirked a little, trying to say, *Yeah, I thought so, you damn coward.*

Was that why Seth smirked in response? Was that why he set down his scrubbing cloth and soap then straightened to unbuckle his vest with such unhurried deliberation?

Raider held Seth's gaze, both of them unyielding, as Seth undid the buckles. But when he shrugged off his vest and bared the smooth musculature of his upper body, Raider lost the staring contest.

His nostrils flared as he took in the sight of that fair skin moving over powerful muscle. He relished every detail: the heavy pads of Seth's pectorals, the notches of his belly, the cut of muscle from each hip angling inward to vanish behind the waistband of his pants. Then there was the delightful trail of dark hair leading down from his navel. And lower … the bulge of Seth's cock against the front of his pants.

Raider closed his eyes as his own cock, already half swollen at the mere tease of Seth's presence, hardened fully.

He remembered perfectly well what Seth's cock had felt like grinding against him. He wanted it again, that hot, stiff length gliding along his own. He wanted that cock in his hands, in his mouth. He wanted it deep inside his body.

Raider opened his eyes to find Seth lingering, watching him. Was he enjoying Raider's gaze? Was Seth teasing him on purpose?

Seth bent to remove his boots, shoulders flexing as he worked. Then he straightened and his hands went to the lacing of his pants. Raider bit his lip, holding back the sound that wanted to escape him. He held still, not quite trusting Seth to follow through.

Then, slowly, Seth turned away, his hands busy. Raider knew he was only unlacing his pants, but the sight of him—broad muscled back, hands working near his groin—made a needful sound escape Raider. He reached down and squeezed himself. He couldn't help it.

Raider meant to take his hand away from his cock, but then Seth pushed his pants down off his ass. He had to bend a little to pull them off, and the view had Raider's hand tightening on himself.

Raider had already known that Seth's body was balanced, that his ass and legs were as well muscled as the rest of him. The way he moved and filled out his clothes said as much. But the sight was another level of reality. Smooth curves of powerful muscle. The light dimpling at his lower back. Then—

Then Seth turned to face the water.

He paused as Raider's eyes locked on his groin, where his cock hung long and thick, half hard. That gorgeous shaft twitched, stiffening further under Raider's hungry gaze.

Raider gave himself a much-needed stroke before forcing his hand away. Seth hadn't touched his own cock.

Raider had spent enough time with Seth to understand that the man was fighting him right now. This was Seth's way of standing ground.

Yes, he was acknowledging that Raider turned him on, but that had already been well established. Seth seemed to be saying that, still, even now, it was of no consequence.

After collecting his soap and cloth, Seth stepped into the water. He was a good fifteen feet away as he sank down into the cool depths, but Raider could see every line of his body above the water. And he could now imagine the rest with perfect clarity.

"The water is nice," Seth said, his voice gravelly.

"Mm," was all Raider managed to reply.

Seth set to work soaping and scrubbing his chest and shoulders. There was color in his broad, handsome face, along his cheekbones.

Before he could think to stop it, Raider's arcane eye zoomed in and focused, showing him the aroused darkening of Seth's eyes. He blinked that away.

The arcane eye was useful, but it wasn't the same as experiencing things naturally. Raider would rather see less and have it feel more real.

Seth's scrubbing moved along each arm. Then it traveled inward. It traveled down.

Raider closed his eyes again as his cock throbbed. An image rose in his mind: Seth's powerful body pressed against his own, Seth's cock hard against his own, Seth's mouth crushed against his own.

Words nearly escaped him.

Put your hands on me.

Put your mouth on me.

Fuck me. Bite me.

Please, please, just touch me.

But Seth wasn't going to. He was making a point. He was fighting Raider, as usual.

Generally, Raider liked that. It was fun. It felt good. But right now, it didn't. Not when he needed something so badly. Not when there was an aching, empty place inside him that could only be soothed by touch, by pleasure, by the right kind of pain.

Raider was so wrapped up in his thoughts that he didn't register Seth's approach until he was only a few feet away.

Raider's eyes popped open to find Seth inching near through the water, those darkened green eyes regarding him intently. Then he felt Seth's hand on his thigh. Raider gasped as the unexpected touch had his cock twitching up against his belly.

"Please," Raider breathed, not too proud to beg—and terrified that Seth would only tease him, that he'd still refuse to touch him like he needed. "Please. I need—"

"I know," Seth said as he curled his strong hand around Raider's cock.

Chapter 14

AS SETH GAVE Raider's cock a slow, firm stroke under the water, he crushed their mouths together, capturing Raider's gasp. Seth swept his tongue into Raider's mouth.

Raider responded like he'd been starving for this, his tongue stroking against Seth's, his sounds of pleasure vibrating against Seth's lips. Seth had never kissed anyone like Raider, whose hunger matched his own, whose body hummed with so much power.

Seth tightened his grip on Raider's erect cock, using it to hold him, to still him. With his other hand, he gripped Raider's hair at the scalp. Seth tugged him back to break the kiss. Raider's lips were parted enticingly. His head was tilted back, his throat exposed. Seth's cock twitched at the sight.

"We're going to do this slowly," Seth growled, his voice so low and gravelly he barely recognized it.

"Why?"

Raider watched him through half-lidded eyes. His hips shifted as he tried to thrust into Seth's grip. Seth held tight, almost too tight, but it made Raider's long lashes flutter, made his lips part further.

"Because I have to be careful," Seth said, forcing himself to loosen his grip a little. Gods, that cock felt perfect in his hand.

"No, you don't, not with me. Fuck me, Seth, hard."

Seth's grip tightened again at the invitation, but he made his hand relax a little. "Absolutely not."

Raider's right eye flashed gold. "Don't you dare walk away."

"Oh, you're going to come," Seth told him and gave Raider's cock a slow stroke to ease his frustration.

Raider made a delicious, needful sound and let his eyes drift shut. Seth had a brief thought of, *I could do anything with him. I could do everything.*

But he insisted, "This has to stay within limits."

"No."

"Yes." Seth gripped Raider's cock again, letting his fingers press into the taut fullness of Raider's balls. "You will behave."

"Fuck," Raider breathed, throwing his head back.

Seth's body rocked forward as his cock throbbed in response. His balls were heavy and full, his whole body primed to fuck this gorgeous man. Seth closed his eyes to center himself, to find his control.

He didn't know why he wanted Raider like he did, but it didn't matter at the moment. His chance to deny himself, to deny them both, had vanished as soon as he'd gotten in the pool.

When he'd discovered Raider here, he'd thought briefly about leaving. But even before Raider's smirk, Seth had known he couldn't leave, not when it would have felt like running away. Seth did not run away. He fought.

And it had felt like fighting. It had felt like power, to tease Raider after all the times Raider had teased him.

But Raider had not responded with the obnoxious commentary that Seth could have fired back at. Raider had watched him in silence, with burning intensity. He had let Seth see his hunger and need.

Seth would give him what he needed—what they both needed. Part of him knew it was a bad idea, that this was the very line he'd vowed not to cross. But with Raider's hot, hard cock in his hand, with his throat exposed, his body so open, with Seth's dick throbbing fiercely for him—there was no stopping this.

But it would stay within limits. Seth needed to know that he was in control.

He stroked Raider's cock under the water, loving the silky hardness of it, loving the way Raider arched into the touch. Gods, this man was the most sensual thing Seth had ever seen.

Raider reached for Seth's cock, but Seth knew that contact would be too much for him. He'd get aggressive. So he released Raider's shaft and slid his hand around to that firm ass, pulling Raider up, bringing their bodies together.

They both groaned at the brush of their erections. Raider's strong arms slid around Seth. His fingers dug into Seth's back as they started to grind together. Raider's leg slipped between Seth's, Seth's between his, locking them against each other.

For a moment, it was enough, that blissful, longed-for contact. Then Raider's teeth found the juncture of Seth's neck and shoulder. The erotic bite spiked Seth's lust. He surged out of the water, carrying Raider with him up onto the smooth shelf of rock.

The movement had forced Raider's mouth away, and he lay back on the stone, amber eyes glittering up at Seth.

"No biting," Seth scolded.

A wicked grin played across Raider's lips. He arched into Seth, prodding Seth's lower belly with his cock.

"Then fuck me."

Seth closed his eyes briefly to let the wave of arousal pass through him. "I promised that you would come. I didn't promise to fuck you."

"We'll see about that."

Raider reached again for Seth's cock. Before he could grab it, Seth planted a hand on his sternum and pinned him to the ground. Then he bent to take the man's gorgeous cock in his mouth. Shouting, Raider drove up, his cock's wide crown bumping the back of Seth's throat.

Seth forced him down, one hand pinning Raider's hip, the other gripping his swollen balls. Seth drew up and down the silky length, lapping at the salty-sweet precum leaking from Raider's slit.

When Raider stopped fighting and gave himself over to Seth's control, Seth moved one of his hands to his own cock, moaning at the relief of contact on his rigid, aching length.

Raider was close and so was Seth. Part of him wanted this to last, but they had both needed this for too long. They both needed, desperately, to come.

So Seth growled at Raider, letting his mouth vibrate around that perfect cock. Raider bowed up, shouting, and immediately flooded Seth's mouth.

That was all it took. With a strangled shout around Raider's pulsing cock, Seth came, his release spilling hot and hard on the ground.

It took Seth a minute to come down from the high enough to pull his mouth free of Raider. Even after his release, Raider's cock lay thick and swollen against his belly. His face was flushed, his eyes half closed. Fuck, he was beautiful.

Seth hauled him up, loving how loose Raider was in his arms as Seth tugged him into the water. There, Raider leaned back against the rocky ledge where he'd been before. He was unusually silent, watching Seth through those half-lidded eyes.

Seth hovered for a moment, breathing hard, more frustrated now than before. He was fighting himself, as he'd previously been fighting Raider—because he wanted more. So much more.

But he couldn't go down that road.

So he didn't reach out to Raider like he wanted to. He didn't try to hold onto him and make this something that it couldn't be.

Instead, Seth withdrew across the pool and pulled himself out of the water. Without a word, he gathered his things and left.

✻   ✻   ✻

Seth busied himself arranging the campsite. They would stay at least one more night, maybe two, to rest themselves and the horses, so he might as well do things right.

He set up the tent, which he hadn't bothered with last night, and built a fire ring. He gathered dead wood and brush. He'd heard birds and suspected there would be other game, but even without meat to cook, he wanted a fire tonight. There had been too many dark, chilly nights lately.

The idea of the coming night, and all the long, idle hours that he and Raider would spend at the oasis, made his stomach knot with unease, so he set himself to work cleaning his weapons and gear. Sand had infiltrated every nook and cranny.

As he polished his sword, knives, and chakram, he thought longingly of his missing multi tool. One of its many features had been a razor. Seth never felt tidy with a beard.

Even with the razor on hand, he probably wouldn't have used it. Freshly shaven skin was a bad idea in the desert. Still, he missed the useful tool, and it bothered the hell out of him that he'd lost it. A thief had undoubtedly lifted it in Shalaa's bazaar. Seth was usually too alert for that, but there was no other explanation.

Lastly, he made a close inspection of the arcane scope, hoping no sand had gotten past its brass casing to damage the delicate mechanisms within. Seth held the scope to his right eye and clicked through its focus levels, locking on the treetops then the distant dunes. He was adjusting down to test its microscopic function when he heard a rustling of undergrowth at the campsite edge.

Seth looked up just in time to register that it was Raider—and that he'd hurled a blade straight at Seth.

Seth dove aside, tucking into a roll then bursting to his feet. As he automatically took a fighting stance, his trained eyes took in details from across the range of the potential combat space.

One of those details was Raider's hands-up surrender.

Another was a wriggling shape at the edge of his vision.

Seth looked back to where he'd been sitting seconds ago under a lime tree. There, mere inches above where his head had been, a five-foot black snake was pinned to the tree trunk with—

"Is that my—"

Seth didn't bother finishing the question because, quite obviously, it was.

He stalked to the tree and wrapped his hand around the handle of his multi tool and yanked it free. The snake fell twitching to the ground.

Seth wheeled to face Raider across the campsite. Raider, who had dropped a jute sack of what looked like fruit at his feet, had also dropped his posture of surrender. He stood there in his silk pants, bare from the waist up, his body language loose and comfortable as though Seth wasn't staring murderously at him.

Seth thought, briefly, of that body stretched out before him, arching against him. He thought, briefly, of the sounds

Raider had made, of how his cock had felt in Seth's hand, in his mouth.

"*When* did you take this?" Seth demanded.

"Are you going to put that snake out of its misery?"

"You stole this from me."

"I did. Now will you kill that snake? I'm serious, Seth."

"*You're* serious," Seth shot back. "There's a fucking joke."

Seth turned and plunged the blade through the snake's skull. Then, with the bloody multi tool tight in his fist, he turned to glare at Raider again.

"When did you take this?"

"In the tavern. When you came to my room?"

Raider voiced it like a question—as though Seth could forget how he'd pinned Raider to the wall, how he'd squeezed his throat, how hard they both had been.

Raider must have lifted the multi tool while Seth had been grinding into him—just as Seth had done at the pool a mere hour again, wanting Raider, wanting more.

It was easy, so easy, for Seth to let all his uncomfortable feelings morph into anger. It was a well-worn path inside him. It was a relief, really, to feel that familiar shift.

He stalked toward Raider.

"You think that's funny? You think this is a toy?" He added blisteringly, "Do you even know how to use this?"

Raider glanced past Seth to the tree where he'd nailed the snake. "I think I used it pretty well."

"*Why* did you take this?"

"I'm a thief, remember?"

They stood only three feet apart, tension thrumming between them. Even furious with the man, Seth could not stop himself from noticing the contours of Raider's sculpted body. He couldn't stop his own body from warming at the memory of what Raider had felt like beneath him.

Raider's right eye darkened as his pupil dilated. The left eye, the arcane one, didn't change. It was a reminder to Seth—that Raider wasn't what he seemed, that he had secrets.

It made him wonder: had Raider been playing him all along as he'd played him in the tavern to steal the multi tool? Raider claimed he couldn't remember anything about his quicksilver. Was that a lie after all?

"You wanted to make me look like a fool," Seth accused.

"No. I just can't help myself sometimes. Are you going to do something about it?"

"What is it that you think I should do?" Seth growled the words. He didn't mean to. They just came out that way.

Raider's eyelashes fluttered and a flush hit his prominent cheekbones. Seth's body answered with similar heat, but he made himself step back. He refused to let this be about anything other than Raider stealing from him.

He swiped the multi tool's knife on his pants then gave it a close inspection. Retracting the blade, he swiped the sequence for the lighter. Raider made a sound of surprise as the flame appeared. Seth enjoyed a moment of satisfaction in knowing that Raider hadn't figured out all of the multi tool's functions.

As Seth continued, sequencing the razor then the lock pick, Raider sighed. "I didn't hurt your precious baby. I know how you love your gadgets."

"Says the man whose body is rife with quicksilver," Seth replied sharply without looking up. "You're practically an arcane instrument yourself."

"It has its advantages," Raider sneered.

Raider didn't sneer often, and it made Seth look up from the multi tool. But Raider had already disengaged from him and was collecting the bag of fruit he'd dropped to execute that perfect throw.

The man was too fucking complicated. Seth couldn't figure him out and, right now, he didn't care enough to try.

For a while, they both busied themselves. There was plenty to do. Snake was good meat, but preparing it was time consuming and messy. Raider left for a while to take care of the horses, and by the time he returned, Seth had the snake skinned and cut up and roasting in the pan over the fire.

Raider peered in the jute sack then frowned at Seth. "You didn't eat any of this?"

"I don't steal," Seth replied stiffly.

"It's not stealing to eat what I gathered for both of us, you over-principled asshole."

"Better too many principles than none."

"Oh, for fuck's sake."

Raider snagged an orange from the sack and threw it at Seth. Seth caught it and immediately ripped through the peel to the flesh beneath. He closed his eyes, barely repressing a moan as the bright sweetness hit his tongue.

"You really are an idiot, you know," Raider told him.

"It tastes better having been given freely."

Raider flung out an arm to indicate the surrounding oasis.

"They're *all* free. I ate at least six while I was picking them."

"My multi tool wasn't free."

With a sound of exasperation, Raider started unloading the sack. He pulled out more oranges as well as dates, figs, and some plump pink berries that he called illu berries.

They feasted on the sweet medley of fruits as the snake cooked and the sky began to deepen toward evening.

When the snake was ready, Seth used a cloth to snag the hot pan from the fire. As Seth set the pan between them on the sand, Raider leaned over to rummage through his saddlebags, digging out what looked like a water skin.

"Raaki?" Raider offered.

"You wasted packing space on raaki?"

"Preparing for a celebration is not a waste. You want some?"

"What are you celebrating?"

Raider shrugged. "The oasis. Surviving. Resting. If those aren't worth celebrating, what possibly could be?"

Seth frowned. He'd never thought about it before. He didn't really celebrate things.

Raider held out the raaki again. He smiled when Seth took it and swigged the sweet, burning liquor. Damn it, but Seth liked that smile.

They settled into the meal, passing the raaki back and forth. After a week of dehydration, the alcohol was quickly going to Seth's head. He knew he should stop drinking, but something kept him at it.

Eventually, when enough of the liquor was in his system, Seth found his eyes lingering on Raider. He found his hand lingering on the raaki as he passed it back. Raider's fingers played over his, brushing lightly.

Holding Seth's gaze, Raider said, "Stop making things so complicated."

"What are you talking about?"

"You know what I'm talking about."

It took Seth a long moment to pull his hand away, to break that eye contact. He didn't trust himself to reply. He didn't trust himself with Raider.

So he got up and walked to the tent.

Chapter 15

RAIDER SWIGGED RAAKI and stared into the fire. He knew what he was going to do, of course. He was already half hard at the thought.

But he needed Seth alone in that darkened tent for a minute, frustrated and restless, having that same thought. Because after what had happened at the pool? Raider was very sure that Seth was having it.

Gods, the way Seth had pinned him down, sucked him so hard, *demanded* his orgasm …

But after, Seth had withdrawn—no, he'd fled—because he'd been feeling more than he wanted to. Raider had seen it in his eyes.

Then that business with the multi tool? Seth had been so damn pleased to have something to get angry about.

Yes, some of his anger had genuinely been about the theft. (More a point of pride than anything given that, obviously, Raider had given the stupid thing back.) But the argument had been a convenient sidetrack from Seth's other emotions.

Raider understood that kind of thing all too well. But that didn't mean he'd let Seth get away with it.

He corked the raaki and set it aside. He had already abandoned his sandals and kaftan, but he took the liberty of loosening his violet sash and the drawstring of his pants beneath. Then he stood up and walked to Seth's tent, making his approach audible. He wanted Seth to hear him, to anticipate his arrival.

Raider pulled up the side of the tent facing the fire and secured it. He didn't like being closed in. He also wanted to be able to fully enjoy the sight of Seth.

Nothing should be wasted—that was a lesson of the desert. And what greater waste could there be than to throw away any possible pleasure?

The distant firelight showed Raider what he expected: that Seth had removed his boots but not his clothes. That he was lying on his back and glaring at Raider in frustration but not surprise. That he was hard.

Raider dropped to his knees outside Seth's thigh, not touching him. Did Seth imagine it like he did? Raider, sliding his hand along that muscled thigh to the bulge of Seth's cock. Squeezing him. Stroking.

"I don't trust you," Seth said. His voice was always deep, but arousal lent it a low, gravelly tone that made Raider's dick throb.

"You don't have to, Seth, not to fuck me. You don't even have to like me."

"That's a fucked-up perspective."

"Not at all. It's just sex. It's just feeling good—because you should feel good whenever you can. And it feels good to touch."

Raider set his hand on Seth's thigh. Seth twitched at the contact, but when Raider slid his hand up that thigh as he'd imagined doing, when his fingers grazed Seth's swollen balls through the heavy arcane fabric, Seth sucked in a breath and widened his legs, opening to it.

Exploring Seth's stiff length through the cloth, Raider grazed his thumb across the underside of his cockhead, shivering deliciously at the size of that fat crown, imagining it deep inside him.

Seth said with obvious frustration, "I don't know why I want you so much."

"It doesn't matter why. Stop overthinking it. It's just two bodies finding pleasure together, giving each other what they need."

"It's not that simple."

"It is that simple." Raider squeezed Seth's erection through his pants.

"No, it's not," Seth growled as he lurched up.

In an expert move, he grabbed Raider's legs, yanking them forward while at the same time slamming his other hand into Raider's chest. In a heartbeat, Raider was on his back on the tent's blankets, Seth pinning him.

Fuck, he loved when Seth pinned him.

"It's *not* simple," Seth insisted, "because when I'm with you, what I need is *this*."

He grabbed Raider's throat. Raider's eyes rolled back and his hips lifted.

"And *this*," Seth growled as he bent to close his teeth sideways on Raider's throbbing erection.

Raider moaned, mindlessly arching into that dangerous hold. He was completely lost in it, so he wasn't ready, didn't even think to resist when Seth grabbed and flipped him.

The hand that had been on his throat now held his head down. Seth's other hand had pulled his hips up and shot between his legs to seize Raider's weeping cock through his silk pants.

"Fuck," Raider gasped, squeezing his eyes shut, trying not to come.

Then he felt Seth's teeth on his ass. He *would* come if he let Seth continue. So he twisted out from under the hand pinning his head. Seth's other hand twisted on his dick, but, fuck, Raider loved it—the danger, the intensity, the way it made nothing exist but the present moment.

Surging up, Raider tackled Seth to the ground, straddling his hips and grinding on him. Seth bowed up under him, shouting as their cocks grazed each other.

Tearing at the buckles of Seth's vest, Raider demanded, "Why is it so hard for you to understand that I *like* the way you are? Why can't you just enjoy the fact that I *want* you to do the very things that you want to do? Take this goddamn thing off!"

Seth lurched up to finish unbuckling the vest and rip it off.

For all Raider's care with the tent flap so he could enjoy the sight of Seth's body, he got only the briefest glimpse of that thickly muscled torso.

It was his own fault. Because the instant Seth's skin was bared? Raider dove in to bite the dense muscle of his pectoral, grazing the taut nub of Seth's nipple with his teeth. Seth let out a fierce growl and grabbed Raider around the waist.

Throwing Raider to the ground on his back, Seth pinned him with one hand on his shoulder, the other on his cock.

"You like this?" Seth demanded, squeezing Raider's cock through his silk pants, the pressure just short of pain.

"*Yes.*" Raider arched into that harsh grip.

"What's wrong with you?" Seth growled, releasing Raider's cock to tear at his loosened sash. He stripped it away then hooked his fingers in the waistband of Raider's pants.

Raider lifted to let Seth whip them off, pleased he'd had the foresight to loosen everything. With Raider fully bared, Seth grabbed his thigh in a bruising grip, forcing him down.

Seth said, "Normal people don't like things that rough."

"But you do and I do and we're the only ones here, so who the fuck cares what's normal? I like your aggression. I like your dick. Give me both of them."

"Is that why you stole my multi tool? Because you like seeing me angry?"

Raider shouted in frustration and wrenched out of Seth's hold, spinning on his back to bring himself under Seth, his mouth at Seth's groin. Raider tore at the laces of Seth's pants, wrenching them open to let that huge, engorged cock spring out. In the same moment, Raider felt the delicious, perfect suction of Seth's mouth on his cock.

As Raider cried out, thrusting into Seth's mouth, Seth's cock drove down between his lips, the wide crown hitting the back of Raider's throat. Tears sprang to Raider's eyes, but he adjusted his throat to take Seth in. But there was no way he could swallow all of that huge cock, so he gripped the thick base of it, loving every ridge and vein, reveling in its intense masculinity, imagining how it would fill him.

Raider had already known how good Seth's mouth felt on his cock, but this doubled experience of sucking Seth while Seth sucked him took him clear out of his head. He gave himself over to the grip of Seth's hands on his thighs, the powerful draw of Seth's mouth on his dick as Seth pumped into his mouth.

When Seth wrenched away, disorienting Raider with the sudden absence of stimulation, he lay there for a second, gasping, his cock leaking precum against his belly. Then he rolled his head to see that Seth was stripping his pants off.

Seth's dick jutted out fiercely, limned by the distant firelight. It was flushed dark, curving slightly from its thick root to its wide, flared crown. Precum spilled from its slit and veins threaded the underside. Seth's balls, heavy and full, were snugged up below it. But when Raider lurched up and reached for that gorgeous cock, Seth grabbed his hair.

"That's quite enough," Seth gritted out.

He kept hold of Raider's hair as he rummaged through one of his saddlebags. He pulled out a small bottle and thrust it at Raider.

Oil. Seth had brought oil. Which meant that, for all his protest, he'd known they would end up like this.

"Take it," Seth demanded.

Raider understood the challenge. It was partly dominance, but it was also Seth forcing Raider to prove that he actually wanted that huge cock inside him.

But Seth should know better than to give Raider opportunities like this.

Raider took the oil and poured some onto his palm. Then he corked it and set it safely aside—because he knew how Seth would react to what he was about to do.

Raider wrapped his hand around Seth's cock, slicking him from base to tip. He stroked up and down that huge length, letting Seth enjoy it for a second, letting him think that Raider was playing nice.

Working his way to his goal, Raider kneaded Seth's heavy balls briefly—then he slipped his fingers back to Seth's tight rim and pushed inside.

Seth had him down so fast that Raider didn't know how it happened. Suddenly, he was face down, ass in the air, with Seth's slick fingers spearing into his hole, stretching him, scissoring inside, shattering his mind with the sudden, rough penetration.

"Fuck!" he shouted as Seth grazed his prostate. Raider's cock jerked up to slap his belly.

Seth's other hand was still gripping his hair, holding him down, but it wasn't necessary at this point. Raider was ready to give in. He needed Seth to take control. He needed that cock inside him.

"Be honest," Seth demanded, fingers still scissoring, stretching him for the cock that would soon take their place. "Did you steal from me to get the better of me? Or to make me angry?"

"I—" Raider gasped. "I—*fuck*, Seth, *fuck*."

"Answer the question."

Raider moaned as Seth grazed his prostate again. "I ... I already told you. I can't help myself sometimes. It's the challenge and—oh, gods, *gods*—"

"And what?"

"You're going to make me come!"

"Don't you dare come," Seth said as he scissored his fingers again. "And *what?*"

"The danger. It excites me. I can't resist. And I wanted—fuck! *Fuck!*" Raider pressed his face into the ground as he fought back the swell of his orgasm.

Seth's other hand reached around his hips and pinched his dick, forbidding him to come even as he continued his assault on Raider's ass.

"You wanted *what?*"

"Your attention!" When Seth stilled at that, Raider shouted, "Now fuck me! I swear, Seth, if I don't feel your cock inside me this second—"

The broad head of Seth's cock pressed against Raider's rim where his fingers had been an instant before. Raider cried out as that huge cock stretched him, pushing past the tight ring of muscle, spearing heavily into Raider's body. Seth only went in a couple of inches before stopping to let Raider adjust, but that wasn't what Raider wanted. He shoved back, taking Seth brutally to the hilt, making both of them shout at the sudden, fierce joining.

Seth grabbed Raider's hips in a bruising grip, drew back, and thrust deep with all the punishing force that Raider had demanded of him. He drove in again and again, ruthless and so fucking perfect that precum spilled from Raider's slit with every deep thrust.

Raider was already out of his head, already close to coming even before Seth yanked him upright on his knees. The change in position shifted Seth's cock in Raider's ass. Raider cried out as he almost came.

Then one of Seth's hands closed on Raider's throat. The other reached around to grab his dick, not stroking but holding him in place.

With one more hard thrust up into Raider's body, Raider, screaming, started to come. The convulsions wracked him, but he was caged in by Seth, who had taken total control of his ass, his throat, his cock.

Seth bent him down as he was still coming, still screaming from the intensity of it. Then Raider's orgasm hit another level entirely as Seth flooded his ass. Seth fucked him hard as he came, shouting, growling, spearing into Raider and drawing out his orgasm until he collapsed, dizzied. His body spasmed through the aftershocks.

For a moment, Seth lay against him, still inside him. Both of them were breathing hard, both of them moaning softly. Raider couldn't possibly have moved. But, all too soon, Seth did.

Raider cried out at the overload of sensation when Seth pulled out of him. Hot cum spilled all over his thighs.

Seth vanished briefly, then he was back, stroking Raider's flank, soothing him. Raider felt a damp cloth sweep between his legs, cleaning away Seth's release. Then the cloth brushed gently over Raider's cock.

When the too-much sensation brought a sharp sound to his lips, Seth laid a gentle hand on his back and murmured, "It's okay. Just relax. I'm almost done."

In the wake of such an intense orgasm, with Raider laid bare, all thought stripped away, something about Seth's tenderness hit him deep. Like it touched some aching, unknown wound inside him.

Seth gently cleaned Raider's abdomen and chest, where his hard release had made such a mess. Then Seth was pulling him across the ground. Raider made a sound of protest, not wanting to move, but Seth shushed him and settled him on his side, laying them together on Seth's bedroll. Seth's arms wrapped around him. Seth's leg slipped between his.

It was too much, too good, feeling Seth's arms around him like that. Raider squeezed his eyes shut.

"You're trembling," Seth whispered. "Are you okay?"

Raider's throat tightened.

"Raider? Are you okay? Answer me."

"I'm okay."

"You don't seem okay."

"I can't think, that's all. Don't make me come that hard if you want to chat after."

Seth's answering grumble was hard to interpret, but he did give up his questioning. As he snugged Raider tighter and buried his face against the back of Raider's neck in a way that felt frighteningly perfect, Raider realized that he might have miscalculated.

He'd been so focused on pushing Seth past his emotions to just enjoy the sex that, somehow, Raider had forgotten about his own.

Chapter 16

Seth sighed as he woke, not thinking yet, just enjoying the warm weight of Raider's body resting against his own. They were lying on their left sides, Raider's back to Seth's chest, his ass pressing against Seth's swiftly hardening cock. Seth had a leg between Raider's, locking them together.

Why did this feel so right?

The blanket had slipped down to their hips, and Seth found himself stroking a hand from Raider's shoulder to his side, loving the structure of muscle and bone, the smooth bronze skin.

Scenes from last night played through his mind: Raider over him, under him, demanding everything he could give. And, gods, the way Raider had come so hard from it, spilling as Seth grabbed and fucked him so roughly. Seth had nearly blacked out as he'd flooded Raider's perfect ass with his own hard release.

Seth had never had sex like that, where his aggression and dominance were wanted, where they were met in kind to create such powerful energy and mutual pleasure.

The memory had his cock throbbing against Raider's ass, but he resisted the temptation to reposition it between Raider's legs. He cut off thoughts of all the things he wanted to do, all the ways he wanted to touch Raider.

Because right now he wanted this even more. The quietness. The settled weight of Raider against him. And he wanted Raider to sleep. He needed rest after their trek across the desert. And after last night.

As Seth woke up more and became more aware of his own impulses, a thread of fear wound through him, just as it had at the pool. He shouldn't feel this kind of tenderness for a man he couldn't quite trust, about whom he knew so little. A man who would vanish from his life as soon as they reached Aqarat.

Soon, Seth could no longer lie still, so he gently pulled his leg free and inched away. Raider murmured then settled, not waking.

Seth grabbed his clothes and left the tent, putting down the side that had been left open last night. The morning sun had not yet burned away the night's chill, and without their combined body heat, it would soon grow cool in the tent.

Seth looked down to where his cock jutted out stiffly, the rigid shaft curving slightly to the flushed head. He wondered if he could ignore it.

But looking down reminded him of how he'd looked down last night, how he'd watched himself pumping in and out of Raider's body. His cock twitched at the memory. Precum leaked from his slit. So Seth dropped his clothes and walked a little ways into the trees.

Bracing one hand on a palm tree, he wrapped his other around his cock and stroked. He worked himself hard, flicking his thumb over the plump, slick head, dragging his fingers across the swollen weight of his balls to bring himself to climax as quickly as possible. It felt good, of course, it always felt good.

But his purpose wasn't really enjoyment. He just needed to come so he could think about something other than returning to that tent. Seth bit back his shout as his body strung tight. He spilled hotly onto the ground.

It didn't help as much as it should have. He was still partially hard, still tempted by that tent. But he seized his goddamn self-control and put his clothes on. Then he busied himself with the fire and breakfast.

Seth had the farro simmering in the pan by the time Raider emerged from the silvery tent. He flung the tent's panel out of his way like it annoyed him and stepped out, scowling ferociously.

Apparently, Raider's customary morning irritability was not lessened by sex. If anything, he looked to be in an even worse mood that usual.

He was wearing only his dark blue silk pants, secured at his lean waist by a drawstring. The breezy, drop-crotch style was growing on Seth. At least, he couldn't deny that it was damned sexy on Raider. Even if he was scowling like a demon.

"I don't like the tent being closed," Raider said sharply.

"You're so goddamn cranky in the mornings."

Seth used the wooden spoon to scoop some butter from its leather wrapping into the simmering farro and mixed carefully. He was giving the task more attention than it needed, busying himself. He wasn't sure how to interact with Raider after last night.

Usually in the mornings, they didn't interact much at all. Seth tended to ignore Raider's morning irritability, but today it bothered him.

This was the problem with fucking someone.

It was never just sex, not for Seth. He'd gotten his warning after their encounter at the pool, but he hadn't heeded that warning. He'd fucked Raider—roughly, deeply, baring a part of himself that he usually kept locked away.

Then there had been what came after. Taking care of Raider after fucking him like that had been necessary, obligatory, but … Seth had enjoyed it. Maybe as much as the sex.

Then, worse, he'd given in to his impulse to hold Raider, to feel the stillness of their bodies together. And not just for a minute, but all night.

It had felt right at the time, so fucking right, but it had changed something for Seth. It had made a connection that hadn't been there before. Or perhaps it had simply made him unable to ignore the connection that had already been growing in spite of his efforts to stunt it.

Whatever the case, that connection made Seth unsure, now, what to do with this surly version of Raider.

(Seth probably wouldn't have known what to do with *any* version of Raider this morning, but this version definitely bothered him.)

Seth's thoughts abruptly refocused when he caught Raider's movement from the corner of his eye. He turned to watch, brows lowering as Raider walked stiffly along the edge of the campsite. Something about the careful steps (and the fact that he'd gone behind Seth instead of in front) said he was trying to hide his discomfort, but the tight play of muscle in his abdomen and the stiff gait …

"Raider, are you—"

"I have to piss," Raider said shortly, not looking at Seth.

Seth frowned as Raider walked off into the trees. He wasn't exactly limping, but he definitely wasn't moving right. Gods, had Seth hurt him?

They'd seemed so in sync last night, their needs so perfectly matched. To think he might have injured Raider …

The idea turned Seth's stomach.

They would have to talk about this. Seth needed to know.

But Raider didn't come back, not even when the farro was done. Ignoring his grumbling stomach, Seth took the pan from the heat and set it aside. He banked the fire. Then he went after Raider.

Seth found him with the horses, who had wandered away from the campsite to graze a patch of lush grass by the pool. Seth's eyes flicked to the shelf of rock where he'd held Raider down and sucked him, when he'd first decided to ignore his better judgment.

Now, Raider was leaning against a boulder by the pool, the morning sun bathing his face. He was slowly working his left shoulder in a circular motion, grunting slightly with each rotation.

Seth didn't remember twisting Raider's arm, but maybe he had? Seth had drunk raaki beforehand. His memory might be skewed.

"You're in pain."

Raider whipped around, wincing at the sudden movement. "What the hell are you sneaking around for?"

Seth said calmly, "Just because you didn't hear me doesn't mean I was sneaking."

What it really meant was that Raider was in too much pain to pay attention. Seth walked from the shade of the trees into the sunlit meadow to face Raider, who eyed him warily.

Seth scanned Raider's body, noting the stiff way he sat, the contracted muscles of his abdomen that said he wasn't breathing easily.

Seth asked, "I hurt you, didn't I? Last night."

Raider closed his eyes with apparent annoyance. "I cannot deal with your exhausting self-recriminations this early in the morning."

"You don't get to blow me off, Raider, not about this. You're obviously in pain."

Raider's eyes opened, the right one flaring as it seemed to do when he was upset. "Whatever I am is none of your goddamn business."

"It's absolutely my business when I saw you walking like …" Seth's gut knotted as he made himself say, "Like I tore you up inside."

"Oh, for fuck's sake, I thought you were an investigator of some kind. That is *not* how I was walking. I was walking like I was stiff as shit from sleeping too hard. I'll be fine in an hour or so. Now can you please fuck off?"

"No, I cannot fuck off. Sleeping hard does not explain—"

Raider lurched up from the boulder. "Goddamn it, you relentless asshole, it's the quicksilver, okay? It settles overnight. I slept too hard, *like I said*—I don't know why the fuck you never listen to me—on my bad side."

Raider was nearly Seth's height and was standing only a few feet away, so Seth got a good look at his face: the tightness of pain around his usually sensual, teasing mouth, the amber eyes so furious at his intrusion.

It frustrated Seth that Raider was being hostile when he was trying to talk to him about something important, so it took a moment for those words to sink in. It took another moment for Seth to do the math—and it added up to something he should have realized before.

"This is why you're shitty in the mornings. You're in pain. Every fucking morning?"

"Since you're so damn eager to blame yourself for something, *you* are the one who made me come so hard that I slept like a fucking rock. Of course, there was also the raaki and the fact that I was still exhausted from trekking the Kesh. I'm stiffer than usual, that's all, I'll get over it."

Seth clamped a hand on Raider's left shoulder. He didn't squeeze very hard, but it still dropped Raider to his knees.

"Goddamn it, you asshole!"

Seth knew he deserved that, so he didn't object, nor did he fight back when Raider slugged him in the gut as he tried to help him up. Raider climbed to his feet and leaned on the boulder again, canting to one side. He closed his eyes, his muscled abdomen contracting as he breathed through it.

"That's not 'stiff,'" Seth argued. "That's serious. Why the hell would you have an arcane implant that causes that kind of pain?"

Raider didn't open his eyes as he said, "I told you that I don't know *and* I told you that I don't like to talk about it. And *you* agreed not to ask me."

Seth had known, even when he'd made that promise, that he would probably break it—and that was before he and Raider had had sex. It was different now. He'd sucked this man's cock. He'd come inside him. He'd cared for him after and had loved it. He'd slept entwined with him all night.

If Seth had believed he could step back from that kind of intimacy into we're-just-traveling-together indifference, he'd been wrong. He couldn't.

Raider had opened eyes and was studying him. He said harshly, "Nothing's changed just because we fucked."

"Yes, it has."

A strange expression passed over Raider's face, a complicated one, like a lot of emotions were jumbled together. One of those emotions, Seth thought, was fear. Another was pain. Or maybe yearning? Raider stood from the boulder and turned away before Seth could decide.

Maybe avoiding him, Raider looked out to the distant sand dunes, that harsh reality almost dreamlike beyond the lushness of the oasis.

Raider stilled suddenly and said, "Caravan. The Sudai."

Seth followed the direction of his gaze, squinting at the undulating sea of sand. "I don't see anything."

"They're at least twelve miles out. They'll be here this afternoon."

"Twelve miles? You can see that far?" Then Seth realized, "Your arcane eyes."

Seth could not imagine having his eyes replaced. Somehow, that disturbed him even more than the idea of the quicksilver. Had Raider's eyes been damaged? Or had he deemed the arcane advantages worth the horror of their implantation? It must have been gruesome.

Raider seemed to hesitate at Seth's observation, but then he muttered, "Yes, they're annoyingly useful." He switched focus. "I should check the snares I set yesterday. It's best to have a gift if we want to ask for something."

Seth frowned. "What are we asking for?"

"They'll spend the night here then move on. We should move with them if they're headed our way. It's always good to travel with a caravan when possible. We'll add two more guards to their roster, and they'll share their shelter and water, more than we can carry on our horses."

"If they need guards it's because they're transporting goods, which means they attract trouble."

"There won't be any trouble, at least not of the human variety, for several days, probably none at all."

"In that case, they're not going to offer us water and shelter for a few measly rabbits."

"No," Raider acknowledged as he turned to walk off into the trees, his movement still stiff.

Seth wasn't done with that subject, but the moment was gone. For now.

Raider said without looking back, "They'll do it because they're good people."

Raider was clearly pleased that the caravan was approaching, but Seth wasn't ready to be excited. Because two men against a whole caravan? They could find themselves robbed. Maybe dead.

"You know them well? You trust them?"

"With my life," Raider called over his shoulder. "And even with yours."

Seth supposed he would have to accept that, but he wasn't sure how much that really meant.

Chapter 17

According to Raider, tribal etiquette required that they show themselves as the Sudai approached the oasis. Once they were seen, they departed, leaving three long-eared hares in the Sudai's path as a welcome gift. After the tribe had set up camp and settled, they would return and speak with the chief.

When Seth and Raider returned near dusk, this time bringing sacks of foraged fruit, Seth's curiosity began to overpower his wariness. He loved encountering new peoples, and nomadic tribes like the Sudai tended to be difficult to approach. But the chief's pleased smile as they drew near said that Raider's relationship with the tribe guaranteed their welcome.

Raider had not explained that relationship. The day had been busy with preparations to resume travel, so during the few times Seth and Raider had spoken, it had been easy to focus on practical, impersonal things.

The fluidity had returned to Raider's body, bringing with it his usual, easygoing manner. Raider had even teased Seth about the tidiness of the campsite, asking if it was truly necessary to stack firewood with mathematical precision. (In Seth's opinion, yes, it was.)

There had been a few times that Seth had felt an intense, scrutinizing look aimed his way, but whenever he turned to meet Raider's gaze, he'd found only that lazy smile.

Now, as they approached the Sudai's camp, a warm smile, a real smile, was on Raider's face. These people meant something to Raider.

The Sudai encampment looked like a colorful city that had sprung up among the trees. Men and women in bright robes, bedecked with tassels, glinting coins, and strings of polished stone, bustled about tending fires and shaking sand from rugs and bags. Dogs barked and children laughed. Horses and camels grazed at the edges.

"Chief Karek," Raider whispered to Seth as they approached a man of about sixty.

Chief Karek wore a billowing kaftan of sunny yellow fringed with light blue tassels. His turban of darker blue crowned a graying head, though he moved with the litheness of a younger man, and his keen, intelligent eyes sparkled with youthful joy, even though his smile was reserved.

Setting down the sacks of fruit, Seth mimicked Raider's bow to the man.

Then Raider offered a knife in what he'd briefly told Seth was a traditional exchange to demonstrate peaceful intentions. It was the curved dagger in the jeweled sheath that Raider held out, and the chief's eyes lit with pleasure at the sight of it. In this setting, the dagger did not look as ridiculous as usual. In fact, it looked entirely proper.

Chief Karek returned the bow and accepted the dagger, offering an ivory-handled one in exchange.

Taking it, Raider spoke as though he could not hold back his words for one more second. Seth didn't know the language he was speaking and only caught one word that echoed the trade tongue: happy.

Chief Karek replied in a gently chiding tone, as though upholding a formality that Raider had dispensed with.

Raider grinned with such delight that Seth's breath caught in his throat. Gods, this man was beautiful. His face so striking, so exotic, his eyes so bright and captivating in spite of their arcane nature, his smile so ... alive.

Raider switched into the trade tongue to say, "This is my friend and traveling companion, Seth, a Curator of the Arcanum in Masir."

Seth bowed again to the chief and said in the trade tongue, "I am honored to meet you, Chief Karek."

It had taken Seth aback to be introduced as Raider's friend instead of simply as a business acquaintance, and he was only more amazed as he heard Chief Karek's reply and understood how much status Raider had given Seth with this tribe—and how much status Raider himself had.

"A friend of our Raider can only be a friend of the Sudai. Welcome, Seth of Masir."

After a few more semi-formalities and a return of knives, they discussed travel arrangements. As Raider had predicted, the Sudai planned to stay only overnight. They had spice to sell and were headed south to Samadesh. Seth and Raider would join the caravan for the handful of days that their paths would align.

When Chief Karek invited them into the camp, they bowed in thanks. After gifting one of their sacks of fruit to the chief, they took their leave of the tribal leader, bearing with them the other sack.

Seth followed Raider into the camp. Raider greeted everyone they encountered by name and was met with smiles and many hugs, even a number of kisses. He laughed and joked with everyone.

Observing that friendliness, Seth recalled Raider's interactions in Shalaa, with Ahmet at the tavern and with the various town merchants. He remembered how Raider had sat in the shade with the camel breeder from whom he'd bought the butter.

At the time, Seth had thought Raider rakish and undignified.

It all looked very different to him now. Raider took time for everyone, was warm with everyone. He was ... kind.

But so much still didn't make sense. Raider's name and what it suggested about his origins. His fighting skills. His arcane enhancements. Even if Raider truly couldn't remember his life before them, he must remember some things. Otherwise, why would discussing it make him so angry?

And there were the nightmares. Those came from somewhere. They meant something. Maybe that Raider had suffered at someone's hands. Maybe that someone had suffered at his.

Raider, Seth had to remember, had a lot of moods, and this friendly, gentle mood was only one of them. Even so, it was very real—a fact that grew increasingly undeniable as Raider led Seth to what was clearly their destination: the cook fire of a woman in perhaps her fifties.

Raider grinned hugely as the woman, graying braids flying, grabbed a dog before it could scarf down a stack of flatbreads being kept warm on the edge of a fire ring.

"Oh, Asha, don't be cruel," Raider teased in the trade tongue as the woman clapped her hands and chased the dog away. "He's hungry."

The woman, who had a pleasant, weathered face, raised an eyebrow and teased back with a heavy accent, "Yours is the one on top. Should I have let him have it?"

"Asha," Raider replied in a reproachful tone that said he had no intention of answering that question.

Asha grinned, much as Raider often did, and threw her arms around him.

"It has been a year!" she exclaimed. "This is too long for an old woman. I might have been withered to dust."

Raider laughed and hugged her back. "My beautiful Asha, why do you like pretending to be an old woman?"

"Because old women have privileges, of course." Asha gripped Raider's arms and leaned back to look at him, smiling. Then she said, "Now introduce me to your handsome companion before Fahet catches up with you and no one else can get a word in."

Raider gestured to Seth and said, "My friend, Seth of Masir, a Curator of the Arcanum."

Seth bowed to Asha. "An honor to meet you."

"And you, friend of Raider," she replied.

How strange it was to hear that. It didn't sound quite right to Seth, but he didn't know what the right word was.

He didn't have to worry over it for long, however, because a slender, grinning boy of about sixteen came bounding into the campsite.

"Nusuru!"

"Fahet, you young rascal!" Raider replied in the trade tongue then said to Seth, "Chief Karek's youngest son."

"Nusuru?" Seth asked.

"Don't listen to him," Raider advised. "He's reckless and bouncy and an awful trouble maker."

Seth snorted. "Sounds like someone else I know."

"I'm not bouncy!" both Raider and Fahet protested at the same time.

A good deal of laughter and lighthearted arguing followed, and Seth mostly settled back to observe, accepting some of the delicious flatbread as he was directed toward a rug by the fire. Soon, however, he found himself busy answering Fahet's questions about Masir and the Arcanum.

The boy's eyes widened at Seth's description of the colossal statues and pyramids, the arcane lamps that lit the theaters at night, and the motors that drove boats upriver against the current. When there was a lull in the boy's questions as he marveled at the idea of cooling boxes to keep meat fresh, Seth took the chance to pose his own question.

"You called Raider Nusuru. What does that mean?"

"It means protector."

Raider, clearly listening in, leaned over from his conversation with Asha to insist, "It's just a foolish nickname. It doesn't mean anything."

Hm. There was something to this, something that Raider didn't want Seth to know. There were so many damn secrets surrounding this man. It drove Seth crazy.

Asha asked with an air of redirecting the conversation, "You are taking care of Umae?"

Raider pretended to be offended by the question. "Of course! I let her be every bit as mean as she likes."

"This is proper," Asha said.

Raider grinned and informed Seth, "Umae is out of Asha's mare, Tamari. Asha educated me in the correct handling of mares."

"They must be respected," Asha put in, "like any woman."

Raider nodded. "Because mares, like women, are quite terrifying."

Asha grinned wickedly.

"Geldings," Seth felt the need to point out, "are much simpler."

"Speaking of geldings, why the hell doesn't yours have a name?" Raider asked it in the tone of a long-repressed question.

"He's not really mine. I bought him in Demir a few weeks ago. I'll sell him somewhere, maybe in Aqarat. He didn't come with a name."

"You could still give him one," Raider argued, "even if it's just … I don't know, Socks."

"Socks?"

"He has two white socks."

"Yeah, I guess. You can call him that."

"That is a terrible name," Fahet complained, shaking his head. "I will name him when I see him."

"Tomorrow," Raider said, getting up from his rug. "We cannot keep you any longer."

Between Fahet's protests and the people who stopped Raider as he and Seth made their way through the camp, it took a while to extract themselves.

As they neared their own campsite, where most of their gear was packed in anticipation of an early departure, Raider said, "You purposefully didn't name him. The horse."

Seth sighed, wondering what had given him away. He almost denied it, but he wasn't a very good liar, so he said, "I'll have to sell him."

"So?"

"So naming him makes it harder."

"Makes what harder?" Raider asked as they stopped at the edge of their campsite.

"Throwing him away. Not caring who has him next. I can't care then suddenly not care. It doesn't work that way. Not for me."

Seth didn't know at what point he'd stopped talking about the horse and started talking about … other things, but Raider had clearly tracked the shift. He took in Seth's words in silence—a silence that grew heavy.

Then Raider said quietly, "I see."

"You can do it?" Seth asked. "Throw things away?"

"I don't think like that. I focus on whatever pleasure I can find in the moment. I think you have to seek it, constantly. It's the only way to balance the pain, which you don't even have to look for. It always finds you on its own."

The tent's silvery arcane material was catching the last of the light, almost bright amid the dimness. It caught Seth's eye, like a reminder of what they had done there together last night.

Looking at the tent instead of at Raider, Seth said, "But sometimes pleasure makes for pain later."

"That's true," Raider admitted. "And you're maybe better at planning for that than I am. But I do wonder if it really makes you happier."

Seth swallowed hard. This was the moment when he needed to reach out, needed to initiate. He could tell that Raider wasn't going to, not after what Seth had just said.

But Seth didn't reach out, didn't initiate. He was already in danger of feeling too much for Raider. He was afraid to make it worse.

Raider could have pushed him past that fear. Seth almost wished he would.

But Raider said, "Goodnight, Seth."

And when Raider walked to his bedroll, Seth turned away and ducked into the tent, where Raider's words would keep him awake long into the night.

CHAPTER 18

R AIDER LOVED TRAVELING with the Sudai: the constant movement, music and stories, good food, and laughter. All the things that had once saved his body and mind, maybe even his soul.

Over the past two days, Raider had gotten to hear about the past year of their lives. He'd grieved to hear of Gelae's death in childbirth but had smiled to see the six-month old baby girl that had survived to become her father's treasure. And he wished very much that he'd seen Kubat's camel spit on the Husaali nobleman's shoes. Everyone had wanted to tell him that story.

It felt good, the way the tribe welcomed him, teased him like Ahmet always did when he was in Shalaa. He felt light and happy. Mostly.

There was, of course, Seth.

Raider didn't know what to think or how to feel about Seth. Raider had meant what he'd said about focusing on the pleasure of the moment. It was how he lived his life, and it was the very reason he'd gotten to enjoy such intense, fantastic sex with Seth. Every time Raider thought about how it had felt to have Seth's cock inside him, how Seth had made him come when he'd gripped him so possessively, Raider got hard.

How could he regret that experience?

He couldn't—but he also couldn't deny that it scared the hell out of him that being with Seth, both during sex and after, had felt a little too damn right.

It scared the hell out of him that when he'd argued that sex hadn't changed anything and Seth had replied, *Yes, it has,* Raider had *wanted* that.

Raider didn't even quite know what *that* was. He only knew that Seth's words had filled him with a deep, almost painful yearning.

Then there were Seth's other words: *I can't care then suddenly not care. It doesn't work that way. Not for me.*

Did Seth mean that he cared about ... Raider?

Raider wanted to say, *No, it doesn't mean that.* It was easier, safer to deny it. Besides, caring had a lot of different levels. Raider wasn't sure what level Seth had meant.

Raider wasn't sure what level he *wanted* Seth to have meant. Because, even though Raider tried to live in the present, the future did loom on that eastern horizon. Where Aqarat would appear all too soon. Where they would go their separate ways.

Everything had gotten a little too complicated—as Seth had clearly predicted. So they'd both taken the easy route and had mostly avoided each other for the past two days.

For Raider's part, he had only avoided *speaking* to Seth. He'd still been watching him. And over these last couple days, Raider had seen new sides of his Curator. Seth was so curious about everything: the Sudai's stories, their gear, their language.

Seth had told Raider that he liked to read, liked to learn new things. Raider saw it now—and what a gorgeous picture it was: the tall, powerfully built Curator in his distinctive black clothing, white kaftan doing little to help him blend in, that sword jutting above his right shoulder, asking as many questions as Fahet.

Seth had plenty of teachers, because everyone was curious about him too. He was bigger than any of the Sudani men. His clothes were strange to them, and they wanted to know all about his arcane scope and lamp, the compact alembic, and his multi tool.

Raider loved watching Seth interact with his friends. He loved seeing Seth take their teasing in stride as he stumbled through the language. Seth wasn't too prideful to try or even to laugh at himself when they explained his mistakes.

Raider had never really heard him laugh before. It was a deep, rich sound. Beautiful.

Apparently, it was only Raider's teasing that put Seth in a state of combat. Raider didn't know what to make of that.

There was, quite frankly, too much about Seth that Raider didn't know what to make of. And as much as Raider enjoyed watching him, he hated being in such a turbulent state of mind.

Fortunately, a caravan of eighty people offered plenty of distractions. One was headed his way right now.

This particular distraction took the form of Fahet, circling back from his place near the front of the caravan on his fine black stallion, bedecked in red and green. All of the Sudai's animals wore rich blankets with intricate trims and tassels. Such beauty traveling through the arid waste.

Fahet's stallion pranced and snorted, showing off for Umae, who put a little dance into her own step. She nickered encouragingly.

Raider sighed.

"There's a reason I'm riding back here," Raider informed Fahet, who already knew this. "She's in season, and you're asking for trouble bringing that hothead near her."

Fahet grinned. "She likes him."

"Of course she likes him. He's gorgeous. I like him too."

"I knew your taste was for men, but I would never have guessed—"

"Oh, shut up."

Fahet's grin deepened, but it didn't last long. He found himself quite busy with his horse's wandering thoughts.

"Behave yourself, you child," Fahet scolded, kneeing the stallion away from Umae.

"Maybe you should return to the front."

"Stop trying to get rid of me. I want to talk to you."

"You've had seven thousand chances to talk to me, but every time we stop, you're busy trailing after Demia like a puppy."

Fahet's expression turned serious. "That is what I wanted to talk to you about."

"Ah." Raider should have seen this coming. "I'm not very good at giving advice, especially about women. Your brother would be better—"

"No! Tulef would only tease me. Please, Nusuru."

"Don't call me that."

Protector. It was ridiculous.

Ten years ago, not long after the Sudai had found Raider near death in the Kesh, a rival tribe had attacked. If Raider had been instrumental in defeating the assault, it was only because he was just that: an instrument. A weapon.

Besides, what had happened that night, the way he'd used the quicksilver inside him, he'd never been able to replicate.

The shoulder guard and armored left arm came easily enough. The rest had lain dormant for years.

"Please, Raider," Fahet amended, looking at him with beseeching eyes.

Raider sighed.

"You know, for all the times I've seen you following Demia, I don't think I've ever seen you actually talk to her, and you talk to *everybody*. So just talk to her! Be yourself!"

"What if she doesn't like me?"

"You've known her since you could walk!"

"It's different now! I want her to like me differently. And she doesn't know *everything* about me. She might not like it all. How do I choose what to tell her?"

"Just be honest. If she likes you, she likes you. If she doesn't, she doesn't. It doesn't do any good to have her like only part of you."

Fahet shook his head. "This is terrible advice. Maybe I will ask Tulef."

On a certain level, Raider agreed. He wouldn't take that advice either. Because when it came to Seth?

Raider could not bear to think of him learning the truth.

✽   ✽   ✽

"Kubat said you wanted to see me?" Raider said, ducking into Asha's tent.

Sitting comfortably cross legged in her loose pants of saffron linen, a sleeveless white tunic baring her strong arms, Asha patted the green and pink rug beside her. A familiar pottery jar rested by her knee.

"Come have tea with me."

This being the midday stop, no fires had been lit to cook or brew. Asha uncorked a flask and poured a stream of rusty-colored liquid into a copper cup. She diluted it with some water from a skin.

"Tea?"

Instead of replying, Asha set out the copper cup where he was supposed to sit.

Given that Asha had her jar of salve out, Raider would put his money on that being a tincture of tisine root. A mild sedative.

Raider sighed, sort of hating that she'd noticed, sort of relieved that she had.

"It's getting worse," she said as he sat beside her.

Raider picked up the cup and took a sip, tasting the expected bitterness of tisine. "This stuff is awful."

"It helps the muscles loosen," Asha said then repeated, "It's getting worse."

"A little."

Asha picked up her own cup and sipped, though Raider could tell from the pink stain it left on her lip that hers was juice.

She asked, "So how did you meet the Curator?"

"Jumping right into it, are you?"

She shrugged, unrepentant. "At the oasis, he was there, then yesterday there were too many people around, everyone demanding your attention. I didn't get to ask about your man."

"He's not my man."

Asha's rather extravagant snort of disbelief made one of her graying braids fall over her shoulder into her cup.

"You deserved that," Raider told her as she retrieved the braid and sucked pink juice from its sodden end. "And Seth and I are just—"

"You are not friends," Asha cut in, tossing the braid over her shoulder. "But the fact that you introduced him that way means you are more than traveling companions."

Raider raised an eyebrow. "Are you asking if we've fucked?"

"I can tell that you have, though not since you've been with us."

Raider rolled his eyes. "You cannot tell that."

"I most certainly can. There is tension between you but familiarity also. But there is a problem, yes?"

Raider sipped the watered-down tisine tincture, considering. If he couldn't talk to Asha, he couldn't talk to anyone.

When the Sudai had found him unconscious in the Kesh ten years ago, it was Asha who had insisted on saving him even when he'd been thought a raider cast out from his gang. The Raider, they had called him. Asha's Raider.

She had cared for him in spite of that. She had cared for him even when he'd been at his worst. Confused and volatile. Even dangerous.

Raider didn't like to remember those times. He had put them behind, with the rest of it.

"Yes, there are many problems," Raider confessed.

"Hmm," she murmured. "'Many problems' are usually one problem. If it had one word, what would it be?"

Raider winced, immediately aware that she had sensed what the problem was. "Who made you so wise and cruel, Asha?"

Asha laid a brown hand over his and said, "Fear is a thief."

"Because it only takes from us, never gives back. I know." Raider drained the cup and rested it on his knee, considering. "But it's not just that. I don't want to hurt him."

"He is also afraid."

"He's just smart. He thinks ahead."

"No one knows what is ahead, Raider. The sand dunes on the horizon are always shifting, because the wind is always changing."

Raider sighed at the familiar axiom. Asha was impossible to argue with.

She took his emptied cup. "Let me help you."

If not for the tisine already working to soothe his nerves, Raider might have found that difficult. But the mild sedative untied the knot that wanted to form in his stomach whenever he thought about Seth. Raider shrugged out of his kaftan and lay belly down on the rug.

He heard Asha uncap the jar, then he felt the warm smear of salve on his left shoulder. It was familiar, having her do this for him, even if it wasn't comfortable. A cup of tisine couldn't change that.

Raider liked to be touched, but this was different. Even though it felt good in a way, this was about pain, about acknowledging that it was there—and it meant thinking about its source.

As Asha started to work the salve into knotted muscles, Raider grunted. He wasn't stiff like in the mornings, but even in the afternoons his fluidity was like a river flowing over and around rocks, a constant accommodation of them.

Near the surface, his muscles loosened under expert fingers, but deeper there was pain—and Asha found it.

Raider winced as a bolt of it shot up his neck into his skull, piercing strangely through his face.

Asha worked on his shoulder until it was supple and the pain became a smooth, almost distant pulse. Then she worked her way down to his forearm, finding knots he hadn't known were there.

She turned her attention to his back. The muscles loosened between his shoulder blades, but when she worked her way down the knotted muscles along his spine, he tensed.

"Stop holding onto the pain," Asha said. "Breathe and let it go."

Easy for her to say.

But she was right, so Raider did what she said. The knots began to loosen. Raider moaned in relief.

When Asha stilled, it took Raider's attention a moment to sharpen. Then he heard the footsteps.

"Wait here," she said, as though, limp and wrung out, there was any chance of his getting up.

She went to the tent opening and stepped out, hopefully to get rid of whoever was lurking. Raider didn't want to see anyone right now, and he certainly didn't want anyone to see him. Not like this.

Chapter 19

SETH HAD BEEN soundly caught. He hadn't meant to get that close. He was not a voyeur. But something about hearing Raider moan had wormed its way past his better judgment, and he'd found himself nearly at the tent entrance before he'd had a chance to think.

"Uh ..." he began oh-so-eloquently as Asha stepped out, dark eyes locked on him.

She was a lovely woman, and Seth would never judge a relationship based on age, but ... he hadn't thought their relationship was like that. He hadn't thought Raider was interested in women at all. And while hearing that moan had sent a bolt of lust straight to Seth's cock, he was also a little pissed off.

He didn't have a right to be. He was well aware of that. Seth was the one who had cut things off, and he and Raider had barely spoken for two days. Raider was not his to claim. And yet ...

For some reason, it didn't feel that way.

"I didn't mean to interrupt," Seth said, more stiffly than he intended. "I was looking for Raider, but he's clearly busy."

Asha's dark eyes twinkled. She regarded him for a long moment before saying, "It is not what you think. You may go in."

Seth wanted to protest that he hadn't been making any assumptions, but those twinkling eyes said she wouldn't believe him. They also said she was making assumptions of her own. Seth felt like all the blood that had surged to his groin a few seconds ago was now in his face. Was he that obvious?

There was really no salvaging the encounter, so he ducked into the tent to escape.

Whatever he'd expected to find, it wasn't this: Raider, stripped to the waist and lying on his stomach, face turned away, a greenish salve smeared all over his left shoulder and down his back.

It upset Seth instantly.

For the past two days, Seth had stolen every possible glance at Raider, but those had been fleeting glimpses. Of Raider's face half shadowed by his dark red kaffiyeh, the material hooding him to offer only teasing slivers of cheek or nose, a flash of white teeth, a searing glimpse of amber eyes.

From a distance, Seth had watched the way Raider handled his sensitive horse so expertly, had watched him talk with everyone, had seen how Raider listened to their stories. Seth hadn't been able to follow most of the conversations as they'd been largely in Sudani. Many of the Sudai did not speak the trade tongue, but Raider switched effortlessly between languages. Seth knew bits of many languages, but he was fluent only in a few. He loved listening to Raider's smooth command of words that Seth didn't know.

But that had been listening, not participating. He and Raider had barely spoken since leaving the oasis—because Seth had been determined to distance himself, to not care.

But looking at Raider now, with that salve telling him everywhere that Raider was in pain, he realized it was already too late—because he already did care.

He absolutely fucking did.

And it bothered the hell out of him that Raider hadn't hidden his pain from Asha as he'd tried to hide it from Seth.

"Asha," Raider said in a relaxed voice, "please tell me you chased off whoever—"

"It's me."

Raider jerked partway up, head whipping toward Seth. Before Raider could get up further than his elbows, Seth came over and sat down, hoping Raider would stay where he was. Seth hadn't meant to startle him and didn't want him to get up.

"It's not just in the morning," Seth said.

Though he remained on his elbows, still partly lying down, Raider's body was tense, his expression wary. "Asha likes to spoil me, that's all."

Seth felt aware of every inch of Raider's body that he'd already touched. His hands had been on that throat and back and chest. He'd gripped those legs and that firm ass. His fingers had tangled in that gorgeous, wavy dark hair, and his cock had been in that beautiful, sensual mouth. It had been deep inside Raider's body.

Seth wanted to reach out and touch that body again, to smooth the wariness from Raider's face, to work the soreness from Raider's muscles. Seth wanted to feel Raider relax under his hands. He tightened his fingers on his knees to resist the impulse.

"I'm glad you let her help you."

A strange look passed through Raider's eyes, the same look that Seth had seen at the oasis when they'd argued about whether sex had changed anything between them. Seth half expected Raider to get hostile, as he had that morning, to tell him to leave, but Raider pushed himself up and pulled his legs into a sitting position, mirroring Seth.

Raider sighed. Then he said, as though resigning himself, "Asha has been scolding me."

"Scolding you? About what?"

"About you."

"About *me*?"

Raider replied with a wry, "Oh, yes. And I don't agree with her completely, but she made me realize something. Since you're here, I might as well say it."

"Okay."

The way Raider's eyes flicked briefly to Seth told him that Raider had heard the wariness in his tone. Then Raider studied the rug in front of him as he spoke.

"The thing is, I don't want to cause you pain, but I don't like avoiding you either. I think I've been doing that. No—" Raider shook his head. "I know I have. I don't want to do that anymore."

Fuck. That wasn't what Seth had expected, and it forced him to be honest.

"Well, I've been doing it too, and it's not your fault, it's mine. I've been … pushy. With my questions. I'm sorry. You're right that it's not my business. I don't know why it feels like it is."

Raider shrugged that away. "It's in your nature to investigate. We all act according to our natures. I would like to point out, however, that I know even less about you than you know about me."

When Seth blinked, Raider asked incredulously, "Did you not realize that?"

"No, I most certainly did not realize that." And shit, it was true. Seth had revealed almost nothing about himself and had thought nothing of it.

"So," Raider said, "did you need me?"

Yes. Seth barely trapped the word behind his teeth.

"No," Seth said. "I just wanted to check on you."

It was partly true. He'd been glad to have an excuse to seek Raider out, had been wanting to for days, but there was a reason he'd come looking for him. He decided not to reveal it.

He didn't want Raider slogging through the sand after his runaway horse. He wanted Raider to stay here and rest and not be in pain.

Seth would deal with that mare himself.

☆   ☆   ☆

Seth was almost back to the encampment with Umae when Raider came trudging out across the sand to meet him. Raider was fully dressed in his dark blue shalvar pants and red kaftan with its gold trim, his darker red kaffiyeh hooding his head. The sun was indeed brutal. If not for the cooling properties of the arcane fabric he wore, Seth would be dropping from the heat, even with his white kaftan shielding his skin.

"This is why you came to find me," Raider accused as soon as he was within speaking distance. "Why didn't you say?"

"I figured I could catch her once Fahet got that horrid stallion under control."

"You're not responsible for her. Come here, demon." Raider held out his hand for the rope, which Seth handed over. Raider spent a long moment looping the rope in his hands. "Thank you for catching her."

"She could be in foal."

Raider's grin flashed, and he patted the mare's arched, coppery neck, deftly deflecting her attempted nip. "I hope you enjoyed yourself, my dear. You certainly caused plenty of trouble."

"It wasn't just her," Seth pointed out as they started walking back to the caravan.

"Did they destroy anything?"

"They ran through Chief Karek's tent."

Raider winced. "Anybody hurt?"

"No. Who told you?"

"I heard the commotion when Fahet returned. Then sixteen people pointed me in this direction. You should have told me. Why didn't you?"

"I wanted you to rest."

"I told you it was just Asha spoiling me."

Seth stopped. "No, it wasn't."

Raider stopped, and Umae danced to the end of her lead rope. Raider looked away. "Seth—"

"You don't have to tell me. But don't pretend it's nothing."

"Fixating on it doesn't help," Raider said sharply. "What's done is done. It just *is*."

But what if something *could* be done? The quicksilver was clearly the source of Raider's pain. An arcanist had put that in his body. Maybe an arcanist could remove it.

But there was no point in arguing a hypothetical now, with no arcanist to ask. So, for now, Seth let it go.

When they got back to the caravan, Raider took Umae to Asha's tent. Seth noted this from afar, tending to his own horse. They would be moving again in an hour or so, once the sun's angle shifted.

A few minutes later, Raider came walking through the maze of camels, horses, and tents. He had the curved dagger in its jeweled sheath in hand, and he went straight to Chief Karek's tent, which had already been propped up with a new pole, its torn panel replaced.

Raider was admitted and was inside for almost an hour. By then, Seth was readying his gear. Raider's saddle and gear lay with Seth's, so he approached to collect them.

"You gave Chief Karek that knife," Seth observed, seeing it absent from Raider's hands and sash.

Raider shrugged.

"Because Umae ran through his tent? So did the stallion. And that knife was worth a lot."

Raider crouched to check his gear. "I wanted to give it to him anyway. Did you see how his eyes lit up at the oasis during the ritual exchange? But I needed an excuse to do it. This was a good one."

"I thought you liked that knife."

"I did. But it was flashy and useless," Raider said, grinning, reminding Seth of how he himself had once described it. "Chief Karek will keep it for a while then trade it."

"Was that a way of paying for us being here? Because if it was, I'm the one—"

"I wanted to give it to him, as I said. I owe him much more than a fancy knife. But it was nice to see his eyes dance."

"Why do you owe him so much? Why do the Sudai treat you like you're one of them?"

"See?" Raider said, tying down the flap of one of his saddlebags. "It's in your nature."

Seth grunted, hating that Raider was right, hating that it didn't dim his desire for an answer.

Raider gazed across the bustling encampment. "These people saved my life. I lived with them for over a year."

That only sparked a dozen more questions, but Seth restricted himself to one. "So why don't you stay with them?"

"Because I'm not one of them. I love them, but I'm not one of them. I'm a feather on the wind, Seth, nothing more."

Chapter 20

TRAVELING WITH THE CARAVAN offered many advantages. The food and water carried by the camels, the shelter offered by so many tents, the sharing of goods and tools. But it was the evenings with the Sudai that Seth came to love.

They told stories and sang. Seth still only understood a fraction of the language, but he could enjoy the rhythms, and usually someone would translate for him. Occasionally Raider did it, but he was often pulled away by other people. Then Asha would take over.

When she would sit with Seth, he felt her warmth and kindness, but he also felt himself under examination. He had the distinct feeling that she was trying to determine whether he was acceptable. For Raider.

Seth had not mistaken her motherly attitude toward Raider. Regardless of what Raider had said about not being one of the Sudai, Asha, quite clearly, regarded Raider as hers to look out for. She chided him sometimes, made him drink water, even took the wine away from him once. She would pat his shoulder and occasionally watch him with a line between her brows.

One night, they had a campfire. The day's travel had brought them to a rocky area where scrub hugged the rugged hills. Some of the younger Sudai had made a great effort to collect firewood for this rare treat of light and heat and the dancing that would go with it.

And the dancing was spectacular.

To the pulsing beat of drums, the trill of pipes, and the plucked notes of a stringed instrument that Seth was itching to take a look at, the dancers whirled around the campfire, silks gleaming in the light then fading into the shadows, metal disks and polished stones flashing on their clothes and swinging out from their necks.

But it was Raider that Seth couldn't stop watching.

Raider grinned and danced with everyone, sweeping here and there, laughing with such beautiful abandon that Seth's heart seized tight. Raider swept up one of the lovely, brown-skinned girls and twirled her around as she laughed. He danced with the men as well, and it made Seth wonder: had Raider been with any of these men?

He was wearing only his shalvar pants, the loose blue silk offering him a fluidity of movement that Seth's arcane clothing did not. His bare feet were quick and light in the sand, his bare torso mesmerizing in the firelight.

"He is beautiful, isn't he?" Asha whispered.

"You caught me."

"I have caught you many times."

She probably had. Seth couldn't help himself. And he couldn't stop thinking about what Raider had said that last night at the oasis after Seth had pointed out that pleasure sometimes made for pain later.

That's true, Raider had acknowledged. *And you're maybe better at planning for that than I am. But I do wonder if it really makes you happier.*

Seth couldn't think of any time in his life when that had made him happier. It certainly didn't make him happier right now.

"Yes," Seth admitted. "He's beautiful."

Everyone knew it. Seth wasn't the only one who watched Raider. Everyone tried to catch his attention. Everyone touched him whenever they passed him. It put a terrible longing in Seth's heart.

Raider's gaze leaped across the campfire to Seth. Raider beckoned him with a hand, but Seth shook his head. He would rather watch.

"Pah," Asha chided and squeezed Seth's knee. "It is not always good to only watch."

"You're watching."

"I'm old!"

"You are not. You're as spry as anyone here."

She grinned and sprang to her feet, proving him right. She caught Seth's hand and pulled him with her. He laughed in embarrassment as he was swung into the circle. He knew how to move in a fight but not in a dance. Asha clapped her hands to the beat, nodding for him to do the same.

Seth did his best. And even if he lacked the smooth rhythms of the others, it was fun. The sand was cool under his bare feet. The night was dark and lovely with stars. The fire crackled with heat, and the sounds of music and laughter filled the air.

All of that vanished, just for a second, when Raider appeared in front of him. He was smiling. Not grinning, as he often did, but smiling. He reached out and touched Seth's arm. It wasn't sexual, but it still sent a bolt of lightning through Seth's body.

"Now I'm happy," Raider said.

"You looked happy before."

"This is different. A different happiness."

Seth drew a breath, though he had no idea what he might say. But it didn't matter because someone grabbed Raider's hand and pulled him away, back into the dance.

When the dance finally ended and the dancers fell, exhausted, to their places around the campfire, the storytelling began. Raider was reclining beside Seth, legs out and crossed at the ankles, leaning back on his elbows. Seth knew Raider was half drunk. He'd watched how often people had passed Raider the wine, had watched the increasing looseness of his body. The firelight was playing over his relaxed form as he translated for Seth.

The old storyteller sat on a mound of cushions on the other side of the fire, his weathered face made beautiful by the light, his aged voice bearing a rich wisdom. The Wind Keeper, they called him.

The Sudai held that the wind carried wisdom and stories across the desert. The Wind Keeper caught them to give to the tribe. Every tribe had a Wind Keeper, or something like it. The Sudai, Seth had learned, belonged to a larger network of tribes that roamed with the sun and sand. The Free People, they named themselves, trading goods in the cities, trading stories between each other's caravans.

There was no way to know, then, where the Wind Keeper's tales really came from or what they meant, but they were wonderful. He told fantastic stories of the djinn, elemental beings whose ethereal garden-cities shimmered in the deserts far to the east. He told of troublesome ifrits, who liked to bargain deceitfully with men and women.

The Wind Keeper spoke, too, of an ancient city, one finer and lovelier than any today, a city full of lost knowledge. Then he clapped his gnarled hands together in a final sort of gesture.

"What did he say?" Seth prompted Raider in a whisper.

"He says they sought too much knowledge and that they found it, and it destroyed them. He says that is what comes of greed."

Then everyone laughed at something the Wind Keeper said. Raider, also laughing, aimed a grin at Seth and explained, "He says that *we* are greedy, keeping an old man from his bed."

As the crowd thinned around the dying fire, people drifting off to their tents, Seth found himself lingering beside Raider. The dimming firelight painted the muscled contours of Raider's abdomen and chest. It brushed his prominent cheekbones and rendered the striking planes of his face somehow even more exotic.

"You're looking at me," Raider said softly, still gazing into the fire.

"I am."

The last of the gathering broke apart, and voices faded into the darkness. Seth let his eyes roam along Raider's body, watching the contraction of his stomach as his breathing quickened. Raider's cock lay partially swollen under his loose pants, but he didn't move, didn't even look at Seth.

Seth had pushed Raider away—a lot.

Even though Raider was turned on right now, he might reject Seth on principle, or to protect himself from future rejection. It would be fair. It would serve Seth right.

But that was a risk he would have to take.

Raider, however, did not draw back when Seth leaned near to brush his lips. A man like Raider, Seth should have known, wouldn't. Because he was fearless. Because he wasn't petty. Raider lived for beauty and pleasure, so he gasped at the kiss, opening to it instantly.

When that happened, Seth had a brief, searing, terrifying realization: that Raider was his perfect counterbalance. He was exactly what Seth needed. He opened pathways that Seth couldn't. He let Seth be himself.

No. He *forced* Seth to be himself.

Maybe it was the wine Seth had drunk. Or maybe it was the night of music and dancing. Or maybe it was just how much he wanted Raider.

Whatever the case, Seth was able to let that terrifying realization flash through his mind and fade away so that he could yield himself to the moment—to the man—before him.

Seth gently explored Raider's lips, learning their contours as he hadn't taken the time to do before, learning how Raider answered him with a curiosity of his own. Seth tasted wine and the particular something that was uniquely Raider.

The man was simultaneously so fierce and so soft, so open. He was so fucking beautiful.

When Seth swept his tongue into Raider's mouth, the vibration of Raider's moan and the answering stroke of his tongue had Seth's cock throbbing in the confines of his pants. Raider had been resting back on his elbows, but now his arms came up, hands grabbing for Seth. He tugged Seth over him. Seth hooked one arm around Raider's torso. His other hand planted in the sand on the other side of Raider as he braced himself to deepen the kiss.

Gods, he loved kissing this man. He loved the taste of him, the feel of him, loved his answering hunger. What a fool he'd been to think he could resist. What a fool he'd been to waste any of the nights he could have spent kissing Raider, touching him, fucking him.

Seth pushed to his feet, hauling Raider up with him. The movement broke the kiss, so Seth let his lips explore any skin in his path. He kissed his way along Raider's throat, loving how Raider's head tilted to give him access.

Raider's pulse beat rapidly under Seth's lips. When Seth gently nipped him there, Raider convulsed slightly, making his hard cock brush against Seth's through the barriers of cloth. Seth needed those barriers gone. He needed to touch that cock, needed full access to the ass that his hands were roaming over, gripping through the slick silk.

Seth felt his head forced back as Raider nudged his way under Seth's jaw, nipping at him in return.

Raider growled against Seth's throat, "You better fuck me after all this."

In answer, Seth grabbed one of Raider's hands and directed it to his engorged cock. Raider let out a breathy sound as he squeezed Seth through the heavy cloth. A fierce wave of arousal had Seth rocking into Raider.

"You're so fucking stubborn, you know," Raider told him, grazing his hand up and down Seth's shaft, letting the material abrade him.

Seth rasped, "I know."

Raider nibbled teasingly along Seth's neck. "How many nights have you wanted to fuck me?"

"Every night. Every goddamn night. But especially," Seth went on, gripping Raider's hair at the scalp and tugging him away so Seth could nip at his throat. "*Especially* since I felt your body tighten on my cock as you came."

At that, Raider's body spasmed, making his hand seize hard on Seth's cock in way that sent a dark need spilling through him.

"Fuck me," Raider whispered. "I need you."

Seth pulled Raider's hand away from his cock. Much more of that and he was going to be tearing clothes off both of them. They were still by the campfire, still visible to curious eyes peering around tents flaps. Seth had never had witnesses during sex, had never wanted any, so he was surprised by how much the idea turned him on.

But this wasn't the place for it.

Another time, he thought, not letting himself ask, *When? Where? Will I get to?*

Tugging Raider's hand, he led him through the shadows to the edge of the camp, where his tent was set up. He ducked inside, not letting go of Raider's hand.

If he'd had any fear of Raider vanishing, it was unfounded—because the instant they knelt inside the tent, Raider slipped behind him and hooked an arm around Seth's neck, choking off his air.

"I can play rough too, you know. And you have *frustrated* me."

Seth could hold his breath for a long time, so he let Raider choke him. He even brought Raider's other hand to his cock as though to play along. He even kind of enjoyed it—at least if his throbbing dick was any indication.

But he still reached silently into his saddle bag to where the arcane shackles were stored. Then he moved fast.

Seth twisted abruptly in Raider's grip, surprising Raider into breaking the hold. He tackled Raider to the ground and clapped the two-inch wide metal cuffs onto Raider's wrists. He pinned Raider with his body. In a real fight, Raider would have kneed him in the groin. Instead, Raider wrapped his legs around Seth's ass and held tight.

Hauling Raider's arms over his head by the bar between the cuffs, Seth sequenced the arcane mechanism to hold Raider's arms to the ground. Somehow, working with the earth's pull, the shackles could lock to any horizontal surface, even sand, like a steel bolt.

Feeling that, Raider froze.

Seth stroked a hand up and down Raider's side, trying to gauge his response, his interest. Even with the moonlight bleeding through, he couldn't see Raider's face clearly in the dimness of the tent.

"I can take them off," Seth said, leaning down to kiss Raider's contracting stomach. "Do you want me to?"

Raider's cock remained as hard as Seth's, but he still hadn't moved, and when he didn't respond, Seth crawled up his body to release the cuffs.

Raider halted him with, "No. Leave them."

Seth's fingers hovered over the release mechanism. "Are you sure?"

His face was inches from Raider's. Raider lifted his head and nipped Seth's lower lip.

Seth didn't let himself grind into Raider like he wanted to. He couldn't be distracted until he had clarity. He said firmly, "That's not an answer."

"Fuck me, Seth. Like this. Hard. *Now*."

Seth growled in satisfaction and slid down Raider's body, scraping his nails from Raider's throat to his chest and belly, feeling the way Raider bowed up into it. Raider's legs had released their grip, falling open to let Seth kneel between them.

Seth tore Raider's sash free and untied the drawstring of his pants. As he pulled them off, the material tugged down Raider's cock, which then slapped up to his belly. It made Raider grunt.

Seth liked that. He curled his hand around Raider's stiff cock. He stroked to the leaking tip, rubbing his thumb there, then let go to enjoy the sound of Raider's cock slapping against his stomach again.

Raider grunted again. He arched. "Fuck, Seth."

"Mm," Seth murmured, rocking back onto his heels. He reached for his saddle bag and dug out the oil and his arcane lamp.

The lamp had a flat bottom and a ring on top to be hung, but it was otherwise spherical and fit into the palm of Seth's hand. He turned it on to its lowest setting and set it aside. It wouldn't bleed through the tent's arcane fabric, but its faint glow, meant for practical purposes, would tonight serve a very pleasurable one instead.

And, yes, it was entirely pleasurable to see what his eyes had not been able to enjoy in the darkness: the sight of Raider, hands locked above his head, stretched out before him, his gorgeous body naked and fully aroused. Raider's cock lay hard against his contracting abdomen. It reached his navel, where precum leaked from its dark-flushed crown.

"Taking your time, are you?" Raider grumbled as Seth's eyes traveled from that perfect cock to that perfect face, where amber eyes were narrowed at him.

Seth smiled. "Oh, yes. You're not going anywhere."

Seth unbuckled his vest and loosened the lacing of his pants. He removed them without hurry, enjoying the way Raider watched him.

He watched Raider in turn as Raider arched, needing movement and not having many options. Raider's cock, untouched, untended, twitched and pulsed out precum.

It made Seth's dick throb so damn hard to see Raider needing him like that.

"*Seth*," Raider pleaded, hooking a foot around Seth's thigh, pitching him forward.

"Patience," Seth chided, catching himself and drawing back to reach for the oil. He poured some into his palm.

"Seth, I *swear*, if you don't—*ahhh!*"

Raider's hips jacked up as Seth took his cock in an oiled grip, stroking him from base to tip, milking the precum from his slit. Seth bent and lapped it up with his tongue.

"*Seth*."

"Mm." Seth crawled up to bring his cock against Raider's, taking them both in his oiled fist, stroking them together.

Seth rocked into his own hand, loving the slick glide of his cock against the hard ridge of Raider's, loving the way Raider's bowed up under him.

Raider started to say something, but Seth crushed his mouth to Raider's, sweeping his tongue inside, claiming and possessing him as he'd yearned to do for days. Raider moaned and pulled against the restraints.

Seth broke the kiss and drew back, kneeling between Raider's legs again. He felt calm. He was hard as hell, yes, his cock leaking, his body practically buzzing with arousal, but he felt in control—and he liked it. He liked how Raider was panting for him, aching for him, leaking for him.

Seth stroked Raider's cock again and massaged his swollen balls—then he slid his oiled fingers along Raider's taint. Raider widened for him beautifully, gasping as Seth teased his tight rim, crying out as Seth pushed a finger into him.

Seth took his time, loving every second of stretching Raider, adding another finger, scissoring inside, feeling Raider shudder every time Seth stroked his prostate.

"Seth, *please*."

Seth gazed up Raider's body to his face, where his jaw was tight with frustration, his eyes dark with need.

"I'm going to take care of you," Seth promised, fingers stroking inside Raider again.

At that, Raider let out a strange, almost desperate sound that turned Seth on so much that he withdrew his fingers and slid his hands under Raider's legs, lifting him. Seth set his oiled cockhead against that tight ring of muscle and watched his cock slowly press into Raider's body. Raider gasped at each new inch of penetration, moaning as he took Seth to the hilt.

Seth groaned at the tight fisting of Raider's body on his cock, the perfect heat and pressure. He drew back and thrust deep. They both tried to be somewhat quiet, but they weren't really. Seth couldn't be, not as he watched his slick cock pumping in and out of Raider's ass. Not with his balls slapping like that.

Then there was the sight of Raider pulling against the restraints, wanting to touch himself, wanting to touch Seth, but wholly dependent on Seth to bring him pleasure and release. Raider's cock leaked a slick trail all over his taut abdominal muscles, jerking erotically with every deep thrust of Seth's cock.

The sight was so damn arousing that Seth started pounding into him, hips snapping, thrusts fierce and deep. Seth lost himself to it, gripping Raider's thighs, driving into his ass. Raider's head was turned aside, teeth gripping his own bicep. He was close.

Seth loved that Raider was going to come just from Seth's cock inside him.

Raider cried out at the first spurt of his orgasm. It snapped something in Seth, watching Raider's seed hit his stomach, feeling Raider's body seize on his cock.

He pounded harder, almost brutally, wild with need as Raider's cock jetted fresh cum with every deep thrust. As it went on, Raider lost it, thrashing in Seth's grip. It was too much. Seth's orgasm ripped through him. He released hard and hot inside Raider, driving deep as his cock spurted, fucking through the last, fierce shock of it.

When Raider collapsed, Seth lowered him with trembling hands. They both cried out a little as Seth pulled free, spilling cum. He crawled up Raider, gliding over his body, loving the erotic mess they'd made together. He kissed Raider tenderly as he sequenced the restraints to release. As soon as Raider's arms were free, he wrapped them around Seth. Seth returned the embrace, holding Raider tight against him as he trembled.

"Are you okay?" Seth whispered.

"Just ... don't let go. Please don't let go."

Seth stroked the back of Raider's head and promised, "I won't."

Chapter 21

THE MORNING'S TRAVEL had seen the sands dwindle and the rocky hills rise in the distance. The caravan wouldn't pass under those hills, not with the treacherous caverns riddling them, but Raider still hated to see them grow with the caravan's approach.

Those hills meant it was almost time for Seth and Raider to part ways with the Sudai. Which meant not only saying goodbye to the tribe—and Raider despised goodbyes—but also that they were within a few days of Aqarat.

Raider didn't like to think about that.

Raider was actually trying not to think about anything, though his efforts weren't very successful.

Even if he was failing to keep his mind empty, at least by riding at the back of the caravan he could avoid talking to people. Normally, he liked talking to people, but right now with the Sudai, it would be those painful, winding-down conversations before parting. And with Seth …

Raider wasn't sure.

It had shaken him to come like that last night. Restrained. Vulnerable.

He'd wanted it. He wasn't sure why, but he'd wanted Seth to fuck him like that: roughly, possessively, in total control of Raider's body. Raider had wanted to trust him. The hard thing, maybe, was that Seth had proven himself deserving of that trust—which made Raider want to trust him more.

And that scared him.

Then there had been after. The way Seth had held him. The way he'd cleaned Raider up, as he had that first night, so fucking tender.

Seth hadn't let Raider sleep on his side again. He'd been subtle about it, hadn't said anything about Raider being so stiff after that first night. He'd simply nudged Raider onto his back when he'd started to doze on his side, making sure Raider was comfortable.

Maybe that was why Raider had needed him during the night, why he'd rolled over Seth and started kissing him, why they'd fucked again.

It had been less rough the second time, almost … loving. They had lain on their sides, Seth entering him from behind. Seth had held tight as he'd pumped smoothly into Raider. He'd told Raider to stroke himself, to make it feel good. And, gods, it had.

It always did, with Seth.

They hadn't spoken much in the morning because mornings were busy with breaking camp and loading the animals, the caravan getting moving in the dimness before the heat began. Raider had drifted to the back of the line, losing Seth in the long train.

But Seth, apparently, had not lost him.

Raider spotted him ahead, off to the side where he'd halted his horse. His white kaftan stood out against the undulating golden terrain, harder and rockier with every footstep. It stood out even against the Sudai's bright robes and saddle blankets.

Seth would stand out anywhere.

Raider's stomach knotted as Umae drew near to Seth's gelding, whom Fahet had named Rompu, which was a tough medicinal plant that grew in rocky places and treated stomachaches. As names went, it wasn't bad. It was definitely better than Socks.

"Why are you back here?" Seth asked.

His kaftan's hood was up, covering his light brown hair, shading his face. The shadows, however, did little to dim the intensity of his expression.

"Someone has to be."

Seth turned his horse to start it walking beside Raider's. Rompu sniffed Umae, who pinned her ears.

After a while, Seth said, "Last night—"

"Was good. Leave it at that."

"I can't. Not when I can tell you're upset."

"I'm not upset."

"Then what are you?"

Raider's heart skipped at the question.

Of course, Seth was referring to his feelings, not to all the quicksilver in his body, but even about his feelings Raider couldn't be completely honest—because Seth had been right. Sex had changed things.

It never had before, not for Raider. He didn't understand why it was different with Seth, and he wasn't ready to talk about that. Besides, there was no point in talking about it, not with Aqarat growing closer with every mile.

But he could still tell Seth something of the truth. Raider felt like he owed him that. "It ... unsettled me."

"To be restrained?"

Raider focused on the laden camel plodding ahead of them, though he could feel Seth's eyes on him. "It wasn't the restraints. It was that ... I liked it, having you in that kind of control."

Eager to shift the tone and focus of the conversation, Raider told him, "I had imagined us doing that actually. Though in my original fantasy, I wasn't the one tied up."

"You imagined *me* …?"

Seth's shocked tone made Raider look at him, and Seth's horrified expression made him smile.

"Oh, yes. Then I realized you would never accept something like that, so I imagined it in reverse, like last night. But I didn't think I could actually do it, not with something I couldn't easily get out of."

The usual intensity returned to Seth's expression. "It scared you. At least at first. You froze."

Raider skipped past that, not wanting to discuss it. "Then I wanted it. I wanted you to take over, to make me come. And you did."

Seth frowned, not content with that. He stared at his horse's ears for a long time before looking aside at Raider.

"I'm still worried," Seth said, his intense green eyes hunting for something. "About you."

Raider's heart twisted up. *This* was the problem. This was why Raider was riding in the rearguard. It was why he'd come so hard last night and why it had shaken him so much.

I'm going to take care of you, Seth had said as he'd stroked so perfectly inside Raider.

I'm still worried. About you.

Raider liked to be free, untethered. Even the Sudai he had left. He didn't understand why he found himself yearning for … something … with Seth. Something more.

Seth went on, "We should have talked about something like that *before* I initiated it. I'm sorry."

"Don't do that, Seth, for fuck's sake. I like how you are—no, I fucking love it. I absolutely don't want you to change or get cautious with me. I *like* that I don't know what you're going to do. I'm sorry I'm being weird, okay? *Don't* change how you are with me."

"Then you're going to have to explain to me—"

"For fuck's sake, it felt *good*. That is what bothered me, all right? It felt good to—" The truth stuck in Raider's throat.

"To *what*, Raider? I don't understand."

"To have you take care of me!" Umae danced at Raider's shout. "It wasn't the restraint, Seth, it was you—it was *you* taking care of me like—fuck, I don't know! What I felt scared me, okay? And I don't want to fucking talk about it!"

As Umae sidled nervously, Raider busied himself with her, trying to calm her down—and himself. He hadn't wanted to say all that. He wished, intensely, that he hadn't. He looked out across the desert, like its vast openness could offer escape.

It was the wind's fortune, the Sudai would say, that he looked out when he did, and in that direction, toward the distant, cavernous hills.

"Raider—"

He held up a hand to silence Seth as his arcane eye zoomed in on the moving figures.

"What?" Seth demanded, the readiness in his tone saying that he knew they suddenly had other problems.

Raider pointed, and Seth slid his arcane scope from his utility belt. He clicked through its settings as he focused it in the direction of Raider's finger—where two dozen mounted men were fast approaching.

✧   ✧   ✧

The caravan drew itself into a circle, securing its most vulnerable people and most valuable goods within. Those who would fight formed a protective ring. While the Sudai were not warlike, they were no strangers to violence. Anyone who transported goods across the desert had to know how to defend themselves and their cargo.

A few were even excited by the opportunity. Fahet, the young idiot, grinned as Raider, stripped to his waist to fight, rode by to check the preparations.

"There are many, Nusuru!"

It was true. Bands of thieves tended to number less than a dozen, but twice that were coming.

"Stay focused, Fahet."

"Very focused!"

Raider exchanged a look with Fahet's older brother, Tulef. Raider would not be the only one looking out for the boy today.

Under different circumstances, Raider might have shared some of Fahet's excitement. He could enjoy a good fight, but only if no one was at risk but himself. Here, there were many at risk, people he cared about—and not just the Sudai.

Seth was a skilled fighter, well armed, well trained. But counting only combatants, the Sudai were outnumbered. Seth would put himself in danger. Raider knew it.

Fahet wasn't the only one Raider would be keeping an eye on.

There was another problem as well: the haze on the horizon.

Sandstorms were unpredictable. This one might miss them entirely, sweeping east or west away from them, bringing only a refreshing breeze. Or it might rip straight through the caravan, scouring flesh, blinding unprotected eyes. It could last for seconds—or days.

But while that danger was uncertain, the danger of the approaching bandits was not.

With high vantage points in the hills—a risky place to hole up—they had likely been waiting for the caravan all morning. They were no doubt timing their attack with the approaching storm, hoping to strike and escape while the Sudai were busy protecting whatever remained of their people and goods.

The bandits came at full speed, shouting ferociously, curved swords flashing, their horses' hooves pounding across the hard-packed earth. Their robes streamed behind them in streaks of purple, black, blue, and red. Teeth were bared in sun-worn faces. Some of the horses carried two—a sure sign that new mounts was one of the things they were after.

Arrows flew from both sides as the band came within range. Scimitar in hand, Raider pressed Umae out to meet the first pass. The bandits would try to sweep by, inflict brief damage, then turn to make another pass. The more Raider and the others could take down in the first sweep or two, the more quickly the band would abandon the tactic to fight hand to hand.

Raider spun Umae out of a spear's path, then swung her around to meet the blue-robed rider he'd chosen as his first target. The bandit yelled like a demon, but all his focus was on his own ferocity. He was unprepared, therefore, for the way Raider ducked smoothly under his sweeping blade, slicing his own upward into the man's exposed armpit.

The bandit screamed. Raider wheeled Umae to track the path of the man's fall as he toppled from his horse. At Raider's signal, Umae leaped into a canter on the man's path. Nearing, Raider leaned to the side, letting Umae counterbalance him as he swept his scimitar across the bandit's throat when the man tried to rise.

The galloping band had finished its first pass and was turning for a second. One of the Sudai was being dragged back into the center ring, but most looked able to keep fighting. Fahet's grin was gone, replaced by a rare seriousness. Seth, his sword red with blood, was tracking the turn of the bandits and maneuvered his horse into their path.

On the second sweep, Raider moved Umae to block the horseman headed for Fahet. Seeing this, the approaching bandit veered to skirt the reach of Raider's scimitar.

So Raider leaped.

He tackled the bandit from his horse, sending them both crashing onto the hard pack. They tumbled and grappled, the combat too close to wield their scimitars.

Quicksilver cascaded down Raider's left arm with a hissing *shhkkt*, wrapping his fist with brutal, gleaming armor. He grabbed the bandit by the throat—and crushed his neck with the ruthless strength of quicksilver.

Raider tossed the body away and climbed to his feet.

Though a few of the attackers were wheeling for a third pass, most of the fight had concentrated around the caravan, the combat now hand to hand. Raider picked up a fallen spear and hurled it at the back of a purple-robed attacker. The man staggered into Tulef's blade.

Raider scanned the scene for Seth. He found the Curator on foot, bleeding from a cut to his arm below the ridge of his black shoulder guard.

Seth swung his straight sword to block a bandit's scimitar. He spun in close to the man, avoiding the long cutting surface of the curved blade, and rammed his sword's pommel into his opponent's gut. As the man's body caved around the blow, Seth's free hand whipped a knife across the bandit's throat.

It halted Raider, watching that. Seth was beautiful in combat, incredible in motion: skilled, strong, focused. He was also, apparently, widely aware of his surroundings. As soon as his opponent fell, he spun, whipping his chakram from his belt. He hurled it—in Raider's direction.

Raider spun as the ring-like weapon flew past him, slicing the throat of a bandit who'd been running toward his unguarded back, scimitar raised. As blood sprayed from the opened throat and the man fell, the chakram made a wide circuit, spinning back to Seth. Seth caught the weapon in a gloved fist and returned it to his belt.

Impressed, Raider shot Seth a grin, which made Seth scowl. Yes, fine, Raider had missed that one.

Raider got busy again, spinning to meet another blade. His new opponent was bigger and more skilled than some of the others. He kept a wary eye on Raider's quicksilver arm, focusing his blows to Raider's unarmored right.

Raider deflected several blows from his opponent, hunting for an opening. He found one at the bandit's knee. Raider's slice across the man's patella sent him stumbling back, exposing his throat long enough for Raider to whip his scimitar across it.

By the time the man fell, Raider could see the Sudai's fighters remained outnumbered. Too many were being dragged out of danger by their friends and family, fighting desperately.

It wasn't often that Raider wished he could fully command the quicksilver in his body. This was one of those rare times. But no matter how much it tore him up to see his friends in danger, he couldn't seem to trigger more than the left-side armor.

Since the day the Sudai had found him half dead in the desert, he had used the full strength of the quicksilver only once, on that day when a rival tribe had attacked the caravan. Like the others, Raider had fought with only blades and fists—until Asha had screamed.

At the sight of a man dragging Asha across the sands, the quicksilver had roared through Raider's body, piercing through at a dozen points. He had become what he'd been made to be: a weapon.

It had been easy, then, to kill the man who would have hurt Asha. It had been easy, then, to kill the rest.

Nusuru, the Sudai had called him after. *Protector.*

Raider had yelled at them to stop.

Nusuru, Nusuru, they had chanted relentlessly—until Asha had scolded them into silence, saving Raider from their praise.

She had led him to her tent. He had lain down, curled up, faced away from her. She had asked, *What happened?*

Raider had squeezed his eyes shut and whispered, *I don't remember.*

She had been silent for a time then had said, *Sometimes it is better that way.*

Since that day, Raider had only ever managed to trigger the quicksilver in his left arm.

Now, guilt made him fight harder. There was something in him that could save his friends—and he couldn't seem to reach it. So he danced through the fight, his scimitar sweeping, his quicksilver fist bludgeoning, killing as many bandits as he possibly could.

When the bandits started to flee, more and more of them leaping onto their horses, the Sudai sent up a cheer. Raider scanned the caravan, relieved to see that the ring had not been breached, relieved that the dead he spotted were all bandits. He laid eyes on Tulef and Fahet.

But Seth, sword stowed in its scabbard, was racing toward one of the bandits. He flung his chakram, but the weapon missed the bandit as he leaped onto the nearest horse—Seth's.

With one hand raised to catch the returning chakram, Seth used his other to aim ... his multi tool? A thin line shot from the device and hooked onto the saddle just as the thief kicked Seth's horse into a gallop. In the instant the horse leaped forward, Seth caught his chakram—and was yanked off his feet.

"Let go!" Raider shouted, heart leaping into his throat as Seth was dragged across the hard pack. The horse wasn't worth it. Even the gear wasn't worth it.

But Seth didn't let go, and the cloud of dust raised by his dragging body streamed into the distance—toward the tunnel-riddled hills.

Chapter 22

THE ARCANE WIRE strung tight from the multi tool's housing to wherever the harpoon-like barb had punched into Seth's saddle as the horse raced across the desert, dragging Seth. His arcane clothing protected his skin from the shredding it would have otherwise gotten from the gritty hard pack, but it couldn't shield him from the bruising impact with every rock.

Seth gritted his teeth and hung on. He could not afford to lose the contents of his saddlebags. Without the letter of credit, not only could he not pay Raider, he couldn't fund the rest of his mission. Without the arcane restraints, he couldn't hope to haul Julian back to Masir. His mission would be over, failed.

Seth sequenced the multi tool to retract. Nothing. Sand must be clogging the mechanism.

He clipped his chakram onto his utility belt to free his hand then grabbed a little way up the wire. The arcane glove prevented the wire from cutting his hand, but the fine strand offered no purchase for his grip and sent him sliding back down to the handle.

The bandit flung a knife at Seth. He twisted to avoid a killing shot, but the blade slashed across his arm. Seth hated sleeves because they always felt like they interfered with his sword work, but he was beginning to wish he had them.

He couldn't see a damn thing. At first the dust had been behind him, but now it was billowing everywhere. The sandstorm that Raider had pointed out on the horizon was catching up.

Seth considered making a wild throw of his chakram or the knife strapped to his thigh, but he would never make the shot. Not from this angle. Not with his body strung out and banging across the ground. Not with visibility so poor.

Grabbing the wire again, Seth managed to haul himself forward a little, slackening the tension on the end of the line. He let go of the wire but not the handle, letting his weight jerk the line. The horse was yanked to one side. The animal stumbled but recovered, and the thief lashed it onward.

The jolt, however, had cleared the retraction mechanism enough to drag Seth closer to the horse—dangerously close to the flying hooves. He got a foot under himself enough to launch himself to the side.

The wire swung him in an arc. He desperately hit the retraction mechanism again. If this didn't work, he might have to let go. Otherwise he would fall straight back into the range of those pounding hooves. But the line retracted, bringing Seth slamming into the side of the rider's leg.

Shouting in alarm, the bandit struck down at Seth's face. Seth punched back at the man, but the angle robbed his blows of most of their force. He couldn't get to his knife, but if he could just get up a little more, he might throw the man from the saddle—

Pain exploded in his shoulder. As the multi tool was ripped from his hands, he went tumbling downward, thudding painfully. Seth had no idea what the hell had hit him or what he was falling down. None of that mattered as much as the fact that he couldn't see a thing.

When he finally skidded to a stop, he lay unmoving for a moment, coming to terms with the pain and slowly realizing that he could, thank the gods, actually see. For a second, he had thought himself blinded.

He had tumbled down a long, rocky slope into a deep cavern. Sunlight, dimmed by the growing sandstorm outside, bled sluggishly down that slope, fading into the darkness. Seth's impact must have been with the rocky edge of the cavern's huge mouth as the bandit rode through, trying to scrape him off.

Hoof beats pounded away through the cavern, but Seth had no time to despair his lost horse and gear—because other footsteps, human ones, were pounding his way. No yell came with the attack, only silent determination as the bandit lunged for him with a knife.

Seth was not so quiet. He leaped up with a shout, catching the man in the gut with his uninjured shoulder. Seth flipped the bandit over his head then spun to meet another attack as the man scrambled to his feet.

The bandit slashed with the knife, but Seth dodged and struck out with a left-handed punch, catching the bandit on the jaw. As the man staggered, Seth swung in with his right, forcing himself through the pain to land a heavy blow to the man's sternum.

As the bandit staggered further, Seth caught his wrist and wrenched the knife away. With a yell, Seth struck the blade into the bandit's neck. The man collapsed. His mouth worked automatically for a second, then he went still, dead eyes staring at Seth.

Seth rolled his shoulder, testing it. The pain burned hot but lacked the sharp bite of a fracture. His shoulder guard had prevented that at least.

Seth looked past the bandit's body to the shadowy belly of the cavern. His horse was long gone, but there was one piece of luck. The bandit had fallen because—between the damage wrought by the wire's barb and the extra strain of Seth's weight—the saddle had broken. It, along with Seth's saddlebags and all their valuable contents, lay in a heap. Seth laughed, dizzy with relief.

At least it hadn't been for nothing.

With the danger gone, Seth took in his surroundings. He was in a vast cavern with tunnels branching in every direction. It wasn't as dark as he had first thought, now that his eyes were adjusting. Dust-clogged daylight filtered down in places. There must be other slopes, other entrances to what seemed to be a network of tunnels.

Wind whistled outside, and dust blew into the cavern from the wide mouth. Seth made his way up the slope until he could see the surrounding landscape, dimmed though it was by the blowing dust and sand. Seth squinted against the grit.

Damn it.

There would be no trekking back across the desert through this. Hopefully it would soon pass and allow him to backtrack to the caravan. Until then, he was stuck.

As Seth walked down the slope into the cavern, unhurried now, he took stock of his injuries. His left knee didn't feel a lot better than his right shoulder, but it was manageable. A bandage would serve the cut he'd gotten from the thrown knife. A scimitar had cut him in the initial fight back at the caravan. That slice should probably be stitched, but he could ignore it for the moment. He was more concerned about his gear.

Seth worked the multi tool's harpoon-like barb from the broken saddle then retracted the line and folding prongs into their housing. The saddlebags were intact, their contents largely undamaged. (Except for the figs. Those hadn't fared well.)

Digging out the arcane lamp, Seth turned it on to full intensity and hooked its ring onto the multi tool, which he hung from his utility belt. After a double check of his weapons, he slung his saddlebags over his good shoulder. He couldn't risk them being found by any returning bandits.

Leaving the broken saddle, Seth headed into one of the branching tunnels to get a sense of where he was—and because he loved to explore strange places. He'd been in more dusty tombs and forgotten temples than he could remember. He'd uncovered artifacts so old that even the scholars of the Arcanum couldn't explain them. He'd found mummies in ancient wrappings and bare bones of every description.

Not everything he'd stumbled across had been dead or inanimate, however. Seth had wrestled with, and barely escaped, a humanoid crocodile in a murky pool. He'd tracked a white light through a dark jungle only to have it vanish into the canopy with a laugh.

Having faced many uncanny dangers, Seth knew what it meant when his scalp prickled—and it was prickling now.

No human had dug these tunnels.

There would be gouges in the rock where they'd sought minerals or precious stones. There would be writing or symbols. There would be left-behind tools and other detritus.

Water, perhaps, could have carved these tunnels. Seth had seen strange landscapes wrought by ancient floods. But …

There was something almost organized about the branches. And they were too smooth, lacking the wavy patterns left by water. They were too perfectly cylindrical— except for the deep groove cut into the ceiling.

Seth directed the lamp's glow onto the floor. Something white and flaky was dusting his boots. He crouched and rubbed some of it between his fingers. It crumbled to nothing.

Spotting a larger fragment of translucent white, he picked it up. He had a brief moment to think that it looked like a flake of skin or maybe a scale before it, too, crumbled to powder.

Chapter 23

THE SANDSTORM WAS whipping up more strongly by the second. As soon as Raider had seen that it would worsen, he'd dismounted Umae, relieved her of his weapons and saddlebags, and turned her loose. She had run back to the caravan, where they would keep her safe, binding her nose and eyes with damp cloth to protect her from the scouring sand.

Raider was slower on foot, but he knew where the bandit had been heading, and he was far enough behind that by now either Seth or the bandit was dead anyway. If Seth was alive—and he'd better be—Raider needed to get him away from those caverns.

With his hand and kaffiyeh shielding his face from the worst of the debris, Raider peered into the storm with only his left eye. Once again, that damn arcane implant was useful. Without the eye's ability to filter input, to zoom and focus, Raider would be running blind.

By the time he reached the caverns, the sandstorm was blowing hard enough to obscure some of the rocky formations rising above the tunnels, their shapes a warning to all wise travelers to keep their distance.

The bandits, clearly, had chosen to ignore that warning in the interests of profit, but they would have known the risk they were taking. They would have known to be quiet.

Raider ducked into the first entrance he reached, throwing back his kaffiyeh and shaking sand from his hair. The relief of escaping the storm, however, was immediately drowned out by the dread of being in this place. Mostly because of what this place was, but also because Raider hated confined spaces.

His heartrate spiked. His breath shortened. He closed his eyes for a second. He would just have to deal with it. He had to find Seth.

Pushing the fear to the edge of his awareness, Raider put his focus on navigating as he crept along the rocky, down-sloping passageway. Narrow and rough, this particular channel could only have been made by the desert's occasional, sheering rainfall. The light faded with every step, but Raider's arcane eye guided him along the rough descent until the channel opened onto a vast cavern.

There, he found a dead man. The fact that it wasn't Seth was almost enough to make Raider thank the gods.

Though the dead bandit gave him hope that Seth was alive, it chilled him too. They had fought here. A man had died here. That would not have been silent.

Raider scanned the many tunnels branching from the cavern. All were dark and silent—except one. Only Raider's arcane eye could have picked out the barely discernable lightness that indicated a distant lamp. Fucking useful eye.

Raider entered the tunnel, this one huge and smooth-sided. As he rounded a few bends, the glow of an arcane lamp intensified until it bloomed bright to show Raider the most welcome sight in the world.

Seth. Alive.

Saddlebags at his feet, Seth was examining the wall of the tunnel. The arcane lamp glowing at his utility belt revealed blood that had seeped from a few cuts on his bare arms, and he undoubtedly had a collection of scrapes and bruises, but he didn't look badly hurt.

He was, however, a filthy mess: his black clothing dusted pale, dirt smudging his cheek, and sand sparkling in the light beard that the desert had forced on him. Something about that, seeing his usually tidy Curator so roughed up, so rugged and powerful, sent a hot pulse through Raider's body.

It didn't matter that it wasn't the time and wasn't the place. Raider couldn't help it. A sound that was half relief, half desire escaped him.

Seth spun his way, whipping his knife from its thigh sheath. His expression went from combative readiness to surprised relief in a heartbeat. He slid the knife back into its sheath.

"You found me," Seth marveled as Raider drew near, his voice gravelly in the way it got when his hunger was stirred. "How the hell did you manage that?"

Raider should have shushed him, should have hustled him away immediately. But seeing Seth alive after being so afraid for him, hearing that delicious, gravelly tone, drove sense and reason clean out of Raider's head.

Raider dropped his gear and stepped in to kiss him. Seth grabbed Raider's hips, hauling him close. Raider's body primed itself with instant, unthinking need. Seth shuddered and moaned, his cock thickening against Raider's as he swept his tongue possessively into Raider's mouth.

Raider grabbed Seth's ass, wanting to feel those muscles flexing as Seth ground against him. Images flashed through his mind: Seth, naked and hard, pinning him against the tunnel wall. Seth spearing into him, filling him with that huge cock, joining their bodies in perfect synchronicity as he began to thrust.

A buzz of danger intruded on that image, an awareness of the tunnel's dark turnings—and what might come slithering around them. The thought snapped Raider out of it. The tunnel was no place for them to fuck. It was no place for them to be at all.

With a hiss of frustration, Raider broke the kiss, but he couldn't immediately tear himself away from Seth. He rested his forehead against Seth's left shoulder for a moment, trying to calm his body, trying to refocus.

Seth, damn him, laid a hand on the back of Raider's head. Seth's tenderness always did something to Raider that he couldn't come to terms with. Seth could be so deliciously rough and dominating, so aggressive and unpredictable. Raider loved that, craved it constantly. But then Seth would do this kind of thing, and something in Raider unraveled.

But Raider couldn't afford to linger against Seth, couldn't let himself feel safe just because he was in Seth's arms. So he yanked back, shoving roughly away.

Scowling at the abrupt separation, Seth demanded loudly, "What the hell—"

Raider clamped a hand over Seth's mouth. The move was automatic and so, it seemed, was Seth's reaction. He grabbed Raider and spun.

Switching their positions, he slammed Raider's back into the wall of the tunnel. The impact bounced Raider's hand away from Seth's mouth, freeing Seth to close his teeth on Raider's throat with a growl.

Seth gripped Raider's cock through his pants, holding him still by it. Raider's eyes rolled back in his head. Why the hell did that turn him on so much?

Seth's other hand seized Raider's hair at the scalp. "You think you get to play like that?"

"Seth, we can't—" Raider cut off, clamping his mouth shut against the loud moan that tried to escape him as Seth's fingers curled deliciously against his balls. He somehow managed to gasp out, "Seth—*stop*."

Frustration boiled in Seth's eyes, but he released Raider's cock and his hair. Instead of backing away, however, he planted his hands against the tunnel wall on either side of Raider, caging him in. His nostrils flared as he took measured breaths, clearly fighting to get his aggression under control.

Raider fisted his hands at his sides, engaged in a similar battle. Raider won his before Seth did—because he knew why it mattered.

"We need to get out of here," Raider whispered.

"Why?"

Finger to his lips, Raider signaled Seth to be quiet. Seth glanced behind himself. Finding only the dark, empty tunnel, he frowned.

"I'll tell you once we're out of here. We have to go. Now."

"There's a—" At Raider's renewed shushing signal, Seth lowered his voice. "—sandstorm outside."

"We're in more danger here."

"So what is this place?" Seth asked, keeping his voice low. "You'll waste more time arguing with me than just fucking telling me."

"These are sand serpent tunnels."

Frowning, Seth stepped back, releasing Raider from the cage of his body. Like Raider, he was still hard, but he managed to focus in spite of it. He glanced along the tunnel, seeming to assess.

"A snake of some kind was my guess. Some ancient behemoth? It's clearly long gone. The shed skin is nothing but dust. There's no evidence of recent meals. Besides, the bandit fled in here to hide."

Raider couldn't help but stare at the Curator. He'd expected disbelief or fear. He hadn't expected an analysis.

Perhaps he should have.

"It's been dormant for centuries," Raider whispered impatiently. "But one was woken once, maybe this one, I don't know. The Sudai have stories of it. It destroyed whole cities, killed thousands, before it went back to sleep. The bandits may have a hideout here, but they know to be quiet. I found a dead man and a broken saddle in the cavern. Was that quiet?"

Seth's expression said that, no, it hadn't been, but his stubborn stance said he wasn't ready to get paranoid.

Raider whispered desperately, "Please, Seth, I'm begging you: trust me."

Seth gave him a long look. Then he sighed and bent to grab his saddlebags. Slinging them over his left shoulder, he gestured for Raider to lead the way.

Retrieving his own gear, Raider whispered, "Turn off the light."

"It'll be pitch black in here."

Raider snagged Seth's hand. "I can navigate."

Seth's eyes displayed a fresh surge of frustration and desire to argue, but he reached for the arcane lamp hanging from his belt and turned it off.

The sudden darkness and sense of confinement tried to swamp Raider, but Seth's hand was in his and it kept him grounded, focused. He had to get Seth out of here.

As they crept along the tunnel, Raider heard nothing but their own movement until the wind's whistling reached him. They were nearing the cavern where Seth had killed the bandit. The storm wasn't over. They could find a place in the hills to crouch and wait out the last of it.

For the second time since he'd entered the network of tunnels, Raider almost thanked the gods.

Such thanks, as usual, would have been misplaced—because from one of the branching tunnels came the sound of a dry, rasping slither.

Chapter 24

SETH KNEW THEY must be nearing the cavern because enough light was filtering into the tunnel that he could have pulled his hand free of Raider's. He didn't though. Not until he heard that rasping slither. Not until Raider looked over his shoulder at Seth and barked, "Run!"

Raider burst into a sprint. Seth bolted after him into the vast cavern where he'd killed the bandit—whose body was now gone.

From the corner of his eye, Seth caught movement in one of the branching tunnels, a gleam of light reflecting off a massive, slithering form.

Heart leaping into his throat, Seth raced after Raider, pounding through the vast cavern toward the slope that cut upward to the dusty light of day. Better the sandstorm than a snake powerful enough to have tunneled through stone, big enough that something on its body had cut a cleft into the rock six feet above Seth's head.

Seth didn't think he could possibly run any faster, but when he heard the shushing, rasping slide of the snake's sinuous body over stone, he discovered in himself a new, higher gear.

But it was too late.

He knew it as they reached the foot of the slope. Raider knew it too, because he slowed at the same time, turned at the same time.

They barely had time to throw down their gear and draw their swords before a black snake large enough to swallow a man whole shot out into the cavern.

Spikes ridged its head and ran down its back, but Seth had no time to observe anything more than that before the snake struck, six-foot fangs flashing toward him and Raider.

Seth swung his sword, catching the serpent's mouth with the tip of his blade. Raider darted close to the thing. He slashed up at its throat with his scimitar, but the serpent's heavy scales deflected the blow.

The serpent coiled away, hissing, its red, reptilian eyes calculating. A long red tongue flickered out from its lipless mouth.

"Go!" Raider shouted.

Ignoring that absurd command, Seth sidestepped, studying the partially coiled snake, its body twice the height of a man and too long to even fit fully inside the cavern. It stretched away into the tunnel from which it had emerged.

Raider barked, "Get the hell out of here!"

"I'm not leaving you."

That was all Raider was going to get. Seth wouldn't waste time arguing and wouldn't damage his focus by glancing at Raider. And that was why he didn't see what Raider meant to do until it was too late to try to stop him.

With a shout designed to draw the serpent's attention, Raider went charging straight at it. The snake's body tightened—then it struck. Raider dove aside.

Somersaulting, he popped back to his feet and leaped for the huge head. He managed to get a hold of one of the snake's horns, but even with quicksilver encasing his hand, his grip lasted only a moment. The sand serpent whipped its head with brutal force, tossing Raider deep into the cavern and out of sight.

"Raider!"

Fuck!

Seth sprinted forward to take advantage of the snake's turned head, hoping he could get his sword to its throat. Raider's slashing scimitar had not pierced the scales, but a thrust from Seth's straight blade might.

He didn't get a chance to find out because the snake wound away so fast he could only make out a blur of motion. The sand serpent coiled and whipped around the cavern, its body too big to move freely but its coils gliding smoothly over one another.

Seth struck his sword as hard as he could into the scaled body. The sand serpent shrieked and whipped around, nearly ripping the sword from Seth's grip before he could yank it free. A coil of the snake's body slammed into Seth, sending him flying into the darkness at the edge of the cavern. He hit a wall and slid down.

Seth rolled to his side and staggered to his feet. Dizzied from the impact, he registered movement but couldn't discern the source. He tried to get his sword up—

"This way!" Raider shouted.

Thank the gods!

Seth lurched after Raider, vision clearing as he tailed Raider through the cavern. Raider had all their gear slung over his shoulder, but he was still fast as hell. He had to be—and so did Seth.

The slither and rasp of the snake's movement was fast approaching. Seth prepared himself to turn and fight. Barely any light reached him this deep into the vast cavern, but even blinded by darkness, he would rather face death than have it strike him in the back.

Then Raider shouted, "Here!"

He vanished into a black hole in the cavern's wall. Seth lost him instantly. He looked behind for the snake. Its massive form shot through the dimness straight for Seth—

A hand, cool and metallic, grabbed Seth's and yanked him into the blackness. A boom shook the tight walls that had closed abruptly around Seth.

Raider hauled at Seth's hand, and Seth found himself scrambling blindly up a rocky slope. A shriek sounded from the cavern then a second boom shook the walls. Grit rained down from the passageway's low ceiling.

Still scrambling, Seth tripped on the uneven ground. His fall yanked his hand free of Raider's. Pain barked through Seth's knees as he hit the ground.

Raider was there at once, scrambling over him. Desperate to see what was happening, Seth reached for the lamp hanging at his belt. He clicked it on.

Cool arcane light splashed over the rough stone walls of the narrow, upward-sloping passageway. The light bloomed across Raider in his brilliant red kaftan, blocking Seth's view of the passageway's opening into the cavern, putting himself between Seth and the sand serpent.

Raider had his scimitar in hand, but he was swaying badly. Seth was already lunging for him as he collapsed. He caught Raider under the arms and hauled him back—just as a long, red, forked tongue flicked into the passageway.

Through the narrow opening, Seth glimpsed glossy black scales forming a lipless mouth.

Seth dragged Raider up the rough slope away from that seeking tongue.

The tongue withdrew. The arcane lamp offered a glimpse of the snake's moving body—then it slammed its head against the opening again. Rock broke from the ceiling, crashing down to block the hole.

Seth scrambled back, pulling Raider farther away from the falling rock, dragging him up the rough slope. When he reached a flat area, he stopped, listening for the snake, but all he could hear was the sandstorm raging outside. The passageway, thank the gods, was not a dead end. Farther up, it opened to the desert. Dust filtered down the slope from that outlet.

Seth unhooked the lamp from his belt and held it over Raider. His skin was pale, his eyelids fluttering. He was trying to stay conscious, but he was losing that battle. The quicksilver had retracted from his left arm. Seth flicked Raider's kaftan open, hunting for injuries. He found none on his torso, but his right pant leg was soaked with blood.

Shit.

Seth set the lamp aside. At the bloody tear, Seth ripped the cloth further, exposing a slash across Raider's thigh—and traces of a clear fluid that Seth had a very bad feeling was venom.

Chapter 25

Raider woke to pain. Someone was cutting him.

Someone was always cutting him. Taking him apart. Putting him back together.

He snarled and wrenched away. The cutter held him down. Raider struck out with a fist, and the cutter fell back.

They had forgotten to strap him down. He was free! He made it only a few inches off the table before they pinned him down again.

A scalpel loomed out of the darkness. The blade glinted as it descended with cool detachment: smooth, fluid, unhurried.

Please, Raider begged, straining against the hold. *Don't.*

"Stop fighting. It's all right. I'm trying to help you."

Arcane light limned a face, but not the one Raider expected. This face was broad and strong and handsome. The expression was intense, the green eyes burning under lowered brows.

Help me, Raider said, or tried to.

But Seth didn't reply. Seth was gone. Everything was gone.

* * *

Raider lifted his head off the table—and screamed.

He had been cut open. His skin had been peeled back to lay bare every muscle and tendon and bone. Silvery liquid shimmered, branching through the raw interior of his body like a network of pearlescent veins.

He screamed and screamed and screamed until he was released, mercifully, into the dark.

* * *

Time passed, maybe.

Raider swam up into a lighter darkness. He hovered there, shivering, cold.

So cold.

Weight pressed down on him, draped him. Something tucked around him.

"It's all right," someone said. "It will pass."

Raider opened his eyes to a vast darkness. A sound of fear escaped him.

An arcane light bloomed and a face came into his field of view. Seth, frowning.

Seth dabbed at Raider's face with a cloth. "Raider? Can you hear me?"

Help me.

Seth's brow furrowed. "It's all right. Just relax. I'm right here."

The blackness was creeping in from the edges. Raider didn't want to relax, didn't want it to take him down into its cold grip again.

He tried to lift his hand, but it was trapped. Bound?

No. Please no.

A blanket tugged free of his side. A hand found his beneath and held it. Relief swept through Raider, but it wasn't enough to keep him there. He spun down into the dark again.

✼ ✼ ✼

Raider lay under the blankets, his body entwined with another's. It should have felt good, but it didn't. Something was wrong.

Raider tried to draw away, but the other's limbs trapped him with dead weight. Raider opened his eyes to see Seth's green eyes staring emptily at him. Blood trickled down Seth's forehead.

Raider yanked back, but he was caught—and it wasn't because Seth was trapping him.

Spears of quicksilver had struck from Raider's body into Seth's. Blood poured out around the shining impalements, soaking the bed, bathing them both in red.

Why, Shashem? Seth's dead lips asked. *I thought you loved me.*

Raider screamed.

Chapter 26

VENOM WAS THE ONLY explanation for such a quick onset of fever and delirium. The slash to Raider's thigh suggested a graze from one of the sand serpent's spines. A bite would have cost Raider his leg. It would have cost him his life.

But surely even a graze from a venomous serpent that size would kill any man.

But then, Raider wasn't just any man, was he?

The quicksilver in his body had clearly altered it on a fundamental level. It was almost like he wasn't even quite human.

Yet, in the ways that mattered, he was.

"Easy," Seth murmured, rubbing Raider's chest through the blanket as he twitched again, his eyes darting back and forth under his closed lids. Another nightmare. He'd been having them almost constantly, mixed in with a half-waking delirium, through the day and now into the night.

Please, Raider had begged. *Don't.*

Help me, he'd mouthed, more than once.

Seth kept rubbing Raider's chest in a soothing, circular motion until he settled. Then, keeping his hand over Raider's heart, Seth lay down to rest. With the storm still raging, with Raider hurt, there wasn't much else he could do.

There had been no further sign of the sand serpent. The fallen rock blocking the way into the passage from the cavern seemed to have discouraged it. It had likely gone hunting for more accessible prey. The bandits were here somewhere, after all.

Seth left the lamp glowing on its lowest setting, just in case Raider woke again. In his confused state, waking in the blackness had frightened him. He hadn't known where he was. He hadn't known that it was Seth's hands on him, trying to help. Raider had thought …

Fuck, he'd thought that Seth—or whoever he'd imagined Seth to be—was hurting him. Deliberately.

Please, Raider had begged. *Don't.*

Seth closed his eyes, trying to shut that out, trying not to think about what that might mean. He needed to rest so he could take care of Raider again. And so he could figure what the hell he was going to do in the morning.

※　　※　　※

Seth woke to a sight he had trouble comprehending. The grayish light of early morning was drifting down the narrow slope onto the shelf of rock … where Raider was rolling up his blankets and organizing his gear.

What the hell?

Yesterday, Seth had feared that Raider would die. And now he was *packing*? To *travel*?

Seth understood that Raider's body healed unnaturally fast, but … Raider had been out of his head for over twelve hours. He'd lost quite a lot of blood, and Seth had put sixteen stitches in him yesterday.

Then again, Raider might be busy packing, but he didn't look like he should be. His hands shook visibly as he lashed his bedroll to his saddlebags. He was moving carefully, obviously in pain, and the dark smudges below his eyes stood out against the pallor of his skin.

Seth, too, had to move carefully as he levered himself up. His left knee was stiff as hell and his right shoulder was black and blue. He also had a few stitches of his own tugging at tender skin.

When Seth finally achieved a sitting position, he regarded Raider's activity with skepticism. True, Raider had managed to dress himself and was clearly coherent enough to get his gear together. However.

Seth said, "There's no way you're—"

"We only have enough food to make it to Aqarat if we get moving," Raider cut in as he checked his scimitar, which Seth had already cleaned. He didn't look up. He hadn't once since Seth woke. "And we need water."

"We have the alembic."

"Is that what was so goddamn important you almost got yourself killed chasing it?"

Seth was vaguely aware that he wasn't awake enough for this conversation, but he found himself answering automatically, "I can't complete my mission without my gear."

"Your fucking mission!" Raider slammed down his sheathed blade.

"It's why I'm here. It's the whole point."

"I am well aware of that," Raider snapped, finally looking at Seth. Glaring at him. "But getting yourself killed for your goddamn arcane shit somewhat defeats the purpose."

"I was chasing a thief, whom I caught and killed, by the way. Everything would have been fine—if not for that giant fucking snake, which I did not expect. You might have mentioned it, you know."

"It was dormant and not in our path. It wasn't relevant—until you risked your life *for gear*."

"And my letter of credit," Seth replied hotly, getting more pissed off by the second, "without which I can't pay you."

Raider's right eye flared gold. "Fuck you."

Seth wanted to shove to his feet and put some distance between them, but the space was too cramped. So instead he closed his eyes and worked his way through one of his breathing exercises. He made himself think. He was reacting to Raider's hostility, but none of the things Seth was saying were the things he wanted to say.

What he wanted to say was *thank you*. Because Raider had not only come after him, he had put himself between Seth and the sand serpent—more than once. (Seth still hated that Raider did that kind of shit, but still. The fact remained.)

What Seth wanted to *do* was take care of Raider. Who was hurt and clearly in pain.

But while Raider's nasty mood made the latter feel impossible, Seth could at least choose the words he actually wanted to say.

He opened his eyes. Raider was refitting the scabbard of his scimitar to be worn instead of strapped to a saddle.

"What's done is done," Seth said, "and I don't want to argue about all that. What I want to say is thank you. For coming after me. Without you, I wouldn't have gotten away from the sand serpent. You saved my life."

Raider glared at him with renewed hostility. "How else would I get paid?"

Seth swallowed down the hot coal of his temper. He reminded himself that Raider was always shitty in the mornings because he was always in pain. This morning was not only no exception, it was a hundred times worse.

It would be best, Seth decided, if they didn't talk for a few minutes. So he scooted away as much as the cramped space allowed and started sorting through his own gear. Without a horse, he had to decide what was worth carrying. That would be a good task for him right now. A simple, quiet—

"You're not going to carry all that, are you?" Raider demanded as Seth sorted his gear into piles. "We don't need the tent."

Yes, they did. Until Raider was healed, Seth needed to have a proper shelter for them.

But he could feel danger in every word he was tempted to say, so instead he replied reasonably, "I'll carry it until I can't."

At least there was no arguing *that* point.

"Your shoulder's fucked up," Raider argued.

Seth glared at him. "If you can travel like that, then I can certainly travel like this."

"My body is rife with quicksilver, remember? It's practically an arcane instrument itself."

Seth narrowed his eyes. Raider's words echoed ones that Seth had spoken at the oasis after Raider had scorned Seth's attachment to his tools. *It has its advantages*, Raider had sneered in response to Seth's comment.

He was sneering now, too.

Seth didn't like that. So even though he wanted to discuss that very subject—namely Raider's quicksilver but also his nightmares and a dozen other things—this wasn't the moment for it.

So Seth ignored Raider's comment and simply told him, "I'm taking the fucking tent." Then he tossed a pouch of dates and almonds at him and ordered, "Eat that."

Raider glared at him. Seth glared back.

Seth didn't know exactly what was going on in Raider's head right now, but it didn't matter. Raider needed to do what Seth had said—because Seth was right. And Seth was going to take care of him even if he was being an asshole.

Finally, Raider yielded. He looked down and let out a shaky breath and reached for the pouch that Seth had tossed him.

Seth wanted more than that. He wanted Raider to talk to him—really talk to him. He wanted Raider to let down his guard so Seth could get close to him. But Seth could tell that none of that was going to happen, not right now.

So, for now, this would do.

CHAPTER 27

RAIDER WAS OUT of breath halfway into their climb up the rocky slope, but it didn't matter. They needed to get out of here—for a lot of reasons. Their limited resources. The fact that the sand serpent was still here somewhere. The fact that the bandits, if they hadn't been eaten, were here somewhere too.

But more than all that, Raider needed out of this goddamn tunnel. He couldn't take another second of the confined space. Especially with where his head had been during his delirium.

He needed some space from Seth too.

That dream …

It was eating him up inside.

Seth had asked him once why he refused to attach himself to anything. He'd asked if Raider didn't trust anyone for more than a meal or a fuck. He'd asked if that was why Raider called himself a feather on the wind.

The thing was … Seth had guessed rightly. And wrongly.

There was a part of Raider, deep down, that always expected betrayal, always expected good things to vanish.

They always did. So Raider preferred to enjoy good things in their fleeting moment—and to drift onward before they could disappear.

But more than that, Raider knew, deep down, that he didn't deserve good things. It was something he'd always known, even before an emperor had changed his life. By always distracting himself with new, superficial pleasures, he didn't have to dwell on that fact.

Raider was so used to staying on that surface level that he hadn't expected things with Seth to be any different, to go any deeper. Raider should have known better. He should have understood from the beginning how different his response to Seth was. But Raider had told himself it was just the challenge. He'd told himself that it was just sex.

If it ever had been just sex, it certainly wasn't now. Not for Raider. His dream was proof enough of that.

But goddamn it, that didn't stop him from wanting it. Wanting this. With Seth. Whatever this was.

At the mouth of the narrow passageway, Seth halted, forcing Raider to a stop behind him. Seth scanned the open ground with his arcane scope. The scope was as good as Raider's eye, and it was better for Seth to lead right now. Raider didn't think he could.

Raider wasn't ready when Seth glanced back at him. He hadn't expected it, hadn't prepared his face. And his face, clearly, was showing way too much because Seth's eyebrows scrunched down and he opened his mouth to say something.

"Let's just get the hell out of here," Raider said before Seth could speak.

Seth didn't look happy, but he faced forward and led the way out.

They kept to the base of the rocky hills that hid the tunnels. If the sand serpent came after them, they would have to climb into the hills and try to find cover. Hopefully, it wouldn't come to that. It shouldn't. They were too small of prey to be worth that kind of effort.

If Raider was wrong about that, they were probably fucked. He, for one, wasn't fit to run right now. Seth wasn't in much better shape. His left knee was clearly stiff, and he had plenty of other minor injuries.

At least they were out of the deep sands of the Kesh. From here to Aqarat, they would be walking across more traversable hard pack.

Walking.

Damn it.

Raider hated that he'd lost Umae. She would be safe with the Sudai, but still.

They headed east along the rocky hills, which rose and fell until they became scattered humps of stone, some with a smattering of scrub. They didn't talk, not for the first few hours while they stayed alert for the sand serpent.

When they were clearly out of range, Seth broke the long silence with, "I'm sorry about Umae."

Of course Seth would be tracking that, how much the mare had meant to Raider. The Curator was way too observant.

Raider said tonelessly, "She's safe with the Sudai."

The same couldn't be said of Seth's horse. Maybe the bandits had gotten it. More likely, the sand serpent had. Raider thought about how Seth hadn't wanted to name the animal, how careful he'd been to not get too attached.

Seth had been right; he'd been smart. Attachment meant loss. Pain. Raider glanced at Seth and away.

"They left us," Seth observed, clearly surprised by that fact. "The Sudai."

"Chief Karek would never risk the lives of his own people for either of us. He wouldn't be a good chief, doing that."

"I wouldn't expect them to risk themselves for me, but they seemed to …"

When Seth trailed off, Raider filled in, "Care about me?"

"Well … yes."

"There are different levels of caring," Raider pointed out. "I think they do care about me on a certain level, but it only goes so far."

Seth frowned, like that didn't make sense to him.

Raider huffed and shook his head. "You're so absolute. So black and white. Life isn't like that."

"It is for me."

"You're fucking impossible sometimes."

Seth's principles could be so exhausting, and Raider didn't have the energy to debate them right now. Keeping his painful leg moving was taking most of his focus. He also had a headache and felt sick to his stomach. That was the venom, no doubt.

When Raider had leaped for the sand serpent's head, hoping to get a blow in at the base of its skull, which legend held to be its only vulnerability, the creature had thrown him off. He had tumbled over the enormous coils of the snake's body, gashing his leg on one of the spines. Any more than that glancing blow and the venom would undoubtedly have killed him. That creature had been made to destroy greater things than men. Its kind were relics, the Sudai claimed, of an ancient battle between the gods. Raider had managed to evade it and get back to Seth only because the creature had been too damn big to maneuver easily in the cavern.

Raider would probably start feeling grateful to be alive when he stopped feeling like shit. That, however, was not going to be today.

As he scrubbed sweat from his face with a kaftan sleeve, his improvised saddlebag-turned-pack lifted from his shoulder.

"Give this to me," Seth ordered when Raider grabbed for it.

"Seth, no—"

Seth pulled it from Raider's weakened grip and slung it over his shoulder. "I'm a fucking pack mule."

"You're a *something* mule," Raider grumbled as he limped onward.

"Yeah, I've heard that too."

Raider glanced at Seth. Scraped and bruised, laden down like, yes, a pack mule, the Curator tromped doggedly onward. So damn determined. So damn strong.

And handsome. And good.

Too goddamn good.

After another hour, Seth said, "Birds." He had his arcane scope trained on a craggy mound of hills about a mile out. "Can you make it?"

Raider grunted in confirmation.

Seth glanced down at Raider's leg, where fresh blood gleamed redly on the already bloodstained silk.

"Yes, I can make it," Raider forced himself to say, even though the words cost him some of his dwindling energy. He didn't want Seth stopping early for him. It was better if they made it to the water source that the birds indicated.

Raider did make it, though just barely.

At the sight of a craggy arm of stone sheltering a shallow pool surrounded by tall, spiky cheffah grass, Raider sat down abruptly. At least, that was what he meant to do. Instead he found himself flat on his back in the dirt. Briefly, he saw the clear sky above him. Then even that was gone.

✷   ✷   ✷

Raider was walking down a long palace corridor. It seemed to go on forever, endless miles of pillars and indistinct mosaics, latticed windows and closed doors.

He had a vague sense of being both lost and trapped. Then a different feeling grew within him, a new awareness. Someone was behind him in the corridor. Someone bad.

Raider tried to run, but no matter how hard he strained, he couldn't pick up speed. He was stuck in agonizingly slow motion with his pursuer right behind him, catching up.

Panicked, Raider looked over his shoulder—and saw himself. A version of himself anyway, one that was pearlescent and gleaming, made entirely of quicksilver. Him but not him.

A hand of liquid metal reached out and closed on Raider's shoulder—

"Wake up! Raider, wake up!"

Raider bolted upright. When a hand touched his shoulder, quicksilver burst from the joint, cascading down his arm with a metallic *shhhhkt!* Raider struck out without thinking—and sent Seth flying to the edge of the blankets.

Blankets?

The scene took a moment to clarify. The silvery awning shaded him and Seth and their gear. Beyond, the sun beat down on the vast openness of the desert. There was no palace corridor. There was no quicksilver version of himself.

Wincing, Seth levered himself up and rubbed at his chest—where Raider had slammed a quicksilver palm into him.

Raider tried to say something, but the words wouldn't come. His throat was too tight. He couldn't *breathe*.

Seth crept forward cautiously. "Raider?"

Raider closed his eyes, hating the sight of Seth's caution, hating that he'd struck out at him. It was too much like his dream of waking entwined with Seth, of Seth being dead, impaled by quicksilver.

When Seth tugged at Raider's shoulder, he flinched. But Seth didn't draw back. He just waited. After a moment, the quicksilver retracted, vanishing into Raider's body with a *shhhhkt*, leaving only its usual wound.

Seth tugged again. This time Raider gave in. As he lay down, Seth laid a hand on Raider's chest, settling it over his pounding heart. He rubbed a circle there until Raider's throat loosened and he could breathe.

After a while, when Raider had calmed down, Seth asked quietly, "Will you tell me?"

Raider's eyes squeezed shut.

"It's okay," Seth said. "Just rest."

But Raider couldn't. He turned his head and looked out at the desert. "The heat's easing. We should go."

"We're here for the night," Seth said.

"I don't think I can get back to sleep anyway. We might as well—"

"We might as well get you cleaned up. There's a bucket of water for you. Then you can rest again."

When Raider started to object, Seth said with finality, "You don't have to sleep to rest." He added, "I need rest too."

At that, Raider sighed in defeat.

Seth brought the leather bucket and washcloth to him. After Raider had washed his face, Seth took the cloth from him and dipped it into the water.

When Raider tried to take it back, Seth said, "Let me. Please."

Goddamn it. Why did Seth have to do this kind of thing? It was different from sex, different from casual touch. Raider was comfortable with both of those, wanted both of those. He wanted this too but …

It was getting complicated. More so every day.

Seth had been right from the start—and Raider had been a fool. But it was already too damn late. Because Raider wanted Seth to kneel beside him. Which Seth did. And he wanted Seth to gently scrub the cloth over his chest and shoulders. Which Seth did.

Seth refreshed the cloth then pulled Raider into him as he scrubbed the back of his neck. Seth must have felt Raider's eyes squeeze shut against his shoulder because Seth closed his arms around him.

For a moment, Seth simply held on. Then he asked gently, "What happened?"

Raider's heart skipped. Seth wasn't talking about the dream. "You promised not to ask."

"I know," Seth acknowledged as he used the damp cloth to sweep sweat and grit from Raider's back.

Raider pulled away. He couldn't handle Seth's gentleness, not right now, not in this context. Raider drew up his left knee and hooked his arms around it. His right leg hurt too damn much to draw in, so he had to leave it extended. He didn't like it though, how it made him feel exposed. Vulnerable.

Seth gave Raider his space, even though it was clear Seth didn't like it. His hands twitched then curled on his thighs, one still holding the washcloth.

Soft but insistent, Seth said, "You must remember something."

Raider's heart skipped again. He had known Seth wouldn't be able to keep his promise to leave this subject untouched. It wasn't in Seth's nature. And sex had changed things, as Seth had said it would.

The problem was ... Raider didn't want to lie to Seth. He hated it. He wanted to tell him the truth. He wanted to tell Seth everything.

But he couldn't.

So he stared at his drawn-up knee and gave what he could. "Only pieces. I don't know how they go together."

"Memory can be confusing. When it's old. When it's from something you ... don't like."

Seth's tone was heavy, and it made Raider look up at him. Raider didn't press, but he hoped Seth would tell him what he meant.

And Seth did, though it took him a moment. He let out a shaky breath. His eyes unfocused. Then he started to speak.

"The last memory I have of my mother is running with her through a bazaar. I was maybe eight or nine years old. Some men were after us. They chased us into a dirty alley. I remember the way she shoved me behind her. I remember her scream. And I remember how warm her blood was when it splattered my face."

Raider sucked in a breath. Shit. Whatever he'd been expecting to hear, it wasn't that.

"By some divine chance, a Curator had witnessed our flight and followed. Marcus, as I came to later know. I don't recall Marcus killing those men. I just remember them lying dead around me and my mother. Then him kneeling in front of me. It's a blank after that, like I wasn't there, even when we buried her. Something so important, and I can't find it in myself. I can almost feel it, the truth, the moment, but it's just beyond my reach.

"Anyway. Marcus took me to Masir University and I became a ward of the Arcanum. It's been my home ever since."

At first, Raider couldn't respond. There was too much to absorb, too much sudden context packed into that brief gloss. No wonder Seth was so devoted to the Arcanum. No wonder he had become a Curator, like the man who had saved him.

But context wasn't the point of this story. This story was about loss. Devastation. There was no way Raider could respond with, *I'm sorry*. Or, *How terrible*. There were no words for this at all.

So Raider unhooked one of his arms from around his drawn-up knee. He reached out and laid his hand over the fist that was balled up on Seth's thigh. It took a moment for Seth's hand to relax, to open. When it finally did, Raider threaded their fingers together.

Seth's brilliant green eyes met Raider's. The intensity was still there, the depth of feeling, but now Raider glimpsed in that depth the pain he hadn't seen before. Seth was *letting* him see it. He was choosing to share Raider's vulnerability—and Raider didn't think anything had ever meant so much to him.

With his eyes, Raider tried to say, *Thank you.*

With his touch, he tried to say, *I understand what you've told me.*

"Asha was my Marcus," Raider said, his thumb brushing Seth's. "After ... this." The quicksilver, he meant. Everything.

Seth nodded, understanding

"The Sudai found me in the Kesh. They mistook me for a raider. That's how I got my name. As a misunderstanding. Then a joke. Then for lack of anything better. Like Jasmine, you know? In the perfume shop?"

Seth closed his eyes, wincing. "Fuck. That's ... not what I had assumed."

Yeah. Raider had figured. He couldn't blame Seth for his assumption. Raider had kept the name on purpose. It had a dozen meanings that felt right to him, but first and foremost it meant, *Don't trust me.*

Seth's thumb stroked the back of Raider's hand. "You said you lived with the Sudai for a year?"

"Yes."

When Raider didn't go on, Seth prompted, "You said you left because you're not one of them."

There was a tone of question to Seth's words, and Raider understood that he was really asking, *Was that the real reason?*

Yes and no.

Raider pulled his hand free of Seth's and went back to having both arms hooked around his drawn-up knee. He looked out at the desert. "I got restless. A feather on the wind, remember?"

Seth made a small but unmistakable sound of frustration. Yes, Raider was closing up. This truth, he didn't want to tell Seth.

The Sudai had seen him at his worst. Angry and confused. Raider had needed to escape that. He had needed to be around people who had never seen him like that—so he could leave it in the past and let it not exist. Every time Raider encountered the Sudai, some of that came back into existence. He loved them. He loved to see them and talk to them. But every time he said goodbye to them, mixed in with his sadness at the parting was a sneaking hint of relief, like the past could vanish again.

A second deletion of his life.

Maybe it was because Raider had closed a door in the conversation, but Seth circled back to the weak point in Raider's story.

"You really have no memory—"

"I told you that. Why don't you believe me?"

Seth grunted in frustration. Raider looked at him from the corner of his eye. Seth's jaw was bunched, his eyebrows down.

"It's just hard to wrap my head around," Seth said. "Not remembering *anything*."

"You said you couldn't remember some things."

It was a low blow and it made Raider feel like an asshole, but he had to shove this conversation in a different direction.

"I know," Seth acknowledged. "That's why I kind of understand. But ..."

"But *what*, Seth?"

Seth's mouth worked for a second, like he wasn't sure whether to give voice to his thoughts. Raider turned his head fully toward Seth, glaring at him, trying to get him to say, *Nothing. Never mind.*

But Seth met his glare. Not with a glare of his own but with a pained look in his eyes. He said softly, "You have such terrible nightmares."

Raider's body locked up. His brain froze.

Seth winced at Raider's reaction. "I'm sorry. I'll let it go."

Raider didn't reply. He couldn't.

Seth dipped the washcloth. "Let me finish this."

Raider unlocked his voice to say, "No."

"Please," Seth said gently.

"No."

"Please, Raider. I'm sorry, okay? I'm sorry."

The problem wasn't what Seth had said. The problem, of course, was Raider. He didn't deserve Seth's gentleness, his concern. He didn't deserve Seth at all.

And yet, when Seth moved closer to him, when he cautiously pulled Raider into him, Raider didn't push back. He was stiff at first, passively resisting, but when Seth closed his arms around him, Raider started shaking. And Seth, damn him, just held on and absorbed it. When the worst of it had passed, Seth resumed sponging the sweat and grit from Raider's skin, taking care of him.

And even if Raider didn't deserve it, he wanted it. So fucking bad. He leaned into Seth, trying to draw all that warmth and security into himself. And when Seth cupped the back of his head, the last of Raider's resistance crumbled. He relaxed and let Seth soothe him until everything else faded away.

CHAPTER 28

SETH WAS RELIEVED that Raider's mood improved as he healed. Raider had been in dark place for a while. It had been hard to reach him there. He had lashed out, pushed back. He'd made Seth work really damn hard to get close to him.

Though Raider's recent attempts to drive Seth away had been the strongest, they hadn't been the first.

The first had been after they'd had sex at the oasis. Raider had gotten hostile in the morning, had sneeringly insisted that sex didn't change anything. But when Seth had soundly rejected that argument, he'd seen the fear and yearning in Raider's eyes. The need.

Something similar had happened when Seth had had to dig so hard to get Raider to admit why he'd been upset on that last morning with the Sudai.

And what had Raider said? He'd been upset—though he'd refused to use the word—that it had felt good to have Seth take care of him. It had scared Raider to want that.

For all Raider's flirtation, for all his casual sexuality, he had a hard time with actual intimacy.

Seth wasn't surprised to find himself being the one who always initiated it. He wanted it. He fucking loved it. Yes, of course it scared the shit out of him too. But he was past the point of resisting it. All the logical reasons that he shouldn't let himself get attached to Raider had lost their power over him.

Walking late one afternoon, three days after the sand serpent tunnels, Raider touched Seth's elbow to get his attention. He pointed to a huge-eared desert fox trotting through some scrub.

Raider smiled and said, "Cute, huh?"

Seth stopped dead. Raider walked on for a moment then also stopped, looking back at Seth with a question.

This man.

Whatever darkness lurked in him, whatever horrors gave him such terrible nightmares, he was so damn full of light. More and more over the last few days, as the haunted look had begun to fade from Raider's eyes, he had turned his attention to other things. Better things.

It sickened Seth to think that once he might have scoffed at Raider in a moment such as this. Once, Seth had not understood that Raider's lightness and playfulness was a *choice*. A damned good choice—and not an easy one. Most people just gave in to darkness. They became bitter, often cruel. But not Raider.

Now, Seth was a little wiser. So he closed the distance between them—and kissed the hell out of this beautiful man.

It clearly startled Raider. Seth had been tender with him but not passionate, not for the past three days as Raider recovered.

Seth had taken the stitches out yesterday. Raider's body amazed him, as did the way he'd already been walking so far each day. He'd been guiding them, focused, in command of himself and their path.

But even after removing the stitches, Seth hadn't initiated anything. Neither had Raider.

In Raider, Seth had sensed a hesitation, a worry. Like he'd thought, for some reason, that Seth might reject him, despite his tenderness. Like he didn't understand that that tenderness was Seth's way of saying, *I want you, but we're not fucking when you're hurt.*

Raider's startlement told Seth that he'd read Raider correctly—and that Raider had definitely misread him.

Seth wanted him with a desperation that had him waking up painfully hard every morning, that had him fighting his sexually frustrated mood like it was a goddamn tiger inside him. Maybe Raider had sensed that tension and not understood it.

Seth had held back because he wanted Raider too much. He still didn't trust himself, not with this man. He was afraid of getting too rough. He was afraid of hurting Raider while he was still recovering.

So, unsurprisingly, Raider was startled by Seth suddenly grabbing him and taking his mouth in a hungry, possessive kiss. Raider's saddlebag-turned-pack hit the ground as he moaned into Seth's mouth, answering with a hunger of his own. He grabbed Seth's ass and hauled him in.

Raider's hand slid between their bodies and gripped Seth's cock through his pants. He murmured against Seth's lips, "I need this. I need you," and swept his tongue into Seth's mouth.

Moaning, Seth speared his fingers into Raider's gorgeous, unruly hair, gripping along his scalp, pulling him back so he could see his striking face. Raider's eyelashes fluttered. How had Seth never noticed before how perfectly those thick, dark lashes framed Raider's unusual eyes? Seth nipped at Raider's sensual, expressive lips, loving his breathy sounds.

Seth stopped himself. He made himself think. This wasn't a place to stop for the night. He leaned his forehead against

Raider's, trying to settle. Raider sighed, clearly sensing the shift in Seth's focus, despite the fact that Seth's cock remained hard as hell in Raider's hand.

Raider let go with obvious reluctance. He bent to retrieve his pack then walked on.

It took Seth a moment longer to recover and get moving. When he did, Raider tossed him something.

Seth caught it automatically. He stopped again, staring at the item in his hand.

Raider shot a wicked grin over his shoulder.

Seth scowled at him on principle, but when Raider looked ahead once more, Seth smiled and returned the multi tool to his belt.

✫   ✫   ✫

That night, they made a more comfortable camp than they had enjoyed for several days. The rocky land was studded with brush, which meant water and game and even fuel for a campfire. The easier landscape felt like a blessing—except that it meant they would reach Aqarat tomorrow.

Seth would have thought himself delighted by that prospect. And, certainly, he was looking forward to a bed and the offerings of Aqarat's bazaar, to a bath and a chance to shave.

But.

Aqarat marked the end of his and Raider's arrangement. Seth didn't know what that would mean. He still had his mission and, though that mission felt more distant to him now after all that had happened over the past month, he still had to hunt for Julian.

But …

It wasn't that simple anymore.

Seth glanced at the man sitting beside him at the campfire. Raider's head was tilted back slightly, his eyes taking in the night sky with its scattered stars. The fire painted Raider's throat with golden light, marking out the strong tendons, pooling in its hollow.

Like every part of Raider, his throat was beautiful.

Like every part of Raider, Seth wanted to kiss it, touch it, claim it.

Then there were his broad shoulders and the muscled planes of his chest and abdomen, the light flex of his lats along his side. Raider wasn't built as heavily as Seth. His body was a more perfect balance of strength and speed, the contours of muscle more elegant.

Noticing Seth's attention, Raider turned his head to look at him. The light now painted his face, playing deliciously with its exotic angles, laying bare the desire in his eyes.

Yes, they were going to fuck. Soon.

But first, dinner. Quartered rabbit, freshly caught by Raider, sizzled in the last of the butter they'd gotten from the Sudai. The heavy pan, Seth thought, had been worth carrying.

However.

He asked, "How long have you been lightening my pack?"

Raider slid him a small, cunning smile. "When did you notice?"

"Not until this evening. This pan wasn't in my pack—then it was."

"I thought you gave me one of your looks."

"One of my looks?"

"One of these." Raider narrowed his eyes and set his mouth in an exaggerated frown.

"I do *not* look like that."

"Oh, yes, you do."

Seth scowled. "You didn't answer my question."

Raider gave Seth one *his* looks, a wry, teasing one that Seth had no trouble interpreting as, *You're doing it right now.* Refusing to yield, Seth kept the expression on his face until Raider gave in and shrugged.

"Since I started feeling better."

Seth narrowed his eyes. That still wasn't an answer.

Raider pointed to the fire. "Who's in charge of this rabbit?"

"Shit." Seth used a stick to turn the meat, revealing some unintended blackening.

Raider shook his head. "After all the trouble I went to skinning those."

"Yeah, yeah. *Damn* it. I hate when I burn the food."

Raider chuckled. "You're such a perfectionist."

"It's very upsetting to me!"

Raider nodded slowly. "I am aware of that. Just like it's upsetting to you if the tent is crooked. Or the firewood isn't arranged with enough structural integrity to withstand gale-force winds."

"That's unfair. The tent, at least—"

"Yes, I know you have your reasons. You explained them to me already."

Raider's tone and warm smile said he was teasing affectionately, and, *fuck*, that did something to Seth. So he sighed, pretending to be annoyed, and focused on his cooking.

He'd had a plan for this meal, and now he'd ruined it. Determined to salvage it as much as possible, he dug into his pack for a handful of the remaining almonds and the last of the dried sage.

Raider, meanwhile, had taken up the stick and was checking the rabbit. "It's fine, Seth."

"It's not how I imagined it," Seth grumbled and sprinkled the sage and almonds into the pan.

"Sometimes things aren't like you imagined them, but that doesn't mean they aren't still good."

It took Seth aback. Such an offhand comment, but it was true, and it spoke so deeply of the man who had uttered it.

All those nightmares. All that darkness. But Raider didn't let it consume him.

"You're doing it again," Raider said.

"Doing what?"

"Giving me one of your looks."

"Yeah, I guess I am. Give me that stick."

When the rabbit was done (more on some sides than others), they ate from the pan. And it was still pretty damn good. Even if it hadn't been, Seth would still have enjoyed it, eating like this. With Raider.

"You know," Raider observed as he polished off the last piece, "for a man who dresses in such bleak color—or lack thereof?—you have a flair for cooking."

"Why thank you, what a lovely backhanded compliment."

Raider flashed him a grin. A real grin. Gods, it was good to see that coming back.

Seth found himself smiling a little as he fished an almond out of the pan. "I do like to cook. Mostly because I like good food."

"Really? You give so little sign of enjoyment."

"I'm enjoying it on the inside." Seth popped the almond into his mouth and looked for more, but the pan was empty. "I don't feel the need to express it."

Raider pushed to his feet and took the pan to the edge of the campsite for cleaning. "Expressiveness annoys you. I know."

Now, that was *not* a teasing tone. That was a sardonic tone, and it said that Raider meant that *his* expressiveness annoyed Seth.

"No," Seth said. "It doesn't."

Raider shot him a disbelieving look as he used a splash of water and the cooking stick to clean the pan.

Seth sighed, knowing he had to explain or else Raider wouldn't believe him. "I just don't always know how to respond to it. And I don't always know how to express my own …"

"Emotions?" Raider supplied when Seth couldn't seem to say it.

"Yes. But sometimes they sneak out. The wrong ones."

"Hm."

"What?" Seth asked, uncomfortable now with what he'd said.

Raider finished his work and turned the pan upside down to dry. He stayed crouched where he was at the edge of the campsite.

"I'm just thinking about what you said. You're hard to read sometimes."

Raider was one to talk. But … that didn't mean he was wrong. Seth knew he expressed anger, and he knew he expressed tenderness (in certain circumstances), but he struggled with everything in between. He actually found it easier to deal Raider's emotions, however volatile, than his own.

Even so, Seth felt the need to point out, "I'm not always hard to read."

"No," Raider acknowledged. "Not always. But since you often are, will you answer a question?"

"It depends on the question."

Raider threw back his head and stared up at the sky in exasperation.

It amused Seth. "Are you asking the gods for patience?"

Raider's head snapped down. "I never ask them for anything. But I will ask you."

"Then I'll answer," Seth promised.

Raider looked at Seth steadily. "When did you first want me?"

"Before you ever wanted me." Seth was surprised by how easy that now was to admit.

"Bullshit. And you can't even know that."

"I most certainly can. You walked into Yusef's shop to sell him silk and that ridiculous dagger, and I saw you from the back room. Before you ever saw me."

Raider stilled. "And you wanted me? Even then?"

"And every moment since."

Raider closed his eyes as his body rocked slightly. But he asked, as though there could be any question, "Even now?"

"Especially now. So get the hell over here. Because my cock's been hard for days, and I fucking need you."

Chapter 29

AROUSAL SURGED so hot and hard through Raider that he had to catch himself with an outstretched hand. Unlike Seth, Raider didn't make a practice of self-denial, so he felt he should be immune to this kind of desperate, starving need. But with Seth …

He *was* desperate.

He *was* starving.

And he'd been afraid—afraid that his nightmares and dark mood might have killed Seth's attraction to him. It had taken Raider a while to work his way out of that darkness, to put aside the feelings he didn't want, to choose better ones. Then, once he had, he'd found himself uncharacteristically hesitant, afraid of Seth's rejection.

For days, he'd been dying for Seth to touch him, kiss him, fuck him. Seth had touched him some, it had been tenderness only. And while Raider couldn't help but crave that tenderness, he needed it balanced with raw, rough desire.

Earlier today when Seth had kissed him, Raider had felt himself come back to life. It had been as though the world had been muted for days and had suddenly burst into vibrant color and sound. But he needed more than that kiss. He needed Seth's hands mastering him. He needed Seth's voice commanding him. He needed Seth's cock driving into him so hard that there was no room in him for anything else.

Distracted by the heat pulsing into his groin, the lighting up of his entire body, Raider hadn't realized he'd closed his eyes, hadn't heard Seth approach.

He gasped as Seth's hands closed on his arms and hauled him up. He moaned as Seth growled, "Come here."

When Seth leaned in to kiss him, Raider responded by sweeping his tongue into Seth's mouth, tasting him, claiming him, demanding everything from him. Moaning, Seth clutched at him, fingers gripping Raider's hips.

Raider reached between their bodies to find the waistband of Seth's pants and worked his fingers inside. He didn't know how Seth could stand such confining clothing, but there was something undeniably erotic about brushing the leaking tip of his cock where it was trapped against his belly.

Seth gasped as Raider's hand forced its way into the tight space, closing around his thick, hard length, which pulsed deliciously in his grip. Raider's mouth watered at the thought of that massive cock tunneling into him. It was hard to believe it could even fit inside his body, but he wanted it. Every thick inch.

When Raider's fingers shoved deeper to curl under Seth's balls and drag upward, Seth barked out a curse, breaking the kiss. He fumbled with Raider's sash but couldn't find the end of it. Raider chuckled and stepped back, drawing his hand free of Seth's cock.

Raider wanted to undress Seth, but he also wanted to tease him. He opted for the latter, which he felt Seth would find more frustrating—and he definitely wanted Seth frustrated. He wanted Seth at the edge of his control. He wanted him rough and raw and harsh.

So Raider quickly tugged his sash free, untied his drawstring, and slipped out of his clothes. Seth's eyes dropped to the rigid length of cock jutting from Raider's body. When his cock twitched at the attention, Seth groaned and reached for him. But Raider slipped away and sauntered to the tent, snagging the oil from his pack as he went.

"You think that's funny?" Seth growled.

Raider grinned over his shoulder as he ducked under the canopy that Seth had made of the tent. "Yes."

Seth had been setting up the tent this way for a while now, leaving the sides up. They hadn't talked about Raider's claustrophobia, but Seth had clearly figured it out. And he had accommodated it without complaint. Raider had never appreciated that more than he did now as he knelt on the blankets facing Seth, the view unobstructed.

Setting the oil aside, Raider wrapped his hand around his cock and started to stroke, pleased when the sight made Seth growl and scrabble at the buckles of his vest. He shucked it off and flung it down.

Raider chuckled, enjoying Seth's little fit of temper—and the sight of his bare torso, thick with muscle.

Glaring, Seth bent to remove his boots, his arms and shoulders flexing deliciously as he worked. His right shoulder was still bruised but didn't seem to be bothering him too much. When he had his boots and socks off, he straightened, tugged at the lacing of his pants, and shoved them roughly off his hips, suddenly baring the huge, brutal length of his cock.

"Fuck, Seth," Raider breathed at the sight.

He needed that body. He needed that cock. He needed that man.

Seth didn't touch himself, didn't tease. He came striding toward the tent, that heavy cock bobbing at his hips. His whole body was power, and Raider shivered in anticipation as all that power headed his way with the clear intention of fucking him.

But Seth, damn him, halted at the edge of the tent. His hands fisted at his sides. Raider narrowed his eyes as Seth took a huge breath, like he was calming himself, slowing himself down. Then Seth ducked under the canopy.

Raider snarled, "If you think this is going to be a sweet and tender—"

Dropping to his knees, Seth knocked Raider's hand away from his cock, replacing Raider's grip with his own. Raider sucked in a breath at the sudden contact, then he closed his eyes as Seth's other hand gripped his hair at the scalp. Fuck, he loved when Seth did that.

Seth pulled Raider's head back and closed his teeth gently on Raider's bared throat. Raider squeezed his eyes shut as his cock throbbed in Seth's firm grip.

This. *This* was what he needed.

Releasing Raider's throat, Seth nuzzled at it and said in a low, gravelly voice, "I know what you're trying to do."

"Get you to fuck me?"

"Oh, I'm going to fuck you. But how I want, when I want."

With that, Seth forced Raider back, lowering him to the blankets. He muscled his way between Raider's legs—and took Raider's cock in his mouth.

Raider shouted at the sudden, hot sheathing. His hips jacked upward, driving his cock to the back of Seth's throat. Seth slid his hands under Raider and gripped his ass, pulling him in harder, taking him deeper. He worked up and down Raider's shaft, moving one hand to Raider's balls to cup and tug in a way that had Raider's eyes rolling back in his head.

"Seth—*fuck*."

Seth drew his mouth up to Raider's tip, gently dragging his teeth over the flared ridge and lapping precum from his slit. He pulled free, sitting back on his heels between Raider's legs.

Rubbing a soothing hand up Raider's thigh, Seth reached for the oil.

But Raider didn't want to be soothed. He wanted to be fucked. Violently.

So as Seth uncapped the bottle and poured some oil into his palm, Raider lunged up. He took Seth's cock in his hand, aching at the thought of that brutal length inside his body. Seth grunted at the contact—then shouted as Raider bit his chest. Seth growled a warning, but Raider only tweaked his nipple while Seth was busy getting the bottle recorked.

As Seth forced Raider's hand away from his cock so he could slick it with the oil, Raider closed his teeth on the crook of Seth's neck, eliciting a ragged shout. When Seth muscled into him, wrestling him down, Raider's heart leaped with anticipation.

"Fuck me," he panted, as Seth forced him roughly onto his side and hooked an arm around him. "Hurt me, Seth."

"You don't seem to understand who's in charge here." Seth's knee shoved Raider's legs apart, and his oil-slick fingers massaged Raider's tight rim. "You're not making those decisions tonight."

"Seth—"

"Let me explain what's going to happen," Seth said gruffly as he pushed a finger into Raider, making Raider suck in a sharp breath. "You're going to relax and let me stretch this fine ass of yours." Raider moaned as Seth stroked inside him. "You're going to breathe and let this feel good."

"*Seth*—"

"You're going to let me do this like I want, and what I want—" Seth added another finger and grazed Raider's sweet spot, making him shout and buck. "—what I *want* is to listen to you moan as I fuck you nice and deep. So you're going to stop fighting me."

Raider moaned at the words, at the anticipation, at Seth's control of his body. When Seth was satisfied with Raider's compliance, he withdrew his fingers and set his broad cockhead against Raider's hole. His arms and legs pinned Raider, holding him in place as he breached slowly.

Pinned, Raider couldn't shove back to force the brutal entry he'd wanted, yet there was something even more erotic about being forced to take Seth slowly, to have no choice but to allow the incremental glide of that huge, hard cock into his body, to feel every inch of penetration. He panted and moaned as Seth pushed into him, filling him so completely that he lost awareness of anything beyond Seth's body possessing his.

"That's it," Seth murmured as he drew back slowly, his cock dragging through Raider's channel, "that's better."

Raider moaned as Seth pushed into him again. Seth's arms and legs held him in place. Raider trembled at the gentle but firm dominance as Seth slow-fucked him into a gasping, shuddering mess. Seth had left Raider's right arm free so he could stroke himself, but Raider only fisted the blankets. He didn't want control of his cock—and he didn't need it. With every thrust, Raider's cock leaked and throbbed.

Seth knew just when to pick up the pace, thrusting a little harder, making Raider's cock brush torturously against the blankets. When Seth took him in an even firmer grip to brace him, Raider shuddered in anticipation then cried out at the deep thrust into his body.

Seth rasped, "That's right, just take it like that."

"I need—*fuck*!"

"I know you need to come. Let it happen. Let me in deep."

Raider turned his face into the blankets, moaning and overwhelmed. He'd never been fucked like this, dominantly—but so goddamn lovingly. He would never have thought something like that would make him come so fucking hard, but his sudden orgasm had him screaming into the blankets, then moaning desperately as Seth tunneled into him again and again.

When Seth's hips snapped forward and his cock kicked hard against Raider's prostate, when he shouted and spilled hotly inside Raider, it made him orgasm a second time, screaming until he was hoarse and shaking and, for some fucking reason, sobbing into the blankets.

Then Seth was shushing him and holding him so goddam tight. Raider lost all sense of time and place as he shuddered through the strange, unexpected release of emotion, but Seth gave him a safe space for it and held on through it all.

The last thing Raider remembered before he passed out in his Seth's arms was Seth kissing the back of his neck and whispering, "It's okay, baby. I've got you."

✧   ✧   ✧

Raider sat cross legged at the edge of the blankets in the predawn dimness. He was rolling his left shoulder to loosen it and staring north across the desert, where the rocky landscape was emerging in ghostly mounds as the night faded. He didn't look east, where the sky was paling. Where they were headed.

They would reach Aqarat this afternoon. What the hell was that going to mean?

What the hell did this thing between him and Seth mean? What *was* this thing between them?

The blankets shifted behind him as Seth stirred. Raider listened to the small, intimate sounds of Seth waking up: the deeper inhalations, the light groan as he stretched, the grunt as he levered himself into a sitting position.

When Seth scooted across the blankets toward him, Raider stiffened. He didn't mean to, but he couldn't help it. Seth sat behind him, extending his legs on either side of him and laying light fingers on Raider's left shoulder. When Raider pulled his shoulder away, Seth's fingers gently stroked the back of Raider's neck.

"Let me help," Seth said, his voice rough with sleep.

Raider drew up his knees and hooked his elbows around them, annoyed that Seth wouldn't just let him deal with it on his own but also …

Embarrassed.

Raider was *never* embarrassed, and he didn't like the feeling. But he didn't understand what had happened last night, and it had left him feeling exposed in a way he wasn't used to, worse even than when Seth had witnessed his nightmares. Something about the way Seth had fucked him—no, made love to him—had stirred up a mess of weird, confusing feelings.

"Why won't you let me help?" Seth asked.

"I don't know. I don't know what's wrong with me. I don't know why I reacted like that. Last night. After."

Seth took a deep breath. He was silent for a while. His hand had drifted down Raider's back. That hand moved up and stroked the back of Raider's neck again as he said, "Because you've had some hard days, that's why."

Raider's throat tightened. "Maybe."

"Let me do this. Please."

When Seth's fingers slid from Raider's nape to his shoulder, Raider sighed and gave in. He let his knees fall open as Seth massaged his shoulder. Seth hunted down knotted muscles, kneading them until they released. Then he started stretching Raider's shoulder, manipulating it in ways Raider wasn't used to.

He grunted as Seth hooked their elbows together and pulled his arm back while exerting pressure on his shoulder blade.

"Fuck, Seth."

"Just breathe."

Raider made himself take a few deep breaths. When Seth finally relented and eased Raider's arm, Raider rolled it experimentally.

"Huh," he huffed, surprised.

"Did that help?"

"Yeah. It did. A lot."

"Good."

Seth's fingers moved to Raider's other shoulder then his neck. None of that hurt as much and the touch had Raider grunting and moaning and leaning back into Seth, where he felt the ridge of Seth's erection.

"Sorry," Seth muttered. "I can't help it."

Raider took Seth's right hand and pulled it around his waist, guiding it to his own hard cock.

"Mmm," Seth murmured as his hand curled around Raider's shaft, stroking leisurely.

Raider let his legs fall open further as Seth explored lower, massaging Raider's swollen balls. His other arm hooked possessively around Raider's torso. Raider let his head fall back on Seth's shoulder. He loved this. He fucking loved this.

Seth's fingers dragged upward along the underside of Raider's cock. "You want to come?"

"You better make me come."

"You're not in too much pain?"

"*Seth.*"

Seth's hand left Raider's cock to settle on his hip. "Answer my question."

Raider's head lifted and he tried to turn in Seth's arms, but Seth tightened his hold.

"You're so goddamn dominant," Raider complained.

"That's right. Now answer my question: are you feeling well enough?"

"Yes! Or my cock wouldn't be so fucking hard! Are you going to do something about it or not?"

Seth nibbled the side of Raider's neck. "Have some goddamn patience."

"Patience!"

"I know that's difficult for you. Now stay there."

Clearly not trusting Raider to comply, Seth hooked his legs around him as he leaned away, hunting for something amid the blankets. Raider smoothed his hands along the muscular legs locking him in place, keeping his ass pressed against Seth's hard cock. Why the hell was that so erotic? Why was *everything* with Seth so erotic?

Seth fumbled with what Raider assumed was the oil. Then Seth sat up a little and unlocked his legs only to hook an arm around Raider. Raider found himself hauled back until he was lying against Seth at a forty-five degree angle. Seth's abs flexed against Raider's back as he held their combined weight. Seth's cock was a thick ridge along the cleft of Raider's ass.

Nudging Raider's leg up, Seth slipped an oiled hand between their bodies and teased Raider's rim, pushing in as much as the angle would allow. Raider lifted to free Seth's cock from under him. It forced Seth's hand away from his ass but allowed him to reposition Seth's cock so it lay hard against Raider's taint and balls as he settled against Seth again.

Raider reached down to curl his hand around Seth's erection.

"Fuck, that feels good," Seth murmured, adding his own hand, the oil from it slicking them both.

Raider enjoyed it for a moment, the heady eroticism of both their hands roaming and stroking. But Raider knew what he wanted—and he wanted it right now. Grabbing Seth's cock, Raider lifted himself over it.

Seth clutched at his hip. "Raider, no, that's going to hurt you—fuck!"

Raider sank down on Seth's oiled cock, shouting at the brutal sheathing. It burned. It hurt. It felt so fucking good.

He collapsed, trembling, against Seth, who still held them both up with one hand stretched behind him.

"Goddamn it," Seth grunted, also trembling. "Fuck. I can't think. *Fuck.* Are you okay?"

Raider let his head fall back on Seth's shoulder as the pain throbbed just like he wanted, pushing out his awareness of everything else.

"You have a huge cock, Seth."

Seth's free hand smoothed its way up Raider's abdomen to his chest, brushing teasingly over his nipples. "That's why I don't do it like that."

"I needed it. Fuck, I love it."

The pain was already morphing into pleasure as Seth's hand roamed down to Raider's cock, which lay hard and leaking against his belly. Stroking Raider from balls to tip, he said gruffly, "Then ride me."

Raider sat up a little, groaning as the movement shifted Seth's cock inside him. When he started to lift and plunge, pleasuring himself on Seth's cock, Seth moaned and fell back. As Raider pounded harder, Seth's hips jacked up, deepening the thrusts, shifting the angle so that every stroke had that massive cock hitting just where Raider needed it. He took himself in a harsh grip, working his throbbing, aching dick with hard, rough strokes as Seth groaned and thrust under him.

Raider let himself race brutally toward his orgasm and came hard, shouting, his whole body clenching, his ass seizing on Seth's cock. Seth shouted and jacked upward, his body stringing tight as his cock unloaded inside Raider.

Raider bowed forward, panting and shuddering. He could feel Seth shuddering through his own aftershocks below, could feel Seth's cock still partially hard inside him. As Seth shoved himself up, it shifted the angle, milking another drop from Raider.

Seth held them up. His arm hooked around Raider's torso once more, locking them together, keeping their bodies joined for a blissful moment before he pulled free. They both cried out at the stimulation and the hot spill of Seth's cum as they sat up.

Locking both his arms around Raider, Seth leaned into him as the shudders passed for them both. They sat there for a long while, both of them a mess, both of them content with that for the moment.

Eventually, Seth spoke quietly against the back of Raider's neck. "I worry sometimes," he said, his hand starting to rub Raider's chest, "when you want it to hurt."

Raider sighed. He'd known this would come up.

"I need you to talk to me about it," Seth said gently.

"I know."

Seth didn't rush him. He waited patiently, hands gently stroking as Raider worked through what he needed to say.

Raider stared out into the morning light, glad he didn't have to look at Seth as he said, "It makes everything else go away for a moment. I try to focus on good things, but other stuff … it's still there. Even when I pretend it's not. It's like … it's right here."

Raider pressed his fingertips below his sternum. Seth's fingers met his there.

"Sometimes," Raider explained as he let his hand drop from the spot, leaving Seth's there, "I want all of that to be forced away."

Raider felt Seth's chest expand against his back as he took a deep, thoughtful breath. Seth's hand smoothed its way across Raider's pectorals again.

"And you need pain for that?"

"Intensity. And the pain … it's good pain. It's pleasure-pain, and I know it will end with release."

Seth thought about that for a while then asked, "So it's something you've done before?"

"A little. Not much. It's different with you."

Seth tensed, clearly not liking that. "Why?"

"Because I trust you, Seth. I feel safe with you. I feel safe doing that with you."

"Oh, fuck," Seth murmured and let his forehead fall to Raider's shoulder.

That was plainly not the answer he'd expected, but it was the absolute truth, and it was the reason Raider couldn't look at him right now, why he hadn't looked at him once since he'd woken.

Because they would reach Aqarat this afternoon, and Raider didn't know what that would mean.

Because he was fucking terrified that when Seth's attention shifted to his hunt, whatever this was between them would become like a mirage, some distant thing in the desert, no longer real.

Chapter 30

Like oases, desert cities always looked a bit surreal upon approach. All that green, such a concentration of life and activity in place of the bleak but beautiful quietude.

Seth suspected that an underground spring had fed the city in its earliest days—because why the hell else would it be here?—but its current agriculture was achieved by means of an aqueduct that carried water from a river somewhere to the north.

The greenery of date palms and fields, likely barley and sesame, dazzled in the distance, sprawling north of the city. Approaching from the arid west, Seth and Raider walked past none of that green, instead following a dusty track made by goats and camels that went out daily to forage amid the desert scrub.

They had passed many such animals and their keepers over the final hours as they approached Aqarat's mudbrick wall. High above, wind towers jutted from rooftops, their clever design drawing fresh air in one side, sending it down to cool interiors that would otherwise grow stifling hot in such close quarters, then venting heat out the other side. In the distance, the bulbous turquoise roofs of the palace rose above the rest.

Aqarat, ruled by Prince Rahim, marked the western edge of the Golden Empire, sometimes called simply the Gold, a vast territory controlled by Empress Zarina. She had ruled since her father's assassination at the hands of his brother ten years ago. Ensconced in the famously magnificent sea-city of Kastari, the empress could have little interest in this remote outpost, but coming from the barren, lonely Kesh, Aqarat looked like an absolute metropolis. And that was even with Seth and Raider entering through the livestock gate instead of the trade gate to the east, where a major road conducted merchant traffic.

"The bazaar is on the other side of the city," Raider informed Seth. "Food?"

"Gods, yes."

Raider smiled slightly. "I thought you seemed hungry."

"It's late afternoon, and we haven't eaten since this morning. Yes, I'm fucking hungry. But what do you mean I *seemed hungry*?"

"You were getting one of your looks."

"Hm."

Seth was surprised that Raider had noticed his expression—because it seemed like Raider had been avoiding looking at him all day. It had started naturally enough when Seth had sat behind him this morning, and he hadn't thought anything of it when they'd fucked. The position hadn't allowed for eye contact.

Heat pulsed into Seth's groin at the memory of Raider sheathing him so abruptly. *I needed it,* Raider had gasped, leaning back against him with Seth's cock hot and throbbing inside him. *Fuck, I love it.*

Seth had never been so passive during sex, and it had been a surprisingly erotic experience to lie back and be ridden like that, to be inside Raider but to not be in control. To know that Raider wanted him like that, that he'd brought himself to orgasm on Seth's cock. And feeling Raider's body seize on him …

Gods, Seth had come so hard.

He made himself take a slow, easy breath. Even though his aroused state was hidden by the heavy material of his pants—not to mention his (now dingy) white kaftan—it wasn't much fun navigating the busy streets with a stiff dick.

His discomfort aside, Seth was relieved to have the distraction of dodging men and women leading animals or pushing handcarts while Raider guided him through the maze of square, mudbrick buildings. If they talked, Raider would realize how anxious Seth was.

Why had Raider barely looked at him today?

Was he distancing himself? To … *leave*?

He'd better fucking not be.

Yet, arriving in Aqarat, Seth couldn't help but remember that he'd hired Raider to get him here, that Raider was owed payment for that.

Why the hell hadn't they talked about what would happen when they got here?

Why the hell hadn't Seth just said, *I love you, stay with me, we need to figure this out*?

But he hadn't said that—and now the moment was gone.

Aqarat's merchant quarter was nothing like the quiet bazaar in Shalaa. Vendors in colorful robes thronged the streets, hawking their wares—everything from rugs and lamps to plucked chickens and meat pies, beads and baubles and promises of magic amulets. Red-lipped prostitutes in gauzy kaftans strolled the streets, bangles clacking at their wrists and ankles. Scruffy children darted through the crowd, and Seth hoisted his packs a little higher and fixed a glare on his face to discourage pickpockets.

Raider, noticing this, grinned.

Fuck, Seth loved that grin. How had he ever scorned it? Why was he such an idiot?

Raider flipped a coin to a fruit vendor and plucked two oranges from the man's cart. He peeled one and handed it to Seth.

"Did you lift that coin from me?" Seth was quite sure that Raider had no money. He'd spent it all in Shalaa before they'd left. On supplies. On his horse. On raaki.

Raider grinned again. "And you were worried about all the little brats running around."

"Brats? Do you not like children?"

"Oh, I love them. But they are brats. I mean, come on, you can't really love a thing if you don't see it for what it is, can you?"

Seth's breath caught. This was the kind of shit Raider liked to throw out as casually as he'd thrown out that coin. Something so deep and real that Seth needed time to process it. He didn't have that time right now, not in this crush of people, so instead he ate the orange that Raider had peeled for him, suppressing a moan of delight. Raider, eating the other orange, threw back his head and groaned freely.

Licking his fingers, Raider asked, "Do you want to check for arcane oddities or anything like that?"

Seth's heart sank a little at the reminder of why they were here. "I guess. But, Raider, we need to—"

"Don't." Raider's eyes squeezed shut. "Please don't."

Fuck.

Fuck.

Any courage Seth had mustered to broach this subject—*the* subject—vanished.

Busying his mind, Seth started scanning the stalls for any sign of valuable arcane goods. He spotted arcane lamps and counting machines, food cooling boxes and other home devices, but nothing that a traveler would have sold.

The merchants and shoppers regarded Seth with curious (and sometimes wary) dark eyes. He stood out here, even with the kaftan draping his arcane clothing. Some of them, noting the sword pommel jutting above his right shoulder, probably knew what he was. Others, taking in his light brown hair and green eyes, only knew that he was foreign. And big.

As Seth was perusing the offerings of a bookseller, he felt the slight, telltale pressure of a pickpocket. He spun, but Raider had already grabbed the culprit by his collar and snatched Seth's multi tool from the boy's hand.

"See?" he said. "Brats."

"Mm-hm."

"Please don't hurt me," the boy begged with obviously practiced drama.

"Oh, go on," Raider muttered, releasing him.

Grinning, the boy vanished into the crowd to steal from someone else.

"You know," Raider said as he reached inside Seth's kaftan to slide the multi tool back into its place in Seth's belt, "you need to keep better track of that thing."

"Apparently. There are a lot of light fingers around here."

Raider's light fingers lingered at Seth's belt and, for the first time all day, he met Seth's gaze. What Seth saw in Raider's eyes terrified him—because he saw confusion and grief. Or fear? Seth's throat constricted.

Don't leave me, Seth begged silently. *Don't fucking leave me.*

Raider's fingers tightened on Seth's belt. His lips parted, but words seemed to catch in his throat. After a moment, he said, "I'm still hungry. The lamb smelled good."

Seth felt a strange mixture of disappointment and relief. It was, if nothing else, a stay of execution, so he said, "I'm hungry, too."

The corner of Raider's mouth tugged. "I'm out of money."

Seth owed Raider money, quite a lot of money, but he couldn't bring himself to say that, even teasingly, so he only said, "I'll buy this time."

"That would save me some trouble."

"Oh, please. You love stealing from me. You love knowing that you can do it. You love having *me* know that you can do it."

"You have me all figured out, huh?"

Seth was spared having to reply to that by the unexpected sound of a cat meowing from around their feet. They both looked down to the sight of a large, handsome tabby staring up at them with brilliant citrine eyes. The cat wound its way between Raider's legs, arching its back to rub against him.

"You should find somewhere else to be," Raider advised the cat and nudged it away with a dusty, sandaled foot.

The cat came straight back, threading now through Seth's legs.

"Go away," Raider said.

"How can you not like cats?" Seth chided, bending to scoop up the tabby. Sensing receptivity, Seth turned the animal onto its back to cradle it in his arms. He hadn't felt a purr in months.

"I do like cats," Raider said, eyeing the rumbling feline in Seth's arms. "But *that* is not a cat."

"What are you talking about?"

Seth scratched the tabby's chin. The cat tilted its head back and closed its eyes in pleasure.

"I don't know what that is, Seth, but that is *not* a cat." As though it had understood, the tabby opened its citrine eye and turned its head to look at Raider. "I think that's an ifrit."

"What?" Seth gripped the cat gently around its ribcage and lifted it. It stared at him with bright, unblinking eyes.

"Put it down."

Seth sighed, unconvinced, but he lowered the cat to the ground. It darted off into the crowd, winding expertly through the chaos of robes and kaftans and sandaled brown feet.

Seth reflexively checked his belt in case a pickpocket had taken advantage of his distraction. "What made you think it was an ifrit?"

"You know they're shapeshifters, right?"

"That doesn't mean every cat is an ifrit. Ifrits are a kind of lesser djinn, right?"

Seth had never encountered one, but the Sudai's Wind Keeper had made them out to be troublesome fire spirits that liked to play tricks and bargain cheatingly.

"In a manner of speaking, though I wouldn't advise you to call one that to its face. They're pretty powerful."

"I still don't understand what made you think it was an ifrit."

Raider shrugged. "Maybe I'm wrong, but it wasn't worth fucking with."

"All right, well, let's get some food."

They backtracked to a vendor selling kabobs loaded with lamb, peppers, and squash, all of it seasoned with salt, garlic, and cumin. They bought four and worked their way through the crowd to a reasonably quiet stretch of buildings, where they found a set of steps to sit on.

Seth pulled a bite of lamb from his kabob, relishing the seasoning. They'd run out of salt two days ago, and though the sage had seemed like a real treat last night, this was a different level of culinary delight.

"So you like cats?" Raider asked. He dragged a piece of red pepper off the kabob with his teeth.

"A few sleep in my room at the College when I'm there."

"Really?"

"Why are you surprised?"

Raider shrugged. "You're so tidy."

"So are cats."

"I guess that's true. Males or females?"

"My favorite is a female. Baast. Yes, yes, I know," Seth said, sensing a revival of their mare-gelding debate. "But cats are different from horses. Baast followed me on a mission once. I was so damn worried about her. I was distracted the whole time."

"Huh."

"What?"

Raider caught a piece of squash that dropped from his skewer before it could hit his lap. He popped it into his mouth then licked his palm.

"I'm just surprised, I guess, to think that something might distract you from Arcanum business. I know how important your missions are to you."

Something about the way Raider said that—and the fact that he looked away after—didn't sit well with Seth. He couldn't pinpoint the problem, though, so he wasn't sure how to address it.

He worked on his kabob for a while, overwhelmed by all the things they hadn't talked about. It wasn't like Seth to leave things unresolved. He liked clarity. But he was having a hell of a hard time achieving any right now.

The last few weeks had marked a deviation from Seth's norm. His hunt had been in abeyance, his progress a matter merely of footsteps. His focus had shifted. Now, being in Aqarat, he felt the returning pressure of his mission, but shit had gotten complicated.

I know how important your missions are to you.

They were. And Seth wanted to complete that mission. His duty to the Arcanum demanded it. But Seth also wanted Raider. His heart demanded that. What the hell would Seth do if he had to choose between them? Would Raider make him choose?

Those agonizing questions assumed Raider even *wanted* to stay with Seth and figure out what the hell was going on between them. Those questions assumed that Raider felt what Seth did.

But ... did he?

Seth commanded himself to stop being such a fucking coward. Unfortunately, that command made his voice come out a lot harsher than intended when he said, "We need to figure some shit out."

"Not right now." Raider was still looking down the street, away from Seth.

"Yes, right now. Raider, we can't keep avoiding—"

"Someone's coming."

Seth followed Raider's gaze to see that, indeed, someone was headed their way. The man's rich purple robes and green turban marked him as a noble.

The man inclined his chin slightly, acknowledging that he'd been seen, making a point of not hiding his intention to approach. What kind of noble not only ventured into a crowded street unguarded but also approached two travel-stained and armed men?

In Seth's experience, only one kind.

This man was powerful, and he was known. Indeed, the bustling crowd parted for him, some bowing, others skittering away.

When the man reached them, he gave a slight bow. White teeth flashed in a refined face bearing a sleek, thin goatee. Pearls studded the man's turban and dangled from his pierced ears. He wore golden slippers with pointed, upward-curling toes.

"Please allow me to introduce myself. I am Lord Malik, a humble servant of our glorious Prince Rahim."

He spoke in the trade tongue, his pronunciation so precise that Seth immediately pegged him for a scholar.

Seth stood, awkwardly still holding his remaining kabob. Raider, notably, did not get up.

Seth could pretty well understand and read Kastalan, the official language of the Gold, but he didn't trust his pronunciation without a few weeks of practice. So when he returned the slight bow, he asked in the trade tongue, "What can we do for you, Lord Malik?"

"I apologize for interrupting your meal, but I promise that I can offer better on behalf of our most esteemed Prince Rahim, who invites you to be his guests while you visit our humble city."

Raider rose to his feet, eyes narrowing on Lord Malik. "And why would Prince Rahim invite two ragged travelers to the palace?"

Lord Malik's eyes flicked to Raider then returned to Seth. "An agent of the Arcanum is always welcome, along with his handsome, if ragged, companion. I trust that a bath would improve you both substantially."

Malik's eyes danced at he threw out his barbed compliments.

It was as Seth had thought. Even with the dingy kaftan covering his arcane clothing, he'd been recognized. At the gate? By a lookout in the bazaar? It didn't really matter. Seth knew why he was being invited to the palace. It wasn't the first time something like this had happened.

Royals and nobles were notorious collectors of arcane artifacts. In fact, they were his main competitors. Prince Rahim likely wanted to know what he was after.

Curators sometimes worked for the wealthy on the side. Seth didn't approve of such practices, but the prince didn't know that and hoped, perhaps, to bribe him.

The truth of Seth's mission would no doubt disappoint Prince Rahim, but Seth might learn something in the palace before that disappointment got him turned out. The fact that Rahim's agent, Lord Malik, was approaching Seth less than an hour after his arrival in the city said that the prince kept close watch of his territory. He might know something about

Julian. The arcanist, after all, would have stood out almost as much as Seth.

Seth felt the familiar thrill of the hunt. It had been muted for weeks, but the possibility of progress, of a fresh avenue, sharpened his focus—and what a fucking relief it was. Seth hated feeling unfocused, unsure, lost.

Even if his heart remained heavy with unanswered questions, his mind seized on the chance to put those questions aside for a moment and focus on a less personal problem.

Seth's relief barely lasted two seconds. Because if he accepted the invitation and Raider refused it …

Fuck. Seth *couldn't* refuse the invitation. Even if not for his mission, refusing an invitation from a prince was always unwise. But at the same time, he *wouldn't* lose Raider.

That realization made things pretty damn simple. He would have them both. Raider was coming with him. Period.

Seth inclined his head to Lord Malik.

"Please call me Seth. My companion"—he used the word that Malik had employed, but it didn't feel quite right—"and I would be delighted to accept the prince's generous invitation."

Lord Malik nodded in acknowledgement but looked to Raider, clearly sensing a question of compliance. "And this is agreeable to …?"

"Raider," came the curt answer. "I guess. Fine."

Seth had hoped for a bit more enthusiasm, but he'd take whatever he could get. He'd take anything that kept Raider with him.

Lord Malik, however, seemed to find Raider's answer entirely satisfactory because his teeth flashed in the sunlight as he said, "Excellent."

Chapter 31

It came as no surprise to Raider when the overdressed Lord Malik snapped his fingers and a quadrant of burly, bare-chested men wearing dhotis and sandals came trotting around the corner bearing a platform-style litter. An expensive rug and assortment of cushions softened the top so the occupants could be borne through the city as though on a flying carpet.

The bearers lowered the litter.

What was Seth thinking accepting such an out-of-place invitation? Generosity had nothing to do with it. Whatever Prince Rahim (or his fancy lord here) might say, he wanted something from Seth.

And while there was no fucking way Raider would have let Seth go alone, it did annoy him mightily that Seth had spoken for them both without consulting him. And there Seth went, climbing aboard the litter as though he hadn't a care in the world, as though all of this was very convenient for him and he expected Raider to blithely follow along.

Wait, no. Seth *was* aware that Raider wasn't pleased—because he looked back at him with those green eyes practically burning, his expression clearly saying, *Get your ass up here. Now.*

And, damn it all, but it soothed something in Raider to see that command.

He stepped onto the carpeted litter, dropped his gear, and angled his scimitar so he could sit down. As the litter was hoisted, Raider went back to work on his lamb kabob. Seth's food had vanished because, surprise, Seth was too well mannered to bring street food onto an expensive litter, but Raider was hungry.

Besides, Seth had bought this for him.

They traveled a major avenue to the palace, so it was a short trip, but there was still plenty of time for silky fine Lord Malik to pepper Seth with questions. Was that a chakram? Would Seth do him the honor of allowing him to inspect it? Oh, a hundred blessings upon him!

Raider narrowed his eyes, not liking Malik's interest in Seth.

"And your gauntlet summons its return?" Lord Malik marveled, turning the razor-sharp weapon with delicate fingers.

After explaining the rudiments of the weapon's function, Seth asked, "You're an arcanist?"

Malik gave a pleased smile. "What gave it away?"

"I've known a few," Seth replied in a wry tone.

Lord Malik, obnoxiously, chuckled. Was the man *flirting* with Seth?

Raider flicked his empty skewer into the street. Malik should have been glad it didn't end up in his eye.

"And the litter is clearly arcane," Seth added. "Four men couldn't carry this with our combined weight."

"An astute observation," Malik commented, making Raider long for his skewer back so he could stab both of them—Malik for fawning over Seth, and Seth for making it so easy for him.

"However," Malik went on, "I am no artificer. The litter caught Prince Rahim's interest some years ago and he, most magnanimously, allows me its use."

"A generous prince."

"Indeed."

The ornate wind towers and bulbous turquoise roofs of the palace loomed from behind its walls. At the approach of the litter, the gates swung open onto a sandstone courtyard with an avenue of palm trees leading to the palace. A mosaic of colorful tiles adorned the palace face with a sun and moon motif. Guards flanked a peaked door with intricate carvings worked into its panels.

As the bearers lowered the litter, Seth and Raider slung their gear over their shoulders and followed Malik into the palace. Between the draw of the palace's wind towers (which likely had arcane enhancements) and the evaporative cooling of a wide, shallow pool in the foyer, the air was quite pleasant.

Servants in dhotis and simple robes hurried through the wide, columned space. Two young males appeared in front of them, bowing to Malik and nodding at his instructions, spoken in Kastalan. Then Malik turned to Seth and Raider.

"I will allow you to refresh yourselves before dinner," he said with his irritating smile.

"We're most grateful for such hospitality," Seth replied politely.

Raider barely suppressed his eye roll.

Seth and Raider followed their guides to a flight of steps then along a hallway to a tiled foyer, where a large potted jasmine flourished in the middle. They were led to neighboring doors and shared a brief look before stepping into their separate rooms.

Raider's chamber featured a wide bed draped in fine white linens and a latticed door that must open onto a balcony. An arcane lamp of blown glass stood on a table beside the bed, and patterned rugs softened the mosaic-tiled floor. A side table held a pitcher, cups, and a platter of bread, olives, and cheese. A standing screen, draped with linen towels, sectioned off a bathing chamber with a small pool sunken into the floor.

The servant, a slim and attractive young man, went to the side table to pour what looked like wine into a blue glass cup. He brought it to Raider, who put down his gear to accept it.

"Thank you," Raider said in Kastalan.

"You would like to bathe?"

"Yes, but I don't need help. You can go about your other duties."

The servant looked offended. "Would you prefer another?"

"I prefer to attend myself. Thank you, but you may go." Raider had no interest in attention that someone was being required to give him.

When he was alone, Raider brought the wine to his lips. A paranoid part of him said he shouldn't drink it, but unless he was going to refuse all food and drink while here, there was no point in abstaining now.

While Raider sipped the wine, which was rich and earthy and probably very expensive, he made a closer examination of the room with its beautiful tilework and fine furnishings. The bed boasted a wool-stuffed mattress and down pillows cased in yellow silk.

Raider loved fine things, and he wanted to love all this, but he couldn't trust it.

The latticed door opened onto a stone balcony with an ornately carved railing, and another door. Seth's door. For the first time since Lord Malik had approached him and Seth, Raider felt an easing of his tension.

He hadn't been cut off from Seth. He could cross the balcony and open Seth's door and see him—and that was very fucking important.

Partly because they were in a place Raider didn't trust.

Mostly because ... well, it just *was*.

He was sorely tempted by that door but ducked back into his own room instead. He wanted to clean up before Seth saw him again.

After returning his cup to the side table, Raider made quick work of escaping his tattered clothes and slipping into the bathing pool. The warm water could only mean the palace benefitted from arcane heating. Sometimes he hated anything arcane on principle, but he did have to admit that some inventions had their appeal. In fact, as he reclined in the soothing water, he was almost prepared to forgive Seth for his rash decision to come here.

But not really. This was a bad idea. Seth didn't understand the people of the Gold. The tricks. The games. The cheapness of life.

It wasn't safe.

But there wasn't anything Raider could do about that at the moment. At least, he thought wryly, there was soap.

As he gave himself a thorough scrubbing from head to toe, he couldn't help but think about the last time he'd gotten to indulge in a full bath. At the oasis. With Seth.

He closed his eyes, recalling the tension of that moment, the knowledge that Seth wanted him but still might refuse to touch him. Then Seth had crossed the pool to him and wrapped a hand around Raider's cock. His own hand wrapped it now, but it wasn't the same. He wanted Seth's hand, Seth's mouth, Seth's body and his voice and all his intensity.

Raider let go of his cock to put his hands over his face. What the hell was happening to him? He'd never felt this before, this kind of ... need.

And the really scary thing was that it wasn't just the sex. Oh, Raider loved the sex, needed the sex—but he needed more. He needed Seth walking with him, talking with him, just fucking *being* with him.

It made no sense. Before Raider had met Seth he hadn't needed those things, so there was no reason to need them now. Before Seth, Raider had flitted from place to place, person to person, enjoying each thing in its brief, beautiful moment. He'd been completely fulfilled by that.

Liar, said a voice inside him. *You were not.*

Raider told that voice to shut the hell up.

No longer enjoying the bath, he stepped out onto the tiled floor and snagged a linen towel from the folding screen.

A mirror hung on the wall of the bathing area, and a table held an assortment of grooming tools, oils, and a shaving basin. Raider regarded his reflection, considering the slightly scruffy beard that had grown in over the past few weeks. Usually, he only trimmed it down but …

He picked up the razor and went to work.

When he was done, he returned to the main part of the chamber to examine the clothes that the boy had brought in while he was wielding the razor. In place of his travel-stained garments, he found a patterned sarong of rose, blue, and gold that fell to mid-calf and a short, boxy vest of blue silk that would hang open, plus a pair of supple sandals.

Oh, yes, he could work with this.

Once he was dressed, he went out onto the balcony and opened the door to Seth's room. The room looked much like his own: plush bed and private bath, sideboard loaded with refreshments. But though Seth's clothes, weapons, and gear made a tidy stack at the foot of the bed, Seth himself wasn't present.

Not liking that, Raider returned to his own room then exited it into the foyer, where he found the boy waiting outside his door.

"Where's my ... companion?" Raider asked, using the same word that Seth had used for him. It wasn't inaccurate, but he didn't like it either.

The boy bowed. "I will take you to the dining hall. He will be there."

Frowning, Raider followed the quick-footed boy down the stairs then along several hallways to a large room where columns supported a high, arched ceiling. Arcane lamps hung on long chains, casting clean white light.

Low tables ran along the two long sides of the hall, and a shorter table stretched across a portion of raised floor. Well-dressed courtiers sat on bright cushions at the two low tables, chatting and lounging. Servants wearing dhotis or sarongs moved through the space, bearing flagons of wine and platters of food.

As Raider was led to a place at the end of one table, he scanned the faces again, as though he could possibly have missed Seth the first time.

"I thought you said my companion would be here," Raider growled at the boy.

"He will be," the boy replied serenely, motioning for Raider to seat himself on a tasseled sapphire cushion.

"Where is he?"

"With Lord Malik."

Dropping unhappily onto the cushion, Raider resigned himself to wait. More people were filtering in. Seth would be here soon. If he wasn't, Raider would go find him, even if he had to tear this place apart.

A young woman bent to fill Raider's cup from a flagon, but he didn't touch it. He needed to stay alert. He needed Seth to walk in.

Raider grew more anxious with every passing moment. The hall was filling up, and Seth still wasn't here.

Then, finally, he was. Seth entered the dining hall with Lord Malik at his elbow, the arcanist's elegant hands pointing out this and that.

Seth had shaved, baring that strong jawline and revealing all the perfect planes and angles of his face. The sun had darkened his skin, making his green eyes stand out even more brightly, even across the room. And, to Raider's delight, he was dressed in silk shalvar pants of rich saffron. A sleeveless tunic of brilliant emerald was bound at his waist by a sash of lighter green.

It looked fantastic on him.

Malik seemed to think so, too, because he kept finding excuses to touch Seth's arm and leaning near to speak. Seth would nod and respond, clearly engaged in the conversation.

Well, then. Apparently Seth was just fine.

So much for Raider's paranoia.

Seth's eyes roamed the hall until they found Raider. Did his body relax slightly, or was that Raider's imagination?

It would have to remain a mystery because Seth did not come to sit with him. Instead, he followed Lord Malik to the raised table and was seated in a place of prominence at the arcanist's right.

Raider picked up his wine. It wasn't raaki, but it would do.

Moments later, everyone stood as a man who could only be Prince Rahim entered the dining hall. A cloth-of-gold turban sewn with rubies crowned his head, and his sarong and tunic bore a dizzying array of color and pattern. Rahim was a distant cousin of Empress Zarina, but he couldn't compare to her in either beauty or grace. Though Rahim's opulent clothing made up for his otherwise uninspiring looks, his body language conveyed more arrogance than authority. Raider's skin crawled. He knew exactly how dangerous that sort of arrogance could be.

As Rahim took his seat, with Malik on his right, he gave a bored wave for everyone to be seated. More wine was poured and the food went around. There were platters of seasoned meat and vegetables, roasted almonds and fresh fruit. Raider stabbed a piece of pork from a tray. The noblewoman seated next to Raider tried to talk to him, but he only made vague sounds in response and she soon, thankfully, gave up.

Raider caught Seth's gaze on him from time to time, but mostly Seth was too busy talking to Malik and the prince.

The more Raider watched, the more obvious it became that Rahim and Malik were lovers. The prince kept passing sweetmeats to the arcanist, kept touching him. And yet … Malik continued his smiling flirtation with Seth right in front of the prince.

It chilled Raider. The two of them were testing Seth. For their bed.

Couldn't Seth see that? Why the hell wasn't he putting a stop to it? Did he … want that?

It was a relief when dancers spilled into the room and gave Raider something else to focus on. Both male and female, they were dressed only in silk ribbons and glittering, tinkling chains. They whirled into a shimmering, undulating belly dance to the beat of drums.

The sensuality intensified as the dancers began to strip away their ribbons. They twirled each ribbon they removed, incrementally baring themselves until only their chains remained. These shimmered over breasts and cocks, lifting to offer fleeting glimpses as the dancers whirled around one another. Their fingers brushed each other's asses and throats. Lips offered passing kisses.

Raider couldn't help but notice the extreme and varied beauty of the dancers. The skin tones ranged from nearly Seth's fairness to deepest ebony. Some of the women had lush curves and full breasts; others were all light delicacy. The men, too, ranged from slender elegance to rippling power.

Instead of rendering the dance chaotic, the diversity made it all the more harmonious. A brown-skinned beauty lifted her slight, chestnut-toned partner into the arms of an ebony man of lean strength. With her chestnut legs hooked around the dark male's torso, the slight female arched away from him, back bending to kiss the lips of her initial brown-skinned partner.

It was … fucking beautiful.

When the prince rose from his cushion and took to the floor, others followed, including Malik.

And Seth.

Seth had not wanted to join in the dance with the Sudai, but here he didn't hesitate. Part of Raider recognized that Seth's body language and expression were less comfortable than they had been at the campfire dance, but part of him only saw that lack of hesitation.

The diners moved among the almost-nude dancers in a blend of dance and flirtation. Raider watched the mingling until Malik once again touched Seth's arm with the excuse of getting Seth's attention. Then Raider looked away.

He didn't know how much time passed, but suddenly Seth was beside him, reaching down his hand.

"Get up," Seth commanded.

"I'm keeping watch."

"You didn't even see me coming."

Seth's hand flexed impatiently, and Raider looked up to see that Seth's jaw was tight, his eyes intense. With Seth, that could mean anything, but the color deepening across his cheekbones and the darkening of his eyes gave him away.

Raider loved the way Seth looked when he was turned on. All that intensity and power channeled into something carnal and beautiful.

Raider wanted him. He wanted him like he'd never wanted anything in his life.

He took Seth's hand. Seth pulled him up and into the crowd. A woman with skin of dark honey twirled by them, her chains shimmering in the arcane light, her fingers grazing their arms.

The erotic atmosphere, the tension, and Seth's sudden nearness had Raider hard—and not entirely happy about it. Seth didn't touch him, and they didn't even pretend to dance, both of them standing amid the movement like rocks in a river.

Seth scowled. "You're in a very strange mood."

"Do you know my moods that well?"

"I don't know this one."

Raider didn't know this one either, and he wasn't enjoying it any more than he was enjoying their current location.

"This is unsafe, being here. These people. They want something."

"I know that," Seth said.

Raider's heart twisted. "You do?"

"I need access here. Information. I can get that through—"

"Your new friend? Exactly how far are you willing to go to get that information?"

Seth's eyes narrowed. "What's that supposed to mean?"

Movement caught Raider's eye. Malik. Approaching.

"You look good like this," Raider said, painfully aware that he wasn't the only who thought so.

Seth frowned. Then, as Malik called Seth's name, he turned. After casting a vaguely critical look at Raider, Seth followed Malik into the shifting, sensual crowd.

Chapter 32

WHEN SETH OPENED the latticed door onto the shared balcony and found Raider there gazing out over moonlit Aqarat, his skittering heart settled. Thank the gods.

Raider had escaped the dining hall long before Seth had been able to, and he'd spent an hour tormented by the thought that he might return to their rooms and find Raider gone. Raider had been off at dinner. He'd been off all fucking day.

Barefooted, wearing only the sarong he'd worn at dinner, Raider was leaning down, his elbows on the balcony's stone railing. Moonlight painted his back.

When he glanced over his shoulder at Seth, the moonlight caught his cheekbone and the line of his jaw. Gods, he looked good clean shaven. His face was so exotic, so masculine, so fucking beautiful. Seth loved seeing every inch of it.

He loved that strong back too, and he couldn't help that seeing Raider bent like that, wearing only that loose sarong, made an image flash through his mind: his hands whipping that fabric away, baring the muscled perfection of Raider's ass. His hands parting those round globes to take possession of that tight rim, to plunder it.

But first.

"What's your goddamn problem?" Seth demanded.

Raider looked away from him, gazing out across the moonlit rooftops again. "I already told you. It's not safe here."

That wasn't at all what Seth meant or wanted to talk about, but he couldn't stop himself from responding to it. "We haven't been safe since we left Shalaa. Why the hell is this so different?"

Raider yanked upright and wheeled to face Seth. Well, at least that got his goddamn attention.

"Are you really that fucking naïve?"

"Do you want to explain what you mean, or do you just want to be an asshole?"

"*I'm* the asshole? You hired me to keep you safe, but you make it so goddamn difficult because you don't fucking listen to me. You should have consulted me before dragging us both here."

"There wasn't time."

"You *make* time. You *make* it work. You tell that prick that we have some business to take care of, that we'll come to the palace later, then we sort some shit out *before* diving head first into the snake pit."

"There was plenty of time to sort shit out, and you kept cutting me off." That wasn't entirely fair, but Seth felt like he'd tried more than Raider had.

Raider's right eye flashed gold. "That's not what I'm talking about!"

As Raider came stalking his way, Seth braced for a different kind of conflict, a physical one, but Raider stormed straight past him into Seth's room, snapping, "Get in here!"

Seth remained stubbornly in place. "Why?"

"Because it's too easy for someone to listen to us out there."

Seth closed his eyes and took a calming breath. (He took a *breath* anyway. It wasn't exactly calming.) Then he followed Raider into the dark room.

Seth didn't like arguing without being able to see Raider's face, so he switched on an arcane lamp on the bedside table.

When the lamp's glass globe bloomed with cool light, it revealed Raider standing with his arms crossed furiously and his eyes trained on Seth like weapons. At the sight, heat spilled into Seth's groin, thickening his cock. Why the hell did that turn him on so much?

"What I'm talking about," Raider snarled in a low voice, "is you not having any fucking clue about this place. Did you *notice* the assortment of dancers? Did you notice their decorative *chains*? The prince is a collector of unusual and beautiful things, Seth. And you, with your fair coloring and green eyes, not to mention your body? *You* are an unusual and beautiful thing. That arcanist? He *belongs* to Rahim. All that flirtation is him testing you for the prince's bed, for *their* bed. You surely see that!"

Part of Seth warmed at the compliment buried in all that criticism, but he couldn't let it distract him. "Give me some goddamn credit. Of course the prince is a fucking collector. They *all* are, every rich man, everywhere. This area is no different from anywhere else. I am *always* navigating *exactly* this kind of thing. What Rahim wants is not *me* but whatever arcane oddity he thinks I can add to his collection."

"Malik has been flirting with you outrageously! You can't possibly be that oblivious—"

Seth gaped at Raider. "Are you *jealous*?"

"Don't you understand that Rahim is arrogant and powerful and will take what he wants—"

"Answer my question, Raider."

Arms still crossed over his bare abdomen, Raider glared at Seth. Fuck. He *was* jealous.

Seth shook his head. "Look. You are way off base. Rahim may want to recruit me. Curators do sometimes abandon the Arcanum to work more profitably for lords and princes. He'll soon learn I'm not that kind of Curator. Tomorrow I'll discuss my mission with Malik. Of course I'll have to bargain with him—and, by extension, Rahim—for what I need. While I have their interest, I have to make use of it."

"Well, you're certainly doing a fantastic job."

"That *is* my job, Raider. I need access here. Access to information, to resources. I need clues. I need a goddamn direction. I can't throw away the possibility of finding one, so I can't overreact just because someone fucking smiles at me."

"Oh, so you *did* notice."

"You're turning it into something it's not! Don't you understand that I have to navigate this court carefully if I want help—"

"You already *had* help. You had *my* help. But if you prefer help from that slimy sycophant, then maybe you don't need me here at all."

Seth felt his lip curl back from his teeth. "So I should just pay you and let you get on your way, is that it?"

"Is that what you think this is about?"

"What the hell *is* this about, Raider? Because it's not about Malik, not really. You've been distant all goddamn day. You wouldn't even *look* at me this morning."

"I'm surprised you noticed, now that you have more important concerns."

"Oh, I noticed. And you better answer my fucking question."

Seth stalked toward Raider, who yielded step after step until Seth had him against the wall. Raider's arms uncrossed and his hands came up. They pressed against Seth's chest, holding him back. Seth's cock, already partially hard, thickened further at the contact, at the tension between them, at the absolute knowledge of where this was going.

"Answer my question," Seth demanded in a low voice. "What is this really about?"

Raider's throat moved as he swallowed. He didn't answer. He wasn't going to.

A growl of frustration, with both Raider and himself, rumbled past Seth's lips as he crushed them to Raider's. Raider opened to the kiss, though his tongue seemed to battle with Seth's, stroking with hunger and a little anger. Raider's aggression took Seth's cock from thick to rock hard, but it also sparked a carnal need to make him submit.

Why couldn't Raider just *say* how he felt?

But then … Seth couldn't seem to either.

Breaking the kiss, Seth nibbled along Raider's clean-shaven jaw, loving the access to his skin. Raider tilted his head, briefly yielding his throat to Seth. Then Raider changed his mind. Bringing his head down, Raider clamped his teeth on the juncture of Seth's neck and shoulder. It sent a hard throb into Seth's dick—and snapped something inside him.

He shoved Raider off and grabbed him by the throat, pinning him to the wall as he'd done in Shalaa.

Raider's eyelids fluttered as Seth choked him. With his free hand, Seth unknotted and stripped away Raider's sarong, baring his swollen cock. Seth closed his eyes as a fierce wave of arousal assaulted his body. He forced his eyes back open to indulge himself in the sight of that gorgeous cock, its long, thick shaft threaded with veins, the head flushed dark and flaring hard, weeping for him. And, *fuck*, was it weeping.

Now, suddenly, Seth understood what this was really about. He felt it, how Raider needed this, needed *him*—just as he needed Raider. Even if neither of them could say it, here, now, with both of them calming down as they showed each other what they needed, it couldn't be denied.

Seth hadn't intended to make Raider jealous. He still thought Raider was way off in his interpretation. But Seth couldn't help that it soothed him to know that Raider wanted him enough to react like that, that he needed Seth to take possession of him. And there was nothing in the world that Seth wanted more than to do just that.

As he choked Raider rhythmically, careful of the pressure, careful to let Raider breathe periodically, he watched Raider's cock twitch upward as his muscled belly contracted. Precum dripped from his slit in a long, tantalizing thread. Seth let Raider's frustration build, idly stroking Raider's thigh as his own cock pulsed and wept at the sight.

When Raider reached for himself, Seth knocked his hand away and rasped, "Don't touch that, it's mine."

Raider's belly contracted harder and his body thrummed with tension as he neared the limit of his submission. Seth made him wait another moment because, gods, he loved watching that cock weep for him, loved seeing Raider need him. Then he eased his grip slightly on Raider's throat and smoothed his other hand up the inside of Raider's thigh to cup the heavy weight of his balls. Raider made a sound of relief at the contact.

Seth hadn't yet found Raider's limit on roughness, but he was pretty sure he'd come close to Raider's limit on denial. Raider wanted to be touched. He needed it. Raider's throat vibrated with a moan as Seth gently tugged his taut sac then pressed his fingertips into Raider's taint behind it.

It was strange to Seth how calm he suddenly felt, how easy it was to control his actions when they did this. All his fears about losing control, about hurting Raider, vanished— because this wasn't about hurting him. It was about using his dominance to give them both what they needed, and, fuck, it felt good.

"That's better," Seth rumbled.

Then he took that gorgeous cock in hand, marveling at the length and girth of it, the heat and hardness, the silkiness. Seth gently squeezed Raider's throat again and groaned with pleasure at the way Raider's cock kicked in his hand. Gods, this man's body was made for Seth to pleasure.

Seth eased his hand away from Raider's throat to the back of his neck, holding him by the nape and the cock as he leaned in to nibble and kiss a path along Raider's jaw to his neck. With his tongue, he lathed Raider's throat where he'd choked him.

Raider's hands worked at Seth's sash, pulling it away then parting his tunic. Seth released his grip on Raider to shrug off the garment. Raider was quick to take advantage of that by tugging at the drawstring of Seth's pants. Seth always felt a bit vulnerable in such unstructured clothing, but it was certainly easier to get out of than his Curator garb.

"I like this on you," Raider said as Seth toed off his sandals.

"And I like you without a beard."

"I thought you would."

That gave Seth pause. "Is that why you did it?"

"It's not like it's the first time I've shaved it," Raider replied, not really answering the question.

As Raider got Seth's drawstring untied, Seth clamped a hand on his shoulder, exerting enough pressure to demand without actually forcing him.

Raider dropped willingly to his knees, but he tugged roughly at Seth's pants to make them drag at his stiff cock and send it slapping against his belly. At Seth's grunt, Raider aimed a wicked grin up at him. Then, as Seth stepped out of his pants, Raider took Seth's aching dick into his mouth.

"Fuck," Seth breathed as he watched Raider's lips stretch around him, cheeks hollowing as he sucked up and down Seth's rigid length. Raider's hands gripped Seth's ass in a way that had him pumping into Raider's mouth.

Raider drew back to Seth's tip, dragging his teeth lightly over the flared ridge before lathing the slit with his tongue, making Seth groan. Then Raider took him deep again, sucking hard.

Gods, that was going to make him come, and Seth didn't want to come in Raider's mouth. He wanted to come buried deep inside his ass. So he pulled back, gliding his cock away from Raider's mouth, and bent to take those swollen lips in a kiss.

"Wait here," Seth commanded and went to dig through his pack for the oil. He didn't even get the flap open before Raider was climbing to his feet.

"You better not move," Seth warned.

"If you want me to stay still," Raider goaded, "you'll have to make me."

Then he turned—and walked out onto the balcony.

It made Seth's cock jerk so hard it hit his belly again. He tore into his pack, making a mess of its tidy contents. Snatching up the oil, he chased after Raider, catching him by the hair at the doorway into Raider's room.

"Where the hell do you think you're going?" Seth demanded, working his grip down to Raider's scalp.

"My bed."

"Hell no. You're not getting fucked in a comfortable bed, not after that stunt. You'll take my cock out here." Seth hooked his other arm around Raider's lower belly and hauled him back, crushing Raider's ass against the stiff ridge of his dick.

"You feel that?" Seth growled in Raider's ear. "Every fat inch of that is going in your ass. So take this oil and fucking get it ready."

Raider was panting and shuddering, his cock twitching up against Seth's forearm where it banded his lower abdomen. Raider's fingers found the bottle in Seth's hand. Seth released Raider's hips but kept a grip on his hair as Raider turned to face him, pouring oil into his hand. Seth took the bottle back from him then groaned as Raider slicked his cock.

Seth forced Raider's face into the crook of his neck, pulling their bodies together. Raider's cock brushed his.

"I need you to listen to me," Seth said intently. "Are you listening?"

"Yes."

"Give me a word that means stop."

"I don't want you to stop. Even if I say stop, I don't mean it."

"That's why you're going to give me a word that *does* mean it. And it doesn't have to mean stop for good, it can mean take a break." As Raider breathed hard against him, Seth planted a kiss behind his ear. "This is the last moment I'm gonna be soft with you until it's over"—Raider shivered at that—"so I need to know if we're crossing a line. Now give me a word."

"Silver."

Seth stilled briefly at the choice then said, "Okay. Say it again."

"Silver."

"Okay. Silver," Seth echoed as he released Raider's hair and stepped away from him, curious about what Raider would do when Seth left him there to set the oil by his own bedroom door.

At first, Raider did nothing, and Seth had a moment to admire how the light spilling onto the balcony from Seth's room marked the outlines of his lean, muscled body. His cock jutted out harshly from his hips, precum still threading from it.

But Raider's compliance didn't last a moment longer than Seth expected it to. He could feel how Raider wanted to fight, how he wanted Seth to force him. So when Raider bolted, Seth did too, cutting him off at the door to Raider's room, grabbing him around the waist and hauling him back to the railing.

Seth didn't even have to tell him to put his hands on the railing. Raider did it automatically as Seth hooked an arm around his hips and yanked them back. He smacked Raider's ass once, twice, three times until Raider cried out. Then he kicked Raider's feet apart and pressed his cock along the cleft of Raider's ass.

"You're gonna find it very hard to escape with my cock buried inside you," Seth growled then stepped back. Clamping a hand on Raider's hip, he ordered, "Reach between your legs and use the oil on your fingers to get ready for me."

"Seth—"

"Do what I said. I want to see those fingers on your hole."

"Fuck," Raider breathed, starting to tremble, but he did as Seth ordered.

Keeping one hand clamped on Raider's hip, Seth used his other to stroke himself as he watched Raider massage his own rim. "Push inside."

Seth's dick throbbed at the sight of those nimble fingers slipping past the tight ring. But Raider couldn't get very deep at that angle, so Seth took his own, now-slick fingers away from his dick and pressed them into that tight hole along with Raider's.

It was hot as fuck, but Seth needed fuller access, so he said, "This is mine now. Hold the railing."

"Fuck, Seth, *fuck*."

"Is your cock still weeping for me?" Seth asked as he speared his fingers deeper. When Raider only moaned and leaned his forehead down onto the railing, Seth demanded, "Answer me."

"Yes!"

"Good. I love when you're dripping for me." With that, Seth withdrew his fingers, lined up his broad cockhead with Raider's hole, and ordered, "Brace."

"Oh, fuck," Raider gasped then moaned as Seth breached him, stretching his rim with his cock.

Seth penetrated him in a slow, smooth glide, fascinated by the sight of Raider's body taking that much cock. It wasn't easy for him though. He was gasping and shuddering at the hard intrusion, and his body's grip on Seth's dick was almost painfully tight.

"Breathe," Seth said as he slowly dragged his cock back through Raider's channel before gliding deep again. He reached around to smooth a hand from Raider's stomach to his chest, grazing his taut nipples. When he delved down to Raider's cock, Seth moaned to find Raider so damn hard for him.

Then he gripped Raider's hips, pulled back, and slammed in deep.

"Fuck!" Raider shouted.

"You can take it," Seth gritted out, drawing back to slam in again. He did it again and again, quickening his pace, deepening his thrusts.

When Raider, moaning, started to reach for his cock, Seth growled, "Don't you fucking touch that."

"You're so goddamn—ah! Fuck, Seth!"

"You'll come on my cock"—Seth bottomed out in Raider again, eliciting a shout—"or not at all."

"I *need*—"

"Clearly a harder fucking, or you wouldn't be arguing with me."

When Seth gave him that, driving harder and deeper, pounding relentlessly into him, Raider indeed stopped arguing. He stopped trying to touch his cock. He was too busy bracing against the railing, moaning and shouting as Seth fucked him with brutal thrusts.

Seth felt his total control of Raider's body, and when he ordered, "Come for me, come now," Raider's body instantly obeyed him.

Raider shouted and bucked as he came violently, his ass seizing tight on Seth's cock. Seth roared as his own orgasm ripped through him.

Seth's hips snapped forward as he spilled hotly into that thrashing body. He fucked Raider through the last of it, both of them panting and spasming through the aftershocks.

But Seth was so damn turned on and needed Raider so fucking much that when he finally eased out, with a grunt from himself and a cry from Raider, his dick was still rock hard.

He'd just have to deal with it. He had a higher priority. Raider was clinging to the railing, barely on his feet. He needed Seth.

"Come on, baby, get up," Seth murmured, tugging at him, pulling him up into his arms and walking him into the room. Into *Seth's* room. He needed Raider in his bed and nowhere else.

Seth half guided, half carried him there, stripped back the sheets, and got him to sit on the edge of the mattress. Seth leaned down to stroke Raider's beautiful face and kiss him, needing to know he was all right.

It seemed to wake Raider up, and he returned the kiss with all the intensity of earlier. There was no anger in it this time. This time, it was all pleasure. Seth broke from Raider's lips to nudge his jaw and kiss the underside of it, gently driving him back to lie down.

"I'll be right back," he promised, knowing that, unlike earlier, Raider wasn't going anywhere.

Seth reluctantly pulled himself away and walked to the bathing area to get a towel, which he dipped into the pitcher of water. His erection had eased slightly, but when he returned to see Raider with his hands over his face and his cock lying hard against his belly, Seth's dick throbbed and stiffened.

When Seth came to the bed, Raider still had his hands over his face, probably not realizing that he wasn't the only one still needing more. Raider's ass was at the edge of the bed, his legs hanging down, his feet on the floor. He grunted when Seth gripped his left hamstring and lifted his leg. He dropped his hands from his face and raised his head, gazing down the length of his body to see the cock ready to penetrate him again.

"Oh, fuck," Raider breathed.

When Seth massaged Raider's hole to make sure he was all right, Seth's cum spilled from it. A ragged sound escaped Seth at the sight. He dipped his fingers into the mess he'd made inside his lover and smeared it across Raider's abdomen, swirling it with Raider's cum where it had splashed his abs. Then Seth pressed his broad cockhead against that perfect hole and shoved inside.

Raider bowed up, shouting, and Seth didn't start easy on him this time but fucked hard and deep into the channel already loosened by his dick, already lubricated with his cum. With every thrust, Raider's cock jerked against his muscled abdomen, leaving a slick trail.

"Stroke yourself," Seth commanded, stretching Raider's leg higher, giving himself deeper access.

Moaning, Raider took his cock in hand and gazed down his body to watch Seth fucking him. Seth's eyes roamed from that beautiful face to the strong, masculine body to the hand pumping that gorgeous cock, plumping the head with every stroke.

"Seth, I—" Raider broke off, moaning.

"You need to come," Seth rasped. "I know."

Raider's balls were swollen at the base of his flushed cock, and his ass was tightening on Seth's cock.

Seth thrust harder and faster, pounding into Raider's sweet spot until Raider orgasmed so hard that the creamy strands shot from his cock onto his chest and throat. That was all it took—that sight, the sound of Raider's cry, the feel of Raider's body seizing on him. Seth shouted as his hips snapped forward and he spilled hotly inside Raider again.

The last delicious, shuddering motions had them both moaning, then Seth bent down to bring his chest against Raider's. The movement shifted his still-swollen cock inside Raider. Raider cried out at the excess of stimulation but still welcomed Seth against him. Seth pressed his face into the crook of Raider's neck. Raider reached up and stroked Seth's head to the back of his neck, holding onto him.

But, goddamn it, Seth was getting hard again, so he pulled out before it worsened, eliciting a cry from them both. Cum spilled from Raider's hole as Seth's cock emerged from it.

"I can't get over the sight of that," Seth murmured, rubbing his hands up and down Raider's legs where they hooked lightly around him. "My cum, leaking from inside you."

"Fuck, Seth," Raider groaned as his cock stirred in the mess painting his abdomen.

Seth closed his eyes and took a deep breath. "We need to clean up and have something to drink and rest for a minute."

Raider's hips lifted slightly. "I don't want to rest."

"I don't care. You're going to rest. *I* need to rest. Because we're going to be doing this all fucking night."

At that, Raider smiled and launched himself up into Seth's arms. Seth pulled him in tight and buried his face against Raider's neck again, shocked by how much that soothed some deep part of him, overwhelmed by how much he needed this man.

How the hell had that happened?

Chapter 33

It worried Raider, how much he needed Seth. They had parted ways less than ten minutes ago, but Raider already felt anxious about the separation. Of course, that probably had something to do with their current circumstances.

True, this was their second morning in Prince Rahim's palace and nothing, so far, had happened. But Raider still didn't like having Seth spend his days with that arcanist.

Of course … that also had a lot to do with the way Malik looked at Seth, not to mention the way he oh-so-casually touched Seth at every opportunity. And Raider certainly didn't like that Seth tolerated it, regardless of his reasons, regardless of his dismissal of the idea that he was being tested for the prince's bed. If Seth was wrong, if Malik tried to take things any further, Raider would put a stop it, and to hell with the consequences.

Seth was *his*.

And he was Seth's.

That had felt clear and simple isolated in Seth's room, with Seth's cum in his ass, on his chest, down his throat. It had felt absolute when Seth had said of Raider's cock the other night, *This is mine.*

Raider didn't understand why he even wanted to be claimed like that. He'd always valued freedom above all else. He didn't know why he wanted Seth to grab him, force him, fuck him so possessively.

All he knew was that when Seth fixated on him like that, wouldn't let him escape, took over his decisions, Raider felt ... safe. He felt centered. He felt *whole.*

And it wasn't just during sex. He'd felt that same sense of certainty when Seth had slept last night with his hand on Raider's chest, his leg over Raider's hip, his breath stirring Raider's hair. He'd felt it when Seth had stretched his shoulder this morning, gently insisting in spite of Raider's surliness, until it had felt natural to let him help.

But that sense of certainty had vanished when a message from Lord Malik had arrived this morning. When Raider had felt Seth's attention shift.

The same thing had happened yesterday. Seth had spent all day with Lord Malik. Because after discussing his mission with the arcanist? Rather than losing interest in Seth, Malik had offered to help him hunt for Julian.

What the hell? Why would Malik care about a fugitive of the Arcanum? And why couldn't Seth see how that indicated that Prince Rahim had no interest in having Seth add arcane oddities to his collection like Seth had argued?

Besides, helping Seth was *Raider's* job.

But Seth didn't seem to see it that way. Totally focused on his mission, just as Raider had feared, Seth had leaped at the opportunity to spend yesterday with Malik, who had shown him around Aqarat like a glorified tour guide.

So Raider had spent yesterday hunting for an escape route—which he'd found. Palaces always had them, and Prince Rahim's hadn't even been difficult to locate. Best of all, the underground tunnel system led beneath the city walls, all the way out.

When Raider had reported this fantastic find to Seth last night (once Seth had finally become his again), rather than being suitably impressed, Seth had actually scolded him.

Seth's words had included: dangerous, foolish, unnecessary, and (most insultingly) *could have been caught*.

Raider *might* have replied with something about needing the escape route himself, just to get away from Seth and Malik's nauseating flirtation.

Seth had scowled gorgeously at that. He'd made some argument about using every possible resource to find Julian so that they—*yes, I mean you and me, Raider,* he'd specified—could get out of Aqarat.

And do what? Raider had asked.

Figure this out.

This?

Yes, Seth had replied, moving in to grip Raider's cock through his pants. (Arguing with Seth always made him hard.) *This.*

They hadn't talked much after that. And everything, for the blissful hours of the night, had been right.

Until a note from Lord Malik had arrived this morning and Seth had started dressing in a hurry to meet his oh-so-helpful guide, who had suggested they start today at a kahve shop in the southern part of the city.

When Raider had snorted and made a few relevant (though possibly sarcastic) comments, Seth had only scowled and warned Raider to *not cause any trouble.*

Raider had no intention of causing trouble. He did, however, intend to break into Malik's workroom.

Raider didn't trust that arcanist one bit. And not just because of the sexual overtones of his—and, by extension, Prince Rahim's—interest in Seth. Regardless of whether Seth was being tested as a potential addition Malik and Rahim's bed, something else was in play. Raider was sure of it—and he intended to find proof.

Maybe *then* Seth would be willing to get the hell out of here.

Raider slipped through the window of Malik's workroom and dropped lightly to the floor. He cast a sharp eye around the room for movement. Seeing none, he retracted his quicksilver armor, letting it slide back from his fingers and up his left arm with a *shhhhkt*.

Damn that quicksilver. Without it, he wouldn't have been able to grip the tiny ridges of stone to drop from the window above to this one. And without his arcane eye, his scouting of the palace—yesterday to find the tunnels and today to find this room—would have been much more difficult.

The workroom, much like its extravagant owner, managed to look both busy and lavish. A book, its cover embossed with gold, lay on a table beside a sumptuous armchair draped with a purple silk robe. A towering bookcase held more valuable tomes. A rich carpet softened the floor, stretching from the armchair to a large worktable.

A shelf above the table was crowded with jars filled with powders of every color, plant matter, dead beetles with iridescent carapaces, an assortment of precious metals, and semiprecious stones.

Atop the table lay a book that appeared to have been subjected to tests of some sort. An arcane magnifying device was positioned over the book, and several colored powders dusted its leather cover. In a glass bowl filled with amber liquid, there floated a clipping of a page.

But it was the book itself, not the tests, that seized Raider's attention. Rather, it was the intricate, gold-leaf symbol worked into the book's cover.

Many weeks ago, when Raider had pressed Seth about the book that Julian had stolen in connection to the murder of a fellow scholar, Seth had described this very symbol. It was unmistakable: the moon overlaid with the eye. That image set within the sun as it burst through a triangle.

He'd *told* Seth. He'd fucking *told* Seth there was something going on here.

Malik had approached them so damn quickly after their arrival in Aqarat. He'd been so damn eager to help Seth with his mission—because he'd been aware of that mission from the start. Malik had already encountered Julian. Malik, somehow, had gotten this book from him.

Was Julian in the palace? Raider had yet to locate the dungeons. Maybe Julian was there. Or was he a guest here, hidden from Seth and Raider, somehow in league with Malik and Rahim? If so, for what purpose?

Whatever the case, this book was exactly the proof that Raider had needed. Seth would have to listen to him now.

Raider's sense of satisfaction, however, lasted only a moment, only until he picked up the book and looked inside. He opened to a random page, curious about what kind of book was worth killing for. Seth had described the book's cover, a detail apparently given to him for his hunt, but Seth had known nothing of the book's contents.

At least … that was what Seth had said.

But that conversation looked very different—everything with Seth looked very different—when Raider started paging through the book.

A few of the drawings could have been found in any anatomy text. The body's branching network of arteries and veins. The interconnecting structures of muscle and tendon and bone when the skin was peeled back.

Those, Raider could dismiss, even if they made him uncomfortable.

But the next one …

To anyone but Raider, the image would likely have looked as innocuous as the others. It was simply a diagram of the human form with silver dots marking a number of points on the body and silver lines connecting them. It could have meant anything.

To anyone but Raider.

He closed his eyes, but the image there was worse: his own body, seen from above, cut open, the skin peeled back. It had happened sometimes during the surgeries. He would seem to leave his body and hover above it, looking down at the living silver threading along the bloody pathways of his exposed muscles and nerves.

No. It couldn't be. He was misunderstanding the diagram. Raider opened his eyes, refusing to read the handwritten notes, and flipped to another random page, desperate to be wrong—

A shiver went down his spine.

The eye. *His* eye. If it could even be called his, given that another had created it.

Beautifully rendered in fine ink, the drawing showed the eye's layers and intricacies. And the notes, which Raider could no longer ignore, detailed its function. The telescopic zoom. The numerous receptors that made the eye more sensitive to light and enabled Raider's keen night vision.

Numbly, Raider started flipping through the book. So many pictures. So much fucking detail. It all blurred together until Raider wasn't sure whether the images he saw were on the page or in his mind.

Raider found himself suddenly on his hands and knees, breath raking through his lungs, the room spinning around him. He didn't remember falling, didn't remember dropping the book. It lay several feet away, the cover open to the book's title page.

Raider already knew whose book it was, *what* book it was, even before his vision clarified, even before that traitorous arcane eye zoomed in on the boldly inked title.

The Masterwork of Kahzir.

Raider lunged toward the book and flipped it shut. But it was too late, of course, too fucking late to deny the truth.

Kahzir's book was the one that Julian had stolen.

Kahzir's book was the one that Seth was after, the one Seth was to take back to the Arcanum.

Of all Raider's hundred questions, only one really mattered: had Seth lied to him?

Had Seth known about the contents of the book all along? Had he known that the book worth killing for was about *Raider*?

Had Seth hired Raider knowing exactly who—*what*—he was? After all, it had only been after Seth had seen Raider's quicksilver that he had sought to hire him as a guide.

Seth had tied Raider to him, had gotten Raider to come along willingly, without need of restraints.

But Seth did have restraints in his possession.

Raider shivered at the memory of those arcane shackles, how completely he had been caught and at Seth's mercy. How much he had trusted Seth. How much he had loved it.

Had it all been a lie? Was Seth planning to seize Raider, along with Julian? To haul Raider back to the Arcanum? Or worse, to Empress Zarina?

Raider wanted to say, *No, no, of course not.*

He wanted to think that what he and Seth had was real. But what was it, exactly, that they had?

Love, Raider wanted to say.

And he *did* love Seth. Even on his hands and knees, shaking and sick to his stomach, with *that fucking book* forcing on him every truth that he couldn't fucking bear, he loved Seth.

But did Seth love him?

How *could* Seth love him, how could anyone? Everything about Raider was a lie. There was nothing real to love. And if Seth knew that, maybe he didn't mind lying too.

Seth's principles were strong, but which one would be strongest? What would matter most to him? Honesty? Or his duty to the Arcanum?

The Arcanum, of course. Seth had devoted his life to it. It had saved his life. It was his home.

Raider would be nothing compared to that.

The thought slid so easily into place that it was almost like Raider had been waiting for it, holding a space ready for it.

And he had been, hadn't he? Good things always vanished. Because Raider didn't deserve them.

He had known that all his life, long before he'd met the emperor, long before Kahzir had used Raider against him.

So he wasn't surprised, not really, to think that Seth, the best thing that had ever happened in his life, would vanish too.

Chapter 34

Normally, Seth enjoyed bookshops. The huge stacks of dusty tomes containing all manner of obscure knowledge and history. A bespectacled bookseller with a long white beard who could somehow find anything amid the chaos.

If Seth weren't in a hurry, if Seth were here with Raider, he would love it.

Raider would be a pain in the ass, of course. He would steal things (or pretend to). He would give Seth shit about every single book he opened. He would light this place the hell up and distract Seth. For fuck's sake, Raider wasn't even *here* and he was distracting Seth.

Seth needed to be ruthlessly focused, like he usually was. He had work to do. He had his mission to complete.

And yet, all Seth wanted was to be with Raider. He *needed* to be with Raider.

During their time in the Kesh, Seth had gotten so used to spending all day with him. Seeing him, hearing him, feeling his nearness. But since their arrival here, he'd seen Raider only at dinner and in bed.

The thought sent images flashing through his mind:

Raider bowing up on the bed as Seth sucked his gorgeous cock and speared fingers into his ass. Raider panting, his cock leaking against his belly, his eyes on Seth's dick as he oiled it. Raider's lips parting as Seth penetrated him.

Other images too:

Raider tilting his head as he shaved, stripping that exquisite face bare for Seth's eyes to enjoy. Raider looking heatedly at him over the rim of his cup at dinner when the prince's nude, flame-juggling dancers emerged to entertain.

But those moments weren't enough to ease Seth's hunger for him.

And those moments only intensified Seth's worry—because he couldn't control what lay outside of them. He couldn't control Raider. And it wasn't that he actually wanted to, but Raider was so damn reckless. What if Prince Rahim had caught him sneaking around the palace yesterday?

It was good they had an escape route (though Seth hadn't admitted that to Raider), but still. Raider needed to stay out of trouble with the prince so Seth could find Julian and finish this mission. So they could figure out what came next.

The problem, though, wasn't Raider (other than Seth being distracted by him). The problem was that everywhere Malik had taken Seth was a goddamn waste of time.

Julian would not have sold the book he stole from the Arcanum, nor would he likely have purchased one here. Seth had already pointed that out to Lord Malik, but the arcanist had insisted on the stop.

A kahve shop, a walk through the bazaar, and now a bookshop? Seth almost felt like he was being paraded around. Yesterday had felt much the same. Seth was getting nowhere, and Malik either had no idea how to conduct a manhunt—or he was stalling Seth on purpose.

The arcanist picked through a stack of books that the bookseller had said were new acquisitions before the white-bearded man had vanished into the back. Maybe Malik's finery and court position intimidated him. Maybe Seth's arcane clothing and weapons did.

Malik's elegant fingers beckoned Seth. Repressing a surge of impatience, Seth left the doorway, where he'd been dividing his attention between Malik and the bustling street.

At Seth's scowl, an eyebrow as manicured as Malik's goatee rose in elegant query. Turban-free today, the arcanist's dark hair was clubbed neatly at his nape, and rubies dangled from his ears. A robe of gold-embroidered blue silk draped his slim, graceful form, and his slender fingers held a book with studied sophistication.

Though Seth hadn't admitted it to Raider, he had begun to see Raider's point of view. (No, that wasn't even true. Seth had seen it from the start, even if he'd pretended not to.) He *was* being tested. Maybe not for the prince's bed, but Malik's flirtation was too obvious to deny, whatever its purpose.

Once, before Raider, Seth might have enjoyed the man's company a little. Malik was well read, intelligent, and witty. He was cultured and smooth, and his flirtation was the sort that Seth, once, had preferred: smiles, light touches, innuendo. All of it designed to tempt but not taunt, easily yielding control to him. Once, Seth had chosen such men for his partners.

Looking back, Seth didn't understand himself at all. Because now, being with Raider? It was so goddamn obvious why none of his past choices had been right. Only Raider was right. Only Raider could balance him.

At Seth's scowl, Raider would have grinned and teased him. He would have said shit just to rile Seth, and it would have ended with Seth's lips silencing his. But of course Raider wouldn't be silent. He never was. He would moan and make those delicious, needful sounds—

Fucking focus, Seth commanded himself.

"Might any of these have come from the Arcanum?" Malik inquired.

"That would be nearly impossible for me to guess, unless you've found the one I described."

"I'm afraid not," Malik replied smoothly, unruffled by Seth's sharpness. "But these are still worth a look."

Malik angled the book he was perusing toward Seth, clearly intending for Seth to look over his shoulder. Instead, Seth picked up a book from the stack and flipped through it without interest. He tossed it down.

"I need to speak with the gate guards, with the healers, and with merchants selling gear and supplies. I need to go to the inns and taverns and stables. Julian would have equipped himself, prepared for his next stage. He wouldn't have wasted time here—and neither should we."

Malik closed his book delicately. "You're assuming this … Julian … meant to continue his journey. What if Aqarat was his final destination?"

"Unlikely."

"What would motivate him to go on? What do you think he wants?"

"I think he'll go on to Kastari. It's a big city, bigger than Aqarat, more like Masir. It's a better place to disappear, besides being a place with more work for an arcanist of his caliber." Seth winced as he realized how his assessment might offend Malik, but the arcanist only studied Seth thoughtfully.

"The book itself must matter to your fugitive," Malik pointed out.

"I assume so, but not knowing the contents of it, I can't guess at its significance. Catalus, head of the Department of Alchemy, glimpsed the book in Julian's arms as Julian left the building. Catalus didn't know Julian was fleeing a murder scene and therefore didn't attempt to stop him."

"And you know nothing of Julian's politics? Nothing of his true purpose? The murder and theft didn't happen without reason."

"I'm sure there is more to all of this, but I can't know what that is until I find Julian. When I find him, I'll find the book. Then I can get some answers."

"What if, when you find those answers, Masir is not the best place to take him?"

"What the fuck does that mean?"

Seth did not have time to wonder if he should have phrased that more politely—because a boom shook the building. Plaster rained down, peppering Seth and Malik. Stacks of books toppled and spilled across the floor.

The bookseller peered out from the back. Seth shouted for the man to get out. Earthshakes could level buildings. The old man turned and fled back the way he'd come. Seth let him go, figuring there must be another door, and hustled after Malik into the street.

Seth struggled to make sense of what he was seeing. A mass of people surged along the avenue, all fleeing the same direction: east. But they should be moving west. The western gate was closer, and they had to get to open ground, away from the buildings.

The second thing that Seth couldn't make sense of was the fact that Raider was on the steps of the building across the street. Seth barely had time to wonder what the hell Raider was doing there before his heart leaped—because Raider started scaling the building to its rooftop.

"Raider!" Seth shouted. What the hell was Raider thinking, getting on top of a building that might collapse at any—

"Great Kasha!" Malik exclaimed, invoking the goddess of mysteries and the arcane.

Seth followed the arcanist's stunned gaze. Beyond the western gate, visible even above the rooftops, reared the massive, monstrous black head of the sand serpent.

Chapter 35

THE INSTANT RAIDER saw the sand serpent rear above the western gate, all other concerns fled his mind. At the moment, it didn't matter whether Seth had lied to him, manipulated him, intended to betray him. It didn't matter that he couldn't decide whether to confront Seth about it. It didn't even matter that he was still shaking from all the times he'd thrown up over the last hour as he'd tracked down Seth and Malik.

No, none of that mattered. Not when the sand serpent could destroy the city. Not when it might kill hundreds, even thousands.

And he and Seth had woken it up.

Long dormant, its hunger must have drawn it to Aqarat's concentration of easy prey.

The quicksilver's overlapping ridges and vicious studs gleamed from Raider's left shoulder to his fingertips, adding power to his grip as he scaled the mudbrick building. As soon as his sandaled feet hit the flat rooftop, Raider burst into a run. He sprinted to the edge of the roof and leaped across the alleyway gap to the next, his kaftan streaming behind him.

Rooftop after rooftop, Raider bypassed the chaos of the streets.

Heavier and burdened by his weapons, Seth would have to fight his way against the movement of the fleeing crowd. He would do it, though. And the damned fool would get himself killed in a fight he couldn't possibly win—which meant Raider had to reach the sand serpent ahead of him. Even amid his awful, desperate questions about Seth, Raider's instinct to protect him still raged with full force.

Whether Raider could actually stop the sand serpent, he had no idea, but he had to try.

The creature's head had vanished from sight beyond the wall. It was no doubt preparing for another assault on the gate. But Raider was almost there.

He launched himself over another alleyway, this one wider than the others. He gave it everything he had, but his stomach dropped mid-leap because, fuck, fuck, fuck, he wasn't going to make it.

Raider's toes brushed the rooftop edge and slipped off, but it was enough to pitch him forward and slam his chest into the ledge. He scraped downward, his whole body raking against rough mudbrick, but managed to catch a scrabbling hold with his quicksilver fingertips. Before he could pull himself up, however, a fresh boom shook the city.

Raider's grip slipped on the shuddering building. He fell for a breathless moment—

Then slammed into a wooden structure. It collapsed under his weight. As he rolled clear of the debris, groaning, Raider dimly registered that he'd landed on a goat-milking stanchion. If only he'd been in the merchant's quarter, he might have landed on an awning and maybe some fruit. Here, near the livestock gate, it was a fucking stanchion.

Raider staggered to his feet and lurched into a run, ignoring a dozen points of pain. He didn't have time for them.

As he careened around the corner into the street, near his goal, Raider felt keenly the absence of his scimitar. He'd left it behind so he could move quickly and silently through Aqarat to tail Seth and Malik.

Of course, the sword wouldn't have done him much good anyway. Not against the sand serpent.

His only chance lay with his quicksilver. If he could reach the sand serpent's point of vulnerability, if he could punch hard enough, maybe he could stop the creature.

Maybe.

Raider raced along the now-empty street to the cracked mudbrick wall and the gate twisting on its hinges. Even the guards had abandoned their posts. Raider couldn't blame them.

Another earthshaking blow against the weakened gate had the wood shattering and the massive, spiny tail of the sand serpent whipping through.

Raider hurtled the debris and leaped onto the mudbrick steps leading to the guards' platform. He raced to the top.

Even knowing what he would see did not prepare him for the full, unobstructed view of the sand serpent. The creature's massive body looped and coiled over the scrubby hard pack. Its innumerable scales and the ridge of black spines gleamed under the sun as it wound around to face the opening that its tail had struck into Aqarat.

Raider flung off his kaftan and climbed to the crenelated lip of the wall. Last time, he hadn't been ready for the fight. Last time, he'd lost his grip on the horns behind the sand serpent's head.

This time, he would do better. He had to.

"Raider—no!"

Raider's heart leaped at Seth's shout. He looked back to see Seth racing along the empty street, sword in hand, chakram at his side. Damn it! Seth was a lot faster than he looked.

Raider faced the sand serpent again, readying himself as the huge head snaked toward the broken gate. With so much potential prey, it didn't respond to Raider's insignificant presence on the city wall.

When the head came within range, Raider leaped down. He landed at his mark, just behind the sand serpent's head, narrowly missing the venomous spines running along the creature's back.

The impact would have been little more than a nuisance to the massive creature, but it still jerked in response. This time, however, Raider was ready. He managed to get a firm grip on the horns with his bare right hand. Drawing back his left, he punched down as hard as he could at the base of the sand serpent's skull. His brutally studded quicksilver fist cracked the scale—and the sand serpent shrieked.

The creature lashed, writhing back from the broken gate, tossing its head with titanic force. For a moment, the world went crazy and Raider could do nothing but hang on.

When the sand serpent suddenly stopped thrashing but instead coiled its body, drawing back to hiss at something, it took Raider a second to get his bearings. Then he heard the high whistle of the chakram. He saw it flash in the sun as it arced back to Seth's arcane glove, clearly having struck the sand serpent.

Seth caught the chakram and hooked it onto his belt. Sword in one hand, Seth reached for something else on his belt. Raider had no time to see any more. He didn't even have time to be furious with Seth for drawing the sand serpent's deadly attention.

Hauling back his quicksilver arm, Raider punched again at the cracked scale. This time, as the massive head whipped in response to the blow, Raider nearly lost his grip—but it wasn't because of the momentum. It was because movement caught his eye. Impossible movement.

For a split second, Raider thought that Seth was actually flying. He soared through the air in a sweeping arc and came zooming toward the sand serpent's head. He had his sword high and ready. His other arm was outstretched ... grasping his multi tool. The wire, its harpoon-like barb lodged somewhere in the sand serpent face, was retracting, drawing Seth straight to the creature's head.

Raider could only watch, dumbfounded, as Seth came flying in to land on the bony ridge of the sand serpent's snout. The instant Seth's feet touched down, he struck down with his heavy sword—straight into the creature's eye.

When the sand serpent screamed and thrashed, dislodging the sword, Seth had no hope of keeping his feet. Raider shouted in horror as Seth was flung off. They were so high, Seth would never survive the fall.

But Seth had managed to keep hold of his multi tool. For a moment anyway. Long enough to delay his fall. But, inevitably, he lost his grip.

When he lost sight of Seth, Raider punched frantically at the weakened scale. The sand serpent's head shook then whipped high. Raider hung on desperately, hitting as hard as he could. The scale shattered.

Raider punched into the raw, exposed flesh, but he could tell even with the first blow that the legends were wrong. The flesh was too dense. There was no vulnerability in this thing, no weak point that a man could possibly break through. Raider would never be able to hammer bluntly through that flesh before the creature's violent lashing managed to unseat him.

But he had a more immediate problem.

As the sand serpent arched high, fangs bared, Raider spotted Seth far below on the ground. He was on his feet, sword in hand—and he had all of the sand serpent's deadly attention.

It didn't matter how fast Seth was, how strong, how precise. The sand serpent's strike would kill him.

The world receded.

Raider ceased to think. He only felt, and what he felt was terror and rage and absolute, desperate need.

And the quicksilver answered.

As it had on that day when Asha had been in danger, the quicksilver roared through Raider's body. It shot through his right shoulder, cascading down that arm. It spiked viciously through his legs and along his spine.

As the sand serpent struck down toward Seth, Raider did not consciously command the quicksilver. It responded as intuitively as his own hands—but with so much more power.

The quicksilver punched, spear-like, through the sand serpent's scaled body to burst through its throat. The liquid metal lengthened and thinned and hooked back to spear through the creature again. Then the strands of quicksilver wrapped around and around its neck.

The sand serpent's broken shriek cut off entirely as the quicksilver bound its punctured throat, tightening and tightening. The creature thrashed in desperation and agony as the quicksilver cut deep into its flesh like razor-sharp wire, slicing muscle, severing nerves and blood vessels until it wrapped around the creature's spine.

Raider didn't hear his own shout of fury. He barely registered the way the sand serpent plummeted—and him with it. But he did hear the sickening crack of bone as the spine broke. And he felt the booming impact with the ground as its body collapsed—and the massive head tumbled free.

The severing dislodged Raider and sent him thudding across the hard pack. The quicksilver whipped brightly through the air as it retracted into the armor.

Raider rolled to a stop and lay on his back, stunned by the impact and the sudden silence and the terrifying foreignness of his own body. Quicksilver still encased his limbs and jutted from his spine. It extended up his neck and across part of his face.

Footsteps pounded across the hard pack. "Raider!"

Raider didn't move, didn't blink. Seth slammed to his knees beside him and dropped his sword. His hands hovered over Raider. Over the quicksilver.

"Are you hurt?" Seth asked, his eyes wide with shock. "Raider? Are you ... okay?"

When Raider still didn't respond, Seth's hands went from hovering to exploring, hunting for injuries amid the metal. Raider flinched away from the touch. He sat up.

The quicksilver armor encased his limbs in pearlescent ridges and spikes. He felt its cool touch over his back and face. He closed his eyes and tried to breathe, but it wouldn't go away.

"Raider—say something."

Raider glanced at Seth's shocked face and away. He climbed to his feet and stared at the colossal, inert body of the sand serpent. Its black coils stretched across the hard pack. Its massive, vicious head had tumbled toward the city wall and lay facing the mudbrick. It seemed to stare at Aqarat, though one eye was ruptured and the other was just as sightless.

Seth, who had also gotten to his feet, followed Raider's gaze and breathed, "*Gods.*"

Seth bent and picked up his sword. He swiped it clean on his pants then sheathed it at his back. Raider could feel Seth's gaze on him again.

Seth said, "Come on," and jerked his head toward the broken gates. He took a step and stopped. "Raider. Come on."

Raider blinked and looked at Seth, actually looked at him. Seth had a nasty scrape along one elbow and would no doubt have some awful bruises, but he was alive. He wasn't maimed. He was *alive*.

Raider breathed out in belated relief, and the quicksilver retracted with a *shhhhkt*, baring his skin and new, unfamiliar wounds.

Seth reached back and took Raider's hand. He squeezed Raider's fingers. Raider didn't squeeze back, but he did let Seth tug him forward. They walked across the hard pack, Seth's eyes flicking sideways to him every few seconds.

As they neared the wall, Seth let go of Raider's hand and walked up to the massive, severed head. Raider stopped and crossed his arms over his bare torso. Movement caught his eye, making him look up.

Malik stood atop the city wall, watching.

Raider dropped his eyes to Seth as the Curator grabbed hold of something on the sand serpent's face and tugged. It came free abruptly, sending Seth staggering back.

Watching Seth inspect his multi tool, Raider felt part of his brain wake up. He said, a little angry, "You're fucking unbelievable."

Seth swiped the prongs clean on his vest then retracted the folding barb into its housing. "Why would I leave it there?"

"Why would you *put* it there?"

Seth slid the device into his belt with a grin.

Raider loved when Seth grinned. He didn't do it often, and Raider wondered how many people had ever seen it at all. It was so damn gorgeous. *Seth* was so damn gorgeous. Tough. Strong. Fucking fearless.

Raider would never forget the sight of Seth flying toward the sand serpent's head, of him landing on the creature's snout and striking his sword into its eye.

Raider wished, deeply, fiercely, that he hadn't found that goddamn book so he could take Seth's grin all the way into himself. He wished he could throw his arms around Seth and feel how alive and whole he was. He wished he could feel Seth's arms around him and believe, even if only for this moment, that it was a safe place to be. That it was *his* place to be.

But all of that was impossible.

Because Raider *had* found that book. And because he was too afraid to find out whether Seth had lied to him. He didn't want to know, not yet. He wasn't ready. Not with so many memories ripping him up inside, making him way too vulnerable.

He had pushed those memories back during the fight, but he could feel them clawing their way through him again, seizing tight around his heart, his lungs, his throat.

Seth's grin faltered. "Come on," he said again, and Raider followed him. Again.

Raider cast a final look back at the sand serpent. He shuddered at the knowledge that he had killed it, that he was capable of such a thing. Because of what Kahzir had made him into.

An arcane instrument, as Seth had once called him.

A weapon.

Raider cast his eyes down and navigated the debris of the shattered gate. Malik had come down from the wall. He handed Raider his kaftan.

If Raider had looked at Malik as he took the red silk, he might have seen how the arcanist regarded him with narrowed eyes. If Raider hadn't been so fixated on the question of whether Seth knew who—what—he was, he might have asked himself whether Malik did.

But Raider was using all of his focus to keep his face from showing every fucking fear and every fucking doubt that was eating him up inside.

He barely even heard Malik say, "The gods must have sent you to us. Come. A magnificent dinner is the least of what Aqarat owes you."

Chapter 36

SETH DIDN'T LIKE how quiet Raider had been since the sand serpent fight. It could have been the shock of the fight, a delayed reaction to the danger, but Seth didn't think so. Except for a brief interaction as Seth had worked his multi tool free of the sand serpent's head, Raider had withdrawn into a tense, troubled silence.

Was it the quicksilver?

This shit, Raider had called it once, and Seth had no doubt that the quicksilver lay at the heart of Raider's nightmares. Beyond that, however, Seth couldn't guess. Raider had told him nothing.

Raider had certainly not told him that the quicksilver could do what Seth had seen it do today. Seth shivered at the memory as he finished dressing for dinner. Maybe he was feeling some delayed shock himself.

When he had raced through the broken gateway to meet the full sight of the sand serpent, with Raider atop it, Seth's heart had stopped. The fight had been impossible. But that hadn't mattered—because it had also been unavoidable.

It was Seth who had, inadvertently, woken the sand serpent. Even if that hadn't been the case, it wouldn't have mattered. He'd had to try. For all the people who would have died. For Raider, who would have died—or so Seth had thought. That had been before he'd seen the full, terrifying power of Raider's quicksilver.

Gods, Raider had *killed a sand serpent*. And he'd done it with chilling arcane weaponry.

No wonder Raider was so confident in any fight, in any journey. Who could possibly defeat him?

It troubled Seth. He wanted to feel nothing but relief that Raider was alive, that he'd managed to stop that creature from destroying Aqarat, but he had too many questions.

Why did Raider have that quicksilver—and why couldn't he remember? Or was that not true?

Those nightmares.

They said, if nothing else, that Raider remembered *something*. Something he had never told Seth.

It bothered him. It always had, no matter how hard he'd tried to put it from his mind. It had always been there, niggling at him—that same niggling he got when people lied.

Something was off. Something bad. Seth couldn't identify it, but he could feel it.

Raider had barely looked at him as they had walked with Malik back to the palace. And when they had reached the doors to their rooms, Raider hadn't even glanced Seth's way before going into his own room. Raider hadn't entered his own room since their first day in the palace. He had stayed with Seth. Until now.

What the hell was going on with him?

And what the hell was Seth's problem that he didn't go over there and demand to know?

Seth's problem was that he knew that Raider wouldn't answer him. He never had. And if Raider refused, still, to talk about it, Seth didn't know what he'd do. Seth had managed, so far, to ignore everything that Raider had refused to discuss. But Seth couldn't ignore it now, not after what he'd just seen. He couldn't let Raider keep hiding things from him, but he wasn't ready, yet, to face the possibility that Raider didn't love him enough, didn't trust him enough, to tell him the truth.

Because what the fuck would Seth do if that was the case? What would that mean … for them?

Stop being a fucking coward, he scolded himself. *Just go over there.*

As Seth tugged on his sandals and straightened his tunic, he eyed his dusty Curator's garb longingly. He didn't like these loose, lightweight clothes. They made him feel too exposed, too vulnerable. Seth never liked that, but he especially hated it now. Something was off, and it put him on edge. It made him feel like he needed to be ready to fight.

Grabbing onto some goddamn courage, Seth walked out onto the balcony. In the distance, the colossal body of the beheaded sand serpent coiled and looped away into the desert twilight. People thronged the wall, eager now to see what had almost destroyed their lives.

It shamed Seth, seeing it again. Raider had risked his life to save all those people. Did it matter what lay in his past, how and why he had the quicksilver, if it had given him the power to do that?

No.

Yes.

Seth wasn't sure. He wasn't even sure what bothered him most. The possibility that Raider's quicksilver was tied to something bad? Or the simple fact that Raider wouldn't fucking talk to him about it?

He rapped on the latticed door into Raider's room. When there was no answer, Seth called Raider's name. At the continued silence, Seth opened the door and found the room empty. Frowning, he returned to his own room and walked through to the hallway door. He opened it—and found Raider waiting in the foyer with a dhoti-clad servant.

Damn it, now Seth *couldn't* talk to him.

This wasn't the first time that Seth's hesitancy had cost him a chance to speak with Raider. It had happened before, when they'd first arrived in Aqarat. Seth was never this hesitant. What the hell was it about Raider that twisted Seth up inside and made him afraid?

Raider's amber eyes flicked to Seth and away. Like maybe he, too, was afraid.

But of what? Of *Seth*?

Surely not. And yet, it kind of felt that way as they both fell into silent step behind the servant as he led them through the palace to the prince's private garden.

The summons, which had arrived as Seth was bathing, had indicated the private nature of the dinner, more exclusive than the usual nightly feast in the grand dining hall. It wasn't out of line, not after the defeat of the sand serpent, but Seth was still relieved, as the servant led them along the grassy pathway to the garden's wide lawn, to see the long, low table already crowded with courtiers.

Why should the presence of others be a relief? Seth couldn't pin down a reason. All he knew was that he felt uneasy.

It was a shame, really, to be on edge right now because even Atri, goddess of love, beauty, and the arts, would have given this garden dinner her blessing.

Bright, multicolored birds twittered in wicker cages. Peacocks strutted through the grass. Courtiers as colorful as the birds sat on silk cushions around the long, low table covered in a white cloth. A woman clad only in ropes of pearls sat apart from the others on a plump cushion, playing a pear-shaped, stringed barboud, filling the air with its deep, hauntingly romantic tones.

On the table, golden bowls held grapes and quartered oranges, candied almonds and plump dates. Servants in gauzy robes or white dhotis poured dark wine from silver carafes, and steam billowed within the glass bellies of several hookahs. Smoky incense threaded through the air, heady frankincense and myrrh and something sharp that Seth couldn't identify, all of it mingling with the garden's sweet scents of jasmine and rose.

Their guiding servant bowed them toward a pair of tasseled cushions at what would clearly be the prince's end of the table, judging by the extreme opulence. Crystal cups and golden utensils. A veritable mountain of cushions. A slender boy standing ready with a palm-frond fan.

To the left of the empty cushions sat Lord Malik, who gave them a sharply elegant smile from within the tidy frame of his goatee. The arcanist was dressed in a kaftan of deep purple silk embroidered with green and silver over matching shalvar pants. Gold bangles clinked together on his slim wrist as he raised his cup of wine.

"I was right," Malik observed over the rim of his cup.

"About what?" Seth asked sharply as he seated himself beside the arcanist, too edgy to mind his tone.

Malik, however, didn't react to his sharpness. He smiled. "A bath improved you both."

"Oh. Yes."

Malik was referring to their first conversation when he had extended Prince Rahim's invitation to the palace, when Raider had questioned why the prince would welcome two ragged travelers.

Raider certainly didn't look ragged now. He was dressed in shalvar pants of rose-colored silk and a sleeveless shirt of fine white linen. He wore no adornments and didn't need them. He was absolutely, completely beautiful.

Sitting here beside him, amid all the romantic splendor of the garden and the elegant table, with the music and the heady scents, Seth wanted him, fiercely and abruptly. He wanted to tear off his own green silk tunic and pants, wanted to tear off Raider's clothes right here, right now, and bear him down into the grass. He wanted to grind his thickening cock against this man he still, somehow, couldn't trust but still, in spite of that, loved.

Seth shook the thought away. Gods. What the hell was wrong with him? This was neither the time nor the place for such thoughts.

As a slim male servant poured wine into Seth and Raider's cups, Malik idly chatted about the garden's exotic plants and the table's succulent offerings, his conversation weirdly sidestepping the monumental events of the afternoon.

It wasn't that Seth had anything he wanted to say to Malik about it, but it felt strange to have it hovering in the background, unacknowledged, while the sand serpent's body lay just beyond the city wall.

As the dusky light faded away, glass-globed lanterns bloomed, casting a mellow, wavering light over the gathered company.

When Prince Rahim entered the garden dressed in silky white, wearing a cloth-of-gold turban studded with diamonds, everyone rose from their cushions, bowing until the prince seated himself at the head of the table. The musician had stopped but began to play again at Rahim's impatient flick of a finger. Then servants brought out tureens of soup, baskets of bread, and platters of meat and seasoned vegetables.

While they ate and drank, Malik made frequent contact with Seth, laying fingers on his arm, leaning near to speak. In fact, there was a lot of that happening around the table.

And Seth ... goddamn it, but he could not get his erection to go away. All it had taken was that brief fantasy of bearing Raider down into the grass, of seeking the hard length of him, of watching his body arch—

What the hell was wrong with him? He needed to talk to Raider, not fuck him. Even if that weren't the case, it couldn't happen right now anyway. He didn't know why his thoughts were running that direction.

Besides, it was *Malik's* fingers brushing his as the arcanist reached for the bowl of candied almonds. It was *Malik's* chuckle in his ear.

Seth glanced at Rahim, wary of his reaction to Malik's flirtation. During the two previous dinners, Seth had exchanged only a few words with the prince, but observation had told him what words had not.

As Raider had so quickly recognized, Malik and Rahim were lovers, but the relationship had many other layers. Malik was Rahim's arcanist and counselor and representative—and Rahim needed him. Where Rahim's speech was curt and sharp, Malik was silver tongued. While Rahim luxuriated in his royal security, Malik navigated the court and city.

None of that, however, changed the fact that power, ultimately, lay with the prince. And the prince, though reserved, had a temper. Seth had heard him snap at Malik and at servants. He was also touchy about ruling such a remote outpost of the empire.

Seth vividly recalled Rahim's response to Seth's compliment when he had feasted at the royal table that first night.

I suppose you did not expect such richness amid the Gold's wasteland.

Only Malik's clever tongue had saved Seth from stumbling through a response to that loaded statement. The prince's hard eyes had softened, and he'd turned his attention to where his dancers had been whirling about in their shimmering chains. As Raider had noted that first night, the chains spoke clearly of ownership.

With the complexities of Rahim and Malik's relationship, Seth wasn't sure how the prince's possessiveness applied to his arcanist. Malik had not hidden his flirtation with Seth, but he'd never flaunted it either.

Until now.

With his wary glance, Seth saw Prince Rahim's eyes harden. In spite of that, the prince's cheeks were flushed. Seth's probably were too.

Malik distracted Seth by reaching past him to take up the nearest hookah. As the arcanist lifted its hose to his lips, a silver shimmer caught Seth's eye across the table. It was a delicate silver bracelet encircling the wrist of a beautiful, dark-skinned woman. She wore a similar decoration around her neck.

But it wasn't a decoration, not exactly, and everyone around the table was thus adorned.

These were Rahim's beautiful dancers, feasting and smoking and beginning to put their lips to more than food and wine. Why would the prince populate this table with his slaves—pampered ones, but still slaves—instead of courtiers?

The smoke from the incense burners and hookahs rendered the scene hazy and almost dreamlike. Seth waved a thread of it away, which seemed to drift from one of the burners straight to him, assaulting him with its sharp, unknown scent. Mixed with the frankincense and myrrh and the muskiness of the hookah smoke, he couldn't parse it out.

Raider's fingers gripped Seth's thigh. He leaned drunkenly into Seth and spoke for the first time all evening. "Seth, I think—" Raider broke off coughing, and Seth coughed too as Malik blew smoke into their faces.

Seth looked angrily at the arcanist, who only gave Seth his usual, unruffled smile, though his cheeks, too, were flushed. Before Seth could say anything, his mind seemed to fog over. Then he totally lost his train of thought as Raider's fingers slid up his inner thigh to his groin.

Eyes closing, Seth sucked in a breath at the shock of arousal—then coughed again on the sharp, almost bitter smoke. For half a second, that alerted him, but then Raider's hand was on Seth's hard cock and nothing else seemed to matter.

Seth turned toward Raider—practically fell into him—and bore him to the ground as he'd imagined doing. Part of Seth's brain recognized that something was wrong, that there was a fog in his mind, that his arousal was too strong and out of place.

But everything seemed to recede as Raider bowed up under him—just as Seth had known that he would. Seth sought Raider's cock through his silk pants, groaning to find him so beautifully hard. Seth ground his own cock against Raider's thigh while his lips explored Raider's throat, enjoying the vibration of his moan.

"Give me more antidote," someone said. "The quiva is strong."

Quiva?

Antidote?

Incense was everywhere, too many scents, and the light dazzled him. Seth couldn't focus on anything other than the hard cock in his hand.

Seth shook his head. Something was wrong.

"Hit him with the smoke again."

Smoke wafted into Seth's nose, dizzying him. He laid his head down and felt the heavy beat of Raider's heart, felt how limp Raider was despite his hard cock.

Like he'd been after the jackal fight. After the quiva.

Quiva.

Seth took his hand away.

"The Curator's getting up. He knows something's wrong."

"Deal with him."

A cloth soaked in something floral-smelling covered Seth's mouth. He drove an elbow back into someone's gut and heard a grunt.

Seth spun, furious, hunting for assailants. Then all his anger disintegrated into a haze. He was falling.

As he hit the ground, he saw Raider's face turn toward him, saw the glaze of his amber eyes, saw his lips part as he mouthed, *Seth*.

Then everything was gone.

CHAPTER 37

SETH DRIFTED TO semi-consciousness to the sound of nearby voices. With his eyes too heavy to open and his body too heavy to move, all he could do was listen.

"Don't be absurd. It was the quiva."

"And was it quiva the first night? Or the second?"

A weary sigh answered that. "Your temper, my prince, is clouding your judgment. This was the plan from the start: for me to test their relationship."

"*Your* plan, I recall. Did you enjoy it?"

"Might we focus on our success? You have, at last, the means of commanding Zarina's attention—"

"You make me sound like a child."

Another weary sigh. From Malik, Seth's hazy brain was beginning to realize. "At least let us focus on what we've learned. The Curator is clearly in love with him and, more importantly, was not wholly surprised by the quicksilver."

"An accomplice, then?"

Accomplice?

Trying to wake up, Seth drew a noisier breath than he intended. The two men fell silent. When Seth blinked his eyes open, he found himself staring blearily at his lap. He was in a chair, his head hanging—and his hands were bound to the chair arms.

Seth's head whipped up. The room spun.

"Easy," Malik said.

Seth closed his eyes until the spinning stopped and the nausea subsided. He had to be calm. He had to think. He had to figure out what the hell was going on.

Subtly testing his bonds, Seth opened his eyes. He was in some kind of arcane workroom. Malik's workroom. The arcanist, still in his finery from dinner, stood beside a worktable. The studied flirtation was gone. He regarded Seth with cool, dispassionate eyes. The prince at his side, however, was glaring.

"What the hell is going on?" Seth asked with as much calm as he could manage. He and Raider had been tricked. Drugged. No wonder the gathering had been populated by Rahim's enslaved dancers. They had no choice but to play along with their master. "Where the hell is Raider?"

"You can't guess?" Malik asked.

Seth stared at him. How the fuck would he be able to guess?

"Your lover," Prince Rahim informed Seth, "is in the dungeon."

The room spun again. Seth's chest tightened. What the fuck was going on?

"What do you know about the death of Emperor Hassan?"

Seth focused on the speaker, Malik, with an effort. The arcanist was studying him, his eyes flicking away only when the prince started pacing. Malik displayed no such impatience but simply rested a hip against the worktable. Behind him, on the shelves above the table, stood rows of jars containing a wide array of powders and other materials.

Malik had never told Seth his specialty, but it was clearly divination. Diviners used the properties of various metals, stones, and organic matter to trigger reactions in items of study. They might determine the age of an object or learn whether a tissue sample showed signs of disease.

They also aided authorities with interrogations ... by administering drugs that rendered suspects more vulnerable to questioning.

Seth thought back to the garden. He'd been drugged with quiva and maybe poppy. They had seized him and Raider by the gentlest and safest means possible: seduction. They had used Seth and Raider's relationship to render them vulnerable.

Had they administered other drugs to Seth while he had been unconscious? Likely so. He felt loose and floaty in his body. Open. He didn't like it.

Resisting a powerful impulse to answer Malik's question about Emperor Hassan's death, Seth demanded, "What the hell does that have to do with anything?"

"Answer the question!" Rahim snapped, wheeling to face Seth. When Malik raised a placating hand, the prince took a deep breath and straightened his silky white tunic.

"Answer the question," Malik echoed more calmly.

Seth's answer spilled out. "He was assassinated by his brother, Kahzir." It was common knowledge. Why were they asking him this?

"Not directly," Prince Rahim said with disturbing relish, his eyes glinting like the diamond pins in his cloth-of-gold turban. "Someone else did the deed. A fact revealed by this book."

Rahim strode back toward Malik, who picked up a leather-bound book from the worktable. As the arcanist handed the book to the prince, Seth glimpsed the cover.

"Is that—"

"The book you've been after, yes," Malik replied.

Seth's anger spilled out as easily as his words. "You've had it this whole fucking time? So why the goddamn charade? You spent two fucking days pretending to help me hunt for—" Seth cut himself off. "Wait. If you have the book, do you have Julian as well? Is he *here*? What the hell—"

"It's not for you to ask questions," Rahim snarled.

Seth yanked at the ropes binding his arms to the chair. "You have no right—"

"I have every right, you insolent dog!"

"My love," Malik soothed. "Please. Allow me to serve you in this."

Rahim made a sound of disgust but relented, stalking away to the window.

"Julian is not here," Malik told Seth. "He arrived in Aqarat four days ahead of you. He was almost as conspicuous as you, entering through the western gate, ragged from desert travel. It's my duty to investigate all suspicious visitors, so I approached him. He tried to flee. I caught him, but he had in his service an ifrit. It helped him get away—but I had hold of his pack, which contained this book.

"I did not know the man's name until you came along, looking for a missing arcanist with a stolen book. By then, I had studied the volume and knew its significance, and I, too, wanted to find your fugitive. I made you visible in the city in the hopes of spurring him to foolish, visible action. I had already, of course, talked to all the people you wanted to talk to."

Seth reeled at the information. "Why the hell didn't you tell me all this?"

"Because I didn't know your connection to him, nor your role in larger events."

"Why not just drug me and ask me from the start?" Seth snarled.

A slight smile tugged at Malik's lips. "Because the answer was worth less than your unknowing participation in my own hunt, though it had not yet yielded anything before certain … revelations shifted our focus."

Seth ignored the parts of that that he couldn't understand. "Julian is a fugitive of the *Arcanum*. His crime was committed in *Masir*. So what the hell do you care about it?"

Malik's eyes flicked across the room. Seth followed his gaze to Rahim, who had put his back to the window and was eyeing Seth once again.

"Are you convinced yet?" Malik asked the prince.

Convinced of what?

Rahim replied, "Even if he's truly ignorant of the book's import and of Julian's purpose, whatever that may be, there's still the other, larger matter."

"Indeed."

The prince fixed Seth with a glare. "What is your relationship with the man who calls himself Raider?"

Seth blinked. Why had Rahim phrased it like that? More importantly: "What the hell does that have to do with anything?"

"Other than fucking," Rahim clarified harshly without answering Seth's question.

Seth's jaw clenched, but he found himself answering anyway. "I hired him to guide me across the Kesh to Aqarat. Which he did. *Why?*"

"And you were aware of his quicksilver?"

"I had seen some of it, yes," Seth admitted, unable to repress the answer, though he did manage to add, "Again, *why?*"

Seth still got no answer but only another question, this time from Malik. "What do you think is its purpose?"

"To fight, obviously. What the hell else would it be—"

"Not its function. Its *purpose*. Why does he have it?"

Seth stilled. That had been his own question for a long time. "I don't know. He never told me."

Seth might have said, *He doesn't remember*, but those weren't the words that had slipped out of his mouth under the influence of whatever drug he'd been given—because he didn't believe that. He never had.

Seth asked more calmly, "What is going on?"

Rahim opened the book to its title page. Walking to Seth, he turned the book to show it to him. Seth read the bold, inked-in title: *The Masterwork of Kahzir*.

Seth's mind reeled. "Why would Julian steal a book about—or written by?—Kahzir? And what does that have to do with Raider?"

Malik said, "We have no more idea than you why Julian stole the book, though it is certainly a book that some would murder for."

Rahim turned the book toward himself and flipped through its pages with the same disturbing relish that Seth had perceived earlier. "This book records Kahzir's process of making the perfect assassin. Due to the unique nature of that work, the assassin's identity is unmistakable."

Seth's head spun as he fought to hold off the conclusions to which his mind tried to leap.

Then Malik spoke, forcing him to those very conclusions. "Seth, the question remains: what do you think is the purpose of your lover's quicksilver?"

The world seemed to shift. Everything shattered. And when the broken pieces settled, they shaped a totally different reality.

Seth shook his head, not ready to accept any of that, desperate for some other truth. "Let me talk to him," he begged. "Please."

✧ ✧ ✧

Free of his bonds, Seth followed Malik and Rahim from the arcanist's workroom down to the lower levels of the palace. The prince and arcanist had briefly argued about bringing the book. The workroom, apparently, had some sort of arcane booby trap that prevented theft, thus keeping the room's contents secure. Malik had wanted to leave the book behind, but Rahim had insisted on seeing Raider's reaction to it.

Seth had asked to see the thing but, being denied, hadn't fought for it. It would take too long to go through the book anyway, and it was more important to see Raider. That was the only thread that Seth could follow among his frayed thoughts. It was all he could think about. Otherwise, he might have recognized the large tabby cat with citrine eyes that came prowling through the shadows of the palace foyer.

Seth, Malik, and Rahim were walking along the shallow evaporative cooling pool when the prince yelped. One knee buckling, Rahim flung up his hands to keep his balance. The book flew from his grasp.

The cat darted out from behind the prince and leaped into the air … where it turned into blue smoke.

Spindly little fingers emerged from the smoke to snatch the book from the air before the ifrit solidified from the waist up into a vaguely human form. Below that, blue smoke continued to drift. Blue skinned and hairless, the ifrit remained about the same size that the cat had been. Small, curved horns protruded from its temples. Only the citrine eyes were unchanged. They flashed with mischief.

"A trade!" Malik cried, clearly thinking fast. "The book for riches! Gold!"

But the ifrit laughed wickedly and darted away, zooming through the air, lugging the heavy volume. Seth raced after it, splashing through the shallow pool, but the ifrit zipped through a window and into the night.

Rahim shouted quick orders at the guards flanking the palace's front doors. They hauled the doors open and hurried after the ifrit, but they couldn't possibly catch it. The devious little thing was long gone.

Seth walked back through the shallow pool and stepped out, streaming water. The bottom half of his silk pants clung to his legs.

Rahim twisted around, inspecting his calf. "It bit me!"

"Julian's?" Seth guessed. "You said he had an ifrit."

And not just any ifrit, but the one that had approached Seth and Raider in the bazaar. It must have been gathering information for Julian.

"It could be no other," Malik snapped, more upset than Seth had ever heard him. "I need to return to my workroom and see if I can locate—"

"You need to conduct an interrogation," Rahim told him. "Neither the book nor the arcanist are as important as the assassin."

Seth's breath caught at the word. Assassin. *Raider*. It couldn't be.

Could it?

They reached the guarded dungeon entrance without further incident. The guard opened the heavy door. They descended the steps, Seth dripping and Rahim limping, and came into the open space outside the cells.

Raider was the only prisoner. Still wearing the rose-colored shalvar pants and sleeveless white tunic, he sat at the back of his cell against the stone wall. His knees were drawn up, his forearms resting on them. If he was worried, it didn't show. He was utterly still and looked, if anything, resigned.

Clearly, Raider wasn't surprised by this.

Seth's hope dimmed, but he still said, "Tell me it's not true. Tell *them* it's not true. They're saying—"

"You killed Emperor Hassan," Rahim announced, striding past Seth. "Admit it." When Raider didn't respond, Rahim snapped his fingers at Malik. "More of the serum! He will talk."

"It's too dangerous to go in there with him," Malik argued. "Half an hour of smoke and he'll pass out, then I can dose him again. In the meantime, I'll attempt to track—"

"The Curator can do it." The prince's eyes glinted, triumphant.

A jolt of fear got Seth's sluggish thoughts churning past the point they'd been stuck on: hearing Raider, finally, explain himself. But that was a bad idea if Raider was guilty. Rahim was a prince, a distant cousin of the empress—and he was far too thrilled by all this.

It wasn't a desire for justice or even revenge that had Rahim's eyes glinting like that. The prince saw advantage in this, advantage for himself.

Scattered memories fitted themselves together into a new picture. The prince's touchiness about his remote post:

I suppose you did not expect such richness amid the Gold's wasteland.

The exchange between Malik and Rahim as Seth had been waking groggily in the workroom:

Might we focus on our success? You have, at last, the means of commanding Zarina's attention—

You make me sound like a child.

Then there were Rahim's varied and extravagant possessions. His beautiful slaves. His feasts. His clothing. His arcane toys such as the flying-carpet litter.

The prince craved status. Significance. Attention. And having the emperor's assassin in his hands could give him all of that.

Seth jumped when Malik handed him a syringe. Fuck. This was really happening.

Seth could refuse. But if he did, they would resort to the smoke, subdue Raider, and dose him anyway. And Seth would then have broken their trust.

But if he walked in there and injected Raider with drugs against his will, he would break Raider's trust. Seth hated that idea, even if Raider had broken Seth's trust first. Unless, by some chance, through some explanation, none of this was true.

Malik unlocked the cell door and pulled it open. Raider made no move. With his quicksilver, he could have.

Hell, with his quicksilver, surely he could have already broken out of here?

Seth stepped into the cell. Raider's amber eyes tracked his movement, but Seth couldn't read those eyes. They were so carefully neutral.

The cell door clanged shut.

As Seth approached, Raider remained still, so damn still. Even when Seth crouched beside him, Raider didn't react.

But when Seth picked up Raider's left arm and rotated it to expose his vein, Raider closed his eyes and shuddered. And, this close, Seth could perceive what Raider had been trying to hide. His short, shallow breathing. His racing pulse, visibly fluttering in his neck.

Maybe it was the confinement bothering him. Maybe it was dread of what was coming. Maybe it having Seth be the one to approach him with that needle.

As Seth pulled Raider's arm into him, the movement exposed the wound in his shoulder, which his shirt had been covering. His other shoulder had a similar wound, and Seth knew that more marked his back. He had seen it, all of it, after the sand serpent fight.

Raider didn't resist and didn't flinch, not even when Seth pricked his vein, but he did make a small sound in his throat. Like it hurt him, on some deep, non-physical level, that Seth would do this.

It hurt Seth too, even though he knew his own intentions. It was the idea of it. Doing this to Raider. Even if he was an assassin. Even if everything had been a lie.

Because if that book incriminated Raider? He had likely intended to steal it from Seth.

Raider hadn't known about the book when Seth had hired him, but Seth had described the book to him during their journey. Though Raider had flirted from day one, it hadn't been until later, until after Seth had told him about the book, that he'd tied Seth's heart in knots. Had he done it on purpose?

Maybe.

But, intentional or not, it had happened. Seth's heart *was* in knots—and no degree of logic or principle could untie it.

And that was why Seth withdrew the needle and squirted the serum onto his already wet pants, outside of Raider's vein, leaving only the tiny blood spot to suggest otherwise.

Raider's eyes opened and met Seth's. They weren't so neutral now. They were full of sorrow and regret and a hopeless sort of yearning.

Seth had seen so many different things in Raider's expressive eyes. Amusement and mischief. Passion and need. Torment and fear. Seth had seen Raider's strikingly beautiful face in so many lights and moods. Seth had seen and touched his gorgeous body in so many ways.

Seth's heart ached at those memories—because they might have been real, but they had never been fully honest. Raider's body and mind had so many secrets. And, even now, Seth would not learn them.

Seth dropped Raider's arm and stood, backing away to make sure that Malik and Rahim could see the spot of blood. Seth passed the empty syringe through the bars to Malik.

With a note of satisfaction in his voice, Rahim asked, "Did you kill Emperor Hassan?"

And Raider, despite not having been injected with the compulsive drug, despite being a very good liar, said, "Yes."

The meaning of the word, the significance of it, took a moment to hit Seth. "What? Why would you say that?"

"Because it's true. I killed the emperor."

"Wait," Rahim all but purred, stepping up to the bars, his tone shifting back to that awful relish. "I remember you now. Gods, I should have seen it from the start. I only saw you with him once, the day he assigned me this post, but I should have recognized you, even if you have filled out since then. You're that street rat Hassan took to his bed."

Seth reeled. "What are you talking about? Raider, what is he ..." Seth trailed off as Raider met his gaze with bleak eyes.

"It's true. I was ... with him. Then I killed him."

Seth staggered and caught himself against the bars. A political assassination was bad enough, but to kill a lover? And his lover had been the *emperor*?

Seth couldn't process it all. It whirled through his brain. Amid that chaos, however, one thought settled, one truth became, at last, wholly undeniable.

"You lied. About your memory. You knew all along what you'd done. That you'd killed a man you ..."

Fucked?

Loved?

Seth's brain scrambled to cast everything in a different light. What if there was a reason for all this, a good reason? What if Raider had done all this to destroy a tyrant? The little that Seth knew about Emperor Hassan didn't suggest that he'd been cruel, but royal reputations tended to be more fiction than fact.

Seth heard the desperation in his own voice as he asked, "Was he a bad—"

"He was a good man," Raider said, clearly seeing the direction of Seth's desperate thoughts. "And, yes, I loved him and I killed him and I lied to you."

For the second time tonight, everything shattered— including Seth's heart.

But Seth had to think, had to speak. So he let the broken pieces of his heart grate together, let the pain of that fill his voice as he said, "I wish I'd never met you, you lying piece of shit."

At Raider's flinch, Seth turned away and stalked to the cell door, which Malik swung open for him. Seth heard it clang shut, but he didn't stop, didn't look back. He walked straight to the staircase and climbed it.

He wasn't important to Rahim and Malik anymore. He was no longer the assassin's lover, no longer a suspect. He was only a fool. So they didn't try to stop him as he left the dungeon and kept going, all the way to his room.

Chapter 38

I *WISH I'D NEVER met you, you lying piece of shit.*
Raider let those words crash through him again and again. He couldn't stop himself.

He'd driven Seth to those words on purpose. Because he deserved them. Because he was so damn exhausted by the hidden truths he'd been carrying, the lies he'd been telling. Because there was no point in lying anymore, not with that book. And because, if he had, Malik and Rahim would have known that Seth had not injected him.

That last fact was a tiny bright spot amid the darkness. Seth had not forced a compulsion on him. Seth had tried to protect him.

Of course, that confirmed what Raider had feared, that Seth had already known the truth. Seth had already known that Raider was guilty—and that could only be because he'd already known about the book.

The thing Seth hadn't known was that Raider had killed not only a political figure but a lover. It wasn't until Seth had learned that fact that he'd shattered Raider with his own truth:

I wish I'd never met you, you lying piece of shit.

But Seth had lied too. About the book. About whatever his intentions were toward Raider. Had Seth meant, all along, for Raider to end up in a cell?

Why, then, had Seth looked so devastated by Raider's confession? Why had he given Raider the chance to lie by not injecting him?

Nothing made sense anymore, and Raider couldn't think. He hadn't been able to think since he'd found that goddamn book.

Only a few things were clear. One, Seth was gone. And two, Raider was exactly where he'd always known he would end up: back in a cell.

He had thought, of course, about breaking out. He could at least try to flee. He should. But it was too inevitable, being here, so damn familiar that there was something almost comfortable about it.

Besides, after Seth had turned his back, Raider simply had no reason to break free. He couldn't go back to his life before Seth, his life without Seth. And now, there was no life *with* Seth. So there was no life for Raider at all and no reason to move.

It didn't even matter that Seth had lied to him, had likely intended to capture him. Even if everything with Seth had been a lie, it was a lie that had twisted too thoroughly around Raider's heart to unravel.

He loved Seth. In spite of everything. Regardless of Seth's intentions. He couldn't help it.

The door at the top of the stairs opened. Something thumped on the steps, then booted footsteps came tromping down. Raider knew that serious, intent tread, but he didn't believe it, couldn't believe it, until Seth stepped into the open space outside the cell. His jaw was set, his green eyes burning. He was wearing his Curator garb and all his weapons. He had his packs—*both* their packs—slung over his shoulder. Raider's scimitar was in his hand.

"Why the fuck are you still in there?" Seth demanded.

"What are you doing here?" Raider croaked, his throat so tight he could barely get the words out.

Instead of answering—or maybe as his answer—Seth set down Raider's scimitar, unshouldered the packs, and pulled his multi tool from his belt. He sequenced it for the lock pick. After making quick work of the cell's lock, he hauled the gate open.

"Get up," Seth ordered. "We have to move fast. We need to get to the tunnels before anyone checks here or in my room. I had to knock out the guard and drag him into the stairwell. Someone will eventually notice that he's gone."

With a hand on the wall for support, Raider pushed himself to his feet. "Why? Why are you doing this? You'll be a fugitive."

Seth's eyes blazed like emerald fire. "I'm not letting them kill you."

"Why not?"

"Because I—" Seth cut himself off. Jaw bunching, he looked away. The cords of his neck stood out with strain. Then he looked back at Raider and said harshly, "You don't need to know my reasons. You certainly didn't tell me yours. Now are you coming with me or not?"

Raider walked shakily out of the cell to meet Seth by the gear. As they each bent to grab their packs, their fingers brushed. They both froze.

In spite of everything, Raider wanted to grab Seth's hand. He wanted, desperately, just for one more second, to believe that everything between them had been real. But he also didn't want Seth to pull away and prove to him that it hadn't.

So Raider grabbed his pack and slung it over his shoulder. He picked up his scimitar. Shouldering his own gear, Seth led the way out.

And Raider followed him.

ABOUT THE AUTHOR

I hope you loved this first part of Seth and Raider's story. I can't wait to bring you more with their second book, *Silver & Gold*.

I can't express how much your support means to me—thank you for reading my work! If you loved Seth and Raider like I do, any extra love you're willing to show them through recommending, sharing, or reviewing is so, so appreciated. It's a huge part of what keeps these books coming!

A bit about me:

When I'm not writing, I'm most likely riding (or acting as servant to) my exceptionally opinionated horse. She has dictated more of my life than it's healthy to contemplate. I also love to draw, so I do most of my own covers. (Yep, I did this one—it took me a long time!) I also like to sew, garden, mountain bike, kayak, and hike. (Not that I have time for all those things …) In a nutshell, I like all things intense and "interesting": food, animals, adventures, and, of course, books.

If you're curious about my other romances, read on. FYI, my past work was MF (except for Book 4 in *The Vampire Defense Agency*, which is a delicious MM).

✶   ✶   ✶

If you're craving heat, action, grit, and just the right touch of humor, *The Vampire Defense Agency* will deliver in spades. This paranormal romance series features five intense, tormented, sexy-as-hell vampires. Working for the VDA (kind of their FBI), they hit the streets at night to hunt demons, the enemy of their people. With all the biting, fighting, fucking, and giving each other shit, you will laugh, cry, and blaze straight through this addictive series.

If you're in the mood for dark intensity, you will love *Her Lord of Death*. (Triggers abound here, so skip this one if sexual trauma is not something healthy or appealing for you to read.) Filled with monsters, witches, and gods, this dark historical fantasy romance set in ancient Greece is an intensely sexual, beautiful, and emotional read.

Beautiful Beast is a dark, gritty romance inspired by Beauty and the Beast. It's got a vaguely Victorian/steampunk feel blended with the intensity and edge of paranormal romance. It's not quite as dark as *Her Lord of Death*, but it's darn close. This is a love it or hate it book. The hate generally comes from readers expecting fairy tale luster. (Look elsewhere for that!) The love comes from readers who crave its harsh, sexy darkness.

Printed in Great Britain
by Amazon